DEAD ISLAND

www.penguin.co.uk

DEAD ISLAND

Samuel Bjørk

bantam

TRANSWORLD PUBLISHERS
Penguin Random House, One Embassy Gardens,
8 Viaduct Gardens, London SW11 7BW
www.penguin.co.uk

Transworld is part of the Penguin Random House group of companies
whose addresses can be found at global.penguinrandomhouse.com

Penguin
Random House
UK

First published in Great Britain in 2024 by Bantam
an imprint of Transworld Publishers

A CIP catalogue record for this book
is available from the British Library.

ISBNs
9781787637016 (hb)
9781787637023 (tpb)

Typeset in 11/14pt Sabon LT Pro by Jouve (UK), Milton Keynes.
Printed and bound in Australia by Griffin Press

The authorized representative in the EEA is Penguin Random House Ireland,
Morrison Chambers, 32 Nassau Street, Dublin D02 YH68.

Penguin Random House is committed to a sustainable future
for our business, our readers and our planet. This book is made
from Forest Stewardship Council® certified paper.

MIX
Paper | Supporting
responsible forestry
FSC® C018179

DEAD ISLAND

'Hello?'

'Hi, Mum, it's me.'

'Jonathan, where are you?'

'I'm at Erik's, we've been crabbing.'

'But Jonathan, it's almost nine o'clock. And you know we're going to Granny's tomorrow morning, don't you?'

'I know, Mum, but listen—'

'No, absolutely not.'

'What? But you don't even know what I was going to ask—'

'You want to ask if you can stay over.'

'Please can I, Mum? Please, please, please?'

'No, Jonathan, you can't. We have to make an early start.'

'Can you come and get me then?'

'No, I've had a glass of wine so I can't drive. Besides, what about your bike? You've got your bike there, haven't you?'

'Yes, but—'

'Good. Then I'll see you soon, all right?'

'OK, Mum.'

ONE

SATURDAY

Chapter 1

Dorothea Krogh was relaxing on the terrace outside the white vicarage, smiling at the sunlight that sparkled in the sea on the horizon. It had been an amazing summer. Perhaps the best ever on the island. The doom-mongers claimed it was the result of climate change. That the planet was heating up, that soon we would need a new Noah's Ark, but Dorothea Krogh had stopped listening to the doom-mongers. Although 'doom-mongers' plural was an exaggeration; it was really only one person, Nora Strand, the pessimistic verger who had just been to visit her. Talk about a downer. Nora Strand was an eternal spinster and chronically offended by everything between heaven and earth, including, of course, the new altarpiece.

'Sponsors in a church? Since when was Mammon in charge of God?'

Dorothea Krogh could see her point, but she also knew that the church was in need of renovation. A new roof. A fresh lick of paint. And that government funds were far from enough. A gift from a more affluent member of the congregation – where was the harm in that?

Hitra was a beautiful island off the coast of Trøndelag county, where she had lived her entire life. The landscape still took her breath away. The smell of seaweed and kelp. Of salty waves washing over the rocks. It was as if God had taken the best of everything he had ever made and created heaven on earth. The light. The sea. The rugged mountains. The windswept trees. It was an oasis. This small island community had been a hidden gem until one family made good and now had more money than pretty much all of Norway put together.

Henry Prytz. He was the founder and owner of Royal Arctic Salmon. Once he had been just an ordinary farm boy, now he was a billionaire, one of the richest men in the world, responsible for the salmon bonanza on the Trøndelag coast, but not everyone thought that was entirely fair.

'As if that family didn't have enough already. Are they hoping to buy the church next?'

Dorothea Krogh shook her head and realized that she was still irritated by the permanently grumpy verger, who had turned up unannounced and cast shade over this beautiful day. No, she decided, she was not going to let that woman get to her. Dorothea Krogh got up in the glorious light and cleared away the coffee cups and the biscuits. The clock by the window showed a quarter to eleven: was it too early for a small glass of port? No, of course it wasn't. Surely she could decide that for herself now that the old vicar had gone to meet his maker. She had carried the bottle and a small glass outside in the blazing sun when her mobile began vibrating on the table.

Oh, for goodness' sake! Would she never get a moment's peace? She had so been looking forward to getting started on today's crossword.

Dorothea heaved a sigh and pressed the green button.

'Yes, Dorothea speaking.'

'Please can you come up here?'

The new vicar sounded exactly as he always did. Anxious and fussy, if possible more than usual. She had noticed it the first time she met him. Aren't vicars meant to reassure people rather than make them more worried than they already are? But then again, she had thought, he would probably grow into his role. He was young and a townie, give him a few years' experience and he would settle in. Except almost a year had passed now and he still seemed like a lost soul who didn't know what to do with himself.

'You have to come up here, something has happened—'

'Have the chickens escaped again? They're allowed to roam, you know. They'll come back eventually.'

'What? No, no, that's not it. It's the new altarpiece – you really need to see it for yourself. Are you at home? Please would you come up here?'

Dorothea sighed again and set down her port.

'Now?'

'Yes, please.'

'Can't it wait until tonight?'

'No, no, I think it's a punishment. From above. I kept saying we should never have accepted that gift—' The young vicar sounded almost on the verge of tears.

'Give me two minutes.'

'Thank you. I'm in the sacristy.'

'I'll be there shortly.'

Dorothea Krogh put away the port and the glass and went to the hallway to get her straw hat. It clearly wasn't going to be a day of rest for her. First the vexatious verger and now the fragile young vicar. Perhaps the time had come? For her to leave the vicarage and move to the retirement flat in Fillan she had been offered?

Yes, she would give it serious consideration.

She had just left her home when she spotted a figure in the church-yard who made her retreat.

Oh, no. Was that today?

She glanced quickly at her mobile: 16 July.

Of course.

Dorothea didn't want to stare, but she couldn't help herself.

Anita Holmen.

His mother. In front of the empty grave.

Three years ago. Here, on safe little Hitra.

Her son had been cycling home from a friend's house, and since then no one had seen him. Jonathan Holmen had been only eight years old.

Dorothea felt ashamed now. She should have gone over and talked to her much earlier. The poor woman had lost her son. It was about time.

Dorothea Krogh was Trøndelag born and bred and she had learned to keep her nose out of other people's business, but surely there were limits.

7

Three years.
Without a trace of the child.
No, the time had come.
Dorothea Krogh put on her straw hat and marched with determined steps towards the churchyard.

Chapter 2

Mia Krüger woke up to the familiar screeching of gulls, but everything else had changed. Last night, the dark-haired homicide investigator had been sitting on the rocks, gazing across the sea, struggling to understand the person she used to be. The sight that had met her in the old white house she had bought on this remote island had shocked her. *My former self.* She had felt sick as she cleared up the living room. Pills of every shape and colour, some prescription drugs, others from places she would rather forget that she had been. Empty, clattering bottles of alcohol on the floor and on the chairs. But the calendar had been the worst. The date she had circled: *18 April.* The day she had decided to die. Be done with it all. Be reunited with her twin sister, Sigrid, who had left this world ten years ago in a filthy basement in Oslo with a needle in her arm. All of them were gone. Her mother, her father. Her grandmother, who had been so like her, who had understood Mia better than she understood herself. *'You see things other people don't, don't you, Mia?'* Her entire family. All of them dead. And then all the wretchedness. She had worked as a homicide investigator in an elite unit led by Holger Munch in Mariboesgate 13 in Oslo. The most disturbing cases. Her responsibility. The misery of the world. On her shoulders.

But not any more.

Mia flung the light summer duvet aside and wandered across the creaking floor. The curtains fluttered in the gentle breeze. Seven weeks ago she had quit her job as a homicide investigator, and she had lived out here ever since. Alone. On Edøya. Her very own island. A short boat trip from Hitra. The sun was high in the sky and the crystal-clear water shimmered quietly below the rocks. When she was last here, she had been completely oblivious to it all. Drugged. Numbed. Off her face. Counting down the days on the calendar. Coming back here had been a shock to the system, with all her senses alive and her body clean. She had got her head straight, and the lump in her stomach was also starting to disappear, the one she hadn't even known she had.

'You see things other people don't, don't you, Mia?'

She went to the bathroom and forced herself to pause in front of the mirror. She had stood like this just over a year ago. Her eyes hazy and swimming. Her long, dark hair hanging limply over her cheeks. Thin, underweight in fact, almost dead already. She had counted her injuries. The physical legacy from ten years with the police. The missing two joints on one little finger. The scar above her left eye.

Mia removed the dressing from her hip with care and was delighted to see how well her most recent injury was healing. Her last case. A stalker. He had shot her from close up. First in her calf, then in her hip. She moved closer to the mirror, studying the wound; the scar tissue looked good. Another day or two and she could ditch the dressing completely. Finally she would be able to get into the sea. Go diving again. She had longed to jump in for a swim from the moment she had moored her boat to the jetty. Her very own jetty. Her very own island. Her emotions had threatened to overpower her. Mia Krüger didn't cry very often, but she had shed a tear on her way up to this lovely house.

She was alive.

But only by the skin of her teeth.

She had been lucky.

If Munch hadn't travelled up here to find her and suggest a case that had brought her back to Oslo . . .

She was better now.

Much better.

Mia sent thoughts of gratitude out into the ether and stepped under the shower. She wondered how much longer she would stay out here at the mouth of the fjord; a few more weeks was tempting, but no, she had made a promise. And it would be autumn soon. And then winter. The January storms out here, no, she definitely didn't fancy them, she had to find another home before that. The houses in Åsgårdstrand, her parents' and her grandmother's, had been sold long ago. So, too, had the flat she had once owned in Oslo. For a long time Mia had been pondering what to do next. She and Sigrid had always fantasized about travelling to northern Thailand and opening a small bar, but she couldn't really see herself doing that now.

But then her old friend Chen had called.

'Hey, Mia, I hear you're looking for something to do? That you're done with the police?'

Her old coach was now running a climbing camp in southern France. Teenagers who had got off to a bad start in life were given the chance to do battle with a rock face while Chen in turn could finance his eternal hunt for new, almost impossible climbing routes.

'I need more instructors. Why don't you join me down here?'

Perfect.

She stepped out of the shower, just the thought of it making her smile.

Being out here on Edøya on her own? Sure, it was great. But she couldn't stay here for ever. So how about climbing in France for a few years? There were worse ways to live, surely?

Still smiling to herself, Mia went down to the kitchen, made herself an espresso and walked barefoot out on to the smooth rocks, already warmed by the morning sunshine. The light out here was incredible, almost supernatural. Day and night. She was nearly grateful that her car was in the garage being serviced so she got a few more days on her island before she had to leave.

'I'll be with you as soon as the Jaguar has been fixed, all right?'

'Absolutely, you just turn up whenever you can.'

Her car. She would need to check on it today, and shop for supplies. Mia was about to wander back to her house when she saw a boat chug across the bay.

Who might that be?

She knew no one out here.

Mia put on a pair of jeans and walked across the rocks. A small dinghy steered by a young girl, not yet a teenager. She could not be more than ten or eleven, with long, blonde, billowing hair, and was wearing a floral summer dress.

'Are you the famous detective?'

The girl climbed eagerly out of the dinghy and on to the jetty. 'Are you?'

Mia smiled. 'I might be. Who are you, then?'

'You have to help me.'

Mia could see the urgency in the girl's eyes now.

'I'm Sofia. It was my fault. That Jonathan disappeared. Can you help me? Please?'

Chapter 3

Luca Eriksen got up from his desk, walked over to a wall in his study and took down the picture of his wife. He carried it solemnly across the room, then put it carefully into a drawer, sat down and stared vacantly into the air. He had to remove as many memories as he could. Her clothes. Her personal possessions. Box them all up. Throw them out – if he was able to. And if he wasn't, then store them somewhere. He couldn't look at them every day. He could put them in the attic, perhaps, or in the basement. As many things as possible. Including all the pictures. Not do what he had done so far, which was to sit alone every night in the empty house with his laptop, watching the old videos, the same ones, over and over, his fingers caressing her beautiful face.

'Tell me you're not filming again, Luca. Oh, stop it, I haven't done my hair yet. I look a sight.'

He got up again, fetched himself a cup of coffee, then stopped with the cup in his hand. It was one year, three months and four days since he had lost her and he missed her so badly that at times he didn't know what to do with himself.

'Hitra Police, Luca Eriksen speaking.'

'There has been an accident.'

'Where?'

'In the tunnel. A car strayed into the opposite lane. It's total chaos here.'

'Have you called 112?'

'Yes, the emergency services are on their way . . . but, Luca?'

'Yes?'

'It's Amanda.'

'*What?*'

'*Amanda. It's her car.*'

Luca Eriksen had a change of heart: suddenly he felt nauseous, and he hurried back to his desk, opened the drawer, returned the photograph to its proper place and caressed the glass.

'I'm sorry, Amanda.'

He nearly jumped when the phone on his desk started ringing. Maybe he should have listened to the advice he had been given. '*I don't think you should return to work yet, Luca. It's still too soon for you. You need to give yourself more time.*'

Not go back to work?

No, he had to go to work.

Sit at home? Without her?

With nothing to do. That would be awful.

He had to return to the real world.

Be of use.

Luca Eriksen pulled himself together and found his official voice before he picked up the handset.

'Hitra Police, Luca speaking.'

'Hi, Luca, it's Dorothea Krogh. Do you have a minute?'

'Of course, Dorothea, what is it?'

'There has been a small incident in the church. The vicar is a bit upset. Do you think you could come down here, or are you busy?'

Luca smiled to himself. Busy?

Hitra police station was open two days a week, from ten in the morning until two in the afternoon, which told you pretty much everything you needed to know about the amount of crime on the small island. Previously he used to commute to Orkanger on the mainland to work at the police station there in addition to his two days on the island, but he had taken some notice of the advice he had been given and returned only to his part-time job on Hitra. Now he worked only Mondays and Wednesdays.

Wednesdays.

'*Oh, do we have to have this discussion every Wednesday, Luca? Surely once a month is enough?*'

Her face in the mirror. The expression he knew so well, a little irritated, but not really, the jingling of her car keys, the scent of her perfume as her lips brushed his cheek.

'*And try to play a bit better today, would you? I'm fed up with losing.*'

Four couples. Always the same people. Laughing and drinking, with him invariably ending up as the designated driver.

Today was a Saturday, and he shouldn't really be working, but of course he would respond. He always answered his phone whenever someone called.

'Are you there, Luca?'

'Yes, sorry, Dorothea. Please would you say that again?'

'There has been a small incident in the church. It's probably nothing, but you know what the vicar is like – he's such a fusspot. Do you think you could pop round?'

'Of course, I'm on my way there now.'

'Great, see you shortly.'

Like a robot.

That was how he felt at times.

As if he were a machine.

He took no joy in anything these days.

He woke up in the big bed.

Alone.

He cleaned his teeth.

Alone.

He ate breakfast.

Alone.

He sat in front of the black TV screen at night.

Alone.

Luca Eriksen got up with a heavy heart, took the car keys from the hook by the door and walked down the steps. For a moment he just sat behind the steering wheel before he finally pressed the button to open the garage door and drove the police car out into the sun.

It was sunny outside. At least that was something. So far it had been a lovely summer, one of the best for years. The bad weather had been one of the reasons behind his original reluctance.

'*There's a vacancy for a teacher on Hitra, Luca. What do you*

*think? How about we move north? Perhaps we can live in my child-
hood home? Wouldn't that be romantic?'*

Coincidences. The butterfly effect. If one thing hadn't happened,
then neither would the other. If he had said no back then, she would
still have been alive today.

It had been perfect.

Love at first sight.

He had moved to Oslo to go to the National Police Academy. He
hadn't been looking for a relationship, not really. He had been too
busy doing his own thing – exercise. Running. He lived for that. He
got up every morning at six. He wore out several pairs of running
shoes that year, and that was how he had met her. A twenty-year-
old teacher-training student working part-time in a shoe shop in
Majorstua.

Amanda.

From Hitra.

Dorothea Krogh was waiting for him on the church steps.

'Hi, Luca. How are you?'

'Oh, you know, not too bad.'

'You're always welcome at the vicarage, you know that, don't
you? If you need someone to talk to.'

'Thank you. You said there had been an incident?'

'I don't know what else to call it. It's probably just a prank. I only
called you because the vicar insisted. You know how he worries,
poor thing. In fact, he has gone to lie down. Come with me, I'll
show you.'

He followed her up the steps.

'It's this way.'

They walked down the central aisle, then Luca stopped and
looked curiously at the wall behind the pulpit.

A large new altarpiece had replaced the old one. Luca smiled and
shook his head slightly.

'Right, now I see what all the fuss is about.'

'You do?' The old woman turned to him.

'You think it's too much?'

'Well, I'm not sure—'

'Too much salmon? That's what I'm wondering. If someone is so annoyed with us that they've decided to send us a message.'

She walked over to a small cloth spread across the floor of the sanctuary.

'These were hanging from the altarpiece.'

Dorothea Krogh pulled back the fabric and stepped aside.

On the floor lay three dead crows.

'A bit gross, don't you think?'

'Yes, I agree.'

Luca knelt down and picked up one of the birds from the stone floor.

'What happened to its eyes?'

Dorothea Krogh grimaced.

'Someone gouged them out.'

'Yuck.' He carefully put down the bird.

'And then, well, there's the other thing, I don't know if it's a message or what it is.'

Dorothea Krogh pointed to a metal tag attached to one of the bird's legs.

Luca turned over the bird and looked at the engraved characters.

'KTTY3?'

'Don't ask me. I have no idea what it means. Perhaps it was tagged. By ornithologists, I mean. But I wouldn't know. And it's still a bit gross.'

'And they were hanging on the altarpiece?'

'Yes. This morning. What do you think?'

The old woman folded her arms across her chest and looked at him, a little concerned.

'Well, it's hard to say.'

'A prank?'

'It most likely is. But it's unpleasant nevertheless. I'm glad you called. I'll ask around.'

'Thank you,' Dorothea Krogh said, gave him a friendly pat on the back and led the way in front of him out of the church.

Chapter 4

The little girl had barely had time to moor her dinghy to the jetty before another, bigger boat came racing around the headland. Mia had seen it before, a grey, rigid semi-inflatable with two sturdy outboard motors. It had been moored by the Co-op where she shopped for groceries. The logo on its side had attracted her interest as it read *Hitra Sport Diving*.

'Oh, that's all I need.' The girl sighed and crossed her slim arms over her chest. 'How old does he think I am? Three?'

She shook her head and stomped in a sulk across the rocks as the attractive grey boat reached the jetty.

'Sofia?' the man on the boat called out.

Mia took the rope from the new arrival and tied it to a post as the clearly experienced sailor switched off the motors and climbed up the ladder.

'Sofia, didn't I tell you to leave her alone?'

The girl ignored him and ran further up the rocks, disappearing behind a mound.

'I'm so sorry.' The man heaved a sigh and brushed his blond fringe away from his eyes. 'She knows better than to do this. Has she been pestering you?'

Mia smiled.

'Oh no, it's nice to have a visitor.'

The man apologized once more and then extended his hand to her. She had noticed him as well as his boat near the Co-op. Slim, good posture, about her age, with blue eyes and a T-shirt with the same logo as on the boat. She didn't do this often, but she had actually paused to watch him while he lugged oxygen tanks on board.

She hadn't been able to put her finger on it, but she had the feeling that she had seen him somewhere before.

'My name is Simon. Again, I'm really sorry about this, but she has been obsessed with meeting you ever since she realized who you were.'

'Mia Krüger,' Mia introduced herself.

The man laughed.

'Yes, and don't I know it. Like I said, she has talked of little else. Only this time I failed to stop her. I should never have bought her that dinghy, but you know. The sea.' He turned and gestured towards it.

'It's better that kids get to know it sooner rather than later, I think. Sofia!'

Simon shrugged apologetically once more.

'I'll go and get her. I'm sure you've got better things to do.'

Mia smiled.

'It's all right. But she seemed upset? Something about it being her fault? That boy?'

A dark gaze this time.

'Ah, yes, I'm sorry. She was with him. The night he disappeared. Jonathan Holmen. I don't know if you're familiar with . . .'

'Oh, yes,' Mia said.

And who wasn't? Norway was a small country. The case had attracted considerable attention at the time. An eight-year-old boy riding his bike home, and then he just vanishes without a trace. It was Kripos, Norway's national crime agency, rather than her unit, that had been tasked with the investigation.

'But she's wrong?'

Mia could smell saltwater and sunshine as the attractive man carefully passed her on the narrow jetty and followed his daughter up the rocks.

'Yes, of course she is. What could she possibly have done?'

'So why does she think that it's her fault?'

He shook his head.

'She's far too sensitive. She lets things get to her. If her mother had been here, perhaps it would have been easier, but there is only me, so . . .'

19

The man turned and chewed his lip as if he had said more than he had intended to.

'Sorry, her mother is in Burundi. She's a doctor. Working for Doctors Without Borders. It's obviously great that some people go abroad to do this vital work, but for Sofia, well, it has been . . .'

'I understand.' Mia nodded and followed him up towards the house.

The girl was sitting defiantly on the steps with her knees pulled up under her floral dress.

She gave her father a stern look as they approached.

'I'm eleven years old and I can make my own decisions.'

'Of course, Sofia, but you can't just—'

'Yes, I can. It's my fault that Jonathan went missing so surely I can ask for help if I want to?'

'Yes, of course, darling, I was just—'

Simon sat down next to her on the stone step and carefully stroked her hair as the girl buried her face in her hands.

'Why was it your fault?' Mia said, and sat down on a rock opposite them.

'Because I could have stopped him.' The girl began to sob. 'I told him not to go home on his bike. That he should just wait. That he could have a sleepover, all he had to do was ask her again. She was like that, his mum. When she had had some wine, you know, then she would—'

Her father stopped her.

'Sofia, we don't talk about that. We don't know anything about that, do we?'

'His mum drank alcohol, is that what you're saying?'

The girl nodded and carried on.

'She always did in the evening. And so she couldn't come and pick him up, do you see? It had happened before. Erik has *Super Mario*, that's why we were there. And we were about to fight Bowser, and Jonathan loved fighting Bowser, and the last time we played, we just waited a bit, then he called his mum again and then she said yes.'

'Sofia, I think that—'

'No, it's true. I should have tried harder to make him stay!' She buried her face in her hands again.

Simon stroked her back to comfort her and exchanged glances with Mia.

'As I said, Sofia is quite sensitive—'

'I'm not!'

'I get it, I do,' Mia said, moving into the shade.

'You do?' the girl exclaimed in surprise.

'I was like that once. When I was your age.'

'What do you mean?'

'It wasn't exactly the same, but I had a sister. She looked a lot like you, come to think of it. Long, blonde hair. Very clever.'

'Did she also go missing?'

'Almost.' Mia nodded. 'Like you I lived by the sea. And one day she wanted us to go sailing. Even though we weren't allowed. I tried to talk her out of it because we didn't have any life vests, but she insisted, and in the end I gave in.'

'What happened?' the girl said, and scrunched up her nose.

'She nearly drowned.'

'What?'

'We capsized. Fortunately someone came to our rescue, but she was in hospital for a long time. She got a lot of water in her lungs.'

'Gosh.'

'So I know how you feel. Do you think it was my fault? That she almost died?'

'Eh?' The girl looked tentatively at her father. 'Well, I don't know . . .'

'We can't tell other people what to do, can we? Everyone has to make their own choices?'

'True . . .'

The girl's father gave Mia a grateful look as he got up and ushered his daughter down the rocks.

'Great, Sofia. You've done what you came to do. Let's leave Mia in peace now, all right?'

'What?' the girl exclaimed. 'No, I'm not done yet.' She freed herself and ran back, stopping in front of Mia with big, pleading eyes. 'Can you find him for me? You're so clever. Can you find Jonathan? Please?'

Chapter 5

Mia moored her boat at the quay below the Co-op, still unable to get Sofia's pleading voice out of her head. Nor was there any respite ashore, with a poster on the noticeboard at the entrance to the shop. A faded colour picture of a boy squinting at the camera. It was three years since his disappearance, but the poster was more recent than that. Someone must still be putting them up. Someone hadn't yet given up hope.

Three years ago.

She had a sudden flashback to a derelict motorhome by Lake Tryvann. Munch and her. A teenage girl had gone missing and they had received a tip-off that she might be there. Mia had been totally unprepared for the man she would encounter there.

Her twin sister's ex-boyfriend.

The junkie who had got Sigrid hooked on drugs.

She had blacked out most of it.

She only remembered brief glimpses, the explosion inside her. She had shot him in the chest – twice. The ambulance. Everyone in the special unit had been interviewed.

If Munch hadn't lied, she would have gone to jail. Self-defence. Which it clearly hadn't been. Murder. She had murdered him.

It had been downhill from there. Darkness. Days and nights she couldn't remember.

Damn it, Mia.

Not that. Don't go there again.

There was another poster next to the poster of the missing boy.

Are you tired of life on Earth?

Come to Jupiter!

She smiled now.

Tired of life?

No.

Not any more.

Hello, new Mia.

She took a deep breath, turned her face to the warm sun and waited until the good feelings came back, then she walked up to the road and continued down towards the garage.

Roar's Autos.

She had her doubts about getting her car fixed at a local garage, but soon realized that she didn't have much choice. This part of the island was called Kvenvær and it was possibly the most beautiful part of Hitra. In the Co-op she had overheard tourists whisper the name almost as if it were magic. As if they couldn't believe that a place like this existed in real life. Pretty wooden houses painted white, red barns, well-tended gardens and fluttering pennants on flagpoles, it was like living postcards, idyllic coastal Norway at its very finest. Roar's Autos, however, looked like a garage from an impoverished small town in the American Deep South. As if someone had picked up the building and its immediate surroundings, moved it across the Atlantic and dumped it on Hitra by mistake. The cream-coloured single-storey brick building had seen better days and the paint was peeling in several places. The hinges on the garage doors were so rusty that it looked as if you couldn't close them. Everywhere she turned she saw old cars in various states of disrepair. There was a thin, white metal door at the front and a large window pane which no one had cleaned since it was fitted. Through the grime you might be able to make out the owner's taste and personality. Topless women torn from various magazines, an old Kenny Rogers record and what had reminded her of the Deep South: a large Confederate flag where the stars had been replaced with cannabis plants.

Her Jaguar was parked exactly where she had left it two weeks earlier, and it stood out like a sore thumb. The English upper-class aesthetic was completely out of place here. Mia was surprised by how quiet it was; there was no ZZ Top music floating across the oil-stained tarmac. That might be because the only loudspeaker she could see was dangling from a cable in the wall, surrounded by holes in the brickwork that looked like someone had taken shots at it. She had yet to meet the owner; she had just called a number she had found on a piece of paper stuck to the front door and got a message to 'leave it wherever the hell you like', and she was curious as to what sort of person would turn up. If the owner was just as much of an American cliché as his surroundings. The only thing missing here was a Ku Klux Klan outfit, but then again, who knew what this place might be hiding?

Mia rounded the corner, and now she could hear music. Muted country songs from a radio in a small workshop with a car on a ramp. Hidden under a baseball cap, a man wearing safety boots and filthy utility clothes was asleep in a camping chair.

'Hello?'

She knocked softly on the metal doorframe.

'Are you Roar?'

The man slowly came to life and heaved a sigh when he spotted her, as if she had disturbed him in the middle of something important.

'Yeah?'

'Mia Krüger. The Jaguar? I've come to find out if it's ready. It's not easy to get around the island without a car.'

'Ready?' He chortled and displayed a set of teeth that would not appear to have seen a dentist for quite some time.

'No, no. The crankshaft and the cylinder linings need replacing. It's a miracle you even made it up here.'

'I see.'

He got up reluctantly from his chair, the simple act of crossing the floor making him wheeze.

'I need spare parts from England.'

'OK? And when are they coming?'

'You want me to order them?'

'You mean you haven't yet . . .'

Mia had to bite her tongue to stop herself from having a go at the guy. She was in the only garage on this part of the island, and if she was to have any hope of getting her car back on the road, her best bet was not to make Roar even more antagonistic or unhelpful than he already was.

'Yes, please.'

'OK,' Roar said, wiping his hands on a filthy rag. 'I guess that will take a few weeks.'

'You wouldn't happen to have a . . . a courtesy car?' Mia asked, but knew the answer before she had finished her sentence.

She wasn't in Oslo any more. She was in the back of beyond.

'A courtesy car?' The mechanic grinned, displaying the row of yellow teeth once more.

'No, I don't suppose so,' Mia said.

'So you've got no transport?'

'No, but thanks all the same.'

She was about to leave when his mood suddenly changed; it was as if he were human after all.

'I got that one,' he said, then coughed and nodded in the direction of a piece of tarpaulin at the back of the crammed workshop. 'Took it as security. Bloody rich kids – the salmon business, you know. They may wear diamond watches, but do they pay their bills? Show-offs – plus-fours and no bloody breakfast.'

Roar put down the rag and pulled off the tarpaulin.

Mia could feel herself grinning from ear to ear.

She was looking at a black Ducati motorcycle with a matte finish.

'Wow.'

'Right? So you like bikes?'

Again she caught a glimpse of an actual human being when Roar looked at her with something that, for the first time, resembled a smile.

'I'm a Harley man myself, I'm not a big fan of these Italian wonders, but yes, it's a nice bike, there's no denying it.' He spat and pushed back his baseball cap. 'So, yes, like I said, it could be a few weeks. Do you fancy borrowing that in the meantime?'

'Absolutely.'

'Besides, it's just taking up space here. So does this *courtesy car* meet with your approval?'

26

'It certainly does.'

'Great. I'll ring through the order today and contact you when your car is ready, how about that?'

'Deal,' said Mia, grinning.

And then she rolled the black wonder out into the sunshine.

Chapter 6

Hannah Holmen took one last look about her before she opened the door. *Fabian Stengel, psychologist.* She had been ashamed the first time she came here, and she still felt a little ashamed now. Not because seeing a psychologist was a bad thing; it was just there was so much gossip out here on Hitra. It was a small place. People were nosy. And if there was anything people had talked about these last few years, then it was her family.

Hannah Holmen, the big sister.

Jonathan Holmen, her little brother.

Three years ago she had been in so much pain that she had barely been able to get dressed. Her feet had struggled to push the pedals on her bicycle; it was as if her body weighed a ton.

She had been early, almost an hour early. Waited on a bench in the shade behind the arts centre, hoping that no one would spot her.

Eleven years.

That's how old he would have been today.

Hannah walked up the stairs and took a seat in one of the light-coloured chairs. There was no one else in the waiting room. He was very particular about this, Stengel; he understood where he practised as a psychologist and the people who lived out here on this small island. No one wanted to bump into their neighbour or the mother of someone they had gone to school with in his waiting room, so he always left plenty of time between appointments. Once, well, and yes, this was indeed gossip and Hannah didn't really like to gossip, but still, this was too juicy to keep to herself. Once, when she had been waiting for her appointment, there had been a handbag on the floor, a very exclusive one, and she had thought, eh?

Who out here can afford a Hermès Birkin? Those bags cost a fortune. And, at that same moment, the door had opened, and who had sneaked out?

Cynthia Prytz.

They had a good laugh at that afterwards in her friend Sylvia's house, the only place they could hang out now. After all, Jessica's mum was mental, so no wonder Jessica had turned out the way she had, and in her own home it was so quiet you could hear a pin drop.

'Cynthia Prytz? For real?' Jessica's laugh had been even louder than usual, and Sylvia's eyes had widened so much it had looked as if they might roll out of her head.

'Seeing a shrink?'

Wearing gloves and sunglasses and a scarf around her head as if she were a movie star from the old days, walking across the floor in her expensive red Marni coat.

Hannah had pretended not to notice her, but she could see that the billionaire's wife was ashamed.

Cynthia Prytz. The wife of Henry Prytz. Mother of Alexander and Benjamin Prytz. The richest family on the island.

'There you go,' Jessica had said. 'Money isn't the answer. It just makes you miserable.'

The girls had nodded sagely at that; no one in their families had much money, so it felt good to see proof that even though the Prytz family had Ferraris and Lamborghinis and swimming pools and their own stable of thoroughbred horses, they still needed therapy.

And it was then that Jessica had said it; she had lowered her voice and told her friends to come closer, and they had huddled together on the pink carpet.

'I know things about them.'

Whispering, her eyes dark.

'Secrets.'

They had been dying to know more, of course, but Jessica had refused to elaborate.

She had just trailed her thumb and index finger across her lips like a zip.

'I dread to think what might happen if it came out. That's all I'm willing to say.'

'Hannah?'

The psychologist suddenly appeared, smiling, and invited her into his consulting room, and she felt good, safer in there behind the closed door.

At her first appointment she had thought it was like entering another world. Calm. Secure. There was no desk or any kind of couch; she had dreaded having to lie on one. Fabian Stengel sat in a beige leather chair, and she sat in an identical one opposite him. The carpet on which the chairs were set out was white and incredibly soft. A bookcase on one wall, not crammed, only a dozen books arranged according to colour.

She had felt so comfortable in there. So comfortable that she almost felt guilty.

I wish I could stay here for ever, that I would never have to go home.

To the dead house.

To the dead eyes.

Her mum.

Who had been so vibrant.

Who had been her great idol.

Reduced to a shrivelled ghost.

Silent on the sofa in the living room.

She didn't even turn on the TV.

Not a sound.

Anywhere.

'How are you, Hannah?'

She pushed the dark thoughts aside.

'I'm fine,' Hannah said, tucking her legs underneath her in the chair.

'And your mum, how is she?'

'Same as always.'

'She still won't talk about it?'

Hannah shook her head.

'Today's a special day, isn't it? Do you want to talk about it?'

She hesitated. She could feel that she didn't really want to.
The sixteenth of July.
The third anniversary of his disappearance.
She had hoped that they could go together. To the place where he
was last seen. But, no.
She had cycled there on her own, just like last year. Picked flowers
along the way.
'Do I have to?' Hannah said eventually, hoping that the lump in
her stomach that had been growing as she cycled here wouldn't
come out as tears.
'No, no, of course not. You're in charge. This is your space. We
can talk about anything.'
She had resisted the suggestion to begin with. Seeing a psychologist. She had thought that everything about him was dumb. His name.
Who calls themselves Fabian Stengel? He sounded like a character in
a children's book. And who dresses like that in real life? A shirt and a
waistcoat? Glasses with thick black frames? Was he running an art
gallery? Did he think he lived in New York? These were not her
thoughts, that was just how people talked about him out here, down
at the café in the shopping arcade, at the bowling alley: *self-obsessed,
arrogant, fancies himself, thinks he's something special.*
But Fabian Stengel had proved to be anything but self-obsessed
and arrogant. He was a really nice guy. He listened. He had kind
eyes. And yes, he was old, over forty at least, and yet there was
something about him that made her feel that somehow he understood her. She had blurted it out during her first session. She had
been to the library, she had borrowed a book by Haruki Murakami,
Norwegian Wood, she had lain awake under her duvet until she had
finished reading it, stunned by the beauty of the story.
'Sometimes I feel like the girl in *Norwegian Wood*,' she had told
him.
He had smiled in surprise.
'Right, so you read Murakami?' Curious, leaning forward in his
chair. 'So what do you mean? Why do you think you're like her?'
She had chewed her lip. It had been so strange to tell someone
what she really thought.

31

'Well, because she's so sad. But she doesn't know why.'

At her next appointment there had been a book on the armrest.

'It's for you,' he had said, smiling.

'J. D. Salinger?'

'*The Catcher in the Rye*. So this is about a boy, but it's also about being different. About not feeling at home in this world of ours. Read it if you like. I'd love to know what you think.'

It was so good. That someone took her seriously. A grown man she could confide in, with whom she could share her innermost thoughts.

'Like I said,' Fabian Stengel continued, 'we can talk about today as something special or we can treat it like any other day. Is that what you want, that we talk about something else instead?'

Hannah nodded. She was already starting to feel better. The lump was diminishing; it was almost gone.

'So you've finished Year Eleven. Do you want to talk about that? Have you thought about what you will do in the autumn? Will you stay here on the island or are you still thinking about moving to Trondheim to continue your education?'

Get her own place. In the city of Trondheim. Far away from all this. She had lain awake recently, mulling it over, but had come to the conclusion that it was hopeless. She couldn't abandon her.

Her mum.

She didn't have the heart to leave her sitting in the dead house all alone.

'I'm not sure.'

'OK. So what about your friends, then? Will they stay here or are they also considering academic options on the mainland?'

Hannah had to smile at this.

Jessica and Sylvia.

Yes, they were her best friends, but nothing about them could be called academic – they probably didn't even know what the word meant. Nothing wrong with that, of course, but there were some things she could never discuss with them.

Maths. That was what she wanted to study. Whereas Jessica was interested in America.

They had been sitting in the back of Andres Wold's car last week with a bottle of hooch and some pills, and they had been quite high, and when she was high, Jessica would always start fantasizing.

'Los Angeles! How amazing would that be? I mean, it's where the Kardashians live. Can't we just run away to America, the three of us?'

Poor Jessica. Sometimes she felt really sorry for her. Everyone knew that her mum partied with dodgy people at home. Jessica didn't even have a proper bedroom; instead, she had borrowed an old boat where she would sleep from time to time.

'And Disneyland! I've read about it online. We could get jobs there – we could be the meet-and-greet characters. How cool would that be?'

The weekends in Andres Wold's car. She shuddered. Her mum would never have let her hang out with that crowd. Not in the past. But now . . .

'You talked about a party the last time you were here? Isn't that tonight? The costume party?'

Fabian Stengel pushed his glasses further up his nose and squinted at the calendar on the small round side table next to his chair.

Hannah nodded.

'Yes, that's tonight, but I'm not sure . . .'

'What's on your mind?'

'Well, I'm not sure if I want to go.'

'Why not?'

She hesitated for a moment.

'Well . . . all the others like to . . .'

Fabian Stengel furrowed his brow.

'Are you worried about drugs and alcohol?'

'Oh, no, or maybe I am . . .'

'But it's only natural, isn't it? For people to experiment a bit when they're your age? As long as it's in moderation?'

In moderation?

Last Friday, she had feared they would have to call an ambulance. Jessica had mixed booze and pills, as usual, and Hannah had struggled to rouse her.

33

'Costume – that's fun, isn't it, or is it just stupid?'

'Oh, no, that's fun.'

'Have you thought about what you'll dress up as? Are you going to be princesses or fairies or mermaids?'

Hannah laughed. 'No, that's for little girls.'

'And you're not little girls any more, I get it. Jessica, was it? And . . .'

'Sylvia.' Hannah nodded.

'It's still the three of you who hang out together most of the time?'

'Yes.'

Fabian leaned forwards in his chair again.

'I think you should go, Hannah. I think it would do you good. Today, of all days. A chance to get out of the house.'

'True.'

'I have a suit and a spare pair of glasses if you want to borrow them, then you can go as a male psychologist.'

Hannah laughed again.

'Oh, no, we already have our costumes.'

'Right, so tell me about them?'

'Well, you know Jessica, she's mad about Disney. She ordered some face masks online.'

'Funny.' Fabian Stengel smiled. 'And which ones did you get?'

'Jessica is going to be Mickey Mouse, I'll be Donald Duck and Sylvia will be Goofy. It's silly, I know.'

Fabian Stengel glanced discreetly at the clock on the table.

'Sounds good, sounds good. Sounds funny. But listen, Hannah?'

'Yes?'

'You're sure?'

'Sure about what?'

'The sixteenth of July? It's three years ago today. Are you sure that we're not going to talk about it?'

'Yes.'

'No problem. I just had to make sure. Is there anything else you'd like to talk about during your time today?'

Hannah pondered this for a little while before she replied.

'I wonder, is it OK if I just sit here without saying anything?'

'OK? Yes, of course. Is there any specific reason why you . . .'

'No. I just like being here.'

'Then that's what we'll do.' Fabian Stengel smiled. 'Would you like me to leave?'

'No, there's no need.'

Just silence. In here. For several minutes.

Hannah Holmen closed her eyes and leaned her head against the headrest of the beige chair.

Chapter 7

Luca Eriksen couldn't remember the last time he had had two phone calls in one day as he sat in the police car outside the entrance to Europris House & Garden at the end of the high street, wishing that the caller could have been someone else. Not that he had anything against Caroline, the hairdresser; no, it was the sign on the door next to her salon that niggled him.

Fabian Stengel.

He had tried to avoid them as best he could after the accident. The three other couples Amanda and he used to hang out with. Card games on Wednesdays. On Saturdays it was usually dinner parties, often eating outside if the weather allowed it. The constant messages and texts on his phone. Didn't they get it? That he was no longer interested? That all he wanted was to be left alone?

Hey, Luca, it's Karin here, we're having a barbecue on Saturday. Fancy joining us?

Hey, mate, it's John, we're thinking of taking the boat to Ulvøya, want to come along?

Hey, Luca, are you there? It's Fabian again, just calling to let you know that I'm here for you if you want to talk. Or we can talk in my consulting room if you prefer? Why don't I make an appointment for you? Just tell me when. I'll be happy to clear my schedule, all right?

The psychologist.

Luca had tried, he really had.

Prawns and crusty bread and home-brewed beer and everyone trying to act normal, as if it were the most natural thing in the world. Eight people around the big table, except they were no longer eight, were they? Now they were only seven.

No, thank you.

He had stopped replying. And in time the messages had almost stopped, thank God. The only one still trying was Fabian. He refused to give up.

Luca had hidden himself the last time he saw Fabian's silver Lexus pull up in front of his house. He had sat in the bathroom, covering his ears with his hands so he could pretend not to hear the doorbell.

A leaflet on his doorstep after the car had left.

Trauma therapy.

Fabian Stengel. Registered psychologist. Specialist in clinical adult psychology and clinical psychological rehabilitation.

No. He didn't want to. He wasn't an idiot. He knew what this was really about. What the ultimate goal was.

Forgetting.

That was what they wanted him to do.

Forget her?

Luca Eriksen could feel the rage surge as he got out of the car and walked up towards the town centre.

He would never forget Amanda.

'Hi, Luca, how are you?'

A mild face under a bicycle helmet greeted him with a beaming smile.

'Hello, hi, Pelle, oh, I'm all right. And how are you?'

'I'm good, I'm really good. I'll be leaving soon. It's true – I was told a few days ago.'

The gentle man kicked the stand to park his bicycle then stood in front of him, shifting his weight from foot to foot on the pavement.

'How exciting. Remind me where are you going, would you?'

'Jupiter. I've been chosen.'

Luca nodded, but didn't know what to say next. Pelle Lundgren was a familiar figure on the island. He was over forty years old, but had the mental age of a child. It was a tragedy. He had been working for a boat builder and he had been good at his job, people had said. There had been an accident. Something about a crane malfunctioning. Pelle Lundgren had ended up underneath a boat, had sustained severe head injuries and had never been the same since. It was a sad story. UFO Pelle was his nickname now. He was an object of derision as he cycled around the island with a rucksack he had packed, ready to leave for space. Always with a smile on his face. A blissfully happy child.

'I'll be leaving soon.'

'They're picking me up any day now.'

'I'll be leaving soon, have I told you that?' Pelle said, his smile broadening.

'Yes, you have, Pelle, that's great. So you're going off in a . . . spaceship, is it?' Luca said.

'Yes!' Pelle Lundgren jumped up and down, clapping his hands. 'I can't wait. Tuesday. Zero-three-zero-zero.'

'Is that when they're picking you up?'

'Yes. By the wildlife tower out in Havmyran.'

'Well, good luck, Pelle.'

'Thank you. Can I come with you?'

'What do you mean?'

Pelle Lundgren kicked the stand back eagerly and grabbed the handlebars.

'I can come with you if you want me to?'

'Eh, where to?'

'Wherever you're going?'

Luca smiled kindly and placed his hand on the man's arm.

'Thank you, Pelle, but I don't think so, I—'

'Are you going to see the psychologist?'

Pelle Lundgren nodded towards the entrance to Fabian Stengel's practice.

'No, that's not where I'm going.'

'I was there yesterday,' Pelle Lundgren said, running a hand under his nose like a child. 'Don't go there. He's not very clever.'

He drew a circle with his finger against the bicycle helmet.

'I'll bear that in mind.' Luca smiled.

'I'll see you when I get back. If I come back, that is.'

'You will, Pelle. Have a nice trip.'

'Thank you!' Pelle Lundgren smiled, got on his bike and set off down the high street.

Luca walked the last stretch, took a deep breath, put on his professional face, ignored the psychologist's sign and opened the other door.

Chaplin Hair.

A bell rang out softly.

'Oh, hey, Luca, there you are.' Caroline walked up to him and gave him a hug. 'How are you?'

Luca steeled himself.

This never-ending pity.

Why couldn't they just leave him alone?

'I'm all right, thank you,' Luca said, faking a smile. 'You said there had been a break-in?'

'Yes, well, I don't know what you would call it, because nothing is missing, but I'm still a bit freaked out by it.'

She led the way through the salon and out into the back.

'Here. Do you see?'

There was obvious damage to the ochre paintwork around the lock on the door.

'Someone was definitely here.' Eriksen nodded and took a look around. 'But nothing is missing, did you say?'

The hairdresser folded her arms across her chest and shook her head.

'No, that's the weird thing. I mean, it's not as if I'm rich, but my laptop is still here, as is the till, both of which are easy to grab, so I can't imagine what they were looking for.'

'How odd. So nothing is missing at all?'

'Not even a pair of scissors.'

'Strange. Perhaps someone caught them red-handed. Or they had second thoughts.'

The hairdresser heaved a sigh.

'You mean they broke in, but then thought better of it?'

Luca gave a light shrug.

'It's possible. Especially if they were teenagers.'

Caroline shook her head, mildly irritated.

'True, true. I'm just glad that nothing is missing. And by the way, it's not happening.'

'What is not happening?' Luca said.

'The wedding.' She returned to the salon and picked up her mug from the counter.

'The wedding is off?' he said. He was surprised.

It was the hot topic around here. It was all that anyone was talking about. Alexander Prytz was getting married. The heir to the empire. The elder son of Henry Prytz. The big event this summer on Hitra. The rumour mill was already grinding. Famous artists were going to perform. They had created a whole shantytown of Portakabins just for the staff. He didn't know how much of it was true, but everyone was obsessed with it. And not just the locals, incidentally; the national gossip press had given it extensive coverage for weeks.

Prince Charming had found his Cinderella.

The billionaire's son had proposed to a local girl.

'So it's off?' Luca said again.

'What?'

'The wedding?'

Caroline laughed and stuck a cigarette in between her lips.

'No, no, sorry. My part in it is not happening.'

She lit her cigarette and walked in front of him out on to the pavement.

'Cynthia has been a client of mine for years, or at least up until she got too posh. So I had been wondering if I would get to do the bride's hair. But no, I've read that they're flying in a celebrity stylist from London.' She was practically whispering. 'Two hundred thousand kroner.'

'Come again?'

'People say that's what it's costing.'

'I know it's upsetting that someone was here,' Luca said. 'But at least nothing is missing. Even so, I'll ask around, OK?'

'Thank you, Luca. Now you make sure you look after yourself.'

As he left, he stopped for a moment and glanced furtively at the brass sign by the other door. Perhaps he should reconsider?

No. He wasn't ready. Not yet.

A message flashed up on his phone.

Choir rehearsal tonight. Are you coming?

He heaved a sigh of resignation. No, thanks.

Why couldn't they just leave him alone?

As he walked back to his car, a cloud slipped in front of the sun.

He had just parked outside the police station and was on his way up the steps when a smart black motorcycle pulled up in the car park.

The rider took off her helmet and he recognized her immediately. The long black hair. The slim body which now walked towards him on the warm tarmac.

'Hello, would you happen to be Luca Eriksen?'

'Yes, that's me.'

'I'm Mia Krüger,' the attractive investigator said, and held out her hand to him. 'Could I have a word with you?'

Chapter 8

Sofia parked her bicycle outside her friend Erik's house, walked down the narrow path to the sea and sat on the rocks. There was mayhem out on the waves. The seagulls were having a feast and fighting each other at the same time. Someone had gutted fish on their boat and thrown the waste overboard. Sofia pressed her lips shut and fought the horrible feeling in her stomach; it wasn't easy, but she had made up her mind, *she wasn't going to be sad*. She face-timed with her mum every Saturday at five o'clock. Most weekends. She had worn her yellow dress. The one her mum really liked. She had put her hair in a ponytail and been ready with a smile, but the time became ten past, then half past, and finally she had realized that her mum wouldn't be appearing on the screen this week either.

Sofia heaved a sigh, picked up a pebble and threw it into the sea.

No: no crying.

There was always next Saturday.

Sofia brushed down her dress and returned to Erik's house.

The Internet connection in Burundi would probably be better then.

Erik was waiting on the doorstep when she arrived.

'What were you doing? Where did you go?'

He pushed his spectacles up his nose and breathed out as if he had run down the stairs from his room. He looked very agitated.

'I just wanted to watch the seagulls,' Sofia said, gesturing towards them.

'Come on, then,' Erik said, putting on his trainers.

'Where are we going?'

'To the viewpoint,' Erik said, starting to jog in front of her. 'Didn't you get my text?'

'Yes, you wrote that you had seen something weird. What did you mean?'

'Shhh.' Erik held up a finger to his lips.

'Don't you shush me. We're the only ones here, aren't we?'

They had now reached the birch avenue. The avenue was a path lined with birch trees, quite dark and hidden away, and it seemed a little unusual for Hitra, but she believed someone had planted the trees like that deliberately. The path led from Erik's house and up to the road. Walking it took only ten minutes if you were quick.

It was where Jonathan had pushed his bike on his way home.

'Seriously?' Erik said, giving her a strange look. 'We're the only ones here? Do you know what kind of equipment they have? For listening in? They have satellites up in the sky that could zoom in on us right now if they wanted to.'

He pushed his baseball cap back and pointed up to the sky.

There wasn't a cloud to be seen.

Or a satellite, for that matter.

Erik had always been like this, even before Jonathan went missing. He was easily spooked. He saw ghosts behind every bush. But since that night it seemed to have grown worse.

'What did you want to show me?' Sofia said, following him into the densest part of the forest.

'Keep your voice down,' Erik whispered. 'I'll show you once we get to the viewpoint.'

'But they can't see us here, can they?' Sofia argued, nodding towards the foliage around and above them.

'Do you really not get it?' Erik said, turning around. 'They can also eavesdrop on us. They have these tiny microphones. They're practically invisible. They can put them anywhere.'

'Are you saying there are microphones in the trees?' She nodded towards one of the slim birches. 'Or in your baseball cap, perhaps?'

Erik gave her a strange look. He was wondering if she was making fun of him.

'I'll be quiet,' Sofia said with a sigh.

She usually enjoyed this game. Playing detective. Being on a secret

43

mission. It was a game they played often. But not today. She wasn't in the mood for it.

'It's out there,' Erik whispered once they had reached their destination.

The calm sea was now sunning itself below them. The fishing boat had disappeared into the distance and taken the seagulls with it.

'Where?' Sofia said, shading her eyes with her hands.

'There,' Erik whispered, and pointed again. 'Not far from Hamnøya.'

Sofia couldn't see anything.

'What am I looking for?'

Erik pushed back his baseball cap and ran his hand across his forehead.

'It's not there now. But it was there earlier today.'

He took a notebook out of his back pocket and flicked to a page to show her.

'Do you see? *The yellow boat at 10.43.*'

'OK, so a yellow boat?'

'Come on, Sofia. *The yellow boat.* What's wrong with you today?'

'I'm sorry,' Sofia said, pulling herself together. 'OK, the yellow boat, am I right?'

Eagerly he turned back the pages in his notebook. 'Look, last Saturday. *The yellow boat.* At 11.05.'

And a few more pages back.

'And here? Two weeks ago. *The yellow boat.* At 12.06. It has to mean something, don't you think?' Erik stuffed the notebook into his pocket and looked about him. 'And it can't be a fisherman.'

'Why not?'

Erik gave her a look of exasperation.

'Because there are no fish out there – everyone knows that. And every Saturday? No, something strange is going on here, I can feel it.'

He pulled his baseball cap down and looked about him again before he came closer and whispered into her ear. 'Don't you remember what Jonathan said?'

'No,' Sofia whispered back. 'What did he say?'

'The yellow boat? Don't you remember him talking about it?'

'No,' Sofia said. And though she was a little upset today, she was telling the truth. She didn't remember Jonathan ever saying anything about a yellow boat.

'Oh, come on, Sofia,' Erik said. He seemed to be losing patience with her now. 'Are we on a mission or not?' He shook his head and walked back up towards the forest in a temper.

Sofia felt a pang of guilt. It wasn't Erik's fault that she was in a bad mood. He hadn't done anything wrong.

'I've talked to her!' She ran from the rocks and caught up with him in among the trees.

'I've talked to her,' she said again, grabbing him by the shoulder.

'Who?' Erik said.

'The famous detective. Mia Krüger.'

'You have?' He spat at the ground and acted all cool, but she could see he was dying to know more.

'She said yes,' Sofia said, and smiled. Which wasn't entirely true, but so what.

'For real?' Erik said, somewhat placated.

Her mobile rang in her pocket. It said *Dad* on the screen.

'Hi.'

'Hey, Sofia, where are you?'

'I'm at Erik's, why?'

A moment of silence ensued.

'Listen . . . I'm a bit busy tonight. And I don't want you to be home alone. Do you think you could sleep over at Erik's?'

How strange. Normally her dad always wanted her to sleep over at Granny's.

'All right? Sure. I can ask.'

'Great, and will you text me if it's OK?'

'I will, and—' Sofia said, and was about to add something, but her father had already rung off.

'Who was it?' Erik said, looking almost as if he had stopped sulking.

'My dad. He wants me to stay over.'

'At my house?' Erik said with a frown.
'Yes.'
'That should be all right, I guess.'
He turned and started walking down the path.
'But you have to promise me to be a little more normal, OK?'
'I promise.' Sofia nodded and followed him down the path.

Chapter 9

Hannah Holmen was standing in front of her bedroom mirror feeling even more awkward than usual. Going to a party? Dressed like this? Why on earth had she agreed to that? She took off the Donald Duck mask and flopped on to her bed. Yellow tights, a pair of yellow slippers that were supposed to look like duck feet, a pale blue oversized T-shirt and a red bow around her neck. At first the idea had seemed hilarious. It was Jessica's, obviously, at the bonfire over at Andres Wold's. *'Let's dress up as Disney characters! I'll order costumes for us!'* They had all been drunk, especially Jessica, who had been barely able to stand up.

Hannah got up, twirled around the floor and shook her head. No, no way. No way would she be seen like this in public. She pulled off the hideous tights and found a white skirt instead. There, that was better. The Donald Duck mask and the oversized T-shirt would have to be enough. Didn't she have some yellow trainers somewhere? No, they were too small. She would have to wear the red ones. Her phone pinged. For the umpteenth time in the last hour.

We'll meet at Andres's, OK?
You coming or what?
Send me a picture of your costume, go on!
You're not staying at home, are you?
She had sent only one message:
I'll be there. See you at six.
Hannah heaved a sigh and looked at the date on her mobile: 16 July.
Three years ago today.

She should be at home; of course she should. Rather than going to a costume party. She took one last look at herself in the mirror and went downstairs to the living room.

'Mum? Are you there?'

Silence.

Hannah went to her mother's bedroom and knocked softly on the door.

'Mum? Are you asleep?'

She opened the door, but there was no one there. She went to the kitchen and then to the larder. Two three-litre boxes of wine, one red and one white. Perhaps she could pour some into a plastic bottle? Her mum would never know, would she?

There was also a bottle of vodka behind the jam. Hannah picked it up. No one had touched it for a long time: there was dust on the cap.

Now we're talking.

She found an empty screw-top bottle on the floor by the potatoes and rinsed it in the kitchen sink.

She checked the level of vodka in the bottle carefully before she started pouring. Right to the top of the label. Alcohol into the water bottle. Water into the vodka bottle. She bent down and checked it again.

Perfect.

Hannah popped the bottle into her rucksack and turned off the light in the larder. Truth be told, she didn't really like vodka. Vodka was a cabbie's drink. Jessica called it that because she knew a taxi driver who always drank vodka at work because no one could tell from his breath that he had been drinking. But it would have to do.

Hannah returned to the living room and stopped in the middle of the floor. The lump in her stomach. She had felt better after the session with her psychologist, but the lump was coming back now.

'Mum?' She practically whispered it.

Her phone beeped again. A picture this time. Jessica in front of Roar's Autos with a bottle in her hand.

You coming or what??

Hannah Holmen popped her mobile into her rucksack, went out into the hall, put on her red trainers and took one last look at herself in the mirror before she stepped outside and started pushing her bicycle towards the main road.

Chapter 10

Mia took a step back; she felt in need of a break. Switching to work mode was taking longer than usual. She had not come to Hitra to work and she had subconsciously resisted it, but there was no way back now. *Jonathan, where are you?* She had always had this ability. Shut out every distraction and focus all her energy on what really mattered, like a chess player who would barely notice if the roof caved in because she was so deep into her calculations.

Damn it, was she really going to go there?

All right, just for a few weeks. Until her car was fixed. And besides, she had already opened the floodgates.

It was too late to turn back now.

She walked down to the jetty and turned her face to the soft light. The orange evening sun had taken a dip in the horizon and had risen again. She could hear distant bass thumping from Hitra. Someone was having a party.

Jonathan Holmen.

Aged eight.

A helpful voice when she had called:

'Kripos, Janne speaking.'

'Hi, Janne. It's Mia Krüger calling.'

'Good heavens, Mia, how nice to hear from you. It's been a long time. What are you up to these days?'

'Funny you should ask . . .'

And not long afterwards she had been standing with the police officer with the sad face in the basement of the small police station on Hitra where Kripos had stored the case files because the officers had always intended to come back.

Four possibilities:
Jonathan was in an accident.
Jonathan was killed.
Jonathan was kidnapped and has died.
Jonathan was kidnapped and is alive.
It couldn't be anything else, could it?

Five hours into the material and she was already starting to sense the outline of a narrative. A feeling that something didn't add up. Because it was hard to believe, wasn't it? A boy cycles home, a bike ride of less than one kilometre. And then, puff, he vanishes without a trace.

Well, there was one lead: his bicycle. It had been found by divers in the sea by a jetty. So was it an accident?

She had tried to visualize it. Jonathan is riding his bike; he is on his way home. For some reason he chooses not to take the direct route. Instead he cycles down to a jetty and there, for some reason, although the ground is dry that evening, he loses control of his bicycle, crashes on to the jetty, hits his head, is knocked unconscious, falls into the sea, drowns and his body is carried away by the current.

Was it possible? Absolutely. But what would he be doing there? Or did he throw his own bicycle into the water? No.

Perhaps some teenagers talked him into getting involved in something they were doing and there had been an accident? Or had he seen something he shouldn't? But there had been no sightings of any activities down by the jetty that night, had there? Only that one car.

Mia closed her eyes and leaned forwards, trying to visualize everything she had put up on the wall.

What was she missing?

Behind all the documents and photographs a voice was whispering to her.

The timeline she had put up on the wall.

20.31 – Jonathan's mother calls the By family.
20.40 – Jonathan leaves the By family home.
20.50 – A car is spotted in Svingen.

21.42 – Jonathan's mother calls the By family again.
21.47 – Jonathan's mother calls the police.
22.05 – The police boat arrives at Svingen.

One hour and twenty-five minutes. From the boy leaving the By family home and the police arriving by boat. Only one witness. He had seen a car. A man in his fifties. What was his name again?

Wallstedt. Jacob Wallstedt. His was the only house with a view of Svingen.

Svingen wasn't its official name or something she could find on a map, it was just how the place was known locally. The spot where Jonathan went missing.

And again there was only one house, with this man in his fifties. Who had been alert as he sat outside his house that evening. He hadn't seen the boy. But he had seen the mysterious car. How come he hadn't seen the boy? Mia got up, stretched out her arms to the sky and resisted the temptation to take off the bandage and immerse herself in the magical water, instead wandering back towards the house.

Jacob Wallstedt. Her first port of call tomorrow morning.

But first, sleep.

Chapter 11

In the old days Luca Eriksen would have treated himself to a glass of wine. It was a Saturday night. Twenty-four-hour sunlight outside the large living-room windows. The light was faint now, true, but even so. These nights. He had loved them. Amanda and him. Together. Out on the terrace. The winters were bad enough in southern Norway, but this far north? Hand on heart, he had to admit it. At times, when the winter was at its worst, he had been angry with her. The snow never settled long enough for him to go skiing. No, up here it just flew around in every direction, wet and sticky and driving him mad.

But the summer nights.

Luca carried his tea and his iPad on to the terrace. Sunshine out here all night. And wine. Lots of wine. He sipped his tea and stared vacantly across the sea. It had been excessive sometimes. The wine. He had lost count of the number of times he had had to help her to bed. He would take her clothes off carefully and gently tuck her in.

Her bloody parents.

Who on earth behaved like this? Towards their own daughter.

He hadn't noticed it to begin with. Her parents were just like the other locals out here on Hitra. But in time he had started to see it.

Her father took no interest in her at all. No matter how hard she tried, he never really seemed to respond. Her mother, however, was almost worse. Criticizing her constantly. Her clothes. Her job. The way she spoke. Never a kind word.

So he never said anything when she drank too much. She needed to numb the pain. And how could he blame her for that? It wasn't until other people started making remarks.

53

Fabian was the first, putting it delicately:

'Listen, Luca. We've been talking about Amanda's drinking. Do you think she might benefit from a session with me? Perhaps that would help?'

He had been furious, of course. What the hell did they know about everything she had been through. In time, however, he had come to realize that something had to change. And so she had started therapy with Fabian.

Sporadically at first, then more regularly. And yes, it had helped. Or at least it had helped a little.

Luca brushed the memories aside and turned on his iPad. He had created a system now, and he was still perfecting it. Pictures in one folder. Videos in another. Luca took another sip of his tea and opened one of them. Oh . . .

He smiled as he felt the tears well up. Diving. Poor Amanda. She had loved the sea, as long as she could stay on the surface. But he had forced her, hadn't he? He'd so wanted her to share his joy. It was another world down there. And she had tried, for his sake. Luca zoomed in on a photo. Amanda with her wetsuit rolled down to her waist, a towel around her hair, her frightened face looking at the photographer.

'I'm sorry, Amanda.'

'I just wanted you to . . .'

Luca broke off. What the . . .

He set down his cup and zoomed in on the photo. In the background.

A boat.

It was beached and half covered by tarpaulin. The name painted on the bow.

KITTY3.

The 'I' was missing.

K TTY3.

Hang on. The crows in the church. The metal tags around their legs.

KTTY3.

The policeman in him woke up. He made a snap decision, ran back inside the house, put on his coat and got into his car. That boat was beached in Setervågen marina. It wasn't far away. A fifteen-minute drive. He felt another pang of guilt as he pulled out on to the road.

Poor Amanda. He should never have put pressure on her, obviously. And now he, too, had quit diving. It didn't feel right any more.

Luca parked, got out of his car and walked down the path to the marina. The sun disappeared behind a cloud at that moment and a darker light spread across the bay.

It was still there.

KTTY3.

An old smack someone had tried to restore, but it seemed they had abandoned their attempt. A large sheet of blue tarpaulin covered the cabin.

Luca walked around the boat. There was a ladder providing access on the port side.

'Hello?'

Tentatively he put his foot on the bottom rung of the ladder. Music in the distance: someone was having a party somewhere. Luca pulled the tarpaulin aside, climbed up on to the deck, took his torch out of his jacket pocket and turned it on.

'Hello?'

How strange. Clothing. A pair of shoes. Some old paperbacks. Was someone living here?

There was enough headroom under the tarpaulin for him to stand up almost straight.

'Hello?'

An empty can of cola. Potato crisps. A filthy sock on the top step of the companionway. Luca let the light from his torch guide him down the steps. He got the same feeling below deck.

Someone was living here.

Small piles of clothes. A mattress in one corner. And what was that smell? Like something had been burned.

Luca froze and then gasped for air.
There was a young woman on the floor.
Covered in blood.
Shaking all over, he cautiously moved the torch beam until it finally reached the battered head. *Her face was gone.*

TWO

SUNDAY

Chapter 12

Holger Munch was sitting in the eighth row of the Oslo Concert Hall engulfed by a profound feeling of emptiness. The orchestra was playing the opening movement of Beethoven's Ninth Symphony, and normally he would have been over the moon. The hush in the auditorium when the lights were slowly dimmed. The clattering of instruments as the musicians carefully took their places. A few tingling seconds of total silence before the conductor arrived. But it was all wasted on him this morning. He had turned up with two tickets for the lunchtime concert. But the seat next to him was empty. No Lillian. So she had been serious. It really was the end of the road for him, personally as well as professionally.

First there had been the telephone call from Oslo Police headquarters. The voice had been trying to stay neutral, but he could hear the glee. *For budgetary reasons a decision has been made to centralize all units in the capital.* He had heard the rumours, of course, murmurings in the corridors, but he had refused to believe that it could ever happen. After all, they had threatened his unit with closure so many times before. The Homicide Unit in Mariboesgate 13 which he led. He was the country's most successful investigator, supported by a team even the best in the world could only dream of. The most complex cases. A clear-up rate of almost a hundred per cent. Naturally that had earned him some enemies, jealous bastards wanting nothing more than to topple him from his throne, but he had always brushed them aside like dust from the shoulders of his old tweed jacket. But this time it really was the end.

'It's over, Holger.'

Anette Goli in his office, softly spoken as always. She had been

59

his right hand for ten years, and he could see his own reaction reflected in her eyes. Crushing disappointment.

He had been short and to the point in the investigation room some hours later. His team: Ludvig Grønlie, Gabriel Mørk, Curry, Ylva and Kim Kolsø, whom he had finally convinced to come back from Hønefoss by promising him the earth.

'Thank you for your commitment, all of you. There is nothing we can do, sadly.'

Holger Munch hadn't touched a drop of alcohol since he was fourteen, but that afternoon he had sought out oblivion. A Glenfiddich with three ice cubes, as he slumped over the bar in some dive in Tøyen, but he hadn't even had the strength to raise the glass to his lips. Thank God for Lillian. Strong, kind-hearted Lillian. He had not known her long, and yet he had grown close to her so quickly. In bed later that same evening, the warmth from her body, her soft fingers caressing his heavy face.

'So what do we do now, Holger? Maybe it's a sign. The past is over, the future awaits. Our future, perhaps?'

And so they had started house-hunting in Oslo for a place where they could live together. At long last he would leave his tiny flat in Bislett, unpack his few belongings from their cardboard boxes and find shelves to put them on. Sort his life out. For the first time since his divorce.

With each day he had come out of his shell, and he had been nowhere near as negative as she claimed. He had really liked some of the suggestions the estate agents had sent them. A lovely four-room place in Frogner with a view of Uranienborg church – yes, absolutely, he had meant it when he said that he could see himself living there. A large maisonette flat in Vika, not far from the concert hall, and again, he had been positive, but there had been something in her eyes, in her voice, and finally she had put it to him bluntly.

'I don't think you want this, Holger. Not really.'

Her hand refusing to hold his now.

'What do you mean?'

'I think you're still in love with her.'

'What?'

He had practically shouted his response, and it was at that moment he had realized that she might be right. He had felt like someone had caught him telling a lie he wasn't even aware of, and yet he had continued to defend himself.

'Oh, come on, Lillian.'

'Holger, just admit it, please? I'm a grown-up. I can handle the truth.'

'Lillian—'

'I think I need a little time on my own.'

The horrible scraping of her chair against the restaurant floor. The silence when she picked up her handbag and left without looking back.

Beethoven's Symphony No. 9 in D minor, Opus 125, his final work, an unrivalled masterpiece, completed in 1824, the finest example of late-classical early-romantic music, and it was meant to be for her. His clumsy way of telling her that he cared about her. Two expensive tickets, the best seats in the house, but the orchestra was now deep into the second movement and for the first time in his life he felt nothing at all.

He didn't return to his seat after the interval. Instead he went outside and stared vacantly across the square; he had taken a third cigarette out of the packet before he had even finished the second one.

His mobile vibrated, but he didn't hear it. It stopped, then started again. His movements were on autopilot when he took the call.

'Yes, Munch speaking.'

An unfamiliar voice far away.

'Hello, Holger, sorry to disturb you. It's Tom.'

'Tom who?'

'Tom Ludvigsen.'

A car with rowdy young people and music blaring out of the windows drove past him.

'Oh, hi, Tom. Sorry. I was . . . lost in thought. It has been a while.'

'Yes, far too long. How are you?'

'What? Oh . . . good, thank you. And how about you? Are you still . . .'

Tom Ludvigsen.

An old colleague. From the time before the Homicide Unit. Ludvigsen had once been an inspector at Oslo Police headquarters.

'Oh, I'm still up in Trøndelag,' Ludvigsen said, laughing. 'I have to say I miss being down south, but if a good man is offered a senior management position in this profession, he really has to take it, wasn't that what we agreed?'

Ludvigsen chuckled. He seemed to be expecting a response, but Munch continued to stare into the distance.

'So,' his former colleague went on, 'is it true?'

'Is what true?'

'That you're between jobs at the moment?'

Munch heaved a sigh and lit the cigarette.

'It is, I'm afraid.'

'Are you going back to Police HQ or do you have—'

'I haven't made up my mind yet,' Munch said, regretting not having turned off his phone altogether. It was an old habit, always being available.

'Great,' Ludvigsen said. He sounded almost cheerful. 'Then I might be in with a chance after all.'

'What do you mean?'

'How do you feel about a trip up north?'

'Come again?'

'I know it's a lot to ask, but we have a case up here and I'm wondering if we might be in over our heads. Don't get me wrong, we've got good people, but I have a feeling we might need someone who really knows this stuff.'

And it was at this point that Munch snapped out of his dark thoughts.

'What are we talking about?'

'A sixteen-year-old girl. On an island off the main coast. Hitra.'

'Go on?'

Hitra.

It was just over one year ago.

He had found her there.

She had been unrecognizable.

Practically dead already.

'I don't want to go into detail over the phone,' Ludvigsen said. 'But I don't like the look of this one. It's like nothing I've seen before. Brutal. And the stuff we found at the crime scene, no, I'm not sure if we—'

Munch heaved a sigh, then cut him off.

'Tom. I'm flattered to be asked, but I don't think that—'

The response came swiftly, as if Ludvigsen had been waiting to tell him all along.

'She asked me to call you.'

'Who?'

'Mia Krüger.'

'Come again?'

'She was there last night. The body was found by a local police officer and he called her.'

'Mia is there?'

'Yes,' Ludvigsen said. 'She wants you to come up here. She asked me to call. Make it more official. So what do you think? Want to join us?'

'I'll be on the next plane. Send me everything you have,' Munch said, and ran towards a taxi rank.

Chapter 13

Mia Krüger was waiting at the express ferry terminal, still wearing the same clothes she had thrown on when Luca Eriksen had called her last night. Luca was leaning against the police car, ashen-faced. Mia had forgotten what it was like to be someone like him. She moved into the shade and observed him discreetly. She liked the expression in his eyes. His reaction on encountering a dead body. The shock. The realization of wickedness. *Someone has taken this young woman's life.* She took another look at him, intrigued now, as she tried to absorb it. His normality. His humanity. She could barely remember what it had been like for her the first time. Old, innocent Mia, the person she used to be. It was the reason she had quit. In the hope of rediscovering her old self.

'*Once a police officer, always a police officer.*'

The words from Munch were seared into her soul. After their first case together. Two boys in a field, practically naked, with a dead fox arranged between them. At that moment she had begun to understand what her old supervisor at the National Police Academy had talked about. The special quality she had.

'*You have something no one else has, Mia.*'

Two nearly naked boys and a dead fox. She had almost been able to feel him. The killer. Sense him, as if he were somewhere inside her.

She had been ten years younger then, and incredibly excited when they had finally caught him in a cabin deep in the woods. It wasn't until later, several months later, that the shock arrived. A total breakdown. She had curled up under the duvet and barely been able to speak.

'*Perhaps you shouldn't carry on?*'
'*Perhaps this isn't healthy for you, Mia?*'
But Munch had persuaded her.
'*Once a police officer, always a police officer.*'
The sheer wickedness of the act. Who kills two children, undresses them, places an animal between them and then takes pictures of the scene?

I don't want to live in a world like that.

She guessed that Munch had sensed as much from the look on her face, because the debriefing that followed had been thorough and she had felt that much of it was for her sake.

An explanation as to why. Who he was, this man. They had found his diaries in the cabin. Long, disgusting accounts. The world as he saw it. He was clearly a paedophile, but refused to admit it to himself. These children had tricked him. Made him do things with them, things he would never otherwise have done. He had no choice but to remove them because these children were no good for the world, they would do it again and again, to others who were like him.

At the time she had reacted to the killer's wording: *remove*, not 'kill'.

Remove them in a way that was beautiful.

It didn't make her feel any better, far from it, but there had been something about the camaraderie during the investigation. The other members of the unit. They were together in this. It was what had made her stay.

'There's the ferry,' Luca said, pointing across the sea as he came towards her.

'Are you OK?' Mia said, placing her hand on his shoulder.

'Eh? Oh, yes. I'm OK.'

'I'm glad you called me last night,' Mia said.

Luca ran a hand across his pale face.

'I don't know, perhaps I should have—'

'It's all right,' Mia said, rubbing his shoulder.

He continued to stand there with a blank expression on his face. He didn't even notice that his mobile was ringing.

'Is everything set up at the station?'

'Sorry, what did you say?' He turned to her, his eyes still distant.

'We'll need a room where we can work.'

'Oh, right. Yes, of course. How about the meeting room at the end of the corridor? Will that do?'

Luca appeared to be waking up.

'Absolutely. And we'll need you, if you don't mind? We need someone with local knowledge.'

'Yes, sure. Of course.'

'Great, Luca. Do you think you could map her relationships?'

'Map?'

'A map of the people who knew her? Parents, neighbours, friends, school, work colleagues – everything we might need.'

Luca nodded and brushed his fringe away from his forehead. He was a police officer once more. It seemed to help.

'Do you want me to—' He glanced towards the ferry.

'No, you take the car back to the station. We need to get started as soon as we can. We won't be long, all right?'

'Good,' Luca said, and returned to his car as the ferry slowly approached the quay.

Chapter 14

The tourists would appear to have read the brochures – or the warnings on the Internet. Going to Norway for your summer holiday? By the coast? Pack extra clothing to keep you warm because there is one thing you can be sure of: you will be freezing cold. This year, however, the weather gods had put all such warnings to bed. The sun was roasting the glittering sea and the faces around him were ecstatic. German, French, American and Japanese; laughter as their mobile phones and cameras snapped the spray around the bows of the ferry. And though Holger Munch had only stepped outside for a cigarette, he couldn't help but stay there and take it all in, this magnificent landscape. Hitra. This lovely island at the mouth of the Trondheim fjord.

She was waiting for him on the quay.

'Hello, Holger.' Mia hugged him and led the way up to a bench in the shade.

Munch wiped the sweat from his brow and sat down.

'So you're the welcoming committee?'

Mia smiled and put down her mobile between them.

'For now. Crime-scene technicians are still at the scene and Trondheim Police have sent us all available personnel, everyone is waiting for you.'

'Good,' Munch said, and took his iPad out of his suitcase.

'Is everything all right?' Mia cocked her head and looked at him.

Norway was a small country. News travelled fast. She had already heard, of course. That their unit had been closed.

'Well, what do you want me to say? Could it be any worse?' He heaved a sigh and took a cigarette out of the packet.

'I'm sure it'll be all right in the end,' Mia said, placing her hand on his.

'Do you think so?'

'Of course.' She smiled briefly under her dark fringe.

'Our bosses are politicians. They come and go. You'll be back once we get a new boss. After all, they know who you are and what you can do.'

'Let's hope so.' Munch sighed again and lit his cigarette.

'And you?'

Mia hesitated.

'Yes, good,' she said eventually.

'So not really?'

'Well . . .' She shifted her gaze to the sea.

'I'm not blaming you, if that's what you're worried about,' Munch said. 'You did what you had to do.'

'Are you sure?' She glanced at him briefly.

'Of course, Mia. Don't give it another thought.'

'Good. I felt guilty, of course. When I heard that they had shut you down. I thought it might be because of me. That me leaving gave them the excuse they had been waiting for.'

'Oh, you're not that important,' Munch said, and winked at her.

'Oh, no?' Mia smiled.

'No,' Munch said. 'I was solving cases long before you arrived, or have you forgotten?'

She laughed out loud.

'We'll be based at the local police station. It's small, but I think it'll be OK.'

'But you wanted to start here?'

Mia agreed. 'I wanted to have you to myself before you meet the others.'

'Good,' Munch said, turning on his iPad.

'Did they send you everything?' Mia woke up her mobile and turned it to him. 'You have these?' Munch nodded. 'OK. So, last night. Around midnight I get a call from the local police officer out here, Eriksen. He was completely beside himself, didn't know what to do.'

'He was the one who found her?'

'Yes, in an old boat which was dragged up on the beach.'

'And why was he there? Something about . . . some birds. In a church, was that it?'

'Three crows on the new altarpiece. With tags around their legs. Look.' She turned her mobile towards him again to show him.

'So he saw those letters and connected them to a boat?'

'Yes. KTTY3. Kitty 3. It's the name of an old wreck in Setervågen marina. The "I" was missing. Well spotted. He's no fool.'

'And he'll be working with us?'

'Yes, I think that would be a good idea.'

'Good,' Munch said, shading his eyes from the sunlight. 'So these birds were on the altarpiece? And what's the story there?'

'There's a fair amount of grumbling on the island,' Mia said. 'Concerning the Prytz family. Does that ring a bell?'

Munch nodded. Henry Prytz. Royal Arctic Salmon. You couldn't miss it. There were few billionaires in this small country.

'The family sponsored the new altarpiece, but some people felt it was going too far. A little too self-glorifying.'

'Too many fish and not enough Jesus?'

'Something like that. I haven't seen it myself, but according to Luca—'

'Luca?'

'Luca Eriksen, sorry. He's the local police officer. At first he thought it was a prank. A crude one, true, but even so.'

'The birds' eyes had been gouged out, am I right?'

Mia nodded and showed him another picture.

'What do you make of that?' he said.

She grew silent and turned her face to the sea. Her eyes took on this unique expression. Munch realized it now: how much he had missed her.

'I'm not sure,' she said softly.

'But it's relevant?'

'What? Oh, yes, definitely, of course it is . . . It's just . . .'

'What are you thinking?'

'I don't know. There's something here, but I can't quite see it yet.'

'Have you been there?'

'The church? No, there has been a lot going on. I've hardly had any sleep.'

'We need to go there, it's a priority, OK?'

Mia nodded and turned her mobile towards him again.

'So this is our victim. Her name is Jessica Bakken. Aged sixteen. She would appear to have been sleeping on the boat, how often or for how long I don't know, but there we are.' She swiped to the next picture. 'Murdered, a brutal attack from the front, it would appear. As you can see, her face is practically gone.'

'Murder weapon?'

'An iron bar?' Mia shrugged. 'My first thought was a hammer, but I'm not sure. Wouldn't the indentations have been more defined?' She enlarged the image and looked at him.

'I agree.' Munch nodded. 'Did you find anything at the scene?'

'No. It was quite dark down there. She didn't seem to have any electricity. Some candles, a couple of battery-powered lamps. The crime-scene technicians will probably find the murder weapon, if it's there. But anyway, a violent, brutal attack from the front, perhaps while she was lying down.'

'She was awake when it happened?'

'It's too early to say. According to Luca, there was a costume party on the island last night, a local event of some sort. I found a Mickey Mouse mask, so she was probably going to the party or she had already been, so I guess she would have been awake.'

'And the time frame?'

Mia shrugged again. 'I don't know. It was all very fresh, but not that fresh, if you know what I mean. The blood on the floor around her was wet, but the edges had started to coagulate. So some hours before we found her, perhaps?'

'Around seven or eight in the evening, say?'

'Something like that.'

'Tech?'

'I looked for her mobile, but couldn't find it. No laptop at the scene. And, as far as I know, no one has been to her home address yet.'

'So she does have a home? In addition to the boat?' Munch lit a fresh cigarette with the previous one.

'As far as I can gather,' Mia nodded. 'The family situation is complicated. Mother an alcoholic? Or a drug addict? Something like that. Like I said, I haven't got all the information yet.'

'Has the family been told?'

'I think officers have tried to track her down, but no.'

'The victim's mother, you mean?'

'Yes. Someone said she often goes to Trondheim. To get drunk, perhaps. I don't know.'

'Nothing gets out until we've spoken to her, all right?'

'Of course.' Mia nodded. 'No press so far, I believe. The journalists have manners out here. There's a local paper. None of the nationals yet, as far as I know. Though rumour has it they're about to descend on the island.'

'What? Why?'

'The wedding. The heir to the salmon empire is getting married. I think it's kind of a big deal.'

'That's the last thing we need,' Munch muttered under his breath.

'I know.' Mia nodded. 'We'll try to keep it under wraps for as long as we can.' She fell silent again.

'What are you thinking about?'

'I'm not sure,' Mia said. 'The level of violence suggests a crime of passion, don't you think? The brutality?'

Munch nodded.

'But then again, when I looked at the scene in the church it seemed carefully planned. I just can't connect the two.'

'Are you referring to this?' Munch said, sliding the iPad towards her.

'Yes.' Mia nodded softly.

The photograph showed a small white teacup.

On the side someone had written BABY WHORE.

And in the girl's blood on the floor, a name:

Jonathan.

Chapter 15

Sofia was standing beneath the pulpit in the church, smiling to herself because it was the same performance every time: two people arguing over who would be the conductor, but, as they were grown-ups, trying very hard not to let on, even though their vying for control was obvious to the whole choir. The girls next to her were giggling, but struggling not to show it. Sofia winked at them and giggled as well. She loved singing in the choir, their voices floating around this fine space, but every time they had to go through this charade before they could start, the two conductors failing to agree. Sofia's favourite hymns were 'Lord of All Hopefulness' and 'Love Divine, All Loves Excelling'. Her father would always shake his head after the church concerts and services and sigh 'Ah, well,' but she wasn't bothered about God; what mattered to her were the hymns. How they made her tingle when she sang them and how all the other voices seemed to dance like warm bubbles in the air around her. Not what the hymns were about. Like every other grown-up, her father had to *explain* everything, and he had sat her down several times: *'You know that people believe many different things, don't you?'* Of course she did, it wasn't as if she was a little kid, was it? She knew that there wasn't an old man with a beard sitting on a cloud in the sky watching everything they did, but surely that didn't matter. What mattered was how singing felt. How happy it made her inside. Rather than the words they sang. That had changed, however, when the new vicar arrived. He had suggested that they sing songs other than the ones about God all the time. Once, when Nora had been ill, he had been in charge of choir practice and brought along different sheet music; he had practically whispered to them, as if they shared a secret: *'Today we're going to sing something funny.'* That had been in December, and they had been rehearsing for the Christmas service. The song he had brought with him was 'All I Want for Christmas is You', which was not only in English but also had nothing to do with God. It had, however, been great fun, especially because the new vicar was nowhere near as good at playing the piano as he thought he was, and it had sounded a bit plinky-plonk, but the English words were amusing; it was almost like moving a boiled sweet around your mouth. They had wondered what Nora would say when she came back. And she had barely been able to contain herself. Her face had gone bright red, she practically had steam coming out of her ears, and after that day they had never sung that song again.

Sofia scratched her knee and used the sheet music to fan her face. The church was unbearably hot today and some people had complained, but they still had to practise for the big wedding. Sofia tingled with excitement when she thought about it. It might well be the biggest wedding in the whole world, and she would be singing at it. She could feel a smile spread across her warm cheeks. How romantic. It was almost like a fairy tale. The prince was getting married and, even though the king and queen would most definitely have preferred him to marry a princess, perhaps one from a foreign land, he had fallen in love with an ordinary girl, someone just like her.

'Yes, but Prytz said he wanted . . .' the new vicar tried to insist at the front, pointing to a sheet of paper in his hand.

Nora's cheeks were flushed, but she did her best not to voice her thoughts, although she looked very cross. She could be like that at times, obsessing over what was right about God and Jesus and so on. However, it looked like the two of them had finally resolved their differences. Nora cleared her throat and surveyed the choir with a smile while the vicar shuffled over to the piano. Sofia felt a little bad now for mocking him. His piano playing was all right; it was just that the English song had been so difficult.

Nora was about to start conducting when suddenly she paused in front of them with a stern expression on her face. At first Sofia thought she was looking at her, but, fortunately, she wasn't. It was another girl, one from Frøya, who was standing next to her. Sofia didn't know her name because she had just joined the choir, which probably explained why she had yet to learn how Nora wanted things done in the church.

'Excuse me,' Nora said with a nod to the girl. 'What do you think you're wearing?'

'Me?' The girl looked up nervously.

'Yes, you there,' Nora said, coming over to them. 'What do you think this is, a lido?'

Nora planted her hands on her hips and nodded to the girl's clothes. Shorts and a crop top which showed her tummy.

'Have you no respect for God?'

'But it's so hot and—'

'We dress properly in church,' Nora said. 'Haven't you got anything else?'

'I have a jumper in my bag,' the girl mumbled, staring at the floor.

'Go and get it.'

The girl kept her head down as she ran down the aisle and returned, crestfallen, wearing her jumper.

'Right.' Nora nodded, returned to her position and raised her arms. 'And now we will sing "Love Divine, All Loves Excelling".'

They were just about to start when the doors at the front of the church opened.

'I'm sorry for disturbing you.' Sofia smiled when she heard the voice.

'Yes, Dorothea?' Nora said with a sigh.

Sofia's grandmother didn't come down to where they were but remained in the doorway.

'Again, I'm sorry for the interruption, but I have to talk to Sofia.'

Sofia turned.

'Now?' Nora said, and sighed a second time. 'The wedding is in less than—'

'Yes, right now, I'm afraid.' Her grandmother's voice sounded strange.

'Very well then,' Nora said, and gestured for Sofia to leave the line-up. Sofia ran down the aisle to meet her.

'What is it, Granny?'

Her grandmother took her hand, closed the doors behind them and said nothing until they were outside on the steps.

'Something has happened, Sofia. Something sad.'

Chapter 16

The local police station was clearly not designed for this. All available police officers in the region had turned up on Hitra in the hope of being included in the investigation team, finally carrying out some meaningful police work. Mia had almost forgotten how commanding Munch could be when he cleared his throat and in a loud voice told everyone to be quiet after the officers had squeezed themselves into the investigation room at the end of the corridor.

'Who is in charge of operations here?' Munch's voice boomed across the room. A couple of uniformed officers exchanged tentative glances before one held up his hand.

'That will be me. Jack Olsen, Orkanger Police.'

'Good, Jack Olsen, Orkanger Police. This is what I want you to do: take everyone, and I mean everyone, in uniform here with you as you leave. I don't want to see a single uniform in here, understood?'

A woman in uniform squashed into a corner quickly raised her hand.

'I'm sorry, are you telling us to change our clothes?'

'No. And I'm talking to Jack.' Munch pointed to Jack Olsen.

'You, Jack, are in charge of everyone in uniform out there, understood?' Jack Olsen nodded gravely.

'I don't want to see a single uniform in here. This room is now for the investigation unit only.'

'But—' said an officer who was standing among a cluster of people outside the door, but Munch simply dismissed him with a wave of his hand.

'You report to me, and I want to hear only from you, understood?'

Jack Olsen nodded again.

'Good,' Munch continued. 'I've been told that the crime scene has been secured, that the technicians are making good progress and that the body has been sent to the pathologist. Is that correct?'

Jack Olsen looked hesitantly at the colleague next to him, who nodded hesitantly in return.

'Yes,' Jack Olsen said.

'Good, keep following protocol and, again, if there are any developments, I only want to hear about them from you, got it?'

'Got it.'

'Our first priority is next of kin. I've been told that there isn't a father and that we're still looking for the mother?'

Another nervous look from Jack Olsen, but his colleague nodded.

'Let me know once we make contact with her, please.'

Jack Olsen nodded, got up and herded the uniformed officers down the corridor. 'You heard the man. Everyone outside.'

There was a chorus of disapproval and sighs of disappointment as every officer in uniform left the room.

'Right,' Munch said, looking around when the room was finally quiet. 'So who do we have here?'

A handful of people, all in civilian clothing, were still sitting down.

'I'm happy to go first,' said a dark-haired woman in her early thirties. 'Nina Riccardo, investigator from Trondheim Police.'

The others followed suit.

'Ralph Nygaard, investigator from Orkanger Police.'

'Hi, I'm Claus, Claus Nielsen. Police lawyer from Trondheim.'

'Kevin Borg, investigator, Trondheim Police.'

Luca Eriksen was standing at the back, looking around hesitantly. 'Er, I'm Luca Eriksen, I'm the local police officer here on Hitra. Now, I am in uniform, but you wanted me to—'

Mia smiled at him. 'Absolutely, Luca. You clearly belong here. You can sit down.'

Luca nodded cautiously to the others and found himself a chair by the window.

'OK,' Munch said, looking across his new team. 'And for those of you who don't know me, my name is Holger Munch, and this is Mia Krüger.'

Mia nodded to the faces in the room.

'We're now responsible for this investigation and, if you have a problem with that, I suggest you take it up with Ludvigsen. By the way, do we have someone here? Who thinks that is a problem?'

A couple of people shook their heads.

'Good. But if we do, the door is over there. I expect you to do what I tell you to and understand that from now on we're working as one unit.'

The investigators exchanged glances and nodded again.

'Some ground rules.' Munch grunted. 'Not a word of what we talk about in here will leave this room. Not to your wife, your husband, your neighbour or to any of your local superiors. Any information will come from me, understood?'

No one said anything.

'Good – and this is extremely important – not a word to the media. I know it can be tempting to be the one who gives the local paper a scoop, but if I find out that there have been any leaks from this unit, then—'

He broke off for a moment.

'We get it.' The woman called Nina Riccardo nodded.

Shoulder-length hair, golden skin, possibly from a father from southern Europe. She was dressed in strong colours: tight yellow jeans, a bright red T-shirt and white trainers. Dark grey eyes. She seemed confident and calm. As if, despite her young age, she had been doing this job for a while.

'Good, thank you. Again, I accept that it might not be your dream scenario for investigators to arrive from Oslo and take over, but that's just how it is. From now on I'm in charge.'

'So not Mia?'

A cheeky remark from Kevin Borg, a man with fair curls wearing a light-coloured summer suit and a white shirt, one of the investigators from Trondheim.

'If there's something you want to say to Mia, but not me, then you're welcome as long as it doesn't leave this room,' Munch said dryly, and took his iPad out of his bag. 'Is there somewhere I can plug this in?'

Luca mumbled something and got up from his chair.

Mia was starting to regret including him in the investigation unit. Luca clearly looked uncomfortable as he fumbled with the screen behind Munch and then connected a cable to a projector in the ceiling.

'There.' He smiled apologetically when the pictures finally lit up on the screen.

'OK,' Munch said, looking across at his team again. 'We will soon get to know each other better, but we can't afford to waste any more time now, so let's get started right away. Please would you—'

He nodded to Luca, who drew the curtains and closed the door to the corridor before sitting down again.

'Jessica Bakken,' Munch said, clicking to bring up the first photograph.

It would appear to have been taken from her social media. A smiling girl wearing cut-off jeans and a cropped pink T-shirt which showed her flat stomach. Braces, and her fingers in a peace sign, grinning at the photographer. Munch turned to his team.

'I only learned about her today. Does anyone here know more than I do?'

Nina Riccardo cleared her throat and looked down at her notepad.

'Jessica Bakken, aged sixteen, born at the regional hospital in Trondheim. Mother, Laura Bakken, aged thirty-three, grew up outside Tromsø. So her mother was only seventeen when Jessica was born. Father unknown. I found a file where she, the mother, I mean, tried to attribute paternity to a man . . .'

She flicked quickly through her notes.

'. . . a man called Ronny Hov from Fauske. A DNA test established that he wasn't the child's biological father. Back to Jessica. I have three different addresses for her since her birth, one in Bremnes, one in Østbyen in Trondheim, and finally out here on Hitra, where she moved when she was nine. So she has, it would appear, lived here for seven years.'

'Good. Thank you,' Munch said. 'Does anyone else have anything?'

'Yes,' said Ralph Nygaard, a broad-shouldered man with a shaved head.

He was wearing a faded Springsteen T-shirt, brown cords, filthy trainers and seemed less confident than the other investigators in the room.

'I'm not – well, I haven't worked on cases like this before, so I'm not sure . . .' He looked hesitantly about him.

'Just say it,' Munch said.

'OK.' Ralph Nygaard cleared his throat. 'My sister lives out here. In fact, she doesn't live far away, so I—'

'Not far from where?' Munch said.

'Er, yes, sorry, not far away from where Jessica Bakken, the victim, I mean, and her mother live. She called me this morning, well, when it became known.'

Munch stopped him.

'Known? The body was found last night. Are you saying it's already public knowledge that . . .' He looked around the room.

'It's a small island,' Luca said by way of apology. 'Everyone knows everything out here. I mean, I haven't said anything, but it's absolutely impossible to—'

'OK.' Munch heaved a sigh and raised his hand to his forehead. Then he glanced quickly at Mia, who knew what that look meant.

We have to find the mother.

Her sixteen-year-old daughter has been killed. She had to hear it from someone who could give her the support she needed, no matter what state she was in. Mia nodded briefly in response.

'I'm sorry,' Munch said to the investigator wearing the Springsteen T-shirt. 'Go on.'

'Well,' Ralph Nygaard said. 'As I was just saying, my sister called me and she said they were well known in the area, Jessica and Laura, I mean. That house had a revolving door, as she put it.'

'Meaning what?'

'People coming and going all the time.' Ralph Nygaard nodded. 'Always partying. Nille said that—'

'Nille is your sister?'

80

'Er, sorry, yes, my sister said that they had called the police several times.'

Munch glanced quickly at Luca, who nodded.

'I have the reports,' he said. 'I found six in total. I myself attended on three occasions. Do you want me to—'

'We'll do that later,' Munch said, and gestured for him to sit down again.

'She described the girl's home environment as very unsafe,' Nygaard went on. 'She told me that Jessica used to come to their house. At night. Several times. Mostly when she was younger. They would give her food, some clothes, a place to sleep – yes, they would help her with whatever she needed, if I can put it like that, when her mum was at her worst.'

Munch held up his hand to stop him for a moment. 'Are we talking child-protection issues? Any reports from social services?'

There was silence in the room.

'Nielsen, was it?' Munch said.

'Yes, Claus Nielsen,' the police lawyer said.

He was a tall man who looked almost as if he had dressed up for the occasion. A black suit despite the warm weather, a white shirt with an attractive blue tie and freshly polished shoes. A wedding ring and an expensive-looking briefcase.

'Please check if we have any files on the family.'

The lawyer nodded and made a note on his iPad.

'Right. Anything else?'

'They haven't seen as much of her in the last few years,' Ralph Nygaard, the investigator from Orkanger, continued. 'They would just say hi sometimes, but I did get this from her.'

He scrolled down on his mobile.

'I'm not sure whether or not it's relevant, but I noted this down. Jessica had just finished Year Eleven, she worked as a childminder for several people. I have some names here: Mary Brun, Anne Mikkelsen—'

'We'll draw up a list later,' Munch said.

'And that's it,' Ralph Nygaard said.

'Good,' Munch said. 'Then—'

'No, wait,' Ralph Nygaard said, scratching his head. 'There was one more thing. Sorry . . .' He smiled apologetically.

'Go on,' Munch said.

'Something would appear to have happened last summer. Jessica changed noticeably, so much so that people started talking about it.'

'And what was it, do you know?' Munch said.

'She seemed to have suddenly come into money.'

'How come?'

'Now I didn't ask in detail, but Nille said that one day she had new clothes, a smart watch, expensive boots, and yes, I'm not quite sure how it came about, but there was certainly a change of lifestyle. Which people noticed.'

'OK.' Munch nodded. 'Great. Good initiative, well done. I'd like to see us carry on like this.' He nodded with approval around the room.

'I . . .' Luca began, and looked about him.

'Yes?' Munch said.

Luca glanced quickly at Mia before he spoke up.

'I've made a list of the people closest to her. Perhaps we should . . .' He produced some folded sheets of paper and a pen from the pocket of his uniform shirt.

'Go on,' Munch said.

'Her circle of friends,' Luca said. 'Jessica mainly hung out with two other girls: Sylvia Green and Hannah Holmen.'

'Holmen? As in?'

'Jonathan Holmen's older sister, yes.' Luca nodded.

Munch looked at Mia. There was murmuring across the room now.

'OK, go on.'

'Those of us who live locally know who they are – very nice girls. Sylvia is—'

'We'll go into detail later,' Munch said. 'Just give us a brief outline of the relationships.'

'OK,' Luca continued. 'So Sylvia and Hannah. Then we have Jessica's mother, Laura, as already mentioned; no other family members, at least not out here. Then she has, or well, she had a boyfriend, Andres Wold. He's twenty years old, so four years older than her. He's the son of Roar Wold, who runs a garage out in Kvenvær.'

Mia nodded softly to herself.

Andres Wold.

She had seen them as she pushed the motorcycle out of the garage. A group of young men hanging around an old Volvo. The owner of the car was impossible to miss. A loud lad with long hair, tattooed hands and rings in both ears. Music blaring through the windows; he had torn open the back door and shouted at one of the boys in the back for some reason or other.

'Now, it appears to have been a bit on and off,' Luca went on, checking the notes in front of him. 'Whether they're an item right now, I don't know, but he has been referred to as her boyfriend, from what I hear.' Luca paused. It looked as if he was mulling over something.

'Yes?' Munch said.

'Well, I'm not sure if I should mention this now or—'

'Go on.' Munch nodded.

'How can I put it? Andres – well, Andres Wold is a familiar face out here. He has been involved in all sorts. Nothing serious, I wouldn't say that – brawling, petty theft here and there, letting off steam . . . is that the right expression? He's no choirboy.'

Kevin Borg heaved a sigh, folded his arms across his chest and shook his head. Munch held up his hand to stop Luca.

'Do you have something to say?'

'Eh?' Kevin Borg said when he realized that the comment was directed at him.

'Yes?'

'Eh, no, I just—'

'You just what? Am I missing something here? You're from Trondheim and you have a problem with people out here on the island, is that it? Please elaborate.'

Kevin Borg looked at the floor and raked a hand through his blond curls. 'No, it's nothing.'

'Right,' Munch said, and nodded to Luca again.

'So, Andres Wold. He's a handful, but, like I said, I've known him for a while, and there's not a bad bone in him.'

'Criminal record?'

It was Nina Riccardo asking. She seemed on the ball. Independent of the others around her. Mia could feel herself liking this colourful investigator already.

'No . . .' Luca hesitated. 'Perhaps he should have one, but I, well, you know.'

'OK,' Munch said. 'Andres Wold. We need to bring him in as soon as possible, and the same goes for the other people on the list, of course, especially the two girls . . .'

'Sylvia and Hannah,' Luca prompted him.

'Exactly,' Munch said. 'Is there an interview room at this station?' He glanced around the room.

'No, not as such,' Luca said. 'But there's a small room down the corridor. Perhaps we could use that?'

'Fine. Set it up, preferably with recording equipment, if you have any?'

'We do.' Luca nodded.

'Good,' Munch said, and looked across the room. 'Does anyone else have anything? About Jessica?'

Everyone shook their head.

'All right,' he went on, pressing something on his iPad. 'Jessica Bakken. Aged sixteen. Yesterday she was alive.'

Another picture on the screen behind him.

'And last night we found her like this.'

Chapter 17

Hannah Holmen was too scared to move her head. She felt absolutely awful. What time was it? The sixteen-year-old girl tried to reach her mobile, which she thought was on her bedside table, but she couldn't manage it. Her arms refused to listen. Not one bit of her body felt good. She was queasy. She ached all over. How late had it been? Shit, was she even at home? Hannah tried to open her eyes. She managed to lift one eyelid a tad. The light pierced her brain like a sword and the nausea was instant, like an eruption from her stomach. Oh, hell, she was going to be sick. No, no, no. She stayed very still. Tried to breathe as calmly as possible. Phew. Luckily the nausea subsided a little, enough for her to risk breathing normally again. Hannah continued to lie with her eyes closed while she tried to remember last night. The party. They had started at Andres Wold's, in his father's garage. About six in the evening, wasn't it? *Where was her bicycle? How had she even managed to get back?* There hadn't been many of them at the garage, just the usual crowd. Sylvia, Jessica, Andres, Morty, Fille, the boys from Frøya – what were their names again? – Jeppe and . . . No, she couldn't remember. Andres had been in charge of the entertainment, as usual; played loud music on his new gadget. Crappy music, as always, pounding electronic dance music with lyrics about all sorts of weird stuff. The boys had been drunk when she arrived. Hooch mixed with juice from big bottles. She had drunk some when it was her turn, of course; if she hadn't, everyone would have been annoyed with her, but it had stung her throat, like the last time. At that point she had made up her mind not to drink too much. She couldn't face the consequences. Feeling this dreadful. Whatever they gave her invariably made her sick. They were going on to the costume party, but their costumes were already a mess. Andres was dressed up like a guy from some horror film, and he looked menacing. The string on Jessica's Mickey Mouse mask had lost its elasticity and the mask was dangling around her neck. *Wait? No. That happened much later, didn't it?* Flashes of memory came back from the old German Second World War bunker where the costume party took place. Loud music there, too, and flashing lights everywhere, but the music had been much better, and for once her body had felt like dancing. She didn't usually dance – she didn't like dancing when people were watching her – but this time she hadn't been able to stop herself. She had laughed out loud and jumped maniacally around as if something had got a hold of her, as if the whole place was bewitched. Costumes and masks everywhere. A horse's head whinnying at her. A witch grinning under a green nose. A devil whispering something in Jessica's ear. Then Sylvia with her Goofy mask and another glimpse of Jessica – was that outdoors? Mickey Mouse right in front of her eyes, her voice that sounded as if it came from a cloud. *'Look, the elastic has gone.'* Oh, dear God, there it was again, the nausea. Hannah pressed her hands desperately over her mouth. *Oh, yuck, how disgusting.* A flashback to a bonfire now, far away somewhere. Behind Andres's garage? They had gone outside, hadn't they? Fed up with the noise and his music. Someone had poured petrol on some planks of wood. Jessica's face again, a small hand coming towards her. Some pills.

Infinity.

Hannah tried opening her eyes again very carefully, this time with more success. There was a Justin Bieber poster by the door. So at least she was at home. In her own bed. *Phew.* That was always something. What time was it really? She fumbled for her mobile on the bedside table, but it wasn't there. She spotted her clothes in a pile on the floor. All right, it was probably in the pocket of her white skirt. She would just have to lie very still for a bit longer, then she would try to reach for it. She had to talk to someone. What had actually happened? Jessica's voice under the setting sun. *'You have to try them, they've just arrived, they're called Infinity.'* She had a feeling she had tried to say no, but it hadn't really worked. The pill on her tongue; she had washed it down with beer. Oh, dear God, no, it was coming. Hannah sat up with a jerk and tried to get out of bed. She attempted to stand, but her feet refused.

Oh, no, shit . . .

She threw up all over the floor and lay back in the bed shaking as she hugged herself. Yuck, that was disgusting. Vomit all the way down her front, her chin, in her hair, and a nauseating stench which made her want to throw up again, but her stomach was empty. She managed to raise her arm and cover herself with her duvet. Her mobile. Luckily her skirt was right in her line of sight. The pocket was bulging. Thank God. It took all her strength, but she finally managed to retrieve her phone. The battery was flat. Bother. The charger was plugged in under her bed. She managed to connect it to her mobile before she flopped back, gasping for breath.

Infinity.

Jessica's face on the dance floor in the bunker. The yellow pills. Was that why she was feeling so dreadful? It had to be. Damn it, Jessica. No, she took that back. It was her own fault. She had made a vow. Not to drink so much. Not to swallow any of the pills she was always offered. Her phone beeped. It had charged enough for her to turn it on, as long as she left it plugged in. Her fingers were trembling as she slowly entered the passcode. *Ping, ping, ping, ping, ping, ping.* The sound hurt her ears. Dear God, how many messages did she have? She moved nearer the screen and tried to read some of them, but everything blurred in front of her eyes. Missed calls, probably fifty. She steeled herself and pressed Sylvia's name.

'Hannah, where are you?' The voice jarred in her ear.

'Oh, Sylvia, keep your voice down, I'm so ill, I feel like crap, I—'

'Jessica is dead!'

Hannah struggled to breathe as the nausea returned.

'I know,' Hannah whispered. 'So am I. I'm completely dead. What on earth happened? How did we get home?'

There was silence for a moment before Sylvia's voice came back, a howl accompanied by an eruption of tears.

'No, I mean it! They found her in the boat! For real! Jessica is dead!'

Chapter 18

Mia parked the motorcycle by the police cordons and walked down towards Munch, who was already standing in front of the old smack. A woman dressed in a white coverall had pulled down her light blue face mask. A hint of a smile emerged in her eyes when she spotted her.

'Hi, Mia.'

'Hi, Rita.'

'We must stop meeting like this, isn't that what they say?' the woman quipped wryly, and shook Mia's hand. Rita Mellbye, a crime-scene technician.

'Have you two been inside?' Mellbye gestured to the deck of the boat.

'Only me,' Mia said. 'Late last night. It was dark. I couldn't see very much.'

'Of course,' Mellbye said, and waved to one of the technicians, who came over to her with an iPad. 'I'll take you inside. We just need to finish up first. I've got pictures of significant findings so far.'

They followed her inside a tent and sat down at a table.

'Have you found her mobile yet?' Munch wanted to know.

'Not yet,' Rita said with a glance at his cigarette. 'You're free to die prematurely if that's what you want, Munch, but do you think you could spare the rest of us?'

Munch shook his head and went outside to stub out his cigarette.

'Do you think he'll ever quit?' Rita said, and woke up the iPad.

'He says he needs them to think,' Mia said.

Mellbye snorted with derision. 'You manage to think just fine, Mia, don't you?'

'I do.'

'There you are then: it's possible to think without them.'

'Right,' Munch said when he was back. 'What do you have that we don't?'

'I don't know what you've been given,' Rita said, swiping across the screen. 'And it took a while before we were able to get our lamps working. Our generator was down, that's why we're a bit behind. I'm sorry.'

'It's fine,' Munch said, and sat down.

A fan had been set up in one corner of the tent, but it was no match for the heat outside. It was almost six o'clock in the evening and yet the sun was baking as if it were the middle of the day in a country much further south.

'Phew,' Munch said, taking off his jacket.

Mia smiled. It was rare to see him like this. He was normally wrapped up in clothes – dark corduroy trousers, a big scarf and the beige duffel coat he always wore – but this was the summer version of him. Light-coloured trousers and a vaguely Hawaii-inspired shirt, which looked as if he had picked it up from the bottom of his wardrobe and failed to check if it still had all its buttons. He wore a pale yellow jacket that also looked as if it had seen better days.

She remembered the look in his eyes. And the knot in her stomach. His blue puppy eyes aimed at her.

'Seriously, Mia. You're not quitting, are you?'

'Not really?'

'You and me? This is what we do.'

He had the same look in his eyes now as he reached for another cigarette before he remembered that Mellbye had put her foot down when it came to smoking inside the tent.

'So,' Rita said, swiping through the photographs. 'We, or rather the local police officer, found the girl like this. On her back on the floor, wearing shoes, a skirt, knickers, a top; now we have to wait for Pathology, but I can see no signs that she was subjected to anything sexual. She's wearing all her clothes, as I just said. The only thing we noticed was a tear in the jacket next to her.'

She zoomed in on the picture. 'Look, a tear at the bottom of the sleeve, a recent one, I think, but then again it could have been caused by anything. She had been to a party, is that right?'

'We're checking the timeline now,' Munch said, and looked longingly at his cigarettes once more.

'Then there's this cup.' She swiped again. 'You saw that, didn't you?'

Mia nodded, urging Rita to continue.

'The writing seems to have been done with an ordinary felt-tip pen. The words BABY and WHORE, and this is either a stain or a full stop, do you see? After BABY?' She magnified the image so that they could see. 'The cup is quite new and it could have belonged to the victim, but it doesn't look like any of her other stuff down there. Everything is quite a mishmash, so it's fair to say that there's no overall sense of interior design. We're thinking that she lived there, is that it?'

'We're still checking that,' Munch said. 'But it does look like it.'

'I would absolutely agree.' Mellbye nodded. 'At least occasionally. We're checking the cup now; it looks cheap. There is a Europris discount store on the island. If we're lucky, that's where it will be from.'

'Good,' Munch mumbled, and pointed to the screen. 'What's that?'

'Something very interesting,' Mellbye said. 'Or rather, that's up to you to decide.'

She magnified the photo Munch had pointed to.

'We found traces of something in the cup, do you see? Hang on, I have a better picture here, from the microscope.'

'Of something in the cup?' Munch echoed.

'Yes,' Rita said, and called out of the tent. 'Benny?'

A young man popped his head in.

'Do you have the bag with the contents of the cup?' asked Rita.

The technician disappeared and returned with a small evidence bag. Rita carried it in and placed it triumphantly under one of the magnifying lamps.

'A hair?' Munch said.

'Almost invisible, but we found it.' She put the evidence bag on the table.

'So,' Rita said. 'A cup with the words BABY WHORE and, as far as we can see, somebody took the trouble to perform a small ritual, i.e. they burned some hair in the cup before placing it on the floor next to her.'

'Jessica's hair?' Mia was curious to know.

'I don't think so,' Rita said, shaking her head. 'We're waiting for the results, but this hair is darker, isn't it?' She held up the bag in front of them.

'Let's see what the lab says,' Munch said, drumming his fingers on his cigarette packet.

'The blood,' Rita said, going back to the photograph. 'It's all hers. Again, we need to double-check, but the preliminary tests we did at the scene show a high probability that it's hers. There's no trace of anyone else's blood, but then again, it's a real mess down there so there could be bloodstains elsewhere, but we've found nothing so far.'

She swiped to the next picture. 'And here you have the name, Jonathan, obviously, traced in the blood, I presume you're thinking that it is—'

'The boy who disappeared.' Munch nodded. 'Do you have anything else we haven't seen yet?'

'Do you want me to go through everything, or don't you?' Rita asked, offended.

'If there's no more news, then we'll do it later.'

He picked up his cigarettes from the table, lit one on his way out and walked in front of Mia down to the boat.

'What are you thinking?'

'I'm not sure,' Mia replied, shaking her head.

'A kind of ritual? Burning someone's hair in a cup with a short message?' Munch said.

'It's possible. *Baby*. I don't know. Do you think she was pregnant?'

'We'll soon know. Are you thinking along those lines? A young woman has an affair with someone else's husband? Revenge?'

'Seems rather over the top, doesn't it? Kill her. Yes, perhaps. But why make it so theatrical? Rather unlikely, don't you think?'

'Perhaps,' Munch said, looking up towards the deck. 'Are you off?'

'Yes. If you take a look at the boat, I'll follow up on Jonathan, all right?'

'OK.' Munch nodded. 'Do you know where I'll be staying?'

'Hjorten Hotel. I think it's booked out because of the wedding, but I believe strings have been pulled. There's probably some pissed-off hack who will have to sleep in a tent tonight.'

'And quite right,' Munch mumbled. 'Will I see you there later?'

'I'll give you a call,' Mia said, and walked towards the motorcycle.

Chapter 19

This was it. This was the house that Jonathan had left one evening three years ago. It belonged to the By family. The last people to see the boy alive. A white-painted 1980s house which had since been extended with a rectangular conservatory at the end of the house that was facing the sea. The first thing that struck her was how normal it all was. There was nothing that stood out, nothing that seemed out of the ordinary. A grey Subaru was parked outside. A treehouse in the garden. A blue mountain bike was dumped near the steps leading to the terrace. A hand-painted ceramic sign by the front door. *Erik, Charlotte and Einar live here.* Mia pressed the brass doorbell and heard it ring somewhere inside.

'Yes?'

A quizzical face appeared in the gap in the door. It was clear that the last twenty-four hours had changed everything on the island. The idyll had been destroyed. The sense of safety was gone. Charlotte By would usually have opened the door widely and with a smile.

Hi, can I help you?

But not any more. The eyes of the forty-something woman flitted as she looked at Mia with suspicion.

'Hi, are you Charlotte By?' Mia said.

'Yes?'

'My name is Mia Krüger. I'm a police officer.'

'Oh,' Charlotte By said. Mia could see the relief in her face.

'I'm sorry, I just—'

'That's quite all right,' Mia said. 'I understand that yesterday's incident has affected everyone.'

'Yes, indeed,' Charlotte By said, and hugged herself. She stepped outside and took a quick look around. 'It was just starting to calm down. After Jonathan went missing, I mean. But a murder? Out here? No, I can't believe it. We've started to lock our doors. I'm almost afraid to let Erik go outside on his own.'

'We're doing everything we can,' Mia said to reassure her. 'But I do understand. Do you have a few minutes? Do you mind if I—'

'No, no, of course not,' the blonde woman said. 'Would you like to come in? I've just made some coffee.'

'Oh, no,' Mia said. 'I'll be quick. I'm trying to get a picture of the night Jonathan disappeared. He was here with you, is that right?'

Charlotte By's eyes took on a burdened expression.

'Yes, he was here. Now, it might sound strange, but it seems as if it were only yesterday. I've been replaying the scene over and over in my mind. The children were playing. The noises in the hallway as he put on his shoes. The way he called out *"See you,"* completely normal, you know? I was in the kitchen, I thought nothing of it. I feel I should, I don't know . . .' She shook her head sadly.

'Please don't blame yourself,' Mia said. 'There was nothing you could have done differently, was there?'

'No, or I don't know. I could have taken him home in the car. There are times when I desperately wish I had. If only I had offered him a lift. Put his bike in the boot of the car. Driven him home safely. But I . . .'

'But why?'

'Pardon?' Charlotte By had been lost in thought for a moment.

'How were you to know?'

She fell silent again.

'No, I don't suppose I could know. Jonathan would always cycle home after being here. But even so?' She shook her head and looked at Mia with sad eyes.

'I get it,' Mia said. 'Are the times right, do you think?'

'What do you mean?'

Mia took out her notebook and flicked through her notes. 'According to Kripos, Jonathan's mother called you at 20.31. And then Jonathan left your house at 20.40? Is that correct?'

'It is.' Charlotte By nodded. 'They asked me several times, and I'm absolutely sure. I saw him outside the kitchen window when he picked up his bicycle. I glanced at the clock. It was twenty minutes to nine. I remember thinking that he'd be home around nine and get to bed at a proper time. Like mothers do, you know?'

She flashed Mia a brief, almost apologetic smile.

'I understand,' Mia said. 'Thank you for confirming it. Did anything happen that night?'

'Like what?'

'Well, anything that was different? Did Jonathan talk about something in particular? Something out of the ordinary. Had he seen anything unusual? Met anyone on his way?'

Charlotte By shook her head. 'No, like I said to the officers who came here at the time, nothing that I can remember. And I've asked Erik and Sofia, too, several times, but no. They had a nice time, I made them some popcorn, which they ate. It was an ordinary evening, right up until . . .' She fell silent again, then heaved a deep sigh.

'OK,' Mia said. 'Good. Can you show me the route he took?'

Jonathan would have gone down the drive, along the field, up through the small avenue; it was all on her map of the island back home, but she wanted to be certain.

'Now I can't be completely sure,' Charlotte By said, and pointed. 'But like I said to the other investigators, he would always walk past the field and take the birch avenue. He would push his bike along the path there. It's a shortcut to the main road.'

'The birch avenue?' Mia said. It was not a name she recognized from her map.

Charlotte By smiled briefly. 'Yes, that might not be its official name, but that's how we refer to it. Erik's great-grandfather planted those birches a long time ago. He didn't think there were enough leafy trees on Hitra. I think he would have liked his own little forest.'

'OK, I'll take that as my starting point. Is your son at home?'

'No, my husband and Erik have gone fishing. But it's getting late so I think they'll be home soon. Should I ask either of them to contact you?'

Mia produced her card from her pocket. 'Here's my number if you happen to think of anything else.'

Charlotte By looked at it and nodded.

'Do you know anything more about—'

'Jessica?'

'Yes? Is it really true that she has been—'

'I'm afraid I can't give you any details,' Mia said. 'But we're investigating. Oh, yes, there was one more thing.'

'Yes?'

'Do you know if they knew each other?'

'Who? Jonathan and Jessica?'

'Yes.'

'I would have thought so,' Charlotte By said, frowning. 'But I don't know for sure. After all, Jessica was a friend of his sister, Hannah. But if Jessica and Hannah were friends at the time, well, I wouldn't know about that.'

'What about your son, Erik? Did he know her?'

She shook her head. 'We talked to him about what happened to Jessica earlier today, and he didn't know who she was.'

'OK, then I have everything I need, I think.'

Mia made to leave, but Charlotte By stayed where she was.

'Is that what you think?' she said anxiously.

'What?'

'That they're related? I mean, Jonathan's disappearance and—'

'We don't think anything right now,' Mia said. 'We're keeping an open mind. Thank you very much for your help. Please call me if you remember anything.'

Charlotte By nodded, and she was still standing outside her front door by the time Mia had reached the end of the field.

OK.

20.40 Jonathan leaves the By family home.

Mia went through a gate in a wooden fence, walked along the field, and then it was almost like entering a magical world. Several birch trees planted close together, an attractive avenue leading to a fairy-tale world. She stopped in a clearing between the trees; she could see boats on the glistening sea further away.

This was where he had walked. Had he seen anything out there? Something unusual? A boat? Something that had stirred his curiosity?

Mia walked further up the path, stopping in another clearing. It had taken her six minutes to get here. He is going straight home, isn't he? His mother has called. He doesn't stop. Unless he has a reason to stop? Here, perhaps? If he saw something out there? Did he notice something?

Mia looked about her. Someone had carved a heart into the bark of a tree.

Thomas + Heidi.

The path ended, and she had reached the main road. She checked the time on her mobile. Twelve minutes. With a few stops along the way. She turned and looked down the path. A boy on speedy legs? Even factoring in him pushing a bicycle? Ten minutes? Possibly eleven?

So he left at 20.40. And arrived here at approximately 20.50?

She slipped her mobile back in her pocket and continued along the main road. It only took her a few minutes on foot to reach Svingen. She looked around. There was nothing here. No houses. No exits from the road. Rocks and sea to one side, spruces to the other. Deserted. So where had the car been spotted? Where did Jacob Wallstedt live? She walked another hundred metres before she could see it. A grey house in good condition with a large terrace up the hill at the end of the bend in the road. It had a good view of the whole area. The sighting must have come from there.

Approximately 20.50. A car is spotted in Svingen.

The timing was right. Absolutely. Mia walked back to the motorcycle, clipped her helmet to the pillion and rode the short distance up the gravel drive.

Jacob Wallstedt.

A man was standing in the garden, holding a rake. She could smell freshly cut grass and see a stone wall and neatly trimmed hedges. Beautiful lilacs. This was a man who knew how to look after his home and his garden.

'Hello?' he called out tentatively, and leaned his rake against one of the attractive trees. He had an air of hesitancy about him as he wiped his hands and came over to her.

'My name is Mia Krüger,' Mia said. 'Are you Jacob Wallstedt?'

'Yes?'

'You're the person who spotted that car, aren't you? That night three years ago? I—'

She didn't get any further. Wallstedt stopped in the middle of the lawn.

'I've said everything I'm going to say on the matter. I don't want any more bother.'

'Of course, I'm sorry,' Mia said. 'There are just a few things I can't quite get to add up. Please could I have—'

'No, no,' the old man said, holding up his hands in front of him. 'Talk to the police.'

'I am the police,' Mia said. 'I won't take up much of your time, I just—'

'No, I've already told you what I saw several times.'

There it was again. The uncertainty in his eyes.

'Just five minutes?'

'Leave me alone.'

The man turned, shuffled back across the lawn and disappeared around the corner of the house.

Mia pushed the motorcycle down to the main road, stopped and then glanced back at the property. She could see a face behind the curtain now.

She was on to something.

She was just about to put on her helmet when her mobile rang.

'Yes?'

'It's Munch. Are you far away?'

'No, only fifteen minutes.'

'We've found something. You have to see this.'

Mia mounted the motorcycle, rode back to the marina and had barely had time to park before Munch came running up the gentle incline towards her.

He must have taken up exercise since she last saw him, as he seemed fitter than he had been for a long time. He was barely out of breath when he reached her, waving an evidence bag in his hand.

'Take a look at this.' He smiled, handing her the transparent bag, which had a black notebook inside.

'You found that on the boat?' Mia said, pulling a pair of gloves from the pocket of her jacket.

'Under the mattress in the corner.' Munch nodded.

Mia opened the notebook and looked at the first page. Names and numbers. And dates. A list. Written mostly in pencil, but in some places with a pen.

14/4: Mr LOL – 1,500
16/4: Big B – 1,200
21/4: Vic – 500
22/4: Mr LOL – 1,500
28/4: Mr LOL – 1,500

'Right.' She nodded as she slowly turned to the next page. The same on the second page. Three names. Dates first, followed by numbers.

'It looks like our friend Jessica had visitors,' Munch said, sticking a cigarette in between his lips.

'Sums of money?' Mia said.

'Don't you think so?'

Mia continued to leaf through the notebook and then pointed to the last date.

'So three men? The first entry in April and the last just a few days ago?'

Munch nodded and smiled faintly. 'But that's not all.'

'Oh?'

'We found drugs in one of the boathouses. Quite a lot. High-end stuff. Come on, let me show you.'

He pulled his lighter out of his pocket, lit his cigarette and walked briskly down towards the boat.

Chapter 20

Sofia lay in her bed, consumed by so many feelings she didn't know what to do with them all. Outside her window the orange sun was setting, bobbing quietly on the surface of the water as if it wanted to tell her something. *I'm here for you.* Or perhaps: *I'll help you.* Sofia knew it was strange, but that was how she felt at times. As if she could talk to the animals and to nature. Not talk to them with words, obviously, but communicate somehow. She hated it when her dad dropped crabs into a pot of boiling water. It was as if they screamed out to her that they didn't want to be there.

She had so many feelings. Bad and scary and weird and good ones, and the last one had taken her by surprise: feeling good at times today – because she was not supposed to.

Her babysitter was dead.

Granny had been very serious, and her dad had driven over to the vicarage as quickly as he could. They had sat her down at the kitchen table and explained everything to her in that voice they used when bad things happened, so many times that she had been tempted to say, *Yes, you've told me that already.* But she hadn't done that, of course. She didn't want to be rude. And yes, it was terrible that her childminder was dead, but the adults had acted as if Sofia and Jessica had been best friends. Only they hadn't. Jessica had babysat her a couple of times, but that was all. And she hadn't exactly been fun company. All smiles until her dad had left the house, but the moment his car was out of the drive, Jessica had changed completely.

'Listen, Sofia, how about you stay in your room, watch a movie or go on your laptop? I've got a visitor, you see. You won't tell anyone, will you?'

Oh, no. She wasn't going to tell. She was no snitch, she had learned that at school, although it was a small place with not many pupils. But it had been boring, sitting in her bedroom on her own. She could hear laughter from the living room. It had made it impossible to fall asleep.

It was almost like now. Sofia heaved a sigh and sat up in her bed. Quite impossible. How was she meant to fall asleep? After everything that had happened today?

She drew the curtains and opened the window a little bit. She preferred sleeping with her window closed now. She used to sleep with it open, until one night last year when she was woken up by a bird in her room, a large crow that seemed to have gone completely mad. It had screeched and flapped its wings, knocking her trophies off the shelf.

Her dad had killed it in the end. Since then, she had closed her window at night. But not now. It was quite simply too hot.

On Granny's radio they had talked about a tropical night. And despite the sad circumstances, it had been really nice. The three of them being together again. Because that didn't happen very often these days, did it? Before, when her grandad was still alive and her mum had been at home, they had been together all the time. Dinners in the garden just like a proper family. But after her mum left, everything had changed.

Divorce.

She had heard them on the phone. She really wished that she hadn't, but she had been so thirsty and the water tasted best from the tap in the old bathroom. Her dad had been standing there, clutching his phone, his eyes red.

Divorce.

Sofia opened the window a little further and spat into the garden. What an ugly word. She had acted as if nothing had happened. She had just returned to her room and climbed back into her bed. The next day, nothing was said. It had never happened. It had all been just a bad dream. Nothing had changed. La-la-la. But deep down she knew it wasn't true.

Her mum had been gone for a long time now, and surely she

would come back if she cared about them, wouldn't she? If she really loved them? No one puts sick people in other countries before their own family, not if you love them more than anything on earth.

Sad, happy, angry feelings. She stuck out her head and spat again. The sun had almost disappeared now. It was dipping its bottom in the water and only its head was peeking up above the surface.

She jumped when she heard the front door open. Her dad appeared on the doorstep, his mobile pressed to his ear. Sofia quickly switched off her nightlight and pricked up her ears. How odd. Who could he be talking to at this time of night? And why had he gone outside?

'Yes . . . no . . . not my fault . . . I'm on my way . . .'

Her dad stuck his mobile into his pocket and started walking across the garden. What was going on?

Sofia quickly made up her mind. She pulled off her nightie, put on a pair of trousers and a T-shirt and tiptoed down the stairs on bare feet.

Not the front door: it squeaked too loudly.

The door to the garden.

She crept across the decking and half ran across the grass until she reached the front of the house. There. He was heading down to their jetty. In the middle of the night? But he knew that she hated him going out. That she struggled to sleep, after that business with the crow. He had taken out his mobile again and was saying something she couldn't hear. His voice was strange. It wasn't nice and good, it was more like . . . scared? Was her dad scared?

Sofia stepped on something sharp and nearly cried out, but managed to suppress it. She bent down and pulled something out of her foot. Stupid thorn.

Her dad had reached the jetty now and returned the mobile to his pocket. Sofia crept along the edge of the path, then hid behind the boxes where the fishing nets were stored. Her dad was standing at the end of the jetty, peering into the distance. A boat was on its way across the fjord. To begin with, its lights were on, but then they were turned off, as was its motor. It glided towards them silently in the dusk. The lamp on the boathouse came on and she jumped when the boat docked. The boat was yellow. Her heart began to pound when she remembered what Erik had told her yesterday.

The yellow boat.

A man tied up the boat and then stepped up on to the jetty. She couldn't see his face, but she could hear his brusque voice.

'Did you bring a dog or something?'

'What? No,' her dad replied, again in that scared voice.

'Right. Only I thought I saw something move over there.'

Quick as lightning, Sofia pulled back her head and wrapped her arms around herself, her heart continuing to race under her T-shirt.

'Are you ready?' the brusque voice said.

'Yes,' her dad said.

'And you're sure there's no one else here?'

Footsteps now. Across the jetty.

THREE

MONDAY

Chapter 21

It was only seven o'clock in the morning, but Luca Eriksen was already at the police station. He hadn't slept well, but for once it had not been for the usual reason. It had not been because of Amanda. He had almost felt guilty in the car on his way to work. Everything was blurring into one; he had had practically no sleep since he'd found the girl in the boat and all those police officers had turned up on the island. And then there was his new role. For once he was at the centre of everything. He had been so excited he had barely been able to sleep. He had actually looked forward to getting up, and he couldn't remember the last time he had felt like that. He had put her picture on the table at breakfast. He had wolfed down his food, but made sure to have a quick chat with her. *Sorry, Amanda, I had to go straight to bed yesterday. I was knackered. What a day. I don't think I sat down once.* If only she had been here now. This would have made her so happy and proud. Not that someone had died, of course not, especially not Jessica, but to see him working. Amanda had always liked Jessica; she had been her primary-school teacher. He had lost count of the nights they had spent talking about her, and the more red wine Amanda had consumed, the more outraged she had become. *'How can you not take care of your child? Tell me that. How is it even possible? If her useless mum was here now, I would . . .'* He had rarely seen Amanda as angry as when they discussed Laura Bakken and her daughter.

Child Services. Yes, they had been involved, but everyone knew what it was like out here. An island. A small community where everyone knew everybody else. So he didn't know if their involvement had made any difference. All he knew was that he had tried to stop the partying at her mother's house whenever he had received complaints about it. It was no easy matter because he knew everyone who drank there. He had never actually seen Jessica there himself, or he would have intervened, obviously. What a mess. Luca poured himself a cup of coffee and carried it to his desk. Of course he should have been more vigilant. A better police officer. A better human being. He should have made sure that the girl was safe. But this past year he had existed in a fog of grief.

A wheezing Munch arrived. His reddish hair was tousled, his short-sleeved shirt buttoned incorrectly and he didn't look as if he had slept much either.

'Good morning,' Luca said. 'Coffee?'

'Yes, please,' Munch grunted, and flopped into the chair next to his. Luca fetched a cup of coffee from the machine and offered it to him. Munch turned up his nose as he studied the contents.

'Filter coffee? Is that all you've got?'

'Yes, sorry,' Luca said. 'Or there's tea, if you prefer?'

Munch snorted with derision, then yawned behind his bushy, reddish beard.

'Just don't offer Mia this rubbish. She's very particular about her coffee.' Munch winked at him and raised the cup to his lips.

'Ah, that's better. That will help me wake up.'

Luca didn't know whether to stay standing, but ultimately opted for sitting down as well.

'So you're not comfortable at your hotel?'

'Eh?' Munch stretched up towards the ceiling.

'Oh, it's fine. I just don't like hotels very much. I sleep best in my own bed. I'm sure I'll get used to it. Has someone organized a car for me?'

Luca nodded. 'It's outside.'

'Good.' Munch yawned again. 'Have you prepared a list of people to interview?'

Luca could feel himself sweating slightly as he quickly flicked through the papers on his desk.

'Here,' he said, trying to hand Munch a sheet of paper. Munch flapped his hand and took another sip of his coffee.

'You read it out to me. Who and when is the first one?'

'Andres Wold. He'll be here at nine. Now, I didn't know how much time you wanted to spend with each individual, so I set aside a whole hour for everyone, is that all right?'

'Yes, that's fine.'

'So we have Andres Wold at nine. The girls – Sylvia and Hannah – will be here at ten.'

'Together?'

'Yes?'

Munch frowned and set down his cup. 'Schedule them individually.'

'OK,' Luca said, making a note on the piece of paper. 'One right after the other, OK? Then I can move . . . Perhaps change the times for everyone else?'

Munch yawned again and scratched himself under his armpit. 'People can wait. It doesn't matter.'

'I have Laura Bakken coming in at eleven, that is, if she has left Trondheim.'

'She's currently in hospital there, am I right?'

Luca nodded.

'Yes, they found her at . . .' He had to check his notebook. 'Bobby's Bar. It's a proper dive, if I've understood correctly. I've never been there myself.'

Munch looked at him. 'In what state, do you know?'

Luca shook his head sadly. 'Quite out of it, as far as I can gather. Like I said, they took her to St Olav's Hospital.'

'Shouldn't she see her daughter?'

'Do you mean—'

'Surely she'll need to see the body?'

'Yes, perhaps, I guess so—'

'She won't make it to Hitra for eleven o'clock.'

'So should I move someone else forward, do you think, or—'

'Oh, no. We'll see the girls separately, and that could take some time.'

'OK,' Luca said. 'And so, yes, it's one person after another, really—'

He was about to resume reading from his list when Munch silenced him with another gesture.

'I can't spend my whole day interviewing people. I'll take the boyfriend and the girls with Mia, then you can deal with the rest, all right?'

'Me?'

'Yes. Is that a problem?'

'No, no, no, only I'm not used to—'

'You'll be fine. Where were they? What was she to them? Have they seen her recently? Did they see her on Saturday? Anyone from that party, by the way?'

Luca checked his list. 'Yes, plenty of people who—'

'Great. We need to map two things. All her relationships in general and then, specifically, what happened that Saturday night. Take Nygaard with you if you feel you might need him.'

'OK. Nygaard, now that was—'

'He was the one from Orkanger Police. In the Springsteen T-shirt. Whose sister lives out here.'

The door opened and Mia entered. 'Have the technicians finished? Have you shown it to him?'

'No, I've only just woken up myself.'

Mia looked as if she hadn't slept or indeed needed sleep. She marched across the floor and stopped in front of them impatiently.

'Shown me what?' Luca said quizzically.

'This,' Munch said, producing an object from his pocket.

'The notebook,' Mia said.

'Jessica's little black book,' Munch said softly, and placed it in front of him.

'Crime-scene technicians found it on the boat,' Mia said. 'We think it's important. Can you tell us what this might mean?' She picked up the notebook from the desk, opened it on the first page and held it up to him.

'Do these names mean anything to you?' Mia said as she flicked through the notebook. 'Mr LOL? Vic? Big B? Dates, names and numbers. We think they might be sums of money.'

'Those three names recur, as you can see,' Munch said. 'Do any of them seem familiar?'

Luca studied the list again, then he shook his head.

'No?' Mia said. 'Mr LOL? Does that ring any bells?'

'Not that I—'

'Big B?'

'No, I—'

'Surely we can assume that it must be someone whose name starts with a B. Perhaps someone in her circle of acquaintances?'

'With a B? Not off the top of my head, but I'll check.' Luca could feel himself starting to sweat again.

'Please do,' Mia said. 'And then the last one – Vic? Is there anyone out here called Victor?'

'We have a Victor who works at the processing plant,' Luca said quickly, glad that he could think of someone.

'The salmon-processing plant?'

'Yes.'

'Royal Arctic Salmon?' Munch said. 'Henry Prytz's company?'

'Yes.'

Munch and Mia exchanged glances.

'OK,' Mia said. 'Is that the list of people to be interviewed?'

'Yes.'

'Bring in Victor today. Sooner rather than later.'

'Absolutely,' Luca said, and made a note in his pad.

Mia returned the black notebook to Munch and looked about her.

'Is there any coffee here?'

'Not for you.' Munch chuckled.

'When is the team briefing?'

'At eight o'clock,' Munch said.

'All right, see you later,' Mia said as she left.

'Oh, by the way,' Munch said to Luca. 'Before I forget. There will be someone from Oslo at the briefing. His name is Gabriel Mørk. He's going to help us with everything – you know, computer, Internet, social media and all that.'

'Do you want him up on the big screen?'

'Big screen, small screen, makes no difference, just as long as I can see him and he can see us.'

'I'll sort it out,' Luca said.

Munch got up with an effort and took a packet of cigarettes from his jacket pocket.

'No chance of an ashtray in here, I suppose?'

'No, sadly, you'll have to go outside, I think.'

Munch shook his head wearily, popped a cigarette in between his lips and walked slowly outside.

Chapter 22

Mia carried her takeaway cup into the meeting room at the end of the corridor and felt like she was entering a classroom. Everyone was early. Everyone was very hushed. Everyone looked wide-eyed at Munch as he held the remote control, which, as usual, he didn't quite know how to operate. Munch and IT. It had been a running joke at their old offices in Mariboesgate 13. Anette Goli, Munch's former right-hand woman, used to say that Munch was a young fifty-four-year-old with the soul of a ninety-year-old and the dress sense of a scarecrow. A fairly apt description. Spoken with love, obviously.

She could see it in their eyes now, their respect for this scruffy detective who needed help turning on the projector. There was also pride: *I'm here, I'm a part of something important.* It felt like a small but good team. Nina Riccardo from Trondheim. Colourful today as well, a yellow T-shirt and green jeans. She, too, had been able to get a room at Hjorten Hotel, which might not have been as full as people had claimed. Ralph Nygaard, who had a sister out here, wearing another Springsteen T-shirt today. Kevin Borg, the swaggering investigator with the blond curls wearing the same light-coloured suit. And then there was Claus Nielsen, the police lawyer, still dressed like an accountant, with two pens ready on top of his briefcase. Mia took a seat and swallowed the last of her coffee. It was not yet eight o'clock, but she could already feel it. It was going to be a hot day. Fortunately there were two fans in the room, ready for use if necessary.

The projector slowly came to life and a familiar face appeared on the screen: Gabriel. Mia smiled and waved to him.

'OK, everyone,' Munch said, turning to his team. 'Our first inter-view is in an hour so I'm going to make this short and sweet. As you can see, we have a visitor today. This is our colleague Gabriel Mørk. He's currently working for the National Authority for Investigation and Prosecution of Economic and Environmental Crime – the fraud squad, basically – but we have been lucky enough to borrow him for as long as we need him.'

'Hello, hello,' Gabriel said from the screen. Heads nodded across the room.

'You're on the big screen,' Munch said.

'All right.' Gabriel cleared his throat. Mia smiled.

Munch had headhunted Gabriel Mørk for his team in Oslo just over a year ago. Mørk had arrived with no police experience at all but had slipped right into the role. He was a computer geek who, at the time, had been living in his mother's basement and spent every waking hour online. He was a really sweet and nice guy. Quiet and shy. Mia realized how much she had missed him. Gabriel's cheeks had gone red as his face appeared on the big screen, and he was trying not to attract attention to himself, an impossible task in the circumstances.

'I don't know about your skills,' Munch said to his team, putting down the remote control. 'But there is an online world out there which I don't really understand. From now on, Gabriel will be our man in cyberspace – isn't that what they call it?'

There were scattered smiles across the room now.

'Social media, anything that happens on the Internet, no one is better than Gabriel, and if we need to take a peek at the databases of NASA or the CIA, he can help with that as well, am I right?'

The latter was said in jest, but even so Gabriel blushed even more.

'I don't think that will be necessary,' he said.

'OK then, let's get started. You have all seen the information we sent out last night?'

More nodding across the room.

'Good,' Munch continued. 'Two things – no, three – from the crime-scene investigators' examination of the boat. Number one: the cup. As you can see, it looks as if something was burned in it. Hair. Any immediate thoughts?'

He looked across the room.

'A kind of ritual?' Nina Riccardo spoke up first and looked around.

'It's possible.' Munch nodded.

'Seriously?' Ralph Nygaard said with a frown, and looked rather nervously at the others in the room. 'Who would burn someone else's hair in a cup?'

'That's what we're here to find out,' Munch said. 'Any other thoughts?'

Luca held up his hand.

'Yes, Luca, and just speak up. You don't need to raise your hand.'

'OK, sorry,' Luca said. 'It's just occurred to me – we had a break-in out here Friday night.'

'Go on?'

'At the hairdresser's down the road. It was a bit odd,' Luca went on. 'The back door had been forced, but nothing was missing. There may not be a connection. But hair in a cup? And someone breaking into a hairdresser's the day before the murder?'

'Good thinking, Luca,' Munch said. 'We'll follow it up. Kevin, will you deal with that? Any cameras in the area? Client lists? What happens to waste hair? Do you follow?'

'I'm on it,' Kevin Borg said, making a note on his pad.

'Now we can't be sure that—' the police lawyer began.

'Yes, Claus?' Munch said.

The pedantic lawyer looked about him. 'Well, what I'm saying is we can't be one hundred per cent sure that the cup is relevant, can we? It could have been left there by someone else.'

'It's possible—' Munch started, but he was interrupted by Riccardo.

'Why would Jessica have a cup in which she burned hair? A cup on which she had written BABY WHORE? I just don't believe that.'

The dark-eyed investigator threw up her hands and was met by nodding from around the room.

'I was wondering, was she pregnant?' Ralph Nygaard still sounded a little timid.

'Thanks for flagging it up,' Munch said, walking up to the files

115

on the table. 'I got the post-mortem report this morning, I haven't managed to circulate it yet, but you'll get it soon.'

He held it up in the air.

'It's all here and, to sum up: no, Jessica wasn't pregnant. However, she was full of all sorts of other things. Very high blood-alcohol level . . .' He flicked through a few pages. 'And a long list of other substances.'

'Drugs?' Kevin Borg asked.

'Definitely.' Munch nodded. 'And lots of them. We have found DMT, ketamine, lorazepam, quite an extensive mix . . .'

'Was she . . .' It was the police lawyer again.

'Was she what?' Munch said.

'Well, I mean, was it recreational use? Did she just want to get high? Or do we think someone drugged her?'

'I've asked the pathologist to examine that possibility,' Munch said. 'However, as far as I can see, we're talking about recreational use at parties, many different substances, but from what I understand, not in quantities large enough for us to believe that she was drugged before she was murdered.'

'You also found drugs out there, didn't you?' Kevin Borg said.

'Indeed we did,' Munch said. 'As you can see from the photos you've been sent, technicians found a not inconsiderable quantity of pills at the scene.'

He corrected himself. 'Not at the scene itself, but in a small boathouse nearby. A total of three hundred pills. What they are we don't know yet, but it looks like ecstasy, party drugs, colourful little pills with small symbols: a star, a skull . . .'

'An infinity sign,' Mia said.

'Yes,' Munch continued, scratching his head. 'Luca, I think we'll need to . . .' He gestured towards the screen.

'I'll put Gabriel on a laptop next time so you can show pictures on the big screen,' Luca said.

'Great, thank you. Please take a look at the pictures on your own devices. I don't know the significance of everything, but we have found colourful pills and small bags. The quantity isn't big enough

116

for it to be a main depot, it's individual-user doses, i.e. it's the stash of a small dealer at the bottom of the food chain . . .'

'And we think that dealer might have been Jessica?' Riccardo said.

'Well, many people have access to the marina, but given what we found in her body, then why not?' Munch said. 'We will consider all possibilities, including that one. Motives for murder here, people, I'm sure you can all see that.'

Munch picked up a dry-wipe pen on the table and made notes on the whiteboard as he talked.

'BABY WHORE. Was Jessica pregnant? No. But could she have had a relationship with someone's, yes, how can I put it, husband, boyfriend, lover? That's entirely possible. Drugs. Was Jessica dealing? And if so, to whom? Were the people who knew her aware of this? Is that why she was murdered? That's also a possibility. Nevertheless, we mustn't get fixated on any of these, am I right? They are just theories. Leads we can investigate.'

There was nodding across the room.

'Then perhaps our most important discovery.'

Munch went over to the chair on which he had hung his jacket, returned with the small black notebook and held it up in front of them.

'Jessica's notebook. Names, dates and numbers, which we're assuming are sums of money. Who were these people? What was the money for?'

'Prostitution?' Ralph Nygaard ventured delicately.

'It's called sex work these days,' Nina Riccardo remarked dryly with a look at Munch. 'Three customers? Not enough, I mean, if she was selling her services?'

'Fair point,' Munch said.

'Or they could have been, well, three good friends with open wallets?' Kevin Borg suggested.

'That's also highly likely,' Munch said. 'Now, I don't want to come across as terribly old school here, but a young woman records transactions in a notebook with three people we presume are men?

Sexual services, perhaps, or selling drugs? The pills we found. Either of those two options seem reasonable.'

Munch made notes on the whiteboard.

Three men. Mr LOL. Big B and Vic.

He put down the dry-wipe pen and continued his briefing.

'Next item. As we talked about yesterday, we have approximately sixty young people at a costume party. We can be pretty sure that most of them had consumed not insignificant quantities of alcohol. Mobile footage, am I right? Who has something?'

Nina Riccardo spoke up. 'I've already received quite a few videos. I think we have between fifteen and twenty already.'

'Excellent, from the party?'

'Some, yes. Most of them before the party in the bunker, hollering in various cars with loud music in the background.'

'Any sightings of her?'

'Nothing yet. But I've also got some pictures.' She picked up her mobile from the table.

'Let's have a look,' Munch said, and she passed it to him.

He swiped quickly through the pictures, then passed the phone to Mia. Jessica wearing her Mickey Mouse mask, alone with a can of beer in her hand. Two pictures of her with her mask pushed up on her head, both with Sylvia Green, an empty bottle in her hand this time.

'Is that all you've got?'

'Yes, I'm afraid so – for now.'

Mia passed the phone around the room as Munch carried on.

'Pictures, videos – there's no need to say what we're looking for. Tell the uniformed officers we have on the island to ask everyone, all right? Did you go to the party? Did you record anything? You get the idea.' Munch turned and pointed to the whiteboard.

'Three men. From Jessica's notebook. Mr LOL. Big B. And Vic. I don't have to stress that this is our absolute top priority right now. Who is hiding behind these names? Search around, ask questions, be nice, be rude, I don't care. We need to find these people, and as quickly as possible, preferably yesterday, understand?'

There was nodding across the room once more.

'Good.' Munch took his cigarettes from his pocket. 'Right. Like I said, Gabriel Mørk in Oslo will be helping us. He's already researching Jessica's online presence and will give you a quick update. Are you ready, Gabriel?'

'I am,' Gabriel said from the screen.

'Go ahead, I won't be long.'

Munch stuck a cigarette in his mouth, headed for the door and nodded to Mia for her to follow him outside.

Chapter 23

Hannah Holmen was standing on the outskirts of the car park from where she could see the entrance to the police station, gripping Sylvia's hand. Since yesterday their hands had been practically glued together. Hannah did not ever want to let it go; she just wanted to stand in the shade with Sylvia until someone came to tell them that the whole thing was a big joke, that it was not real, just a hoax someone had thought up. There were people all around them here, a stark difference to the usual quiet. Police cars, but also other vehicles, civilian ones with important, serious people in them. Mobile phones. Fingers pointing. Mouths whispering. Hannah shielded her eyes with her hand and looked up at the sky. It was warm today. A few white clouds, small cotton balls, but not many. It could have been just an ordinary, lovely day. Which day was it today? Was it still Sunday?

Hi, Hannah, do you want to come to Ulvøya for a picnic?
No, it's too far, Jessica, I can't be bothered to cycle all that way.
No worries. Andres will give us a lift, so how about it?
'Hannah.' Sylvia squeezed her hand hard and she came round.
'What?'
'Where were you?'
'Sorry, I was just—'
'Don't disappear,' Sylvia said sadly, and squeezed her hand again.
They had been together ever since Sylvia had called. Hannah had stopped throwing up. She almost didn't feel ill any more either. It was as if the shock had cleansed her whole body, her blood and everything. They had walked straight up to Sylvia's room and stayed there. Sylvia's mum had been nice: she hadn't said much, hadn't

disturbed them, just left food outside the door, knocked and then left.

'I'm dreading it,' Sylvia said in a low voice. 'What are we going to say?'

'What do you mean?' Hannah said, also in a low voice.

'Well, you know . . . about Saturday night?'

'That we can't remember anything, is that what you're saying?'

'Yes. And what about everything we took?' She whispered the latter. 'I mean, it's fine for you, your mum doesn't care, but my parents do. My dad will kill me if he finds out.'

Hannah was a bit hurt, but she didn't say anything because she knew that Sylvia didn't mean to upset her.

Your mum doesn't care.

And because it was true. Sylvia didn't know how lucky she was with her family. Being shouted at was preferable to silence.

'I don't think anyone is worried about that now,' Hannah said.

'You don't?' Sylvia said, chewing her lip.

'That we got high? I don't think it matters now. Not compared to . . .'

'*Go on, Hannah, don't be so boring!*'

'*You're out of your mind, Jessica . . .*'

'*America!*'

'*We can't just go to America. Are you mad?*'

'*Of course we can. I've got loads of money!*'

'Hannah?' She snapped out of it when Sylvia elbowed her side.

'Yes? Oh, sorry . . .'

'Stop zoning out all the time. I'm frightened. I'm scared to be here alone.'

'I'm here now,' Hannah said, squeezing her hand.

'What are we going to say?' Sylvia said, looking at her desperately.

'What do you mean?'

Sylvia looked about her, then she whispered, 'About all the *things*, you know?'

'What things?'

'Oh, come on, Hannah? You know what she got up to in the boat . . .'

'What?' Hannah said.

'Oh, stop it, of course you knew! What she did?'

'What do you mean?' Hannah frowned. 'I knew that her living in the boat was a secret. I haven't told anyone, I promise.'

'Not *that*,' Sylvia whispered. 'Seriously, she didn't tell you anything?'

'Eh?' Hannah said, letting go of her hand for a moment. 'What kind of things?'

'Shh,' Sylvia said. She pressed her lips shut and nodded to the entrance.

Two people were walking across the car park towards them now. A man with a red beard and a floral shirt and the pretty female investigator everyone was talking about.

'Hello,' the man said, holding out his hand. 'Are you Hannah and Sylvia?'

They nodded.

'My name is Holger Munch, and this is Mia Krüger. Are you ready for a little chat?'

'OK.' Sylvia gulped.

'We would like to talk to you first, Hannah, if that's all right?' Sylvia gripped her hand hard.

The woman called Mia Krüger looked at them, then back at the man with the beard.

'Perhaps you'd like to come in together?'

'If that's all right?' Hannah whispered.

'It's fine. Just follow us,' said the man called Munch.

And he led the way across the car park.

Chapter 24

Munch was pleased that they had decided to interview the girls at the same time after all. They had huddled together behind the table, looking more than anything like they wanted to disappear into each other. Hannah Holmen was quite tall for a teenage girl, with medium-blonde hair reaching halfway down her back. She was wearing a summer dress that highlighted her long, slender arms, but her blue eyes, normally radiant, were red and sad. Sylvia Green was shorter but just as slender. Shoulder-length strawberry-blonde hair and pale skin on which the sun had brought out her freckles. Neither girl seemed to be fully present. Their gaze was distant. Their shoulders were slumped. The girls were doing their best. They sat politely in their chairs, but they looked as if they could break down at any moment.

'So.' He cleared his throat. 'Like I just told you, my name is Holger Munch, and this is Mia Krüger. We're police officers from Oslo, and we are in charge of this investigation. I'd like to start by saying how sorry we are for your loss. We understand that you're mourning, Jessica, but I hope you also understand that we have a job to do and that we are here first and foremost to solve this case. So if I seem harsh, then that'll be why, all right?'

Both girls nodded.

'Good,' Munch said. 'So perhaps you could start by telling us a bit about what happened on Saturday night?'

Sylvia glanced furtively at Hannah, who seemed to be the more mature.

'Who wants to go first?' Munch said.

'To be completely honest, we don't remember very much,' Hannah said.

'Go on.'

'Only bits and pieces,' Sylvia mumbled.

'Is there any particular reason why you don't remember very much?' Munch said.

The girls exchanged glances once more.

'We took some pills,' Hannah ventured cautiously.

'Who gave them to you?' Munch asked.

There was another pause.

'Jessica,' Hannah replied in the end.

'Any of these?' Mia said kindly, and took some photographs out of the envelope in front of her.

The girls stared at the pictures and then looked at each other.

'The yellow ones,' Sylvia said, placing her finger on one of the pictures.

'And the red ones,' Hannah said.

'So the ones with the wings?' Munch said.

'Yes, Skywalkers,' Sylvia confirmed.

'It has a name?' The girls nodded in unison.

'They all do,' Hannah said.

'Please would you tell me what they are?' Mia said, arranging all the photos she had in front of them.

'The blue ones are called Autobahns,' Hannah said.

'I think they contain amphetamines,' Sylvia said carefully. 'I haven't tried them, but that's what people say.'

'And these ones?' Mia said, pointing to some black pills.

'Deathcrushes.'

'Deathcrushes?' Munch echoed.

The girls looked at each other again.

'I think it's from a song,' Hannah said cautiously.

'By Mayhem,' Sylvia added.

Munch noticed Mia smiling, probably at him, who didn't know much about the music teenagers listened to.

'Mayhem, yes? And Mayhem is?'

'It's an old death-metal band,' Sylvia said. 'The boys are into them. They're Norwegian, and they were one of the first ones, I think, to paint their faces white, use real blood on stage and all that. It's complete rubbish, if you ask me, just noise.'

'But the boys like death metal?' Mia said.

'Yes.' Hannah nodded. 'That and electronic dance music. They have truly terrible taste in music.'

For the first time the two girls seemed to exchange a smile.

'And you took them last Saturday? The one with the number eight on its side?' Mia said.

'They're called Infinities,' Hannah said. 'They're the new one.'

'New as in?' Munch said.

'Jessica never had them before. Or at least it was the first time I tried it.' Hannah looked to Sylvia, who nodded.

'Yes, it's the first time I've seen it.'

'So you would take these pills often?' Munch wanted to know.

'Well, not that often . . .' Sylvia said hesitantly.

Hannah, however, seemed to have made up her mind not to hold anything back.

'At every party, pretty much since last summer.'

'Last summer?' Munch said. 'That was the first time?'

'Yes, the first time that Jessica had those pills. We've seen pills before, but nothing like these . . . not anything so . . .'

She looked to Sylvia for help with finding the right word.

'Top quality, like,' Sylvia said.

'Yes,' Hannah resumed. 'The pills people had before were, like, well, they just looked like fluoride tablets or, you know, regular stuff.'

'But these ones first turned up last summer?'

They nodded again.

'Do you know how Jessica got hold of them?' Mia asked.

Another silence.

'No,' Hannah said eventually. 'It was like we shouldn't be asking.'

'She was very strict about it,' Sylvia mumbled. 'We had to promise not to ask. If we didn't ask, then she wouldn't have to say anything, if you know what I mean?'

It was some years since Munch had grasped teenage logic, but Mia nodded.

'So you weren't supposed to ask any questions?' Munch said.

'No,' the girls said.

'And you didn't?'

They looked at each other. 'No, of course not. We had promised.'

Munch looked at Mia, who smiled, again probably at him.

'OK, good,' Munch said. 'So you didn't ask any questions, but do you know who her supplier might have been? Do you have any ideas? I mean, if you were to hazard a guess, a wild one?'

A long silence followed. They bowed their heads, glancing furtively at each other.

'Nothing you say will leave this room,' Mia said. 'We should have told you that to begin with, shouldn't we, Holger? This stays between us. You're safe here.'

Munch nodded and tried to produce a friendly smile behind his beard. The girls were quiet for a while before Hannah finally opened her mouth.

'Andres Wold,' she said in a low voice.

'Yes, same here,' Sylvia said.

'You think that was what everyone thought?' Mia said. 'That the drugs ultimately came from Andres.'

The girls nodded now, their heads still bowed. Mia looked at Munch, and he nodded in return. Andres Wold, the boyfriend, should have been the first person they interviewed – except he had not turned up.

'So were they a couple, or how was it?' Mia said. The girls hesitated.

'They weren't an item, or rather . . .' Sylvia said.

'Were they sleeping together?' Mia wanted to know.

'Yes,' Hannah whispered. 'But mostly in the past, in the spring. Not so much now – they had a row about something.'

'When did it happen, this row, I mean?' Mia said.

'Around the time of her birthday,' Sylvia said.

'In March.' Hannah nodded. 'We thought that was the reason why.'

'Yes,' Sylvia said. 'Jessica had asked for a spa weekend as her present, but he just gave her a bottle of alcohol.'

126

'Yes, one he'd already opened and drunk from,' Hannah said.

Munch raised his eyebrows and looked at Mia.

'So they argued on her birthday? And after that they weren't together? I mean, they broke up?'

'I think that was when it happened,' Sylvia said. 'It was certainly different after that.'

'You said you thought that they had argued about her present, but could it have been about something else?' Mia said. The girls shrugged.

'Not sure,' Hannah said. 'He was never generous with presents and stuff, so it's not like it was news.'

'For Christmas he gave her a Little Tree,' Sylvia went on. 'One of those pine air fresheners you hang in cars, you know?'

'OK,' Munch said. 'So back to Saturday, can you tell us anything at all? You must remember something, surely? Seeing as it was the last time you saw her.'

They looked at each other again.

'I'm not sure about the time,' Sylvia said, with Hannah nodding in agreement, 'but we were together in the bunker so it must have been after eight.'

'The bunker, was that . . .'

'The venue for the costume party,' Mia said.

'OK, so you remember being there together. Do you have a final memory, something that can be connected to a time?'

'The elastic on her mask had come loose,' Hannah said. 'That's the last I remember.'

'Then she got a message on Telegram,' Sylvia said. 'I think, unless I dreamed it. The music was very loud so I couldn't hear what she said, but she showed me her mobile.'

'Could you read what it said?' Mia asked.

Sylvia seemed sad now and she shook her head.

'Sorry, no. After I took those pills I don't know what really happened and what I'm just imagining.'

'You're doing fine,' Mia assured her. 'So Jessica got a message, and that was the last time you saw her?'

Sylvia nodded.

'Telegram?' Munch said. 'What's that?'

'It's an app,' Mia said to Munch, and then she asked Sylvia: 'Do you use it a lot?'

'Yes, all the time. Everyone does. It's encrypted. Nothing on it is registered anywhere. It's untraceable, if you know what I mean?'

Munch glanced at Mia, who nodded.

'Do you think Jessica left the party after getting that message?'

Sylvia squirmed and then she shrugged. 'I really don't know. Sorry.'

'It's OK,' Mia said, placing her hand carefully on her arm. 'We know that this is difficult for you, and you won't have to sit here very much longer. We're nearly done. I'm assuming you brought your mobiles to the party. Did you take any pictures? Videos?'

The girls looked cautiously at each other.

'I have nothing on mine,' Hannah said. 'The battery had died when I woke up.'

'I only have some from when we were getting ready,' Sylvia said.

'Could we have those pictures, please?' Munch said. 'Would that be all right, do you think?'

'Yes, of course.' Sylvia nodded.

'Great, please speak to Luca Eriksen on your way out and he'll take care of it. You won't need to be here very much longer. I've just got one last question.'

Mia slid a piece of paper across the table.

'Do you recognize any of these names? Mr LOL? Big B? Vic?'

Hannah looked carefully at the piece of paper, but Munch noticed that only the other girl, Sylvia, had an emotional reaction.

'No idea,' Hannah said.

'Sylvia?' Munch said, somewhat stern this time.

A tear rolled down Sylvia's freckled cheek. 'I promised not to say anything.'

She buried her face in her hands.

'What?' Hannah said. 'Was that what you were talking about outside?'

Sylvia sobbed behind her fingers.

'If you know something, Sylvia, you have to tell us,' Mia said, more firmly now.

'This is for Jessica's sake, do you understand? Did she ever talk about any of these?'

Sylvia nodded.

'All three of them?'

She shook her head.

'So which one of them? Mr LOL?'

Her cheeks were wet now.

'Yes,' she whispered.

'Neither of the other two?'

'No, just him. An older guy.'

'Older? How old, do you think?'

'I don't know,' Sylvia said.

'Are you sure?' Mia said. 'Don't forget that we're doing this for Jessica. Anything you can remember is important to us.'

Sylvia looked across to Hannah, who merely shrugged.

'I've never heard anything about this,' she said.

'Nothing more, Sylvia?' Munch said.

'Was he someone she knew?' Mia went on. 'I mean, someone in her immediate circle? Was it a relative? A casual acquaintance?'

'She just said that he liked her.' Sylvia chewed her lip and shook her head.

'Was that all?' Munch said.

'Yes,' the teenager mumbled. 'And that he was generous.'

'Generous?' Mia said. 'As in he paid her for something?'

'I don't know anything else,' Sylvia said, covering her face with her hands again.

Mia opened her mouth, but Munch placed his hand on her arm.

'That's all right, Sylvia. I think we'll stop at this point.'

The teenage girl could hold back the tears no longer.

'Poor Jessica,' she sobbed.

Hannah put her arm around her friend and looked at them.

'Are we done? I think it might be best if we—'

'Nearly done,' Munch said in a kind voice. 'Just a few

practicalities. Your mobiles – do you mind if we take a quick look at them before you leave?'

'That's all right with me,' Hannah said. 'How about you, Sylvia?'

The girl nodded behind her hands.

'We can have a little break first,' Munch said. 'Would you like something to eat? Some water?'

'Water,' Sylvia sobbed.

'We'll get you some. I'll be back in a moment, all right?' Munch said, and left the room.

Chapter 25

Mia left Munch to conclude the interview with the girls and walked outside to her motorcycle with a certain amount of reluctance. The time had come. It wasn't something she was looking forward to, but it had to be done. Anita Holmen. She had to talk to Jonathan's mother. She had always found this to be the hardest part of the job. Dealing with the bereaved. Munch was much better at this. He embodied serenity and warmth and instilled confidence, which appeared to help, while she always wore her heart on her sleeve and suspected that relatives often felt even worse after she had spoken to them. She was just about to mount the Ducati when her mobile rang. It wasn't a number she recognized.

'Yes? Mia speaking.'

A male voice on the other end.

'Hi, Mia. It's Daniel Lie from Kripos. I don't know if you remember me. We met at a party a few years ago?'

The cogs in her brain turned slowly while she tried to think back. And yes. A slim man her age. Blond hair and glasses. She remembered him as being nice. He hadn't tried to flirt with her like people usually did on the rare occasion that she went to a police get-together.

'Hi, Daniel. How are things?'

'Not too bad. A bit of internal restructuring, new management, yes, so we're a little all over the place at the moment – you know what it's like. Listen, I don't want to keep you, but I heard about your case up there. A teenage girl in a boat, was that it?'

'Yes, were you up here back then?'

'When the boy disappeared? No, I didn't work that case. Myrboe did, and it's no secret that we don't get on. I wanted to talk to you about something else. Have you come across the name Longden Shipping?'

'Longden Shipping? No, that doesn't ring a bell, why?'

Lie heaved a sigh. 'Well, I might be on a wild-goose chase here, but I had to try when I heard that you had gone to Hitra. People say you have a nose for these things. I'm working on a trafficking case, but I'm not getting anywhere. My new boss wants me to shelve it, but I just can't let it go.'

'Right, tell me about it.'

'These cases are all the same, aren't they? Girls from Eastern Europe and Asia. They're brought to Norway and promised money and a better life by the sick bastards behind the racket. They end up in prostitution mostly and, as long as it doesn't go large scale, it's not a priority for us. Whatever, I had a tip-off some time ago about this company, Longden Shipping. That someone working for them might be involved. I'm checking the route logs, and Hitra is one of the places where their ships have called a few times.'

He disappeared for a moment.

'Last autumn on 16 October and this spring on 4 March. Two different ships, MS *Salazar* and MS *Rover*. Does that mean anything to you? Have you come across those names?'

'I'm afraid not,' Mia said.

'Ah, well, it was worth a try.'

'I'll keep my eyes peeled. Longden Shipping, was that it?'

'Yes. British-owned, but registered in Cyprus.'

'I'll give you a call if anything turns up.'

'Super, and I'm sorry for disturbing you.'

'That's quite all right. Good luck.'

'Thank you.'

Mia stuck her mobile in her pocket, put on her helmet and rode out of the car park. The sun was high in the sky now and the wind warm around her body as she resisted the temptation to speed. She hadn't ridden a motorcycle for a long time. She had missed the tingling sensation in her body, the feeling of total freedom with the roaring engine underneath her. She had been like this ever since she was little. Loved anything extreme. Anything dangerous. It had carried on into adulthood. Parachute jumping. Climbing. Diving. The Ducati was like a warm, mechanical animal under her, Italian perfection, and she ended up giving in to the temptation, rolled the throttle towards her and grinned broadly under the visor when she felt the acceleration underneath her.

OK. Easy now, Mia.

There was a campervan in front of her. She reduced her speed and kept it down until her exit came into view. She parked the Ducati near the road and walked towards the well-kept house at the bottom of the hill.

It had already crossed her mind, of course. The name written in Jessica's blood.

Jonathan.

A mother's rage? Had his mother discovered something?

The bicycle dumped in the sea near a jetty as if the boy had caught someone in the act or walked in on an incident he should not have witnessed. Drugs? A courier handover? Perhaps a meeting between Jessica and a supplier? The kingpin behind it all? Jonathan could have been in the wrong place at the wrong time, and reacted in such a way that they thought they had no choice but to get rid of him.

And then perhaps recently his mother overhears a conversation that makes her realize what really happened.

She doesn't trust the police – after all, they have already failed her – and she decides to take matters into her own hands.

A final ritual down in the boat. The hair in the cup. The name in blood.

Goodbye, Jonathan.

Now we're even, this whore and me.

It was definitely possible.

Mia walked through the gate and knocked on the front door. It was all very attractive. A nice house, well maintained, as was the garden. She had expected it to be different. Signs of neglect. The place overrun with weeds. But not at all. The windows shone and looked like they were cleaned recently. The doormat lay in perfect symmetry on the clean stone doorstep. Perhaps that was how the mother was dealing with it. She kept her environment spotless. Control. There wasn't a pebble out of place.

It took a while, but then the door opened and a sad face appeared in the gap.

'Yes?'

'Anita Holmen? My name is Mia Krüger, I'm a police officer.'

A second's delay, then the dead eyes came alive.

'Is this about Jonathan? Do you have any news?'

'No, I don't. I'm sorry,' Mia said. 'But I would like to ask you some questions, if that's all right?'

The tiny flame that had been lit was quickly extinguished. Anita Holmen nodded softly and opened the door fully. She was just as well presented as the house itself. She was in her mid-forties, wearing light make-up, her hair scraped back in a tight ponytail. A grey, knee-length linen skirt. A pink blouse with long sleeves. It was like watching a wax doll. A lifeless person.

'Come in,' Anita Holmen said quietly, and walked in front of Mia down the hallway.

It was just as neat inside the house. Rows of pegs in the hallway, ruler straight. Shoes placed perfectly on the rack. One of the pegs was empty, but the name sign underneath was still there.

Jonathan.

The tidiness carried on into the living room. The floor appeared polished. A pink sofa with cushions neatly arranged in the corners. An armchair from the same suite in front of a bookcase with the books arranged according to colour. Curtains with tiebacks that almost looked starched. A few plants in good health. Three pale pink orchids in identical pots next to each other on one windowsill.

Anita Holmen gestured towards the sofa.

'Can I offer you anything?'

'No, thank you, I won't keep you long.'

Mia sat down, but Anita Holmen continued to stand in the middle of the floor as if Mia was not there. Her gaze empty, her arms hanging by her side as if she was waiting for something. Finally Mia had no choice but to cough lightly.

'Would you like to sit down?' she said gently.

'Pardon?' Anita Holmen said, as if she had already forgotten that Mia was there.

'Wouldn't that be more comfortable?' Mia said, nodding towards the pink armchair.

'I'm sorry,' Anita Holmen said, and sat down carefully, perching on the edge of the armchair and folding her hands in her lap.

'It's quite all right,' Mia said. 'Like I said, I won't keep you long, I just have a few questions.'

'Who did you say you were?' Anita Holmen said. She seemed to wake up a little now, and squinted at Mia as if it were far too bright in this tidy room.

'I'm Mia Krüger,' Mia said. 'I'm a police officer. We're investigating the murder of Jessica Bakken—'

'I'm sorry,' Anita Holmen interrupted her. 'So you're not here to talk about Jonathan?'

'Oh, yes, absolutely. I've just—'

'When will they send someone new?'

'I'm sorry?'

'Kripos? When are they sending someone? They weren't here for very long, were they? I put flowers on his grave, but that's just for something to do. Because he's not there. He's still out there somewhere. Who will help me find him?'

'We're looking into it,' Mia ventured cautiously.

'Oh, are you? I thought you were here for Jessica? She matters, is that right? But my boy doesn't?'

'Did you know her?'

'Jessica?' Anita Holmen heaved a sigh and shook her head. 'Only slightly. She is – she was – one of Hannah's friends, but they didn't come here very often. They'd go off somewhere. I don't know where.'

Anita Holmen disappeared again, shifting her gaze and staring vacantly towards the windows. A clock was ticking somewhere in the quiet room.

'Did they know each other? Jessica and Jonathan?'

'Pardon?'

She woke up and turned to Mia again.

'Jonathan? And Jessica? Did they know each other?'

Anita Holmen snorted slightly, as if she regarded the question as an insult.

'Jonathan was only eight years old. And what would a nice boy like him want with a girl like her?'

'*A girl like her* – what do you mean?'

'Well, you know.'

'No, I don't,' Mia said. 'Did you not like her?'

Anita Holmen raised her eyebrows and shook her head.

'I wouldn't say that I disliked her. But she didn't exactly have a great reputation, did she?'

'I wouldn't know,' Mia said, taking her notebook out of her pocket. 'What was her reputation? What did people think she was doing?'

'It wasn't what she was doing. Rather it was a question of where she was from.'

'You mean her mother? Laura Bakken?'

'Do you know something?' Anita Holmen said. 'I don't think I feel like talking about Jessica right now, if you don't mind.'

She adopted a stern expression and brushed something off her skirt.

'Of course,' Mia said, putting down her notebook. 'On the night that Jonathan disappeared, you were at home, weren't you?'

Anita Holmen nodded softly.

'I'm sure that Kripos went through this with you several times, but I would like to hear it for myself,' Mia went on. 'Did something happen that day? Or in the days leading up to it? Something out of the ordinary?'

'What do you mean?'

'I just wonder if there was anything that struck you at the time? Something that wasn't as it should be?'

Anita Holmen frowned.

'Are you referring to that business with Lucien Frank?'

'Who?' Mia picked up her notebook again.

'How do you lot actually work? Lucien Frank? Haven't Kripos told you anything at all?' Anita Holmen sighed.

'Well, I don't work for Kripos, I just—'

'Lucien Frank,' Anita Holmen said firmly. 'I said it then and I'll say it again. I saw him skulking around here that evening. And no, I don't believe he has an alibi, or whatever those idiots have concocted. Lucien Frank was out here. Out there.'

She got up suddenly and walked over to one of the windows facing the road.

'Look.' Mia followed her across the floor. 'Out there. Do you see? Up there. By the fence.'

'You saw a man there that evening?'

'Not a *man*,' Anita Holmen snapped. 'I saw *Lucien Frank*. Loitering up there. And no, I hadn't had too much to drink, as that rude investigator implied. That useless idiot should mind his own business.'

'When was this?' Mia said.

'I'm not actually sure. I used to think around seven, but then it struck me that the news had finished, so it can't have been until after seven thirty.'

'And you told Kripos this?'

Anita Holmen was fuming now. 'Many times. *Many* times.' She stood rigidly in front of the window before finally walking back and slumping on the edge of the armchair. 'But they won't listen to me.'

'Lucien Frank? Who is that?'

'A pig. We all know what he gets up to out at that dodgy place of his.'

Mia rested her pen on her notebook. 'Such as?'

'Oh, it's more what doesn't he do. Filthy pig.'

There was hatred in the eyes of the beautifully presented woman now.

'Just ask the police – they know him. Everybody out here knows him. Keep your children away from that man is all I'm saying. You ask any parent on the island.'

'He's a paedophile?'

Anita Holmen seemed to nod.

'Has he been convicted of anything?'

'I don't know, but he certainly should have been.'

'Have there been incidents? Has anyone—'

'Listen,' Anita Holmen said. 'A mother just knows, am I right?'

Her gaze darkened now. 'I went there myself, yes, I did. If the police won't get me justice, then—'

'You went to see him?'

'Of course I did.' She nodded proudly.

'What happened?'

'Pah, he hid away inside, too scared to face me. The bastard then called Luca Eriksen, and then I was . . .'

She pressed her hand against her blouse and shook her head.

'I was taken away in a police car. *Me?* While he just—'

'I'll look into it.'

'You do that,' Anita Holmen said sarcastically. 'I'm sure that will make all the difference. After all, you can always rely on the police.'

Anita Holmen straightened her back and looked towards the windows once more. The room fell silent.

'I really am so sorry,' Mia said. 'If Kripos didn't do their job, I can't do anything about that, but I'll look into this, I promise.'

Anita Holmen lowered her gaze and nodded softly.

'You have two children, don't you?' Mia continued. 'Jonathan and Hannah?'

'Yes.'

'I saw from the files that they don't have the same father?'

Anita Holmen fell silent again and brushed another invisible speck of dust off her grey skirt.

'No, they don't,' she said at last.

'And who is Jonathan's father? Is he in the picture?'

Anita Holmen shook her head again.

'No, he isn't *in the picture*,' she said tartly.

'May I ask you who he is?'

Anita Holmen looked at her with a gaze that Mia hadn't seen before. Fierce, almost hateful, now aimed straight at her.

'No, you may not,' Anita Holmen then declared.

'So he isn't—'

'Did you not hear what I said?'

'Oh, yes, I just—'

'It's getting late,' Anita Holmen said, faking a yawn. 'I think I need to rest. Was there anything else?'

Mia checked the time on her mobile.

It was barely noon, but she decided it was probably unwise to argue with Anita Holmen at this point.

'No, that was everything,' Mia said, returning her notebook to her jacket pocket. 'Thank you for your help.'

'Lucien Frank,' Anita Holmen reiterated once more when they were back on the doorstep.

'I'll see what I can find out,' Mia said, and gave Anita Holmen her card. 'You call me any time if something should come up, all right?'

Anita Holmen nodded briefly, then she closed the door.

Up by the road, Mia stopped next to the motorcycle.

Well, that was weird.

Her phone vibrated in her pocket.

'Yes?'

'How did it go?' Munch asked.

'We have another potential suspect.'

'OK?'

'A Lucien Frank. Will you run his name through the system for me?'

'I'll check with Luca Eriksen. How about the church? Should we take a look at the notorious altarpiece?'

'Sure. I'll meet you there.'

Chapter 26

Munch parked his car in the shade of a large copper beech by the entrance to the churchyard and had taken a cigarette from the packet just as Mia arrived at the car park. She dismounted, hung the helmet from the handlebars and looked up at the white, wooden church before she joined him. An old woman wearing sandals and a straw hat dashed across the car park and disappeared inside the church.

'So how did it go with the girls? Anything else after I left?'

'Nothing major. How about you?' He could see Mia's reluctance.

'I think she would have been capable of it.'

'You do?'

'Yes, definitely. If Jessica was involved in her son's disappearance in any way.'

'So she's on our list of suspects?'

'She is, for now,' she said, taking a bottle of water from the motorcycle's tail bag and raising it to her lips. 'Did you manage to check out Lucien Frank?'

'Luca knows who he is.' Munch nodded. 'Their paths have crossed a few times, but there's nothing serious on his criminal record. Petty crime, mostly. Where did you get his name from?'

'Anita Holmen claims to have seen him outside her house on the night her son disappeared. I don't remember the name from the notes that Kripos made, but I'll double-check when I get back. And then there's the question of Jonathan's father.'

'Who is he?'

Mia raised her eyebrows and shook her head. 'She refused to tell me.'

'So you don't think it's relevant to our case?'

'I've no idea, but she didn't like me asking, if I can put it like that.'

Mia looked up towards the church again.

'Are they expecting us?'

'Yes, I phoned ahead.'

'So why are we still standing out here?'

Munch took his lighter out of his pocket and lit his cigarette.

'Just a quick catch-up. You and me?'

'See where we have got to?' Mia said.

'Yes, how about it?' Munch said, wiping the sweat from his brow.

'Go through everything from scratch?'

'If you like.'

Mia screwed the cap back on the bottle and sat down on the motorcycle.

'OK. Jessica. Age sixteen. Bad home life. Lives on this boat, but not officially. One year ago something changes in her life; she gets access to money.'

'Drugs. Men,' Munch said.

'Yes,' Mia went on. 'But only three clients. Or she only recorded three names in her notebook, and that's important.'

'Because?'

'If she was selling drugs, she must have had more than three customers, because if she didn't, no one would want her dealing for them, do you agree?'

Munch nodded.

'She's a small-time dealer, 200 kroner here, 300 kroner there. She sells to friends and acquaintances, it's a small circle, there's no need to list every transaction,' Mia went on.

'Because?'

'They mean nothing to her. But these three people do, isn't that what we're thinking? It's not just the amounts of money because they're not that extreme, but it has a kind of symbolic value, don't you think? Three men, at least one of whom is an older man.'

An older man.

The only kind that poor young woman knew.

'And she uses abbreviations. Mr LOL, Big B, Vic. She wants to keep their identities secret. But is it because she has to or because it makes it exciting?'

'Perhaps both?' Munch said.

'Maybe.' Mia unscrewed the bottle again and took another gulp. 'Whatever the reason, I don't think her notes were about drugs. Not enough customers to stay in business. I think the notes referred to something else.'

'Sex?'

'Most likely.' She shrugged. 'What type of sex I don't know – after all, each to their own – but I think we can be pretty sure that some kind of transaction took place.'

'I agree,' Munch said, taking another drag on his cigarette. 'The cup? The hair? The writing in blood?'

She fell silent. He remembered that look on her face. And he liked it. She disappeared from the world for a moment before she came back.

'OK, let's start with the cup. After all, it's our link to this place, isn't it?'

She nodded up towards the church.

'Last Friday night. Three crows on the altarpiece. KTTY3. A clear message, isn't it? *I'm coming for her.* So, definitely planned.'

'I agree,' Munch said. 'The break-in at the hairdresser's. Was that the same night?'

'Yes, it was, wasn't it?' Mia said. 'Plus or minus a few hours, perhaps?'

'So the killer decides to go for it . . . *my time has come?*'

'Don't you think so? The killer may have been thinking about it for a while. Then something sets them off and they let rip . . . the crows, the break-in, the murder – everything in a short space of time. It sounds plausible, doesn't it?'

'To me, absolutely. So what about the writing?' Munch said.

'BABY WHORE. Yes, that is irritatingly intriguing.'

Again she disappeared into herself for a minute.

'I'm surprised by the choice of words.'

'Oh, right, why?' Munch said.

142

'Well, it's that particular word. *Whore*. It's rare these days. And that's why I'm not as interested in her boyfriend as you are. I don't think he would have chosen *whore*. I think "slut" is more up his street.'

'So, an older person?' Munch said. 'Such as Mr LOL?'

'But Sylvia didn't know his actual age, did she?'

'No, she just said that he was an older man. I don't know what that means to a teenager, but forty or fifty?'

'At least he can't be a teenager. I can't imagine that.' Mia shook her head and emptied the bottle.

'But why these props?' Munch wondered out loud. 'Or the ritual? Why not just kill her?'

'Exactly. That's what is so weird, and it's what I mentioned to you earlier. The violence. It looks as if it was a crime of passion, doesn't it? But the hair, the crows . . .'

'That's planned.' Munch nodded.

'Yes. And that's what I can't get to add up.'

'And then?'

'The million-dollar question?' Mia said.

'Precisely: what could the link possibly be? Between a boy's disappearance and a girl's murder? Jonathan was Hannah's brother. Did Jessica and Jonathan know each other somehow? Do we have any information there? Something that I have missed?'

'Writing his name in blood,' Mia said, and fell silent again for a few seconds. 'I don't know. It seems so . . .'

'Theatrical?'

'Yes, true, but it's not only that. I just . . .'

Those bright eyes again. She was gone for a while this time before she came back.

'. . . no, I can't make sense of it.'

'How are you doing otherwise? What about the eyewitness from the Kripos file?' Munch said.

'I've asked Gabriel to check him out.'

'Wallnes, was that his name?'

'Wallstedt. Jacob Wallstedt. I don't know if there's anything there – it could be nothing. It's just a hunch.'

143

'And who was he again? I mean, in terms of Jonathan's disappearance.'

'He was the only witness to a car he says passed Svingen at the time Jonathan disappeared.'

'If there even was a car in the first place,' Munch said. 'Could he be hiding something else?'

'You mean, could he be involved in the boy's disappearance?'

'Yes.'

'I don't know.' Mia hesitated. 'It's always possible, but then why would he implicate himself? *I saw a car, but I'm not sure of the colour or the make?*'

'But isn't that perfect? *I don't know what I saw, but I saw something so I've done my bit?*'

'Yes, perhaps you're right,' Mia said, then fell silent once more. Munch wiped the sweat from his brow again and moved further into the shade as he looked about him.

'What are you looking for?' Mia said.

'It's an old habit,' Munch said. 'Last Friday night someone sneaked into the church. I just wondered if they were caught on CCTV.'

'Good luck with that out here,' Mia said, and raised the now empty bottle to her lips. 'Gosh, it's hot today.'

'I think I have a lukewarm bottle of mineral water in there,' Munch said, pointing to the passenger seat.

'So what's next?' Mia said.

'Andres Wold.'

'I can take him. I need to talk to his father anyway, to see if he has ordered the parts for my car. Anything else?'

'This Victor from the salmon-processing plant,' Munch said.

'What did Luca say about him?'

'Not a lot. Apparently he's away at the moment, but he should be back the day after tomorrow.'

'OK, we'll speak to him then.'

'Are you sure we can't do anything about that app? Telegram? Speak to the software designer or something?'

She shook her head.

'Impossible. Secrecy is how they make their money. We're never going to get anything out of them.'

'But we believe that's the chain of events, don't we? She goes to the party. Gets a message from someone. And then she goes to the boat.'

'It seems likely. Otherwise, why leave the party that early?'

'I agree.'

Munch stubbed out his cigarette just as the church doors opened. The old woman who had crossed the car park earlier waved to them from the doorway.

'Hello, we're up here.'

'Are you coming with me or are you going straight to the garage?'

'Oh, I'm coming with you,' Mia said. 'I have to see that altarpiece.'

'I really hope it's cooler inside the house of the Lord,' Munch remarked, and started walking.

Chapter 27

Munch didn't like churches. Truth be told, he couldn't stand them. Respect for other people's religion? Absolutely. Allah, Shiva, Buddha, Jesus. People could believe in whatever they wanted. But actual churches? No, he shuddered on the rare occasions he had to enter one. He had been to Rome once, a long time ago with Marianne, and visited St Peter's Basilica, which had really put him off. Festooned from top to toe, a mishmash from another world, and at whose expense? The poor throughout the ages, that was who. Who, when threatened with hellfire and eternal damnation, had given away what little they had. It went back to his childhood. Munch's father had worked on the railways and been a dyed-in-the-wool communist. At home, the only gods had been Stalin and Lenin. His mother had been less of a firebrand, but she had shared her husband's beliefs. When he was younger and had yet to see the light, Munch had asked for permission to go to Sunday school. The attraction had been considerable. You got gold stickers and a cute girl from his class went there, so why not? He was given a huge telling-off. His father had been angrier with him then than the only time in his life Munch had got drunk, at the age of fourteen, on his father's home-made cherry brandy.

'Now be nice,' Mia whispered as they approached the steps.

'Me? I'm always—'

'Shush,' Mia said.

The old woman with the straw hat smiled and held out her hand to them.

'Hi, I'm Dorothea Krogh. And this is Thomas.'

She nodded towards the slight man next to her. He was in his late

146

twenties, wore a black shirt with a white dog collar and seemed strangely nervous. He wiped his hand on his trouser leg and cleared his throat before he extended his hand to them.

'Thomas Ofelius. I'm the vicar.'

'Munch,' Munch said. 'And this is Mia Krüger.'

'Hi,' Mia said.

'Yes, we've heard about you,' the old woman said kindly, and held open the door for them. 'You're very famous, aren't you? People have talked of little else since you arrived. I believe you're staying out in Kvenvær?'

'On Edøya.' Mia nodded and followed her inside the church.

'Oh, Edøya. Old Monsen's house? I have been there many times, but it's a long time ago now. My husband – he was the previous vicar – and Old Monsen were good friends. It's lovely out there – glorious, in fact. Do you live there permanently? Or is it a holiday home?'

'I'm living there for the time being. We'll just have to see for how long.'

Mia smiled and glanced quickly at Munch. Munch nodded back discreetly. He had thought the same thing.

What was up with the vicar?

They were halfway up the aisle, but the vicar still lingered near the entrance. Munch looked about him. Crucifixes and large candlesticks. Arched stained-glass windows with images of scenes from the Bible. Munch wasn't terribly familiar with the Bible, but he was able to recognize some of them. Eve with the apple in the Garden of Eden. Moses with the tablets on Mount Sinai. At least the temperature in here made it preferable to being outdoors.

'Are you joining us, Thomas?' Dorothea Krogh turned to the vicar, calling out to him in a chirping voice, almost as if he were a child.

The vicar nodded, then he took something out of his pocket.

'Yes, I just need to . . .' He blew his nose on a handkerchief.

'Poor Thomas, he has caught a summer cold,' Dorothea Krogh explained on his behalf.

'I'm allergic, I'm sorry,' the vicar mumbled as he came up to them.

'Really?' Dorothea Krogh said. Munch picked up a hint of irritation in her voice now.

'You should probably show them, Thomas. After all, it was you who found them.'

'Eh, yes, of course.'

'So this is Sandstad Church,' the old woman said. 'Many people think it's called Hitra Church, but it isn't. Hitra Church is that beautiful old stone church on Melandsjø. Perhaps you have seen it?'

'I don't think so,' Munch said.

'It's definitely worth a visit. Very pretty. Built with local stone, it has a bell tower in the middle, an incredibly fine copper dome. It's very fine, isn't it, Thomas?'

'Er, yes.' The nervous vicar nodded. 'It's very fine. But—'

'It's a bit small, unfortunately,' Dorothea Krogh said. 'So we use this church for most events. Christenings, services, weddings – it all happens here.' She smiled and gestured to their surroundings.

'So this is where the big wedding will be held?' Munch said.

Dorothea Krogh looked to the vicar, who nodded.

'Yes. This is where it will be. We, or rather I, will be in charge of the ceremony. I'm sure it'll be beautiful. We're still discussing what we're going to—'

The old woman rolled her eyes. 'Please excuse Thomas. He is, as you can see, not on top form today. Grass is it, Thomas? That you're allergic to?'

'Yes, I'm afraid so,' the vicar mumbled, and ran his hand under his nose.

'You have my sympathy,' Mia said. 'My sister suffered with it, too. It ruins the summer, doesn't it?'

'Eh, yes, it does. Very much so. Thank you.'

'Shall we?' Munch said, with a nod towards the altar.

They could see what everyone was talking about. The new altarpiece. Big and impressive, looming on the back wall. The decor in the rest of the church was heavy with religious symbolism, but it was almost absent here. A figure in the centre, clearly Jesus on the cross, but otherwise the motifs were more secular. A wriggling salmon in a net. Another salmon in someone's hands.

'So this is our new altarpiece,' the vicar said, clearing his throat. 'And yes—'

Dorothea Krogh shook her head and took over again.

'It's no secret, is it? Let's be honest, Thomas. The church has little means and so the parish council accepted a gift from the Prytz family. Is this design exactly what we wanted? Well, that's up for debate, but does it ultimately matter? is what I ask myself now. What's wrong with including something from our local history? Fishing? It's how people have made their living out here for generations. No, come to think of it, I think it's fine, I really do.'

'This is where they were hanging? The crows?' Munch walked right up to the altarpiece.

'Yes, on those.' The vicar came up behind him and pointed.

'What do you mean? Where were they hanging?'

The slight man reached up as high as he could.

'Up there . . . and there . . . and there.'

Munch looked at Mia. 'You mean they were attached to the fish-tails that stick out?'

'Yes.'

Mia pulled out her mobile from her trouser pocket and took some pictures.

'Do many people have access to the church?' Munch wanted to know.

'Oh, the doors are never locked,' Dorothea Krogh said.

'So anyone can enter?'

'Yes, everyone is welcome here.'

'Are there any cameras here? Inside? Outside?'

'No, I'm afraid not. We've never needed them. We're a small, tight-knit community. No one would—' She broke off and didn't complete her sentence.

'I understand,' Munch said. 'We're still investigating. We will find out what happened.'

'Her poor mother,' the old woman said when they were back outside.

The vicar had made his excuses and disappeared out of the back door.

'Did you know the girl?' Munch said.

'Jessica?' She hesitated briefly. 'She would babysit Sofia from time to time. And yes, I've seen her around. But I didn't know her personally.'

'Ah, so you're Sofia's grandmother?' Mia said.

'Yes, I'm her maternal grandmother,' Dorothea said. 'Simon is my son-in-law. They live in our old house out in Kvenvær. Ugh, I can't imagine how I would feel if it was my child who—'

Munch put his hand on her arm. 'You have no need to worry. Like I said, we're on the case. So no cameras, then?'

He looked about him.

'No, I'm afraid not.'

'What about the immediate vicinity? What's up there?' He pointed towards a house on a hilltop across the road.

'Oh, that's the old mink farm. It attracted quite a lot of attention some years ago. Protesters demonstrating – you know. There are no animals in cages up there these days. That's some progress, at least.'

'So no one lives there now?'

'I'm not sure, but I think someone's there. I've seen trucks go in and out. I don't know who has taken it over.'

'So you never lock the church? People can come and go as they please?'

'We can lock it if we need to,' the old woman said. 'I'm not quite sure where the keys are, but—'

'Didn't you house a family of asylum seekers here some years ago?' Mia wanted to know. 'Or was that in one of the other churches?'

'Oh, no, that was here,' Dorothea said proudly. 'My husband and I took them in. Four children, poor things. Surely there has to be a limit to border control. Ultimately, we are all God's children, aren't we?' The old woman smiled.

'Would you like me to show you around the rest of the area, or—'

'Thank you, but I think we have to get going,' Munch said.

'Nice to meet you,' Mia said, shaking her hand.

Once they were back by the car in the shade, Munch could finally help himself to another cigarette.

'So what are we thinking?'

'About the fishtails?' Mia said.

'Yes? Were they chosen deliberately?'

'It's hard to say. There were few other places where you could hang the crows, but even so.'

'A reaction to the altarpiece? An act of revenge against the Prytz family?'

'I'm not sure. After all, we have nothing linking them to this yet – or do we?'

'You mean the girl and her rich men?'

'Yes.'

'Nothing that I can see right now,' Munch said, shaking his head. 'But then again, it's only been a few days. Let's keep an open mind, see if we find a connection.'

'What about the vicar?'

'He was an oddball.' Munch nodded. 'Let's put him on our list. Give his name to Gabriel, see if he can find anything.'

'OK,' Mia said, putting on her helmet. 'Are you going to the station?'

Munch looked up towards the building across the road.

'No, I think I might take a look around up there. The old mink farm. As Mrs Krogh said, such places attract controversy. Perhaps they installed cameras in order to protect themselves against intruders.'

'OK. I'll see you later.'

Munch waved goodbye to her, crossed the road and was soon wheezing as he made his way up the hill. The sun was roasting him now and he wished that he had brought a hat. At the top of the hill was a rather derelict house, white like most places out here, an old farm comprising two storeys and offering a view of the strait. The gate and the fence looked new. He could see several other buildings up there now, a small barn and rows of what must have been the cages where they had kept the animals. Animal rights activists. He was reminded of Miriam. His daughter was a committed animal rights activist and he had retrieved her from police custody on many occasions.

Munch opened the gate, carried on up the dusty drive and noticed movement behind the curtains in the main house. He stopped and looked about him. Silence. A lorry bearing the name NorSalmon was parked near the barn. The door to the main house opened and a man started walking towards him. He was in his early thirties. His head was shaved. Tattoos on his muscular arms.

'Hey, this is private property. Can I help you?'

'Holger Munch, Homicide Unit, Oslo Police,' Munch said, showing him his warrant card.

The stocky man fell silent and glanced quickly over his shoulder at the house. There were several people inside it. More movement behind the curtains.

'All right? Is it . . . well, is it about that girl?' The man ran a hand over his smooth head. 'Jessica, isn't it? I've seen her around, but I didn't know her myself. It's awful. What a tragedy.'

'So this place used to be a mink farm?' Munch said.

'What? Yes. Yes, I think so. Why?'

A glimpse of another face inside the house, this time from the first floor.

'And who are you?' Munch said.

'I'm Steve,' the man said, holding out his hand. 'I'm a bit busy right now, so if . . .' He glanced over his shoulder again.

'I won't take up much of your time, I just wanted to check something. Would you happen to know if there used to be cameras anywhere around here? I can see that you have a view of the church?'

The man stroked his scalp again.

'Cameras, no . . . not that I've noticed. Now, I wasn't here when the property changed owners, but I've never heard anything about that.'

'OK, that was all. Thank you.'

'Sure. Happy to help.'

Munch made to leave, but then he stopped.

'So what's this place being used for now?' He nodded to the lorry parked near the wall.

'Salmon transport. All over Europe. The lorry drivers stay over here whenever they need to.'

'Is it your business?'

'Eh, yes.' The man waved the mobile in his hand. 'Like I said, I'm a bit busy right now, so—'

'Of course,' Munch said. 'So no cameras?'

'Not to my knowledge.'

The man remained outside right until Munch had closed the gate behind him.

Steve?

That didn't sound very Norwegian.

Munch took one last look up at the house, then he walked down to his car.

Chapter 28

Mia arrived at the garage to find Roar under the bonnet of an old Ford. His utility trousers hung low and revealed more of his backside than she needed to see, quite frankly. She parked the Ducati near the wall and went up to him.

'How are things?'

Roar looked up from the engine and wiped his fingers on a rag.

'Not great. The carburettor has had it. I don't think I can bring this car back to life unless I fit a new one.'

He produced a tin of snuff pouches from his pocket and popped a piece under his upper lip.

'I meant my Jaguar?' She nodded towards her car, which was still sitting in the exact same spot she had left it.

'Oh, that, yes. I must get round to ordering those parts. But I don't suppose that's the only reason you're here?' He spat on the floor and looked at her.

'Is he here?' Mia said.

Roar wiped his forehead and nodded towards the house.

'He's round the back.'

'He didn't come to the station this morning. We were told he's ill, is that right?'

'Well, not that ill. I guess he thought you would come out here if it was important enough. It's not the first time we have had a visit from the forces of law and order, as it were.'

'I heard they were a couple,' Mia said. 'Did you know her?'

'Jessica? No, I wouldn't say that. She was just one of many kids hanging around here. They come and they go, his girls. He's popular, you know. It's probably his car.'

He grinned, showing his crooked teeth, and nodded towards the low flame-painted Volvo parked by the entrance.

'Were you here that evening? I gather everyone met here to drink before the party?'

'Saturday?'

'Yes.'

'Nope, Leangen.'

'Leangen?'

'The racecourse. The V75 horse race. No luck, sadly. Those so-called experts don't know what they're talking about, do they? I should have trusted my gut instinct. And I will next time.'

'And you didn't drive home afterwards?'

'No, no, I'd had a few beers at the racecourse so I couldn't drive. We've had more than enough accidents out here. No, I ended up at a party at a mate of mine's in Byåsen. I've only just got back. You have created havoc, haven't you? Coppers all over the island. It's impossible to get a moment's peace now.'

'He's round the back, did you say?'

Roar nodded and spat again.

'In the shack. Just bang on the door, he'll wake up.'

'Call me when my car is ready, will you?'

'Will do.' He raised two fingers to his forehead in a salute and bent over the engine once more.

Shack wasn't a misnomer; the lean-to behind the garage couldn't be called anything else. It was a small outbuilding with a crooked roof and filthy windows. A door with no handle, just a rope looped around a nail on the frame.

Mia knocked and took a step back.

'Andres? Are you in there?'

There was silence for a moment, then she heard noises coming from the inside.

'Yes?' A tired face appeared in the doorway.

'Hi. My name is Mia. I'm sure you can guess why I'm here.'

Andres yawned and scratched his cheek.

'Hang on, let me put some clothes on.'

He appeared a few moments later, barefoot, wearing ripped jeans and a pale pink vest bearing the wording 'FBI – Female Body Inspector' – and sat down on a plastic jerry can by the wall.

'I would ask you in but, well, the place is a mess.'

'It's fine,' Mia said.

The young man ran a hand under his nose and seemed reluctant to meet her eyes. His eyes were red. As were his cheeks.

The tough guy had been crying.

'I'm sorry for your loss,' Mia said, sitting down on an oil drum.

'Thank you, but so what. Stupid words. What good will they do?' He blew his fringe from his forehead and stuffed his hands into his pockets.

'I know. My condolences. It's an old expression, I imagine. Like *whore.*'

'Like what?'

'Oh, nothing. I want to start by telling you that I don't think you have anything to do with this.'

His brows knitted over his grubby nose.

'Eh? Why would I have anything to do with it? Kill Jessica? Why the hell would I—'

'No, that's what I just said,' Mia replied. 'I don't believe you would.'

He looked at her suspiciously.

'But other people do, is that what you're saying? The cops? They're sitting around the station, having already made up their minds, is that it? Oh, Andres? We know all about him. Morons.'

He picked up a pebble from the ground and threw it at the garage. It hit the wall, bounced off it and went through the missing window of an old Vauxhall with no wheels jacked up on some bricks.

'I'm happy to tell you again: no. And yes, your name came up, obviously, but we don't think that you have anything to do with this.'

'Good,' the young man muttered. 'Thank you.'

'But you were with her, weren't you?'

'On Saturday? Not together like that. We were there for a while. It was just a party, nothing special. Then she freaked out, as she usually does, and left with her mates from school. The three of them are always together. Her and the sister of that boy who disappeared, and that third one whose name I can never remember.'

'Sylvia?'

'Yes, that sounds about right.'

'So the three of them left together.'

'Yes, in Gekko's car, I think.'

'Gekko?'

'Listen, are you a parrot? Do you have to repeat everything I say?' A hint of a smile now, the first one, as he picked up another pebble and blew his fringe away again.

'Sorry,' Mia said. 'Is Gekko a friend of yours?'

'Not really. We mess about with cars together from time to time. He drives a nice Toyota MR2. Sweet ride.'

'You said she freaked out – what did you mean?'

'Jessica?' He rolled the pebble in his hand as he thought about it. 'Well, I don't really know. She had started acting weird. After that business last year. It was like she stopped being normal. It was all howling and crying, oh, I don't know. Girls. Impossible to make out.'

'Last year – what do you mean?'

He looked at her through his fringe.

'You're supposed to be clever, aren't you?'

'I don't know about that,' Mia said.

'That's what they say. The famous detective who suddenly turns up here on Hitra for no reason. We've all googled you.' He smiled wryly.

'And why is that important?'

'That you're clever?'

'Yes?'

'I'm no snitch, just so you know it.'

He spat at the ground and ran a finger across his throat: '. . . Get it?'

'Yes, I get it.'

He leaned towards her.

'But seeing as you're so clever, you've already worked out what she was up to, haven't you?'

'It's possible,' Mia said with a nod.

'And unless you're completely blind, you may also have found her stash? Which was so well hidden in a boathouse under some sacks?'

'That's also possible.'

'Well, then you know most of it.' He threw the pebble, on to the roof of the garage this time.

'So she started last year?'

'Dealing?'

'Yes.'

He nodded.

'She changed completely. Got very full of herself. Suddenly nothing I did was good enough.'

'And who was her supplier?'

He narrowed his eyes.

'Oh, no, no. You won't get that from me.'

'But you know who it is?'

There was silence for a moment.

'I have an idea,' he said eventually.

'Someone here on the island?'

'Listen, cop, seriously. Are you trying to get me killed?'

Then he fell silent again, as if he had just realized the magnitude of his own words. He picked up another pebble and rolled it between his palms.

'Do you think that's why she was killed?' he said in a low voice.

'We don't know. What do you think?'

He shook his head softly, his eyes elsewhere.

'I take it back,' was all he said.

'You take what back?'

'That I know who it is. It was just something I said. I have an idea, yes, but that's all.'

'So which is it? Do you know or don't you?'

He leaned closer to her again.

'Listen, I get my weed from a dude in Trondheim, yeah? At first I thought it might have been him, but having thought about it, it doesn't add up. Weed, cannabis, perhaps a little resin, yes, but he doesn't sell stuff like that. No, I take it back.'

'OK,' Mia said. 'And what if I tell you that people think it came from you?'

'Me?' He snorted. 'Do I look like the local drug dealer?'

He looked down at himself.

'All right, maybe I do, but seriously, no, it's not me. No way. I won't touch that crap. Synthetic? No, I only do organic. Homebrew and home-grown. Don't step on the grass, smoke it, if you know what I mean.'

'What if I were to come back with a warrant?' She nodded towards the dilapidated shack.

'Be my guest. Like I said, it's a bit messy. You might find my iPad. I haven't seen it for a while.'

'All right,' Mia said. 'Gekko, where will I find him?'

'His real name is Geir-Ove Karlsen. He's the chef at Ansnes Brewery.'

'Get in touch if you remember anything you think might help us, will you?'

'I will.'

At the front of the garage everything was quiet again. Mia ran her hand over the bonnet as she passed the jade-green Jaguar then went over to the motorcycle and put on her helmet.

Chapter 29

Luca Eriksen was standing in his hallway. He was so tired that taking off his shoes was a struggle. Talk about having your life turned upside down. No more working two sleepy half-days a week. He felt that he had worked harder today than in the last two years put together. He unbuttoned his uniform and went upstairs to shower. He stood under the water for a long time. The pace of those Oslo people. Full steam ahead the whole day. A team briefing in the morning where people were given tasks and set to work. Then another meeting later in the day with updates. He was their liaison officer. *'If we learn anything while we're out in the field, the smallest detail, then call Luca. Not me or Mia, we can't have our phones ringing all the time. Call Luca, OK? And then Luca will call me. And no, I don't need to know what you're having for lunch, only call about essentials, OK?'* He had taken as many notes as he could; it was like being caught up in a whirlwind, but he was enjoying it. The phones were ringing non-stop, and it felt good to be important, at the heart of it all. And then there was the evening briefing, and they had finished late tonight. The clock in his kitchen showed eleven before he had put on his pyjamas and was ready to carry the plate with his dinner into the living room. He reached for the remote control, but realized he didn't have the energy to turn on the TV. Not tonight. Too many voices in his head; not a moment's peace all day.

She had praised him. Mia Krüger. He had glowed.

'Well done, Luca. What would we have done without you?'

To be honest, he had been intimidated by her to begin with. Her intense eyes boring into him, almost as if she could read his thoughts.

160

Quiet and softly spoken at every briefing, but once she opened her mouth, it was always to say something which made them, or at least made him, understand more and more about what was relevant and what wasn't. Like this business with the cup. *Whore.* And why it was the reason she had already eliminated Andres Wold. Luca regarded himself as reasonably bright, but he would never have thought of that. Fascinating. And now they were working together.

Luca carried his plate to the kitchen and had just rinsed it off and put it in the dishwasher when a car pulled up in front of his house.

Oh, no.

Luca made a beeline for the light switch by the window, but it was too late. Fabian Stengel had already stepped out of the Lexus and was waving to him.

'Luca?'

Luca heaved a sigh, went out into the hallway and opened the door a little.

'Hi, Luca,' Fabian said. He was already on the doorstep.

'Hi, listen, I've been working all day, I really need to go to bed—'

'I just wanted to see if you're all right,' Fabian said. 'You're not taking my calls. Do you mind if I come in briefly?'

Fabian pushed his glasses up the bridge of his nose and looked past Luca into the hallway.

'So you took my advice, I see? You've put away some of the pictures? What about the videos on your computer? It's not healthy, you know, you really need—'

'I've done it.' Luca yawned. 'Thanks for your concern, but I really need to hit the sack. I'm knackered.'

Fabian Stengel nodded, but he still didn't move from the doorstep. He seemed reluctant to leave.

'So how are you getting on?'

'With the investigation?'

'Yes? Are you getting anywhere? Do you have any suspects?'

'I can't talk to you about that.'

'Sure, I get it.' Fabian smiled. 'But hello, it's me. I have a duty of confidentiality. I won't tell anyone. She was found in that boat, wasn't she? Was anyone seen out there? Do you have witnesses who saw someone come or go, anything like that? Karin is beside herself. You know what she's like. She's almost too scared to leave the house now. It would reassure all of us hugely if we, well, got a bit of information, so we could feel safer.'

'I can't tell you anything, Fabian. I'm sorry. But thanks for stopping by.'

Fabian Stengel smiled and nodded. 'You take care of yourself. I'll come see you another evening, all right?'

'OK, and say hi to Karin from me.'

'I will. Speak soon.'

Chapter 30

Mia walked with her coffee down to the rocks as a mild, warm breeze wafted in from the sea. On the radio they had talked about the hottest summer on record, and the pink glow on the horizon where the sun had just disappeared promised another fine day tomorrow. It was almost a shame that she had to work. Her bandage was gone now. She hadn't been diving for a long time and she missed the silence of the dark deep. She had been through all the files Kripos had given her again, but hadn't found much on Lucien Frank. Just a brief note: *The boy's mother believes she saw him outside the family home that same evening. Eliminated. He has an alibi. He wasn't on the island. He was in Trondheim with his sister, Emily Frank.*

There was an address in Knarrlagsundet below. Mia knew the area well. She had driven there to enjoy the view a few days before the Jaguar had packed up.

Right, that meant a trip to Knarrlagsundet tomorrow. To double-check that alibi.

She sat down and raised the cup to her lips. She probably shouldn't be drinking coffee this late in the evening, but she had no intention of going to bed so it didn't matter. Night-time around her. She loved this time of the day. It was so much simpler to think, being alone with herself and her thoughts. Suddenly memories from her childhood came back: the small attic bedroom in the house in Åsgårdstrand. Her mother had got up for a pee and found Mia awake in front of a window.

'*Why, Mia, can't you sleep?*'

'*No, I'm thinking.*'

She stretched out her legs in front of her on the rock as a night-time fisherman chugged past her out on the sea.

OK. The timeline. Once more:

20.31 – Jonathan's mother calls the By family.
20.40 – Jonathan leaves the By family home.
20.50 – A car is spotted in Svingen.
21.42 – Jonathan's mother calls the By family again.
21.47 – Jonathan's mother calls the police.
22.05 – The police boat arrives at Svingen.

She got up and quickly went back to the house. She stopped in front of the large map she had stuck to the wall.

The home of the By family.
There.
The birch avenue.
There.
Svingen.
There.
The jetty where they had found his bicycle.
There.
No, damn it, it still didn't make sense, did it? What was it that . . .

Her train of thought was interrupted by her mobile ringing. She would have preferred to turn it off, but Munch had said no.

'*I must always be able to contact you. Always.*'

She smiled when she saw the name on the display and stepped outside the house before she took the call.

'Hello, Gabriel.'
'Hello, Mia. I know it's late. Am I disturbing you?'
'I always have time for you, Gabriel.'
'Phew, thank you. I just wanted to share my discovery.'

He disappeared for a while, there was some crackling, and Mia had started walking down to the jetty by the time he came back.

'Can you hear me?'
'Yes, I can hear you now, Gabriel. Sorry, bad signal up here.'

164

'It's about this man you asked me to check out, Jacob Wallstedt?'

'Yes. Did you find anything?'

'Well, that's a good question. Yes and no.'

'What do you mean?'

He hesitated for a moment. 'Well, according to the National Population Register, he doesn't exist.'

'What?'

'I found only two Jacob Wallstedts, and both of them are dead.' It sounded as if he was flicking through some papers.

'One died in Bergen in 1997 and the other died in Tromsø in 2008.'

'Are you serious?'

'Yes, but listen – and this is where it gets really strange: he's listed in *our* database as being alive.'

Mia shook her head.

'I'm completely confused. Is he dead or isn't he?'

'Well, I found two references to him. One in Indicia, which has him listed as living at the address 112 Forsnesveien, 7246 Sandstad? Is that where you are? Sandstad?'

'Yes, that's in this area. How very strange . . .'

'It's about to get stranger. You know Palantir? The international register? I found him there as well.'

'Where did you get a hit?'

'In the Netherlands. Not a lot, just a name and an address. But I think someone noticed me.'

'How do you mean?'

'Well, it's hard to explain. But I had a sense of an echo there.'

'A what?'

'Sorry, I'm sure there's a technical term for it, but we just tend to call it an echo. It's a way of registering visits. If I take a look at something, someone will get a message saying I was there, do you understand?'

'And who gets the message?'

'I've no idea. I could probably find out, but in order to do that I would need to get into the software and, strictly speaking, I'm not allowed to do that.'

'But you could do it?'

'Yes, if someone twists my arm, then . . .' Gabriel chuckled to himself.

'But nothing in the National Population Register?' Mia said.

'No, he's dead.'

'How odd.'

'Yes, very.'

'All right, I'll have a word with Munch. You'll hear from me tomorrow, OK?'

A small boat was approaching the island now. Mia could see the light from a torch on board.

Good God, wasn't that . . .

'Listen, Gabriel, I have to go, but I have a list of more names I would like you to run for me. And a couple of other things. I'll send you an email once I'm at the station, OK?'

'OK, I'll wait to hear from you.'

Mia stuck her mobile into the pocket of her shorts and ran down the rocks as the boat glided towards the jetty.

'Sofia? Good heavens? What are you doing out here at this time of night?'

The little girl trembled as she climbed the ladder and flung her skinny arms around Mia.

'My dad's gone. I can't find him anywhere. Can you help me? Please?'

Chapter 31

Forty-three-year-old Pelle Lundgren was well aware that people out here on Hitra talked about him behind his back, that they had nicknamed him UFO Pelle, a nutter and worse, but why on earth would he care? No, he had forgiven them a long time ago. Because they didn't know what he knew, did they? How it was all connected? Life and death, the universe and everything?

Pelle Lundgren smiled and pushed his bicycle over the ditch, then parked it carefully next to a tree at the entrance to Havmyran nature reserve.

He was travelling light. He had only packed the bare necessities. One set of clean pants. He would hate to find himself in perhaps the world's best spaceship only to discover that they didn't have any clothes in his size. Crispbread and cod roe. Who knew what they ate up there? Perhaps robot larvae or some kind of astral powder that wouldn't agree with his stomach.

It would take a while – he had given the matter considerable thought – until he became like them; or perhaps he wouldn't ever become like them? Perhaps he would still be a human being? Because they were not very specific; the messages he had been sent had said nothing about that. Only that they were coming to pick him up.

Tonight!

He smiled again and walked with his rucksack deeper into the nature reserve. He was wearing his wellington boots because it was always wet in here, at least in some places, and he would hate to meet his future with wet feet. It would be most uncomfortable.

He could feel his cheeks grow warm as he bent under a tall pine and made his way towards the wildlife tower. Ultimately, it was a little sad. Him having to leave them all behind. Because he did care about some of the people out here.

There were a few good ones who definitely deserved to be here with him now rather than toiling through this sad life on earth without ever knowing what would happen to them at the end. But he had seen the look in their eyes. At the Social Services meetings he had to attend.

'Jupiter?'

Yes, Jupiter, as it happens. During his sessions with the psychologist who always treated him as if he were a child.

'They're picking you up in a spaceship, is that what you're saying?'

Yes, for Pete's sake. How many times do I have to tell you?

'I've been chosen.'

Pelle set down his rucksack at the foot of the tower and looked up at the sky with a smile on his face. He checked the time on his watch.

02.47.

Excellent. Perhaps he was a little early, but he had been so keen to get here that he had been pacing up and down his hallway at home.

Wait, what was that?

He saw something across the wetlands. A light? Were they here already? He rubbed his eyes: he could hardly believe that it was true.

Yes, there it was again! Moving from side to side now, as if someone was signalling to him.

They were here!

Pelle Lundgren was so excited he could barely breathe as he put on his rucksack with trembling hands.

And walked slowly towards the flickering light.

FOUR

TUESDAY

Chapter 32

A beam of sunlight fell through the flimsy curtains and landed on the floor, where she was lying under a blanket. Mia hadn't slept much. She had let Sofia have her bed, having promised the girl repeatedly not to leave the room. Sofia had been scared and further unsettled by sleeping in a strange house. Mia had eventually managed to contact her father by phone. Simon had sounded distracted. And by then it had been very late. So Mia had made the decision. *'Sofia will stay here with me tonight. We'll speak tomorrow morning, all right?'*

Mia stood up and watched the little girl. She was sound asleep. Her long blonde hair spilled over the pillow, a mild and calm expression on her pretty face. Poor kid. Mia glanced at her mobile. It was five thirty in the morning. She stretched towards the ceiling, her muscles sore after lying on the hard floor, and went over to the window. She opened it quietly and cool air filled the room. She peered out behind the curtain; it was going to be another fine day, but it wasn't too hot yet, fortunately. Mia stroked the girl's hair and made her way downstairs. Sofia's eyes had widened on entering Mia's house. *'What's all this?'* And who could blame her? The walls were covered with notes and photographs, including some the girl probably should not have seen.

'That's Jonathan, isn't it? So it's true? You are looking for him? That's so nice of you!'

And more of the same. She had stayed close to her. Held her hand. Squeezed it. As if Sofia had a deep need to feel safe. It was unusual, wasn't it?

Mia had great respect for all the mothers in the world, though she herself was not the maternal type. Children? It would never happen. Her life did not permit it.

Mia carried her coffee cup from the kitchen and found his number. She had expected a tired voice to answer, but Simon sounded wide awake.

'How are things?'

'Everything is fine. She's still asleep.'

'Oh, I'm so glad. I'll set out now, if you don't mind. I didn't sleep a wink last night.'

'Of course. I'll see you shortly,' Mia said, and rang off. She put her mobile on the table and stopped in front of the photographs. She checked the map of Hitra yet again. No, she still couldn't make it add up.

'Mia?' Sofia suddenly appeared in the doorway with sleep in her eyes.

'Hello, sweetie.'

'I couldn't find you and I got a bit scared.'

'Oh, I'm sorry. I just needed a cup of coffee.'

The girl padded across the floor on bare feet, yawned and sat down on the sofa.

'What are you doing?'

'Nothing, just working. Are you hungry? Would you like some breakfast?'

'No, thank you.'

'Your dad is on his way,' Mia said. 'He won't be long. Have you got all your things?'

'What?' Sofia looked around with bleary eyes.

'I've really enjoyed your visit,' Mia said, stroking her hair lightly. 'But I need to work so I think you had better go home with your dad when he gets here, all right?'

Sofia pulled her legs up under her dress.

'Can I stay here just a little bit longer? I promise I won't disturb you.'

'No, I'm afraid not,' Mia said.

'But I'm scared,' the girl said. 'Dad is being so weird. He left the house last night, but it's not only that. He has secret conversations on his mobile. And the other night I saw him with the man in the yellow boat.'

'The yellow boat?' Mia said.

'Yes. The one Erik saw out by the viewpoint.'

'Erik? Do you mean Erik, the boy you were playing with on the night that Jonathan disappeared?'

Sofia nodded. 'Sometimes we play detectives. Erik writes down everything he sees. And he says he has seen the yellow boat lots of times. At first I thought he might be making it up – he does that – but then I saw my dad with that man, and then, well . . .'

Mia sat down on the sofa next to her and stroked her shoulders.

'Let me just make sure I've understood you correctly. The viewpoint, is that the place near those birch trees from where you can look across the sea? The avenue that Jonathan passed through on his way home?'

'Yes.'

'And this boat, the yellow one? Erik saw it from there?'

Sofia nodded again.

'I know it's a really long time ago, but do you remember if *you* saw it on the night Jonathan went missing? The yellow boat?'

She shook her head. 'I've never seen it. Not until the other night.'

'Tell me again where you saw it, please?'

'By the jetty down by our house. My dad got a phone call late the other night and went down to the jetty, and I followed him. Then the yellow boat arrived and the man was on it and they were doing something.'

'Could you hear what they were doing?'

'No. And I thought they might see me, but they didn't, then I climbed along the rocks and ran back home behind the redcurrant bushes. It was really, really scary.'

'Well done. You're a tough cookie, Sofia. Your dad loves you very much, but he also has his own life to live. And he's allowed that, don't you think?'

Sofia bridled a little and said, 'Yes, but he was out again last night.'

173

Mia stroked her hair again.

'But that was just a misunderstanding. We discovered that when you came here. He couldn't sleep so he went for a short walk; he didn't go very far, he just took a walk around the house. When he came back inside and couldn't find you, he got very scared, isn't that right? It was great that he realized you might have made your way here, just like you did the last time. So it all worked out in the end.'

'I know,' Sofia mumbled.

'Good, now go and get your things and we'll walk down to the jetty. I bet he's already there.'

'OK.' Sofia nodded and shuffled reluctantly back upstairs to the bedroom.

They reached the jetty just as Simon arrived on the semi-inflatable. He turned off the motor and climbed up the ladder, shaking his head.

'Sofia.' He bent down towards her and squeezed her tight. 'You must never do that again, do you hear me? We've talked about it many times before. I got so worried when I discovered you were gone. What would I do without you?'

'It was fine. I was here. But perhaps the next time you could visit me during the day? How about that, Sofia? And after your dad has given his permission?' Mia said, and ruffled Sofia's hair.

'OK,' Sofia muttered.

Simon straightened up and shook his head wearily.

'Again, thank you. I don't know what to say. I felt sick when I couldn't find her. It's not the first time she's gone off without telling me, but never that late. I was just so scared.'

He looked different to the last time she'd seen him. Unshaven. His eyes flitting. Restless fingers through his blond hair.

'Luckily it all worked out in the end,' Mia said.

'Thank God for that.' He heaved a sigh of relief. 'Come on, let's sail back together. You can tie your boat to mine. Say thank you to Mia, Sofia.'

'Thank you, Mia.'

'You're very welcome.' Mia waved from the jetty until Simon's boat had disappeared behind the headland. Then she ran back to her house.

Where was it, where was it . . .?

She had to go through four stacks of files before she found what she was looking for.

Interview with Peder Eftedal, local fisherman, 26 July: mentions a boat he believes he has seen in the waters around Skorvøya, an island east of Hitra, at the relevant time. Pale yellow hull, make Nordkapp or similar. To be followed up.

She picked up a pen from the table and walked up to the map. She made a note of the name Sofia had used.

The viewpoint.

She trailed her finger south across the map until she found it. The island of Skorvøya.

It wasn't far away.

She took her mobile and went back outside to the rocks.

'Yes, Munch speaking.'

'Are you awake?'

'Yes, what's up?'

'I'm just calling to tell you that I'll be in later today.'

'OK.' Munch yawned on the other end. 'Any particular reason?'

'There's just something I need to check. I'll be at the station around lunchtime.'

Chapter 33

Twenty-five-year-old Lissie Norheim was standing on the manicured lawn with a vague sense of dread on hearing the helicopter in the distance. Two years ago she would have laughed out loud if someone had told her that this would be her story, and yet she had taken to her new life with surprising ease. Elisabeth 'Lissie' Norheim. An ordinary girl from Stavanger. Her parents were called Henrik and Eva. Her father worked in a warehouse. Her mother worked at a jeweller's. She had grown up in a terraced house not far from Vaulen beach. She was happy with her life. She had not been sure what she wanted to do after school, but had finally decided to read architecture at the Norwegian University of Science and Technology in Trondheim. The entrance requirements were tough, but not a problem for her. Her grades were good, so good in fact that they had made fun of it at home. Was she some kind of foundling? No one in her family had ever made it to higher education. They were working class and proud of it. Hence her sense of dread as she waited on the lawn in an expensive dress and wearing a pair of shoes which cost more than her mother earned in six months.

As the sound came closer, Lissie shaded her eyes with her hand in order to spot the helicopter that had picked up her parents from Trondheim airport. The two sets of parents had met once before and it had not been a success. It was at an expensive restaurant in Oslo, and she remembered only too well the look in her father's eyes when he saw the prices on the fancy menu. The mini quarrel when the bill arrived, her proud father insisting on paying his share, even though she knew it was pretty much their food budget for several weeks.

Her mother had been the complete opposite. She had practically had stars in her eyes. Giggling like an excited little girl, her jaw had dropped when the cosmopolitan Cynthia and Henry Prytz held forth about their most recent adventures. Diving for pearls in Fiji. Setting up a children's home in Nepal. Her father's eyes had darkened, his stooping body dwindling in the chair. When it was all over, he had not said a single word, just nodded politely and left.

The son of a billionaire? Except she had not known that was what he was. They didn't believe her, of course they didn't, her old or her new friends, when she came back from her holiday in Naxos and told them that she had got engaged.

'To Alexander Prytz?'

'Oh my God.'

'Cinderella has found her Prince Charming.'

There had been a social media explosion. Overnight she went from having twenty-six followers on Instagram to having more than five thousand. Not all the online comments had been kind; of course not.

Gold-digger.

Norway's most desirable bachelor and that grey mouse?

She hooked him good and proper!

Lissie had despaired; she had tried to defend herself as best she could, but in the end she had given up because no one wanted to believe her. But it was the truth! She had had no idea who he was. Alexander Prytz. The son of one of the richest men in Norway.

First, she had never heard of him. And second, he hadn't introduced himself as such, had he? Svein Hansen. That was the name he had given her.

Lissie's paternal grandmother had left her a bit of money and she had treated herself to a holiday. Her course of study was hard, competitive, much more demanding than she had imagined, and the days were long. Two weeks on Naxos on her own – she deserved that. And that was where she had met him, one warm evening in a small, whitewashed café with a view of the Aegean Sea. Another Norwegian travelling on his own. Very nice. And attractive.

Svein Hansen. He had told her he was also a student. Reading engineering. And she had fallen head over heels in love with him. Incognito. She hadn't even known what that meant. She knew what the *word* meant, of course she did, but not why someone might choose to live such a life, the desire to hide away, to get a little privacy.

She had not understood until she visited him in Trondheim that his circumstances might not be quite as straightforward as he had told her. The enormous apartment. With its own lift going right up to the penthouse. Astounded, she had found herself on an enormous terrace with a view of the whole city.

'You love me, don't you, Lissie?' The almost mournful eyes and the hand squeezing hers.

'Of course I do, but—'

'We love each other for the people we are on the inside, don't we?'

'Yes, sure, but what—'

She was shocked. At the magnitude of the deception. But then again, he was right. And later she was pleased that that was how it had all come about. She had fallen in love with an ordinary guy called Svein. Not with the money. Only with him.

Alexander.

She could feel herself smiling on the inside as he came walking towards her.

He squeezed her hand. He leaned closer to her as the helicopter came into view.

'Have you seen Benjamin today?'

'No, why?'

'The police have cordoned off an area around the nature reserve. Where that party was. Something must have happened.'

'Oh? No, I haven't seen him.'

Alexander took his mobile out of his pocket, checking it quickly. 'I hope he hasn't—'

'What?'

'Oh, nothing.'

He put his phone back in his pocket and smiled at her. They could see the helicopter more clearly now as it approached the island. Alexander put his arm around her.

'Are you OK?'

She nodded.

'You'll help me, won't you? Try to tone it all down a bit?'

She looked at him plaintively. He let out a light sigh.

'You know what my mum is like.'

'Yes, but a *rehearsal dinner*? Isn't the wedding itself enough? Can't we do something more fun instead? How about we go over to Kvenvær tonight? Have a beer down by the seafront?'

He sighed again and said something, but she didn't hear it; the helicopter was too close.

The wind was lashing her face now.

'I'll try,' he shouted, then squeezed her hand hard and followed her to the helipad.

Chapter 34

Munch lit another cigarette and looked across the car park as his new team arrived for the first team briefing of the day. He was in a foul mood. He had had another bad night and knew himself well enough to realize that if he turned up for the meeting without calming down first he would ruin everyone's day. Back in Oslo, his staff had had a code word for this: cyanide. Meaning *Munch is toxic today, better stay clear of him.* Cross. That was what he was. With himself. Overtired and, after tossing and turning on the far-too-thin mattress, he could no longer control his emotions. He had picked up his phone and poured out his heart. Sent messages. *Hi, Lillian. I'm on Hitra at the moment. I don't know for how long. How is your cat? Hi, Lillian, are you getting these messages?* He had called her as well, several times, in the middle of the night; she hadn't picked up, obviously. Finally, he had got dressed and left his room. Stood alone outside the hotel under the dark night sky. Him and his cigarettes, total silence all around him.

OK. Time to snap out of it.

He threw his cigarette aside and crossed the car park. It was early, but he could already feel that today would be another hot day. He had visited a shop in the small shopping arcade yesterday and bought himself a sun hat. They had not had a vast selection and he probably looked like an idiot, but it would just have to do.

'Hi, hi.'

He greeted people as he walked down the corridor, then sat down near the screen. He waited until everyone had found their seats before he began.

'Good morning, everyone. Thank you for your efforts yesterday. We'll keep at it today.'

'Did we get a hit on the hair?'

It was Ralph Nygaard who wanted to know; no Springsteen T-shirt today, instead Bob Dylan.

'That's right – my apologies if Luca didn't manage to send the information to all of you?' He looked to Luca Eriksen, who still insisted on wearing his uniform, even though it was boiling hot outside.

'I believe I sent it?' Luca said hesitantly, then checked his phone.

'Whatever,' Munch said. 'For those of you who are not yet aware: the crime-scene technicians from Kripos have done a great job and we now have a DNA profile of the hair. We're talking about the hair that was found in the cup—'

'Would you like me to—' Luca interrupted him timidly, nodding towards the projector.

'Yes, please,' Munch said, and waited until his iPad had been connected to it. 'Here it is,' he went on a moment later, bringing up a picture. 'So that's a good start.'

'Is this person already in our system?' Nina Riccardo wanted to know. She was dressed for the summer again today in a yellow T-shirt, a floral skirt and sandals.

Munch realized that he cheered up considerably when Nina Riccardo was in the room. Her personality. Her professional skills. This was exactly the kind of investigator he had been looking for when he hired for his team in Oslo. Alert. Clever. Unafraid to speak her mind, the courage to be herself. That was not always easy for women in this male-dominated profession.

He had sent Anette Goli a text last night.

Any news? About the unit?

She had replied early in the morning.

Nothing, sadly.

'No,' Munch said. 'We have a DNA profile, but it doesn't match anything in our databases.'

'We're not talking about the killer now, are we?' Kevin Borg looked about him.

'That's right,' Munch said. 'Unless the killer burned some of their own hair and got off on that. Which is still a possibility. Because we don't yet know the point of this little stunt, the burning of hair in a cup. Unless anyone has had a bright idea overnight?'

No one said anything.

'The DNA profile of the hair,' Munch continued. 'It's obviously a priority for us now to test as many people out here as we can. Pathology has sent us kits. Let me know if anybody needs help using them.'

'And what about the legalities of this?' said Claus Nielsen, the police lawyer, who had also changed to a more casual look today, khaki trousers and a white short-sleeved shirt.

'Good point,' Munch said. 'The procedure is as follows: we can ask anyone for a DNA sample. I mean, ask the person in question for their permission to take one, and if they agree, yes, then we go ahead and do it, obviously. But . . .'

He gestured towards the police lawyer.

'Yes, if we want a DNA sample from someone,' Claus Nielsen said, 'but that individual refuses, then we have a choice to make. We either change their status to suspect, which gives us the legal basis on which we can take a DNA sample, but it will have other consequences, of course.'

'Such as?' Luca said.

'They'll have the right to legal representation, for one.'

'What Claus is saying here,' Munch said, 'is tread lightly. But try to get DNA samples from as many people as you can, please.'

There was nodding around the room.

'OK,' Munch said. 'Anything else?'

'I spoke to the hairdresser.' Kevin Borg cleared his throat and checked his notepad. 'Very nice owner. Showed me around. She does actually know what happens to waste hair – it goes into a bag in her back room. Apparently there's an artist who uses it for weaving or something?'

He turned to Luca Eriksen, who merely shrugged.

'She doesn't have a client list. When I asked her who her clients are, she replied: *"Anyone on the island with great hair."*'

There was muted laughter across the room.

'OK, thank you, good,' Munch said, holding up his hand. 'But we still don't know if there is a link there, so let's not spend any more time on it now. Videos and pictures from the party? Where are we with that?'

He looked to Nina Riccardo, who tucked her hair behind her ear and let out a gentle sigh.

'We have a few more, but not all that many, unfortunately. We're working on it.'

'So nothing with Jessica?'

'Not yet. Nothing apart from what I've already shown you.'

'OK,' Munch said. 'You'll be in charge of that. Try and make some progress. Find more people who were there. Check their mobiles.'

Nina Riccardo nodded.

'Good. OK. Does anyone have anything on the three names from Jessica's notebook? Mr LOL? Big B? Vic?'

'I've spoken to Victor Palatin, as I said I would,' Luca said. 'That's the guy who works at the salmon-processing plant. He's away, he has been to the nunnery on Tautra—'

'He's a nun?' Kevin Borg chuckled and looked at the others.

'I presume it's a tourist destination, isn't it, Luca?' Munch said.

Luca nodded and continued. 'I believe he's back tomorrow. He lives out by Akset. It's on the island of Fjellværsøya. I'm happy to take you there by boat, it's the quickest way.'

'Good, let me know when he's back and Mia and I will come with you.'

'I have something,' Ralph Nygaard said. 'Nille – that's my sister – thinks she has heard people refer to a guy from Ulvøya as Big. He's a bodybuilder, I think. And his first name is Birger. So Big B? He works in a pub there. Would you like me to follow it up?'

'Definitely, Ralph. Good work,' Munch said. 'Anything on Mr LOL?'

There was silence in the room once more.

'As we can see,' Munch said, scrolling through the photographs until he found one of the notebook, 'Mr LOL is the most frequently occurring name on the list. More than four times as often as the second person, Big B. Vic is mentioned only three times. So without prejudicing our enquiries, I would say that I'm most interested in Mr LOL.'

'Does anyone have any thoughts on what the acronym might mean?' Nina Riccardo said, looking around the room. 'I mean, "laughing out loud" is the obvious explanation, but can it really be that simple? That we're just looking for somebody who is funny?'

'Are you thinking he might be a comedian?' Claus Nielsen asked, running the back of his hand over his forehead.

The fans were on and the blinds were down, but they could all feel the temperature rising in the room.

'I don't know,' Nina Riccardo said. 'It does sound a bit silly, but maybe that really is the explanation. I mean, the person in question might not be a stand-up or anything, they might just be a local resident who is well known for their sense of humour? Someone who is the life and soul of the party?' She looked at Luca.

'No one springs to mind, but I can ask around.'

'OK,' Munch said. 'Then it's more interviews today, tomorrow, for the rest of the week, for as long as it takes until we have spoken to absolutely everybody and their dog on this island. Kevin?'

'I have twelve names on my list today. The first person will be here shortly.'

'Good. Ralph?'

'It's about the same for me. My first person is already waiting.'

'Great. Any other questions?' Everyone shook their head. 'Super, then let's get going. Don't forget—'

He was interrupted by a police officer in uniform who knocked and popped his head round without waiting for a reply.

'This had better be important,' Munch said.

'Er, yes, sorry. I think it is. There's a guy out here who wants to talk to somebody.'

'About what?'

'He says he owns the boat. The smack. Where we found her. He says he was out there that night.'

'Show him into the small room,' Munch said, and took a cigarette from the packet.

184

Chapter 35

Lissie Norheim covered her ears with her hands as the helicopter took off and felt the lump in her stomach starting to dissolve when she saw the two smiling faces coming towards her. Her mother had dressed up. She had put on her smart floral dress and the pearl necklace she had bought in a market in Gran Canaria. Her father, too; he wasn't in his Sunday best, but she could see that he had made an effort. Nice shorts with pockets and a white short-sleeved shirt. And he wasn't wearing his Crocs today, but proper shoes which had laces.

'Hello, sweetheart,' her mother said, setting down her handbag and giving her a big hug.

Her father carried both suitcases. He was struggling with the weight, but for once he wasn't stubborn and proud, he actually said *yes, please* when Alexander offered to help him with them.

'Phew, you're having quite the summer,' her father said, and took out a handkerchief from his pocket. He wiped his brow, then smiled and came over to stroke her hair.

Oh, thank God. She could see it in his eyes. That everything was fine.

'Everyone back home is so jealous,' her mother said, and clapped her hands together. 'We've had rain for days.'

She nudged Lissie with her elbow and giggled.

'Everyone from your old job sends their love, and erm, Granny, of course.'

'How is she?'

Her mother tilted her head and looked at her father.

'Reasonably well? I think we can say that?'

'It's a real shame she can't be here,' Lissie said.

'It is, but she's old, you know. She can't manage the trip up here. But she sends lots of hugs.' She gave Lissie another big hug.

'Can I get you anything?' Alexander asked politely. 'We'll be having lunch soon, but before that? Something to drink? An alcoholic drink. Is it too early?'

'Oh . . .' her mother said, looking at her father again. 'Something sparkling, perhaps? That would be lovely.'

Her father nodded, but said, 'Nothing for me. Where will we be staying?'

'You're in the big guesthouse.' Lissie pointed it out to him.

'I'll bring you something to drink.' Alexander smiled. 'Just leave the luggage. I'll get someone to bring it down to you.'

She saw her father frown for a brief second, but that was all. It was clear that he had made up his mind to be positive. Set aside politics for a few days.

Thank you.

Her mother, too, was beginning to relax and enjoy herself. She took in her surroundings, then clasped her hand over her mouth.

'Good heavens. Is that really . . .'

'Calm down,' her father said.

'No, I just have to . . . look at that, Henrik.'

She touched one of the rosebushes planted in a ruler-straight line along the well-manicured lawn.

'Is that . . . marble paving?'

'Eva—' Her father heaved a sigh.

'Oh, humour me just this once, please. And the fountains too? Anyone would think they had their own gardener.'

'They do,' Lissie said. 'But—'

'Oh, wow,' her mother interrupted her. 'That must be the biggest garden pond I've ever seen. Do they have fish in it, I wonder? Look, Henrik, some orange ones? Are those carp?'

'Mum,' Lissie said gently, trying to hold her back.

'Yes, sweetheart?'

'Would you mind if we don't talk about all the things they have? I don't want us to . . .'

Her mother looked sad for a moment, but then she nodded.

'Of course, sweetheart, that's just what I'm like. You know how easy I am to impress. Sorry, I will try to control myself.'

'You'll soon get used to it,' Lissie said, taking her arm. 'Did you have a nice trip?'

'Eh, what? Oh, yes. Though your father insisted on parking a mile from the airport – no surprise there. It was so far away we had to catch a bus.'

'It was just a minibus.' Her father heaved a sigh.

'We might as well have caught the bus from home it was that far away.'

'No one in their right mind parks at Gardermoen airport multi-storey. That place is a rip-off.'

'But the helicopter from Trondheim was OK?' Lissie wanted to know. 'You managed to find it all right?'

'There was a very nice man waiting for us.' Her mother smiled. 'Holding up a sign with our names. Very posh – I felt like royalty. Good heavens, there's more?' She stopped and looked around. 'What's that?'

'The stables.'

'They have horses?' She practically whispered it.

'Eva . . .' Her father sighed again.

'Let me enjoy myself,' her mother said. 'Goodness, what a car collection!'

It was now a matter of urgency to reach the guesthouse before her father could no longer contain himself, but when it came to the cars, Lissie was of the same mind as him.

The big house, the stables, the two garages, the four guesthouses and the spa that continued down over the water – all that was one thing, but the cars made no sense to her at all. That was just show-ing off.

The Prytz family style was fairly minimalist overall. Wealthy, yes, but elegant and understated. Even the statues in the park behind the house had an element of restraint to them. But the cars? No, she could do without them.

'This is where you'll be staying.' Lissie smiled as she opened the door to the guesthouse.

'Oh, my,' her mother said, stopping in the doorway with her hands on her cheeks. 'This is lovely. How many rooms does it have?'

She set down her handbag on the floor and disappeared inside.

'Ah, well,' her father said, wiping his forehead. 'So how are you? Is everything ready?'

'Everything is fine,' Lissie said, slipping her arm around his waist and giving him a small squeeze.

'We're here quite early, aren't we? Five days before the big day? We would hate to be in the way.'

'You're very much not, Dad. I'm so pleased you're here. And we have lots to do. There's a rehearsal dinner tonight, tomorrow my dressmaker arrives for the final adjustments to my wedding dress—'

'Well, your mother will enjoy that, I guess,' he said, patting his pockets and pulling out a leaflet from his shorts. 'I picked this up at the airport.'

It said *Whale safari by boat, Hitra and Frøya* on the front.

'Do you think we'll have time for that?'

'You want to go whale watching?'

'Yes, please, if you can spare the time?'

'Of course.'

'Great.' Her father smiled and flicked through the leaflet. 'It says here: *Mondays and Thursdays, two departures, at eleven and three, sailing from*—'

'Dad,' Lissie interrupted him. 'They have boats here. Alexander will take us out whenever you want to.'

'My oh my, we have a four-poster bed, Henrik. And a sauna. And we have separate bathrooms, and—' Her mother was interrupted by Alexander, who entered with a bottle in a bucket of ice.

'Are you settling in all right? I thought champagne might be in order. After all, we want to celebrate that you're finally here.'

'Wonderful.' Her mother smiled.

'A toast to welcome you to Hitra,' Alexander said in a solemn voice.

'And to the happy couple.' Her mother nodded and raised her glass.

They were interrupted by a din outside. Another colourful monster of a car came speeding up the avenue and screeched to a halt in
front of the main house. The doors slid open and a girl in a skintight
white dress emerged. She lifted up her sunglasses and raised a bottle
to her lips. She appeared to have some difficulty balancing on her
high heels.

'Is that—' Lissie said.

'That'll be Benjamin's girlfriend,' Alexander said tersely. 'Please
excuse me. I'll go and talk to him.'

He shook his head, set down his glass and marched towards
the car.

Chapter 36

Munch returned after his smoking break and heard barking in the corridor. Waiting in the interview room was a man his own age, sitting down with an Alsatian on a lead by his side. The dog growled and bared its teeth as Munch entered.

'Quiet, King,' the man said, resting his hand on the dog's head, not that it made much difference.

'Hello, my name is Munch, and the dog has to go,' Munch said.

'Oh, no, he's a very nice dog, aren't you, King? You're a good boy, you are. Now don't you disturb the nice man.'

The dog barked again. Munch sighed and called out down the corridor.

'Luca!'

'Yes?'

'Could you come in here, please?'

'No, no, King won't bother us. He can stay, can't you, King? Yes, there's a good boy.' The dog bared its teeth and growled again.

'Are you blind?' Munch said.

'Er, no?' the man said.

'Do you have any conditions – loss of hearing or physical disability – which makes it necessary for you to have a service animal present?'

'No, King isn't a—'

'Great,' Munch said.

'Yes?' said Luca, who had popped his head round.

'Take this dog for a walk around the block,' Munch ordered him. He closed the door behind Luca and King, and sat down.

'There. Hello again. My name is Holger Munch. And you are?'

'Roger,' the man said, looking a little put out as he stuck out his hand.

'Hello, Roger. What can I do for you today?'

The man was around fifty, with a bald head and a greying beard. He looked like Pippi Longstocking's pirate father back from one of his many voyages. A gold hoop in one ear. A T-shirt. Leather waist-coat, cut-off denim shorts stained with several flecks of paint.

'It's my boat. And I know the man you're looking for.'

'You do?' Munch reached for a pad and a pen.

'I'm sorry I didn't get in touch with you sooner, but I was in Trondheim. I opened an exhibition yesterday in Gallery SG in Kjøp-mannsgata. Well attended. I even sold a few pictures, as it happens.'

'But you were on Hitra last Saturday?'

He nodded.

'I should never have let her use the boat, of course. It was a stupid idea, wasn't it? But that's what I'm like. Soft. It's just the way I am. If anybody needs anything, well . . .'

The big man threw up his hands and shook his head at himself.

'So you did know that she was staying there?'

'Oh, I did. Not officially, of course. But on the quiet. Or some busybody will show up and lecture me about health and safety and God knows what, and that's always the owner's responsibility. Even though it's just an old smack, but that's what it's like these days, isn't it? The government telling us all what we can and can't do – whatever happened to freedom? A man's right to his own property and all that?'

'OK.' Munch heaved a sigh. 'So Jessica was living on your boat. How long had she been staying there?'

'Oh, not very long.' The artist scratched his beard. 'A few months? Since March? Something like that. Guilty conscience, you know.'

'Because?'

Roger raised an imaginary bottle to his lips.

'Drinking. I'm better now. A beer when I'm painting, that's all, but before . . . well.'

He ran a hand over his scalp and shook his head at himself.

191

'So you feel guilty because—'

'Well, because I used to hang out there. When the muse refused to visit me.'

'Hang out where?'

'At Laura's, of course,' he said, as if Munch must surely know what he was talking about.

'You mean Laura Bakken, Jessica's mother?'

A quick mental note.

Mother. Hospital. Arrive when?

'Yes, I'm afraid so,' the big man said, fiddling with his fingers. 'And that's where I saw it, that the girl was not OK. Christ, she would run around in nothing but a nightie while we partied. No, it wasn't good. Some years later I saw her down by the cinema. And I just thought—'

'So you offered her your boat?'

He nodded.

'Perhaps I should have let her stay at my place, but it's a bit cramped, you see, and my stuff is everywhere.'

'OK,' Munch said. 'You said just now that you know the man we're looking for?'

Roger's eyes took on a more confident expression as he leaned back in the chair and nodded softly.

'Oh, yes, I knew all along.'

'You knew?'

'That there was something not right with that rich lot. Isn't it always the way? Abracadabra. Overnight riches. That's never a good sign, is it?'

'You're referring to the Prytz family?'

'Exactly. I'd gone to get one of my palettes, and there he was. He had parked that yellow Lambo of his further up the road – fat lot of good that will do.' Roger laughed out loud.

'Are we talking about Henry Prytz?' Munch wanted to know.

'What? That idiot? I thought he was busy saving koala bears in Australia? No, no. Benjamin Prytz.'

'Benjamin – is he the one who is getting married?'

'No, that's Alexander. He's the golden boy. I don't suppose he has ever put a foot wrong in his life. No, I mean Benjamin, of course. The younger brother. Totally different kettle of fish. I would have thought he was on your radar already. Does he have a record? Or perhaps rich people don't have those. They buy their way out of trouble, am I right?'

'It's early on in the investigation,' Munch said. 'But it goes without saying that we will follow up anything of interest. When was this, did you say?'

'Last Saturday.'

'Yes, but at what time?'

'Well, when could it have been? Eleven, twelve?'

'Are we talking about the morning now?'

'What? Yes, yes. I drove to Trondheim afterwards. I had pictures to hang, you know. Things to do.'

'OK,' Munch said. 'Have you seen him out there before?'

'No. Or, yes, hang on, once. Now I can't be sure if he had been to my boat, but he was walking away from the marina. He was heading back to his car. You can't miss it, can you?'

Munch made a note on his pad. Benjamin Prytz. Big B?

'Is there anything else you think is worth mentioning?'

'What do you mean? I've just told you who did it.'

'And I'm grateful to you. But I'm trying to understand the bigger picture. Do you know if she had other visitors?'

Roger scratched his beard again.

'Well, I didn't go there very often. Now there was Pelle, of course, but he wouldn't hurt a fly.'

'Pelle?'

'Pelle Lundgren.' The pirate nodded. 'Also known as UFO Pelle. I would often see them together. Oddballs, both of them. Birds of a feather, isn't that what they say?'

'So you saw him out there on Saturday? This Pelle?'

'No, only the rich guy.'

'OK, thank you,' Munch said, getting up. He knocked on the window and waved to Luca, who was walking the dog on the grass.

'Was that all?'

'Yes, thank you. We'll be in touch if there's anything else.'

The pirate got up and disappeared down the corridor.

Munch was about to follow him when his mobile vibrated. He took it out of his pocket and saw the name on the display.

Lillian.

'Hello, Lillian.'

'Hello, Holger. You called me?'

Munch took a cigarette out of his pocket and opened the window.

'Yes. I'm sorry. I couldn't sleep.'

'Are you working?'

'Yes, a case on Hitra. And what about you? How are you doing?'

Chapter 37

Mia drove across the bridge that offered her a view of Knarrlagsundet strait and followed the road until she reached Ulvøystien. She found the sign for Prestvikveien, turned off and decided that she must be in the right place when she spotted the dilapidated smallholding at the end of the road. She parked her motorcycle by the roadside. She was more alert now. Her holiday was truly over. The detective in her was back. Her eyes scanned her surroundings as she walked up to the old property at a leisurely pace. Lucien Frank. The man Anita Holmen claimed had been in her garden. She had called him a filthy pig. Mia was reluctant to be prejudiced, but so far she could see no reason to contradict her. Roar's Autos was almost neat compared to this place. Three buildings, all equally run-down. A residential house that looked as if it was inhabited, yet still abandoned. The front door was open. The paint peeling. An old curtain flapped in the wind through a broken window. There was rubbish lying around everywhere. Plastic bags, rusty metal parts; a moped with no wheels had been dumped in the middle of the drive next to a rotting mattress. The stench of something wafted towards her as she approached the house. She stepped over a pile of flattened cardboard and realized where the smell was coming from. A big pig was lying on its side in a sty that had not been cleaned for a long time. She could hear noises from inside the house now as she walked up to one of the filthy windows and peered tentatively inside. A man was sitting in an armchair with his feet on a table and a can of beer in his hand. The TV was on.

She walked over to the front door and knocked on the doorframe.

'Hello?'

'What do you want?' a grumpy voice called out from inside.

'Mia Krüger, police. Are you Lucien Frank?'

She heard something fall and smash against the floor. Lucien Frank muttered curses under his breath, then came shuffling to the door.

'What?'

He was in his early fifties. Slightly tubby, wearing jogging bottoms and socks, a filthy vest and a baseball cap. Bags under his red eyes, traces of chewing tobacco under his upper lip and a row of brown and yellow teeth.

'Come again?' He squinted at her and scratched his stomach. He still had the can of beer in his hand.

'Mia Krüger, police. Are you Lucien Frank?'

He pushed the baseball cap to the back of his head.

'Why is that any of your business?'

'I'm investigating the murder of Jessica Bakken. May I come inside?'

He narrowed his eyes and then glanced quickly over his shoulder.

'Eh, why? Why do you want to come inside?'

'Or we can talk out here,' Mia said. 'Did you know her?'

'Know who? You mean the girl who was killed in the marina?'

'Yes. Jessica.'

'No idea. What are you doing here? Is someone *else* claiming to have seen me?' Frank shook his head and snorted with derision. 'I know how you lot work. It's that woman with the kid, am I right? Who ran away from home because his mum's a bitch? She has seen me again, has she? Messing about in the marina this time? Because I was also in her garden, wasn't I? Either that woman is blind or she has a problem with me – what the hell do I know. Not my problem. I know as much about some dead teenager as I do about that other kid. Or is it the neighbours again?'

He spat towards the fence and nodded in the direction of a farm on the far side of the field.

'My trees.' He pointed to them. 'The boundary line runs there and I can chop down whatever the hell I like, can't I? As long as it's on my own land.'

'So you weren't there?' Mia said.

'Where?' Frank said. 'In that stupid cow's garden or down in the marina? You already know I have an alibi for that night. Just how thick are you? It is because my sister gave me my alibi – is that why? You think she did it to help me? Yeah, right.'

He laughed and showed his stained teeth once more.

'She wouldn't cross the street to piss on me if I was on fire. We were seeing a solicitor in Trondheim, as it happens. I even have the proof here. Do you want to see it?'

'Sure,' Mia said.

Frank frowned, as if he had not expected her to reply in the affirmative, but then he shook his head and disappeared into the house. He returned with an envelope.

'Here, see for yourself.'

He opened the envelope and handed her a crumpled piece of paper.

'A meeting? Didn't I tell you? Family stuff.'

Mia skimmed the document.

'You had a meeting with a solicitor in the evening?'

'Yes? What about it?'

She held the piece of paper up in front of him.

'And you're saying this summons is evidence that you were there?'

Frank heaved a sigh and spat.

'Of course not, smartarse. But my sister got one as well, didn't she, and though she hates my guts, it was difficult not to admit that we were there together. Especially seeing as that idiot solicitor was there too. Is that alibi good enough for you or what?'

Mia nodded and returned the document to him.

'And what was the meeting about?'

'That's none of your business.' Frank took a swig of his beer and looked about him briefly. 'So is that it? Is it just you here, then? No paperwork or—'

'You mean a search warrant?'

'Yes. Do you have one?'

'No, I just—'

Frank grinned again.

'In that case, I think we're done here.'

He scratched his stomach again and waved her away. He stayed on his doorstep until she had left his property.

Mia took out her mobile from her pocket and called Munch.

'Where are you?'

'I'm at the station. Did you learn anything from Frank?'

Mia glanced back up at the derelict house.

'It would appear that his alibi stands up. But I'm not sure. I would like to have a look inside his house, but I don't suppose that's possible?'

'Not unless you can link him to Jessica in some way.'

'OK. How about you?'

'I think we might have found our Big B.'

'Really?'

'Or at least a potential candidate. The owner of the boat saw Benjamin Prytz in the marina on Saturday.'

'The rich guy?'

'Yes, not in the evening, though, but earlier in the day. How about we pay him a visit? Hear what he has to say?'

'I'm on my way,' Mia said, donning her helmet.

Chapter 38

Hannah Holmen was sitting on her bed, wearing her headphones and resting her laptop on her lap. Sylvia had sent her a lot of messages, but she hadn't replied to any of them yet. She had read them, but they contained no news. Just requests to hang out. *Are you coming over? We're all going to lay flowers by the road to the marina. Are you coming?* She was starting to feel guilty and took out her mobile. After all, it wasn't Sylvia's fault. None of it was. She was just as rattled as Sylvia. Both of them were distraught after the murder, and that was the problem. They had spent the whole day together and done nothing but cry and look at pictures of Jessica. They had talked about what could possibly have happened. Looked at some more pictures. Cried a bit more. In the end Hannah had been drowning in emotions. She had made her excuses and cycled home. Her room had been quiet and empty; she had a sense she was missing pieces of herself. She sent Sylvia a quick text message.

Not feeling too good. Leave some bluebells from me, will you?

Hannah switched her mobile to silent, then got up and put it in a drawer. She climbed back into her bed and resumed numbing out on her laptop. Her mum used to be very strict about her not spending too much time online. Escaping from reality. But not these days, not since Jonathan had disappeared. And it was what she needed right now. To escape for a bit.

She clicked on the bookmark and logged on to Friendz. She was staying away from Facebook today: it was impossible to find any relief there. Jessica's page was filled with comments, each more mournful than the last. *Goodbye, my friend. Miss you. You were the best, Jessica!* Friendz was different. She didn't know many from Hitra there. It was just a place for people her age from all over the world to meet, though she usually selected Norway; her English was all right, but it was easier to write in Norwegian. She was starting to make some new friends there. Mainly girls her own age. A few boys: she had lots of requests, but they mostly wanted to know if she had a boyfriend, and that wasn't why she was on Friendz. It was just for regular, social stuff. She was a member of two groups. BookFans and MathsFans. The latter didn't have many followers – no surprise there – but those who were there were kindred spirits. It was nice to chat to them and just be herself. Not having to pretend all the time. Fabian, her psychologist, had talked about it once, the importance of being yourself. And she had thought that one day she was going to be more open. That she wanted to give it a try. Not just echo the opinions of others and like the things they approved of. Perhaps she was adopted? Perhaps she came from another place? A big city somewhere in Europe with a different culture? It crossed her mind at times, especially when she hung out with Andres and the gang. The boys there, and the girls for that matter, had totally different interests to her. And she didn't have a father, did she? Perhaps he lived abroad? In Amsterdam? Or Rome? Perhaps that was where she had got it from? His genes? Perhaps he was a university professor. Or an author. Perhaps he was sitting in a white house underneath an orange tree with a view of the Mediterranean, writing an important novel which people all over the world were just waiting to read.

She had asked her mum many times; she hadn't pestered her, no, but had approached her with sensitivity. Her mum, however, refused to talk about it. Hannah had written an email once, to the authorities, asking if they could help her find out who he was, and the reply had stated that she was absolutely entitled to that information, but not until she turned eighteen. Then they could only help her if her mother had registered her father's name with them. After that her enthusiasm had waned a little. If her mum didn't want to talk about it, her father's name probably wasn't registered anywhere. But she could always hope.

Hannah logged on to MathsFans, but there was no one else online today. No wonder. It was a small group. It was just like at school; ever since she was young she had pretty much been in a set of her own. Her teachers had allowed her access to the books which those in the year above her were studying because she had already read the ones for her own year. Books that made her classmates groan and scratch their heads.

She left the chat room and joined BookFans instead. Two people were logged on today. One person she didn't know; the other was one of her friends. Nina from Kristiansand. Hannah smiled to herself and pinged her.

She had a response almost immediately.

Hi, Hannah!

Her fingers moved across the keyboard. She felt calmer already.

Hi, Nina! How are you? Have you read anything good lately?

She could see from the dots on the screen that her friend was typing a reply.

On the fourth Harry Potter book. Have you read it?

Hannah had read the first one, but she hadn't been that impressed by it. It didn't make sense to her. If the boy was a wizard, why didn't he just do some magic and fix everything? But OK. It was all right. She liked Hermione. She was tough. Only she wasn't into this potion and magic business; she preferred realistic stories.

She wrote back.

No, haven't read it. Is it any good?

New dots on the screen from her friend.

Oh, yes, it's brilliant . . . I don't want it to end.

A follow-up came when she didn't reply immediately.

I know it's childish, but then again, so am I!

An emoji of a smiling face crying with laughter.

And you? What are you reading?

Hannah glanced at the stack of books on the floor by her bed.

John Green. The Fault in Our Stars. Nearly finished it.

Her friend responded quickly.

Great title! What's it about?

She typed her reply.

A girl who is very ill, she has cancer. Then she meets a boy who's also sick. I don't want to give away any spoilers . . .

The room was getting hot now. It was a nice summer's day outside, but she didn't have the energy to walk down to the rocks to cool down. She leaned towards the window and opened it a bit.

How tragic. I have to read it!

Yes, I recommend it! It's really good!

Dots on the screen again before Hannah had replied.

But I have to go. Speak soon!

The chat room was almost deserted now. There was just one boy logged on, a boy she hadn't seen before. She clicked on his profile.

Ludvig, sixteen years. Location: Trondheim.

Oh, right, Trondheim? Well, that wasn't far away.

She read on.

Hi, I'm Ludvig. It's a bit lonely being me at times, but then I read books and forget real life for a while ☺

Hannah smiled to herself.

I get you.

She clicked on his profile picture. He had chosen an ordinary one; she liked that, rather than one of him showing off his muscles or holding up a fish or something. Just a simple portrait, a shy gaze behind a curly fringe.

She clicked on the link to her right.

My favourite books.

She scrolled down and raised her eyebrows.

Murakami, Norwegian Wood.

Hmmm . . .

Normally she didn't read boys' profiles.

But this one seemed OK?

She clicked and waited.

The dots on the screen started to move slowly. Then:

Hi . . . ?

She typed her response.

Hello. I've just seen that you're in Trondheim. I'm on Hitra. It's hot today.

202

A pause, and then he replied.

Yes, same here. Very hot. But am inside. I'm reaching the last page, and I can't bear the thought of it ending . . .

A smiley with its tongue sticking out.

Hannah typed and smiled.

Same here. Inside, I mean. What are you reading?

The answer came more quickly this time.

Jeff Noon. Vurt.

Don't know it. What kind of book is it?

Hannah stretched to open the window a little more.

Science fiction. Except not really. Cyberpunk, I think they call it.

New dots appeared so she paused her reply.

. . . the genre, I mean, sorry.

Hmmm . . .

Exciting. I don't know it. What's it about?

It took longer this time. It was clear that he typed quite slowly.

People are hunting feathers. Which you can place on your tongue. There are dreams in the feathers. And you can travel in them. It's really cool. I don't want it to end.

She smiled and wrote back.

Right, that sounds cool. I've got to read it. Has he written many books?

This time the answer came quite quickly.

I think there are four in the series. I can send you the titles. Are we going to chat on here or can I dm you?

She pressed the friend request button.

We can be friends. I have added you.

She waited for him to reply. However, it took some time. As if he was mulling it over. Finally the dots appeared.

OK. I have accepted your request. I just need to check my bookshelf.

Hannah peered out behind the curtain. Something was happening down the road. A car had arrived. Sylvia got out of it and said something to her mother, who was behind the wheel. Her mother had given her a lift. Sylvia nodded, then ran up the drive to Hannah's house.

Hannah sighed. No more peace and quiet for her. Her fingers quickly skipped over the keyboard.

Got to go, sorry. Please send me the list, OK?

She logged off, turned off her laptop and smiled as she walked downstairs.

Chapter 39

Munch was waiting in the car when Mia arrived and his mood seemed changed since the morning briefing. The expression in his eyes was more serious, his face haggard, and he didn't say anything until they were on the main road.

'Ah, well,' he sighed, and helped himself to another cigarette from the packet on the dashboard.

'What's wrong?' Mia said, pressing a button to open the window.

'Sorry?' Munch said, lighting his cigarette. 'Oh, nothing. You would think that after thirty years of doing this job I would be used to it, but no.'

'I don't suppose you ever get used to it,' Mia said. 'I couldn't sleep last night either so I just stayed up.'

'A young girl, for pity's sake,' he said with a shake of his head. 'Older people, sure. That's bad enough, but I can come to terms with it. But a teenager? With so much life ahead of her? No, it makes me sick.'

'How was the owner of the boat?'

He turned to her.

'Sorry? Oh, yes. He was a character, but he seemed honest enough. He used to drink with Jessica's mother, felt bad about it, had known the girl since she was a kid, let her use the boat to make himself feel better. That is my impression.'

'Will we have to make a trip to Trondheim, do you think?'

'To talk to Laura Bakken?'

'Yes?'

'I spoke to the duty nurse at the hospital just now. He said they're not discharging her yet. She poses a risk to herself, as he put it. I asked to speak to her on the phone, but he said there was no point.'

'Is she an addict?'

He shrugged his shoulders.

'It's hard to say. Besides, it would take us two and a half hours to drive there, I reckon. So a round trip of five to six hours? Is that a priority now? I don't think we have enough hours in the day as it is.'

'Are you stressed?'

He didn't reply, but he nodded faintly, almost imperceptibly and took another drag on his cigarette.

'I'll try to speak to her on the phone tonight, but if I don't succeed, we will have to rethink it.'

'How about sending an officer from Trondheim Police?'

'They visited yesterday,' Munch said. 'They said the same. She doesn't make much sense, but they did their best.'

'At least she has been informed,' Mia said as they drove past Kvenvær.

'True.' Munch nodded. 'I would like to talk to her, but she may not be able to give us anything that will help us anyway. According to her friends, Jessica hadn't been at home for a while. She was practically living on the boat.'

'Remind me, what did the boat owner say about Prytz again?'

'Yes, Benjamin Prytz,' Munch said, and opened the window on his side at last. 'Is it just me or do the locals really not like this family?'

'Both, I think,' Mia replied. 'Officially, they're popular. The family provides jobs, tax revenues and all that. But privately? It's not much fun working your backside off filleting fish just to pay your rent while that family drives around in luxury cars. Basic jealousy, I reckon.'

'I certainly wouldn't mind a little of their money,' Munch said, leaning towards the windscreen as they turned off the road and caught a glimpse, through the park in front of them, of the imposing buildings at the end of the avenue.

There was a roar further up, then a low, bright yellow sports car came zooming down the avenue. Mia recognized the distinctive Lamborghini bull on the hood as the car stopped right in front of them and the driver left the engine idling.

'There's the son and heir himself.'

Munch stubbed out his cigarette in the ashtray and opened the car door.

'I think the son and heir is the other one,' Mia said. 'That's the black sheep, from what I've heard.'

She got out of the car and followed Munch over to the yellow sports car.

'Listen,' a smiling face behind the wheel said. 'You're blocking my way. Are you delivering the champagne? The tradesmen's entrance is round the back. Don't park at the front of the house or Cynthia will blow a fuse.'

'Cynthia, is that your mother?' Munch said, holding up his warrant card.

Benjamin Prytz looked at it and raised his eyebrows slightly. Apart from that he didn't look noticeably contrite.

'Police, well, all right. Have you come to arrest the bride? I thought she must have got the wrong house.'

He laughed, then pressed a button and the window opened fully.

Benjamin Prytz lived up to his reputation as a vacuous billionaire playboy heir, certainly as far as his clothes and appearance were concerned. A tanned face with a row of pearly-white teeth that had probably had a little help. A short-sleeved white shirt with a chequered cravat, a gleaming ring on each hand. Mia could make out his khaki shorts, which were likely to be followed by a pair of deck shoes on his feet. Benjamin Prytz ran a hand over his smooth hair and bent over his mobile, which was attached to a stand on the dashboard.

She saw how Munch jumped when music suddenly blasted from the car. The car itself was shaking on the inside now. The boy had probably had it fitted with a sound system that cost as much as the car itself.

'Just checking out my new bass speakers.' Benjamin Prytz grinned and nodded to the rhythm of the heavy beat. 'What do you think?'

He was looking at her now with that gaze with which men often looked at Mia, irrespective of income and age. Eyes that didn't meet hers but sized up her body instead.

'Please would you turn that down?' Munch said.

'Speak up,' Benjamin Prytz mocked him, cupping his hand behind his ear. 'I can't hear you.'

Munch made a rotating gesture with his hand. Benjamin Prytz laughed again, then turned off the music.

'Is that great or what?' He went back to leering at her.

'Please would you turn off the engine as well?' Munch said.

Mia could see how Munch struggled not to lose his temper.

'Sure, boss,' Benjamin Prytz said, and saluted him with a hand to his forehead.

He pressed a button on the steering wheel and the din was finally silenced.

'Thank you,' Munch said with a smile he employed when more than anything he wanted to grab someone by the scruff of their neck and punch them in the face.

'So how can I help you?' Benjamin Prytz grinned. 'I'm guessing you're looking for me? The girl in the boat? Did someone spot my car?'

He looked at Mia again, and she could see it in his eyes now. He was nowhere near as stupid as he pretended to be.

'That's right.' Munch nodded. 'Were you out there?'

'At the marina? Was that last Saturday?' He pretended to think about it for a moment, but again Mia could see that he had already prepared his answer.

'Yes, yes, I must have been out there last Saturday. There was a yacht I wanted to have a look at. You can never have too many boats, am I right?' Again he was only addressing her.

'A yacht?' she said calmly. 'You can't moor a yacht down there. The water is too shallow, isn't it?'

'Eh, yes . . . or, no, maybe not, but it wasn't moored there. I'm not interested in small boats. It was anchored in the bay further out.'

'Can you show us, please?' Mia said.

'The yacht?' Prytz said. 'No, no, it's not there any more. And besides, it wasn't my kind of thing. So, is that everything? I'm sweating like crazy – it's like the Mediterranean here right now. I need to get going and test these bad boys. Rogue Acoustics. They'll blast your eardrums. You're welcome to join me. I only have room for one passenger, so how about it . . .'

He smiled and looked at Mia again.

'Did you know her?' Munch said.

'Who? Jessica?'

'Yes.'

He hesitated, this time for real.

'I wouldn't say I knew her well. I knew who she was, I'd seen her around, but I didn't know her personally, if that's what you mean. I don't spend a lot of time on the island these days. I'm only back for *the big wedding.*'

He raised his eyebrows and put a sarcastic emphasis on the latter.

Another car was coming down the avenue now, a van. It slowed down and stopped a short distance away.

'Right,' Prytz said, checking his rear-view mirror. 'Best get out of the way. Anyway, nice chatting to you. Bye for now.'

He smiled, pressed a button on the steering wheel, started the engine and disappeared down the avenue. Munch gestured for the van to drive past him and took another cigarette out of the packet. He shook his head and looked at Mia.

'So what do we think? Should we bring him in for a proper interview?'

'He was spotted at the crime scene. That should be reason enough?' Mia said.

'I would think so.' Munch nodded. 'Eight hours too early, but even so.'

He was still looking up at the palatial house when Mia's mobile rang. When she saw the caller's name she walked a little further away before taking the call.

'Yes, Mia speaking.'

'Hello, Mia, it's Simon here.'

'Hello, Simon.'

Then there was silence on the other end.

209

'I . . .' he began.

'Listen,' Mia said. 'I'm at work, so I'll have to—'

'I'm sorry,' he said quickly. 'But I need to tell you something.'

'Aha?'

'I haven't been completely honest with you.'

'Go on?'

'Could you . . . could you come to my house? How about tonight?'

'Not even a hint?'

'I'd rather not do it on the phone. Please?'

Munch summoned her.

'Sure. I'll come over after work.'

'Thank you so much.'

'See you later,' Mia said, slipping her phone back into her pocket.

'Listen, Mia, I've had a thought,' Munch said, opening the door to the car. 'This business about Jonathan's father?'

'Yes?'

'This is a small island, isn't it? Surely someone must know? Or have an opinion about it?'

'You mean local gossip?'

'Yes.'

'That's not a bad idea.' Mia nodded and got in. 'Let's check with Luca.'

'Have you had lunch?' Munch said.

'No.'

'How about some food at Hjorten Hotel before the afternoon briefing? Do you have time for that?'

'Yes, as long as it's quick. I need to go back to Svingen. I can't get the times in the police reports to add up.'

Chapter 40

Lissie Norheim kept rocking her weight from foot to foot as she stood in the doorway near the row of mirrors in her parents' bedroom, waiting for her mother to pick an outfit. It was already eight o'clock and she knew how Cynthia felt about punctuality. The invitation was on the bedside table, on her mother's side of the big four-poster bed.

Dinner in the great hall at 8 p.m.

'Who sends out printed invitations to people who are already in their house?'

Her father had scratched his head at this particular custom.

Right now he looked very relaxed. He was sitting in one of the armchairs by the window, resting his feet on the footstool. He had pretty much sat there since their arrival, with his nose buried in a book he had picked up at the airport.

'This is an excellent chair, Eva, perhaps we should get one like this?'

It had made Lissie smile. Finally, he seemed to be settling down.

'Do I look all right?' her mother said, twirling again. 'I think the dress is bunching up at the back? Henrik?'

'You look great,' her father said, without lifting his head from his book.

'What do you think, Lissie?'

'I agree with Dad.'

'All right,' her mother said, smoothing the dress with her hands. 'Then this is it. And then I need some—'

'Shoes,' Lissie said, pointing.

'Oh, yes.' Her mother smiled. 'Which do you prefer?'

211

'These match your dress the best.'

'Are you sure?' her mother said, sticking out a foot in front of the mirror.

'I'm quite sure, Mum, and we should be going. They're waiting for us. Dad, are you ready?'

'I'm always ready.'

Her father yawned and put down his book.

'Wait,' her mother said, just as she was about to leave the bedroom. 'My handbag.'

She seemed to linger in front of the mirror again, then, thankfully, she joined them at last.

'The invitation? Do we need to bring it?'

'No, no.' Lissie smiled. 'Now come on.'

Cynthia's smile was somewhat strained as she greeted them by the door. Her outfit was immaculate: a beige Chanel dress, shoes handmade in Verona and a string of pearls around her neck and one wrist. She had put up her hair in a chignon, probably with some help from the hairstylist who had arrived a few days earlier and who was also in charge of Lissie's hair for the wedding.

'Welcome, welcome.' Cynthia smiled before bending down and kissing Lissie's mother on both cheeks.

'Oh, right, hiya,' her mother said, somewhat flustered.

'Thank you for having us,' her father said with a slight bow.

'Come in, come in. Help yourself to a drink on the way.'

There were no waiters here, thank God. Lissie had asked Alexander repeatedly if they could hold off at least until the dinner and, to her delight, she saw that the aperitifs were set out on a silver tray in the corridor.

The big dining room, which Cynthia referred to as the great hall, was at the back of the house, beautifully furnished, as every room in the house was, with chandeliers hanging from the ceiling and impressive paintings on the walls. In here it was mostly nineteenth-century Norwegian painters. Henry Prytz had a large collection of contemporary art, but the majority of that was kept in their house in Marbella, thankfully, so she didn't have to listen to her father's comments.

'Would you take a look at this? I could paint something like that myself, don't you think, Eva?'

A large damask tablecloth covered the whole of the long table, which took up almost half the room, although they were unlikely to be more than six people.

'Will your father be here?'

'I don't think so. He's in Asia somewhere.'

'But he will be here in time for the wedding, won't he?'

'Let's hope so.'

Alexander had uttered that last comment flippantly, but she could see that there was more to it. That was how it was around here. Lissie had seen a great deal of Cynthia; she was the lady of the house and ran everything with a firm hand, and with considerable attention to detail. Henry Prytz, however, she had met only a handful of times.

He was very nice, no doubt about it. Attentive and obliging. But busy. Always on the go, and with his mobile pressed to his ear most of the time.

Alexander entered the room and her heart skipped a beat. So handsome. He was wearing his new suit and that tie she had suggested. He winked at her and kissed Cynthia on both cheeks. That was another custom she had yet to get used to.

'Benjamin won't be joining us,' Alexander said. 'She . . . Natalie wasn't feeling too good, so they'll stay in the rotunda.'

'Oh, you have roundabouts here, too.' Her mother smiled. 'My sister lived in Sweden for many years and I've always thought it was such a funny word. It's like it tickles your tongue. R-r-rotundas.'

Cynthia smiled and patted her shoulder gently.

'No, that's the name of the round guesthouse at the bottom of the garden. Benjamin stays there sometimes when he's at home.' She clapped her hands and showed everyone to their seats. 'So it's just us, but I'm sure we'll be fine. I need to check with the kitchen one last time and then we can begin.'

'What are we really doing?' her mother whispered once they had sat down.

'We're sampling the menu. For the wedding,' Lissie whispered back.

'Oh, so we'll be having the same thing on Saturday as we're eating now?'

'No, tonight we're choosing what we'll have on the day. We will taste different things and then decide.'

'Oh, right, OK,' her mother said, and glanced at her husband, who was more interested in the art on the wall.

'Is that a copy of a Werenskiold? It's very fine.'

'No, that's the original,' Alexander said politely, and spread out his napkin on his lap. Her mother noticed it and did likewise.

'Good heavens,' her father said, stroking his chin. 'I'm impressed. It's almost like being at the National Museum.'

Lissie was expecting an acerbic comment, but none came. He almost looked a little proud as he sat there.

'And here we are,' Cynthia chirped as she returned, followed by several waiters.

She positioned herself at the head of the table as small plates of the various starters were set out on the table.

'Where are the menus?'

She summoned one of the waiters, who rushed back to the kitchen and returned with a menu for each guest.

'Super, then we're good to go.'

She gestured to the dishes in front of them.

'Yes, as you can see, we have opted for traditional Norwegian dishes. After all, here we are on beautiful Hitra and, of course, we would like to reflect that in the food we serve. All the ingredients are locally sourced and prepared on site by our chef. Obviously, you'll get the chance to meet her and her team when we have finished eating.'

She smiled and carried on.

'To begin with, we have blinis with cured leg of lamb, roe and prawns. There is also ceviche from raw, marinated halibut in an apple, cucumber and citrus marinade. And finally we have a tartare made from venison tenderloin on a bed of turnip purée. Enjoy.'

Cynthia sat down and waited for her guests to start.

'I think I'll try one of these,' Lissie's mother said, cautiously lifting one of the blinis on to her plate.

'Just take the whole plate.' Cynthia smiled. 'The table cloth will be dry-cleaned afterwards, but it's just more practical for all of us.'

'I'm sorry,' her mother said, picking up one of the orange beads of roe that had fallen off in transit.

'Don't worry about it. Like I said: it's just easier that way. Especially with the venison, that purée can quickly get sticky.' She looked at Lissie. 'Perhaps we should just scrap that right away? Is it a little too much?'

Lissie cut off a piece and tasted it.

'No, why? I think it's delicious.'

Cynthia clutched her forehead.

'Oh, what am I like. Phew, it's just as well we don't have a wedding here every day. So much to keep track of. My apologies. The wine, of course.'

The waiters filed in from the kitchen now, each carrying a different bottle. Two white and one red.

'I hope we don't have to drink them all?' Lissie's mother giggled. 'I don't think I can manage all that.'

'The wine has already been chosen,' Lissie said, putting her hand on her mother's. 'The chef has selected one for each dish. This is just so that we can see how they go together.'

'Oh, right,' her mother said as several glasses were lined up in front of her. She lifted up one.

'Which one is this for?'

'The blinis.' Cynthia smiled.

Her father had already knocked back half a glass of red wine, tasted everything, and now he patted his stomach.

'I don't know about the food, but whatever goes with this wine gets my vote,' he said with a smile.

'Really?' Cynthia said, sounding surprised. 'Didn't you like—'

She nodded towards the dishes.

'What? Yes, all of them. I like everything, me. Bring it on.'

He waved to one of the waiters, who poured him more wine.

'So what do we think?' Cynthia said. 'Do we wait until we have sampled all the dishes or shall we give our verdicts right away? It's not an easy call to make and each dish has its own charm, but ultimately everything needs to go together. What do we think?'

'I'm sorry, I have to take this.' Alexander picked up his mobile from the tablecloth and nodded towards the door.

'Don't be long,' Lissie said, and kissed him.

'Of course.' Cynthia nodded. 'The next dish will be here in a few minutes, so if anyone would like to stretch their legs?'

Lissie's parents stayed seated, each holding a glass.

'I think I will.'

Lissie smiled and went to the lavatory in the corridor.

When she was done, she put the lid down, sat on it and took a deep breath.

It was going well, wasn't it?

Much better than she had dared hope for.

Her dad even looked as if he was having fun, didn't he?

Amazing.

It couldn't have gone any better.

She got up and went to wash her hands.

Voices outside suddenly; the window was ajar.

Alexander? But he was on the phone?

She turned off the water, tiptoed across the floor and stopped with an ear against the curtain.

'Damn it, Benjamin, you really need to get a grip.'

Benjamin?

'So what is it this time?'

Both men were whispering, but she could still hear them.

'Did you have to bring her here? Lissie's parents have arrived. You knew they were coming.'

'Natalie? But she's my girl.'

'She's this week's girl. Well, try to keep her sober at least. You're letting the side down.'

'What side?'

'You know what I mean. Why did you want me to come outside? You know we're in the middle of dinner?'

A silence ensued. Had they walked further away? No, there was Benjamin again.

'I think I'm in trouble.'

'What is it this time?'

'The police were here today.'

'The police? Seriously, Benjamin. Did Mum see them?'

'No, no. Fortunately I caught them as I was heading out. I had a quick chat to them through the car window.'

'What did they want?'

Another silence. Quite a long one. Lissie pulled the curtains slightly to one side, and now she could see them: they had walked further down the lawn. Alexander was gesticulating. Benjamin was nodding and staring at the ground. Alexander jabbed his finger into his brother's chest before he turned on his heel and marched back to the house, clearly frustrated.

She was quick. She was back in the corridor before he reached the door.

'Oh, hello.'

'I just needed the loo.' Lissie smiled. 'Is everything all right?'

'Eh, is what all right?'

'Your phone rang? Who was it?'

'Oh, that. It was just Kyrre. He wasn't sure if he could get here on Saturday, but it's fine.'

'So he's still coming?'

'Eh, yes, sure.'

Cynthia suddenly appeared at the end of the corridor.

'We're ready, are you coming?'

'We're on our way.' Alexander smiled.

And together they walked back to the great hall.

Chapter 41

The sun was signalling that evening was approaching when Mia rode the motorcycle down the short gravel road to Simon's house; she was still annoyed that she couldn't pin down whatever was troubling her. The map on her wall at home. The times. She had gone back to the birch avenue. Been up and down Svingen. Visited the jetty where the boy's bicycle had been found. It was as if the answer was staring her right in the face, and yet she still couldn't see it.

Enough.

OK.

She was keen to get home as soon as she could. Have yet another session in front of all the pictures on her wall.

Simon's house was another pretty postcard, and it lay right down by the water on the western side of the island. They were practically neighbours, the two of them; the exit to her jetty was only a kilometre away. She could see apple and cherry trees, redcurrant and gooseberry bushes. At the far end of the garden was a small strawberry patch where someone had put out a scarecrow which the wind had undressed. A large rhododendron nearby reminded Mia of her mother. Smiling, kneeling on the grass in the garden in Åsgårdstrand, wearing her favourite clothes: utility trousers, an anorak and garden gloves.

'Would you like to help me garden, Mia?'

No. Mia had never had green fingers, but she liked to watch.

In the garage with her father, however, now that was where she belonged. The radio on in the background as he bent over the engine of the jade-green Jaguar.

'Pass me a plug spanner, will you, Mia?'

218

'Can I have a go, please?'
She could still hear his happy laughter.
'Of course you can. Come here, let me show you how to use it.'
A tomboy. That had been her nickname at school. The other children had used it to tease her, but they soon stopped when they realized that she genuinely could not care less about other people's opinion of her.

She had bought her first motorcycle the day she turned sixteen. A second-hand Honda CB 100, glossy red with the trademark white wing on the tank. And while the other girls had fluttered their eyelashes and pulled their chewing gum by the petrol station in the hope of being invited into the back of one of the souped-up cars with fluffy dice hanging from the rear-view mirror, she had zoomed off to Horten or up to Borrevannet to swim.

Mia followed the flagstones along a flower bed of honeysuckle and twinflowers that took her to the end of the house, where she found Simon sitting on the terrace.

His eyes lit up and he rose quickly when he saw her.

'Hi, Mia. Thank you for coming.'

'Hi, Simon.' She stopped at the edge of the terrace. 'Where's Sofia?'

'Having a sleepover with her granny. Would you like to sit down?' He adjusted a cushion on a garden chair.

'I'm in a hurry. You wanted to talk to me about something?'

She didn't know him well, but he didn't seem like himself. He looked exhausted and anxious. His eyes were red and his gaze flitting and there was a worried expression on his unshaven face. Mia felt sorry for him.

'Are you sure?' He extended an arm hesitantly, his eyes begging her to stay.

'All right then.' She heaved a sigh and gave in.

'Wine?' His hand was trembling when he held up the bottle to show her.

'No, thank you.'

He gazed across the sea for a moment as if he were wondering where to start.

'Am I here as a police officer or as a friend?' Mia said.

'Both, perhaps. Can people be friends after two meetings?'

Mia smiled.

'No, not me. Not usually.'

He ran a hand across his blond hair and shook his head.

'No, no, no.'

'Is it that bad?'

'It's worse.'

'Are we talking prison here? Am I about to arrest you?'

He smiled at this, fortunately.

'It's much more serious.'

'Is it really?'

'Yes, I'm afraid so,' he said, and buried his face in his hands for a moment. 'Is it all right if I start at the beginning? Do you have enough time for that?'

'Oh, go on then.' She heaved another sigh and let the keys to her motorcycle fall on to the table.

'Thank you. Let me just . . . two seconds, do you mind?'

Simon jumped up from his chair, ran inside the house and came back with a long, rolled-up piece of paper. He positioned himself next to her and unfurled it so that she could see.

'What's this?' Mia said, studying the drawing.

A building; his logo had been drawn on the front.

'It's a new diving centre,' he said, pointing. 'The jetty has been extended here, glass all along the front, you see, shops there, and up there guest accommodation for visitors.'

'Great,' Mia said. 'Why am I looking at this?'

'You haven't been down to my shop, have you?'

'No.'

He left the drawing between them and sat down in his chair.

'The place is falling apart. I'll have to close unless I can come up with something. And don't get me wrong, I don't mind doing something else. I'll happily fillet salmon 24/7. Sofia is obviously the most important thing here, but I thought, why not try, give it one last go, do you understand?'

'And?'

'Right, so this was my idea: expand. Invest. Be bigger and better than the others. I contacted an architect and I spent the last money I had on this drawing.'

'Great,' Mia said again. 'But I still don't see the problem.'

'The bank said no.'

'OK?'

He rubbed his eyes.

'Or rather they didn't refuse me outright, they said my credit rating wasn't good enough, I would have to invest some of my own money.'

'And you didn't have any?'

'No, sadly.'

'Are we getting to the point here?'

'Sorry, I'll fast-forward. One day a guy came to my shop, he was interested in diving. I'd seen him in town a few times, but I didn't know him. He wanted some lessons, paid cash, so I said yes, obviously, and I went out with him a couple of times. I showed him how to check the tanks and, well, you know the drill, but he didn't seem all that interested in learning about diving, which I thought was odd. Instead he started talking about money. And he wanted to know if I was good at diving. At deep-water diving. Had I tried that before.'

'And?'

'So the third time we went out was when it happened. I guess the first two trips were just him checking me out. He said he was working for someone who needed help.'

'He wanted you to dive for something?'

'Yes. They had lost something, he said. Out by Mausundvær. That it was deep down. That the guy they had originally hired to do the job couldn't do it any more.'

'How much did he offer?'

'A hundred thousand kroner.'

'I see. For one dive?'

'Yes.'

'Whatever they lost, it must have been very valuable.'

'Yes, that was my thought too.' He shrugged his shoulders. 'No, actually, I didn't think that at all, not then. All I could think about was the money and the new build. A hundred thousand kroner? It wasn't enough, but it was a start. So I said yes.'

'So now you have a hundred thousand kroner? Congratulations.'

'No, unfortunately that's not what happened. I got home, and then I started thinking about it. Lost something in the sea? What could it possibly be? Drugs? It had to be, didn't it? There must be a route out there somewhere.'

He nodded towards the sea.

'So I called him and said that I had changed my mind.'

'End of story?'

He shook his head and gazed across the garden.

'Oh, no. That's when the real trouble started.'

'Let me guess, no more pleasantries?'

'Correct. He said it had to be done. Now, soon.'

'Or?'

Simon trailed a finger across his throat.

'Seriously? He threatened your life?'

'Not directly, but there was no mistaking him. He said that I had probably failed to appreciate what was at stake. That he was willing to give me another chance. And for me to get back to him in two days.'

'Was that the guy you were talking to the other night? When Sofia couldn't find you?'

He nodded shamefacedly and stared at the ground.

'I'm sorry. I never meant to lie or for her to wake up and not be able to find me . . . but I just didn't know what else to do.'

'Do you know his name?'

He nodded.

'Steve. Tattoos, muscles, the whole caboodle. Sorry for troubling you with this. I'm at my 'wits' end.' He shook his head in despair and buried his face in his hands. 'I've really messed up.'

Mia got up and placed her hand on his arm.

'I'll see what I can do, all right? It's a bit late now, but tomorrow?'

'You would do that for me, seriously?' His eyes smiled at her. 'Thank you so much, Mia. Thank you so, so much.'

There was that spark again. She had felt it the very first time they met.

A single father and his daughter. In this picturesque location.

Another life? An opportunity?

A warm breeze wafted across the terrace now. The sun cast soft shadows across his anxious face.

'Are you sure you don't want a glass of wine?'

She paused for a few seconds, then she made up her mind and stepped down from the terrace.

'Some other time, perhaps. I need to get back to work. By the way, there was something I wanted to ask you.'

'Yes?'

'Anita Holmen, do you know her well?'

He looked a little disappointed, as if he had hoped that she had changed her mind about staying.

'No, not very well. Why?'

'The boy's father? Jonathan's? Are there any rumours out here about who it can be?'

He mulled it over for a moment, but then he shook his head.

'No, not that I've heard. Is it—'

'Thank you. I was just curious.'

'Call me, please,' Simon said.

'OK.' Mia nodded and followed the flagstones around the house back to her motorcycle.

Chapter 42

It was approaching midnight and Munch was drowning his sorrows in a glass of mineral water with ice and a slice of lime in the bar at Hjorten Hotel. The small bar was quiet, just him and a young woman who came and went. Her name badge said *Ruth* and it was clear that she had several jobs apart from bartending. She reminded him of his daughter, Miriam, who had had a grand wedding earlier that summer. Munch had proudly walked her down the decorated garden outside his ex-wife's house.

'Can I get you anything else?' Ruth smiled.

'Everything is fine.' Munch nodded and placed a cigarette on top of the packet. He was trying to cut down. Get fit. Four intense weeks. The worst he had ever experienced in his life. No contest.

Lillian was addicted to exercise, and she had ribbed him so much about his spare tyre, especially when he had to sit down to put on his shoes. He had finally had enough.

Bring it on.

He had regretted it immediately. Sit-ups, squats, lunges, burpees, dips, jumping jacks and planks and whatever the hell they were all called, in a gym with dreadful music blaring out of the loudspeakers. He had been sick in the changing room afterwards, bent over the lavatory bowl, so dizzy he could barely breathe.

Lillian behind the steering wheel in the car on their way home.

You look terrible. Are you giving up already?

So, no. He couldn't do that. And it had paid off, it absolutely had. Run up the stairs to his flat? No, he had never believed he would one day be able to do that.

'Are you a journalist?' Ruth asked him.

Long, medium-blonde hair, blue eyes, a freshness, and that glow about her which everyone out here seemed to have – it must be something about the air, the constant proximity to the sea.

'What? No, no.'

'So you're not here for the wedding?'

'No, I'm not.'

'I don't care about it all that much either, to be honest.'

Munch didn't normally have much time for small talk, but tonight it suited him fine.

Don't call me again, OK?

Yes, but Lillian—

No, it's enough now. It's over.

Munch rolled the cigarette between his fingers and looked towards the door leading outside, then he put it down.

'I'm guessing they'll be here by the weekend – we're fully booked from Thursday.'

'Is that when it is? The wedding?'

'This Saturday. Down in Sandstad Church.'

'Do you live locally?'

'I live on Frøya,' Ruth said.

'And that is . . .'

'The next island along.' She smiled.

She leaned towards him and whispered, 'It's even more beautiful than this one.'

'Really? Is that possible?'

'You've not been out there? To Frøya?'

'No.'

'You should visit.'

'I'll see if I can find the time.' Munch smiled.

Ruth frowned as she studied him, then she looked at the white sun hat on the bar counter.

'Hang on, I know who you are. You're the detective, aren't you?'

'That's right.'

She chuckled.

'Martha in the clothes shop told me that a police officer from Oslo had come to the shop and bought a hat, and it made her laugh.'

'Did it now?' Hitra really was a very small place.

'You know it's a woman's hat, don't you?'

'Er, no, I didn't know that.'

'She only sells clothes for women.'

'So you don't think it suits me?'

Munch put on the hat. Ruth laughed again. She leaned over the counter and adjusted it.

'At least wear it the right way round.'

Munch popped the cigarette into the corner of his mouth and got up.

'Will you keep an eye on my drink?'

She smiled.

'Are you sure you don't want something stronger?'

Munch looked up at the shelf of bottles behind her.

For the first time in forty years?

In that case, tonight would be the night to go for it.

'No, thank you. This will have to do.'

It was cooler outside now, but still pleasant, a light breeze from the sea rustling the leaves on the birch trees.

Otherwise, all was quiet.

Munch lit his cigarette and stood with his face to the sky.

To hell with it all.

He rubbed his finger where, until recently, his wedding ring had been. It had been ten years since his divorce, but he had continued to wear it. Finally he had taken it off. He felt naked now.

'Munch!'

He turned and saw Nina Riccardo run across the road. She looked like she had jumped out of bed and got dressed in a hurry, her colourful shirt hanging outside her trousers.

'Why aren't you answering your phone?'

'It's charging. What has happened?'

'They've found another body.'

'They have?'

She bent down to tie the laces on her trainers.

'A man. Out in the Havmyran nature reserve.'

'I'll drive us. Give me two seconds.'

'Ralph Nygaard is on his way, as is Mia. Kevin Borg didn't answer his phone,' Nina Riccardo said once Munch was back.

'Pathology?'

'Flying out from St Olav's Hospital. We're getting extra support from Orkanger Police. I called them as I left my room. Crime-scene technicians are already on their way.'

'Good. Will you give me directions?'

Nina Riccardo nodded and brought up a map on her phone.

'Is it far?'

'No, twenty minutes, that's all.'

It was quiet around them now and they had the road to themselves. A deer in a field. Some farms. A cluster of houses and then they were on the 713 road with the forest to one side, the sea to the other.

Luca Eriksen was waiting by his car, his own car. The passenger door was open and an older man was perched on the edge of the seat, a blanket wrapped around him.

Munch parked a little further away and got out. Luca came up to him, for once not in uniform.

'He called you at home?' Munch said with a nod to the man in the car.

'Yes.'

'And who is he?'

'His name is Hans Oliver. He's the chair of the local branch of the ornithological society, a twitcher.'

'And what was he doing out here at this hour?'

'He said he thought he had left his binoculars in the wildlife tower a few days ago. The tower they use when they're birdwatching.'

'And did he find them?'

'Eh?'

'His binoculars?'

'Er, no, I didn't ask him. I was busy . . .' Luca glanced anxiously at the man. 'Well, he was just standing rigid by the road. In shock.'

'OK,' Munch said, putting his hand on Luca's shoulder. 'Listen to me carefully. The pathologists will be here soon. They're arriving by helicopter.'

'OK?' Luca nodded nervously.

'There's a scene-of-crime box in the boot of my car. Inside it you will find four red lights. I want you to fetch them and set them out somewhere nearby where the helicopter can land, understood?'

'Eh, yes, understood.'

'You'll also find rolls of barrier tape. Can you see the area I'm pointing out now?'

'Yes.'

'Cordon it off. Not the road itself, mind – we'll need vehicular access. And make sure the twitcher doesn't wash his hands. Crime-scene technicians are on their way from Trondheim by car. They'll be here in a couple of hours and he mustn't leave until they have taken samples from his fingers and his clothes.'

Luca nodded.

'Do you have a torch?'

'Yes, I think so.'

'Go and get it.'

Luca ran back to his car and returned with a big Maglite.

'Here you go.'

'Thank you. What's your shoe size?'

'Er, eleven.'

'Give me your boots.'

'What?'

'I need your boots. The ground is wet in there, isn't it?'

Munch nodded towards the trees.

'Yes.'

'Right then.'

Luca took off his boots while Munch bent down and untied his shoes.

'You take these,' Munch said.

Nina Riccardo came over to them.

'Are we going in?'

'Yes. Where is this tower?' Munch said.

'About three hundred metres in that direction,' Luca said, pointing.

Munch switched on the torch. The nights out here were relatively light, yet it made a significant difference. A small path led the way between the heavy pines.

He nodded to Nina Riccardo.

'Let's go.'

FIVE

WEDNESDAY

Chapter 43

Munch waited until everyone had sat down. He was feeling slightly more patient today, as last night's operation had been impeccable. Nina Riccardo had impressed him at the scene – she was highly professional – and even Ralph Nygaard, who had come across as inexperienced to begin with, had followed procedure to the letter. He had helped to get the uniformed officers working in the correct way so that they did not contaminate the crime scene and the surrounding area.

This morning's review might be unnecessary. They had all been present at the scene except for Kevin Borg, who hadn't responded to phone calls until the early-morning hours, and Claus Nielsen, the police lawyer. Munch could see Mia's head nodding over her coffee at the back of the room; she had left the crime scene only a few hours ago, but he had insisted she came to the briefing.

No, everyone. We need to look at this together. Now. *Again.*

Luca Eriksen stifled a yawn and connected Munch's iPad to the projector while Munch looked across the room, then clasped his hands together.

'OK, team. Welcome back. I know that some of you are tired, but I want to go through everything again while it's still fresh in our minds.'

'Yes, fine.' Kevin Borg nodded, keen to get started for once.

He tugged at his shirt collar and looked about him, a little embarrassed at being the only investigator not to have turned up at the scene.

'So let's take it from the start,' Munch said, turning to the screen.

'At approximately five minutes past midnight this morning, Luca received a telephone call from a man called Hans Oliver. He's the head of the Hitra and Frøya branch of the Norwegian Ornithological Society, so he's a twitcher. Out in Havmyran nature reserve he had discovered the body of a man who had been the victim of a violent crime. At approximately twenty minutes to one we arrived at the wildlife tower from where Oliver had seen the body. And this is what we found.'

He brought up the first photograph.

'A man, fully dressed, lying on his back on the ground. Pathology will confirm this in due course, but it was clear to us when we arrived that the man was dead. Based on our initial observation, he would appear to have lain there for a while. Not too long though. I think we're looking for a killer who may have been in the area, let's say, at some point in the last twenty-four hours before we found the body.'

'Stabbed?' the police lawyer wanted to know.

Munch nodded and brought up another picture.

A close-up showing stab wounds to the neck and a lot of blood around the man's head.

'The body has been sent off for a post-mortem,' Munch continued. 'And we're in ongoing contact with the pathologist.'

He looked to Luca, who nodded and suppressed another yawn.

'She'll call me.'

'Good. As we have already observed and, given what we saw out there, this was undoubtedly a deliberate attack, intended to kill.'

He brought up another picture.

'Deep lacerations to the carotid artery. The victim was covered in blood, and I estimate that he bled to death after the attack in ten to fifteen minutes.'

Claus Nielsen, the police lawyer, paled at this. He undid the top button of his shirt and looked away from the screen.

'Perhaps we could get some fresh air?'

Munch nodded to Luca, who opened the window.

'Hans Oliver claimed', Munch continued, 'that he had gone to the nature reserve because he thought he might have left his binoculars behind in the wildlife tower after a previous trip out there some days ago.'

'And we found them.' Nina Riccardo nodded.

'Which backs up his account. We took all the usual samples from him, and I expect that we will have the results in due course, but he showed no obvious signs of having been involved in the incident – until he discovered the body, I mean. No visible signs of injuries or blood on his hands or his clothing.'

'He could have used them as an excuse?' Kevin Borg said, clearly keen to contribute. 'He could have left the binoculars out there first? Then arranged to meet the victim there? Killed him and then set in motion last night's performance?'

'It's an option, yes,' Munch said. 'And it's possible, but it doesn't seem likely to me right now. Obviously, at this point in time we can assume nothing and so we can't eliminate him completely.'

Kevin Borg nodded smugly to himself and looked about him. Munch produced another picture.

'Due to our excellent local knowledge, i.e. Luca, we have already identified the victim. His name is Pelle Lundgren. He is forty-three years old and well known to everyone here on the island. As is his sad story. Pelle Lundgren was involved in an accident some years ago in which he sustained serious head injuries which made him . . . how shall we put it, Luca?'

He turned to Luca again.

'Well, he changed dramatically,' Luca said. 'It was like he got a different personality. He became, ahem, I don't want to say *backward*, but something like it.'

'You knew him well?' Claus Nielsen said, carefully turning his gaze to the screen once more.

'Yes, or as well as anyone could know him after the accident, I would say. I spoke to him not long ago, last Saturday, in the town centre. He told me he had been given a time.'

'A time?' The ears of the police lawyer pricked up at this.

'Yes. For his departure.'

'Departure?' Kevin Borg echoed. For once there was no hint of sarcasm in his voice.

'When the spaceship from Jupiter would arrive.'

'He was going to be picked up by . . . a spaceship?' Kevin Borg said.

Mia shook her head irritably.

'We went over this several times last night. Can't we just—'

'Yes, so we did,' Munch interrupted. 'But I'm happy for us to do it again. Luca?'

He nodded for Luca to continue.

'Yes, like I said. Pelle was injured some years ago. And after that he was different. He was convinced that he had been chosen somehow. That he would be leaving Earth. He told me when and where when I spoke to him five days ago.'

'In a . . . spaceship?' Kevin Borg said again, and looked about him.

Mia was just about to open her mouth, but Munch stopped her.

'Yes, so he believed,' Munch said. 'And he had been given a time and a place when and where this was going to happen, hadn't he?'

'On Tuesday at 3 a.m.,' Luca nodded. 'Out by the wildlife tower.'

'Where we found him killed,' Munch continued.

'Please can we just . . .' Mia mumbled, and threw up her hands.

'I don't get it?' Kevin Borg said, looking at Munch.

'If Luca knew when and where it would happen,' Mia said impatiently, 'then chances are that other people did too, am I right?'

'Exactly,' Munch said. 'If Luca knew where Pelle Lundgren was going to be at 3 a.m. on Tuesday morning, we can presume his killer waited for him in the same place.'

'So we don't think the victim went there with anyone?' said Ralph Nygaard, who was struggling to keep his eyes open and who had been quiet until now. 'With a friend or an acquaintance? That perhaps they ended up having a row?'

'Pelle never argued with anyone—' Luca began, but Munch interrupted him.

'That's another possibility, Ralph, but we know from Luca's description that Pelle Lundgren was an open book, happy to tell anyone his business. And it is highly likely that he told several other people where he was going to be and when.'

'At three,' Luca said. 'Three o'clock in the morning, I mean.'

'By the way, how did he get these messages?' Mia said, calming down now. 'What if the killer had told Pelle the time and the place? I mean, if someone wanted to kill him, why wait? If it were me, then I would just have dropped a hint and made sure he would be there. *Hi, Pelle, I know when your spaceship is coming.*'

She looked towards Luca.

'Do you know that? How he got the messages?'

'No, it never occurred to me to ask him.'

Mia raised her eyebrows and looked at Munch once more.

'That's obviously a priority now,' Munch said. 'Can we answer these two questions: Who knew that Pelle Lundgren would be present out by the wildlife tower early on Tuesday morning? And does anyone know how he got these alleged messages?'

'Will you text me his address?' Mia said.

Luca nodded again and took his mobile out of his pocket.

'Yes, OK, but hang on,' Munch said, bringing up a picture of Jessica Bakken on his iPad. 'Let's not forget why we were originally called out here. Jessica. Remember? Two murders on a small island in a short space of time. Statistically speaking, it's highly likely—'

'We think they're connected?' Kevin Borg said.

'One hundred per cent.' Mia nodded. She was already on her way out of the room.

'No, no,' Munch objected. 'At this stage we assume nothing, but we can be sure that—'

He was interrupted again by a man in uniform outside the door. 'Yes? What is it?'

The new arrival popped his head round cautiously.

'Er, I'm sorry, but the mother is here.'

'Who?'

'Laura Bakken. Jessica's mother.'

'OK,' Munch said. 'Please put her in the interview room, we're just—'

'She doesn't want to come in. Doesn't like cops. I didn't mean to disturb you, but she says she'll leave unless someone comes outside.'

Munch went up to the window and pulled the curtain to one side. A woman in a tracksuit was standing outside. A young man was hugging her and stroking her head.

'Fine,' Munch said. 'Tell her five minutes?'

The officer nodded and closed the door as he left. Munch looked across the team.

'OK, people. That was a long night, but today it's important to think straight. Nina, please would you allocate tasks as we discussed earlier?'

Nina Riccardo nodded.

'Good. I want us to meet back here fairly soon. Let's say at three o'clock this afternoon. If that changes, I will let you know.'

Munch took a cigarette out of the packet and turned to Mia.

'Pelle Lundgren's home?'

'I'm on my way.'

'Take someone with you,' Munch said, but Mia was already halfway down the corridor.

Chapter 44

Victor Palatin pulled into the drive, parked the car in front of the garage and grabbed his bag from the back seat. He was greeted by his cat, a scruffy red-striped stray which had turned up one day and decided to stay.

'Hello, little one, did you miss me?'

The cat meowed and rubbed itself against his trouser leg. He smiled as he bent down and scratched it behind its ear.

'Sssh, let's not wake up the witch or she will throw us both in the pot and have us for dinner.'

He winked at the cat and glanced at the small house across from his. It was quiet, fortunately. He checked his phone. Thirteen minutes to noon. Great. His timing was perfect. His mother had her fixed routine. Every single day. All year round. Over and over. Exactly the same.

Eleven to twelve thirty morning nap.

'Sssh.' He smiled again and walked over to his own house on the other side of the drive.

There was a bouquet of flowers on the doorstep. Roses. A small card was attached.

Forever yours.

Victor Palatin shook his head wearily, then carried the bouquet and the card to the rubbish bin by the shed and tossed them both in.

'There,' he said, stroking the cat's head. 'Let's get ourselves something nice for lunch, shall we?'

The cat meowed again and slipped past him as he let himself in. He took off his trainers and went to the kitchen, where he found one of the more expensive tins of cat food and a bowl.

'There you go. Here's an extra treat for you, seeing as you've been home alone for so long.'

The cat purred happily and started eating the food.

He opened his bag and was setting out his shopping on the kitchen table when he heard a rhythmic noise. He went into the living room and frowned. The door to the terrace was open and banging lightly against the doorframe. Surely he had remembered to close it before he went, hadn't he? Bother. He would probably have to replace it soon, certainly before winter came. The little house was cold enough as it was during the dark months, and when the wind was at its worst he needed two blankets on top of his duvet to keep warm in his attic bedroom, but then again, insulation was so expensive.

Maybe next year.

The cat had finished eating and strolled contentedly into the living room. She licked her chops, stretched her paws and jumped up on her usual spot on the pale blue blanket on the old sofa.

'That was quick, little one.'

Victor Palatin sat down next to her and stroked her fur.

'I guess we should pick a new name for you, shouldn't we? You're not that little any more, are you?'

She had been just a kitten when she turned up outside, soaked and wretched in the rain. A little gift from above.

He returned to the kitchen, put the jars he had bought into a small box and looked out through the kitchen window. Still no noise from across the drive. He looked up at the picture of Jesus hanging above the kitchen table and suddenly felt a wave of guilt.

'Yes, Father.' He nodded at the picture and bowed his head. 'I'm sorry. I've had bad thoughts about her, my own mother. I ask for Your forgiveness. Thank You, Father, for looking down on me in mercy.'

He made the sign of the cross, kissed his fingers and ran them lightly over the picture. The flowers on his doorstep?

Forever yours.

He wasn't going to be with anyone. He didn't deserve that.

Victor Palatin carried his bag to the laundry room to empty out the clothes he had taken with him. He hadn't worn everything, but it was always good to have clean clothes. To be clean for the Lord.

His mother used to say that to him when he complained that her hard scrubbing hurt his skin as he sat trembling in the bath tub in the always too cold water.

Don't you want to be clean for the Lord?

Of course he did. He folded his socks and underpants so they would not be visible until they went into the washing machine and put his jumper and trousers on top.

Clean for the Lord.

He carried the empty bag upstairs and stowed it away in its regular place at the top of the wardrobe on the landing.

He returned to the kitchen and checked the jars in the box.

Paul the Apostle says that we Christians should be like a pleasant scent for the Lord. We should always smell nice and thus reflect God's overwhelming goodness.

Hand lotion, foot lotion, three different herbal soaps, skin lotion and lip salve.

He nodded. He had remembered everything.

Four times a year he drove to Tautra Abbey.

To get his mother her creams and soaps.

It made him happy. He didn't leave the island often – or the house, for that matter. He liked the drive to the abbey, he enjoyed every second really; he got some time to himself and could listen to whatever he wanted on the car radio. Again he felt a pang of guilt and glanced up at the picture on the wall.

'Yes, Father.'

He bowed his head and paused for a moment before he made the sign of the cross again, then he returned to the hallway, put on his work shoes and went out into the back garden.

Victor Palatin picked up the green watering can from its usual place and went to the tap on the outside wall. He filled the watering can almost to the brim, then walked down to the flower beds at the far end of the garden. He knelt down by one of them and stuck his fingers into the soil. Oh dear. It was terribly dry. The sun had been fierce for days and no one had tended to them. His mother couldn't;

she wasn't able to get all the way down here in her wheelchair. He had seen the weather forecast before he left and had considered turning on the sprinkler, but he couldn't let it run for days and use so much water; it was wasteful.

'I'm sorry,' Victor Palatin said to the flowers as he picked up the watering can. 'Here you are. This will make you feel better.'

The phone rang inside the house. No, it could wait until he had finished. Or could it? His mother had a doctor's appointment this week. Perhaps they were calling to reschedule.

Victor Palatin set down the watering can, ran back to the house, took off his shoes and reached the kitchen just as the phone rang again.

'Yes, Victor Palatin speaking.'

'Hello, Victor, it's Luca Eriksen.'

His heart sank. He had had a lump in his stomach as soon as his phone started to ring.

'Hi, Luca. What can I do for you?'

'I just wondered if you were back yet?' the police officer said. 'The investigators from Oslo would like a word with you.'

Victor Palatin's hands were trembling now. He bowed his head in shame in front of the picture.

'I'm home now.'

'Would it be OK for me to stop by?'

'Yes, sure. Just come on over.'

'Great, see you shortly.'

Victor Palatin carefully put down his mobile and looked beseechingly up at the picture on the wall.

'You have to help me, Father. Please?'

Victor Palatin closed his eyes, folded his hands and stood with his head bowed for a long time.

'I have sinned.'

Chapter 45

Hannah Holmen was sitting on a slope leading to Setervågen marina, looking at the things people had left by the side of the road. There were flowers, lots of them, in every colour. Some mourners had left small cards, written messages with pictures of Jessica on them, and there were teddies and other cuddly toys. Hannah regretted coming here, but Sylvia had refused to take no for an answer; she had come to Hannah's house for that very reason. *'I don't want to go without you. Please, please, would you come with me?'* So Hannah had snapped out of her lethargy, the cocoon she had created upstairs in her bedroom, put on a T-shirt and a pair of shorts and gone with them. Sylvia's mother sat behind the wheel with a worried look on her face. *'I don't want you being out there on your own, girls. What with everything that's going on. Please be careful who you talk to, promise me?'* She had been very reluctant to let them do this unsupervised. She only agreed after Sylvia had promised to call her the moment they were ready to leave. Sylvia had been annoyed, but Hannah thought the request seemed fair enough.

Someone who cared. Who watched out for them.

Sylvia sat down next to her, her cheeks flushed. She hadn't stopped talking since their arrival. About who had left what and where and that some people had no business being here in the first place. Like why had Malin and her friends left something? They hadn't even liked Jessica, had they? The area leading down to the marina was still cordoned off with yellow and white tape. In a short space of time several cars had pulled up and there were people by the side of the road, looking down and pointing. *It was there. She lived in that boat.* Hannah couldn't hear them except inside her own head and yet she could imagine what they were saying. Caroline from the hairdresser's was there, along with Fredrik, who worked in the sports shop. She'd heard they were a couple now. Further away she could see Malcolm from the Rema supermarket and his friend, the one with the curly hair; she couldn't remember his name. Heads shaking, hands pointing. A campervan had driven past slowly, idling near the shrine. The woman in the passenger seat had taken out her mobile. Held it up through the window. The sun was high in the sky, but it made no difference. Hannah was freezing cold on the inside. She was desperate to get home. Turn off the light, close the curtains and just disappear inside herself. Disappear into the screen, get away from all this.

'Look.' Sylvia elbowed her in the side.

The dark blue, flame-decorated Volvo belonging to Andres Wold had just parked up by the side of the road. The door to the driver's side opened and Andres got out.

'Eh?' Sylvia whispered, and yanked her arm. 'Would you take a look at that.'

Veronica Engen emerged from the passenger side and adjusted her clinging dress. She walked around to join Andres and positioned herself close to him. Like the others, they stopped and pointed towards the marina.

'She didn't waste any time – what a bitch.'

'Calm down,' Hannah said. 'It might not be what it looks like – perhaps they're just comforting each other. Like we are.'

She slipped her arm under her friend's and pulled her closer.

'Yes, sure,' Sylvia mumbled. 'I know how she comforts people. She's such a slut.'

'Oh, Sylvia, really.'

'I hate her.'

She grimaced at them again and stamped on the grass.

Jessica and Veronica Engen had had a run-in just a few weeks ago. It had almost turned into a fight. Over Andres, of course. Hannah had had to intervene.

'You'll pay for that, bitch!'

Veronica had been frothing at the mouth, as usual when she'd had way too much to drink.

'I bet she did it,' Sylvia said in a low voice.

'No, Sylvia . . .'

'I mean it. Didn't you hear that she hit someone over the head with a bottle at a party during SummerFillan Festival last year?'

'Oh, that's just gossip.'

'Is it though? Didn't Kyrre say that he had seen it?'

'Kyrre will say anything to get attention.'

'No, he won't. It's true – there was blood and everything. The police turned up.'

Hannah heaved a sigh and pulled her friend even closer.

'She wouldn't come here if it was her, would she?' Hannah said.

'Why not? That cow is capable of anything.'

Sylvia clenched her teeth and gave the couple the evil eye, just as Andres noticed them and pointed in their direction.

'Shit, they're coming over,' Sylvia said. 'Why don't we bash her head in with that?'

She nodded to a stone in front of them.

'Stop it, Sylvia.'

Veronica Engen shook her head and tried to hold Andres back, but he freed himself and walked over to them all the same.

'Hi.'

'Hi, Andres.'

He looked incredibly sad.

'Have you been here long?' he said, sitting down on the heather next to them.

'No, only a little while,' Hannah said.

'So, are you dating Veronica Engen now?' Sylvia said archly.

'What?' Andres said. 'No, no. She just . . . wanted a lift. She wanted to leave something by the roadside. For Jessica, you know.'

'Sure,' Sylvia muttered.

Hannah elbowed her.

'So have you heard?' Andres said, pushing up his baseball cap.

'Heard what?'

'People are saying that Pelle Lundgren was found in the nature reserve last night.'

'What?' Sylvia exclaimed, startled.

He nodded.

'Gekko drove past there this morning and the area had been cordoned off. There was a helicopter and everything. I didn't hear it myself, but someone told me. Ambulances with flashing blue lights and lots of cars.'

'But that doesn't automatically mean that—' Hannah said.

'That's what they're saying,' Andres said. 'I spoke to William just now and he said the same. Pelle Lundgren. Dead in there. So you didn't know?'

'No,' Hannah said.

'OK.' Andres nodded. 'Just checking. Seeing as—'

'Seeing as what?' Sylvia said.

He hesitated.

'Well, seeing as you were best friends with Jessica and all that.'

Andres looked down towards the boat again.

'After all, he used to visit her.'

Sylvia and Hannah looked at each other.

'UFO Pelle? Visit Jessica?' Sylvia exclaimed.

'Yes. I saw them together down there several times.' Andres nodded in the direction of the marina.

'Are you coming or what?' Veronica Engen called out from down the road.

'Sure, I was just checking something.'

Andres got up and left.

'What did he mean?' Sylvia said. 'Found in the nature reserve? Did he mean Pelle's body was found there?'

'No idea,' Hannah said, feeling she couldn't take much more. She brushed off her shorts and started walking down to the road.

'UFO Pelle?' Sylvia said nervously. 'What if some mad killer is loose on Hitra?'

'We don't know if that's true,' Hannah said.

'Yes, but a helicopter and everything? I'm scared,' Sylvia said, clinging to her arm. 'Please can we go back to my place? I can't be on my own. Please?'

'Yes, all right.'

'Oh, thank you.' Sylvia breathed a sigh of relief and took out her mobile. 'Perhaps my parents can tell us what has happened.'

A police car pulled up now, not very far away from them. Two officers got out and started walking down towards the boat.

'What are they doing here?' Sylvia said.

'I don't know,' Hannah said. 'Perhaps they haven't finished yet.'

'Please would you sleep over?' Sylvia looked at her beseechingly.

'We'll have to see,' Hannah said. 'OK?'

Chapter 46

Mia had closed the front door to Pelle Lundgren's maisonette flat behind her and was walking down to the bike shed by the road when Munch arrived and got out of his car.

'Is this where he lived?'

Mia joined him and nodded.

'Social housing, am I right?' Munch said, wiping the sweat from under his white sun hat and looking up at the small brown terraced block.

'I think they call it council housing now.'

'Whatever,' Munch said, moving into the shade of a tree by the entrance to a playground. 'This was where he lived? In one of these houses where *tenants are eligible for housing benefit in order to secure their own accommodation*, as they say?'

'What has got into you?' Mia said.

'Sorry. I'm just tired. I've been swimming in a pool of human grief and misery for almost an hour. Jessica's mother. Some people should never be parents.'

Munch sighed, took a cigarette out of the packet and shook his head.

'So have you been inside yet?'

He looked up towards the six identical maisonette flats that made up the block. Each had a small garden and there was a big playground at the front. The location was not far from the town centre and offered a view of the strait on the northern side of the island.

'Yes, I was just leaving.'

'Did you find anything?'

'Potentially. I was about to call you. Do you want to come inside with me?'

'Sure, let me just . . .'

Munch lit his cigarette and shook his head again.

'No, poor woman. I felt sorry for her.'

'Laura Bakken?'

He nodded.

'Goddammit.'

'That bad?' Mia said.

'She was completely out of it. I've no idea what they've given her – she could barely stand up. She struggled to talk. Let's hope it numbs her pain, whatever it was.'

'Did you get anything out of her? Anything useful to us?'

He shrugged his shoulders. 'Perhaps. I don't know. She had been in Trondheim all weekend. Partying. New boyfriend, a young man barely older than Jessica.'

'So nothing useful?'

'Well, I don't know. She mentioned something about a diary. Says Jessica keeps all her secrets there, or words to that effect. I've sent people down to the boat to check it again. See if we can find anything.'

'And her room at home? Are we checking that again as well?' Mia wanted to know.

'What's the point? A mattress in a corner, two empty packets of crisps on the floor?'

Mia nodded. The house had barely been fit for human habitation. They had understood immediately why Jessica had sought refuge in the boat.

'We'll have to see if anything new turns up down in . . .'

'Setervågen marina,' Mia said, and led the way up to the front door at the end of the block.

She put on her gloves and entered the small flat.

'I think we might need a team out here. I'm not sure. That's your call.'

'I get to make the call? Lucky me. Anything else you would like to give me permission for, your ladyship?'

249

'Christ, you really are in a foul mood. Is it one of those days?' Mia said. 'You know we used to have a word for that in Oslo?'

'I do. *Cyanide*. I'll try harder, I'm sorry.'

Munch went in front of her into the small living room and took a look around. It was as sparsely furnished as the rest of the house. An Ikea sofa in one corner. A small TV. A coffee table with a half-finished jigsaw puzzle of the Moomin troll family. Some posters on the walls. A map of Hitra and the surrounding islands.

'Do you have one of these?' Mia said.

'A map? Yes, one very like it.' Munch nodded. 'It's in my hotel room. I'm starting to get my bearings, I think.'

He went up to the map and pointed.

'Fjellværsøya?'

She nodded.

'Knarrlagsundet?'

'Yes.'

'Here's Fillan, and . . . this is where the police station is?'

'Good.'

'And this is where we found Jessica, isn't it? Setervågen marina, did you say it was called?'

Mia nodded.

'It's a bit weird, isn't it?' he said, still studying the map.

'What is?'

'Well, there is only one road around the island, isn't there? You come out of the tunnel from the mainland . . . here? And there's only one road, the 713. It starts here and it goes all the way round – you can't drive anywhere else, can you?'

'What's your point?'

'Well, Jonathan disappeared somewhere around here, didn't he?'

'Yes, in Svingen.'

'And Setervågen marina is . . . here. Both locations are near or on this one road, the 713, yet no one saw anything?'

'We're in the middle of nowhere,' Mia said. 'Have you been outside at night? Do you realize how few people are here? How few cars?'

'True, true, but even so.'

Munch wiped away the sweat under his hat with his glove and continued to shake his head in disbelief.

Mia followed him through the flat, making sure to stay behind him so that he could explore the property in the same way she had a little earlier. Once they reached the bedroom on the first floor, she stopped in the doorway.

'OK,' Munch said. 'So this was his control room, or whatever we call it?'

Mia nodded.

In contrast to the ones downstairs, this room was crammed with stuff. A desk below the window with an amateur radio to which a pair of headphones was connected. A microphone on a small stand in front of it. The walls were covered with posters, all of Jupiter from various angles, and in between them were printouts from the Internet, most of them in English.

UFO sighting in Boise, Idaho.

It's real! Man tells story of visit to Area 51.

A few in Norwegian.

Light phenomenon confounds scientists.

The UFO mystery in Hessdalen.

'So could this be it?' Munch said with a nod towards the headphones on the desk. 'He received messages through amateur radio?'

'He may have thought so.' Mia nodded.

'Is it plugged in?'

'I think so. It certainly has power.'

Munch flicked a small switch.

A green light came on and the speakers crackled.

Munch bent down and pressed the button on the microphone.

'This is LA3Z1. Is anyone out there today?'

There was no response; the white noise just continued.

Munch sat down and fiddled with a few more dials before he tried again.

'This is LA3Z1. Come in?'

He paused before repeating the message.

'This is LA3Z1. Come in?'

Mia nearly jumped out of her skin when a male voice suddenly came out of the speaker.

'Hello, LA3Z1. This is JW5E. Longyearbyen calling. What's your location?'

Munch turned to her and smiled.

'Hello, JW5E,' he said, pressing the microphone again. 'I'm on Hitra in Trøndelag county. Apologies, I just wanted to test my equipment.'

'Understood, LA3Z1,' the voice replied. 'I can hear you loud and clear.'

'Thank you, JW5E. Have a good rest of the day. Over and out.'

Munch released the button and got up.

'Good heavens,' Mia smiled. 'You never cease to surprise me.'

Munch looked a little embarrassed.

'Well, a boy has to do something when he can't play football.'

'So Pelle really was in contact with people?' Mia said curiously.

'No,' Munch said.

'He wasn't? But you just—'

'He hadn't set it up properly.'

'So he . . . he just sat here, pretending to talk to people?'

'I don't know about people – I thought they were aliens?'

'True, but even so?'

'The way it was set up before I reset it, he wouldn't have been in contact with anything other than his own head.'

He looked around the room.

'Have you been through everything here?'

'Yes.'

'Including the rubbish?'

'Upstairs and downstairs.' She nodded.

'OK. I think it's worth the resources. We'll get a team out here. If that's all right with you, your ladyship.'

He winked at her and walked past her downstairs. They had just stepped outside when his mobile rang. He answered it, nodded, said a few words. Then he put it back in his pocket.

'That was Luca.'

'What's new?'

'He has made contact with Victor Palatin. Vic. He thinks it's quicker for us to take the boat.'

'You're not a fan of boats, are you?' Mia said, walking down to her motorcycle.

Munch looked across the strait.

'It should be all right in this weather.'

'Where is it moored?' Mia asked.

'Viken. That's just down there, isn't it?'

'Yes.'

'You see, I do know my way around Hitra.'

Munch stuck another cigarette in his mouth and headed for his car.

'I'll see you there.'

Chapter 47

Munch was well aware that Mia was enjoying the sight of him clinging to a handle in the cabin on board the white police boat; he felt a little seasick and was annoyed with himself for not driving to the location instead. The express ferry from Trondheim had been one thing; it was so big he barely noticed that he was at sea. But this tub? No, thank you. But it was obviously too late for him to change his mind now.

The two people behind the wheel, however, looked like they were having a whale of a time. Bright sunshine and the sea around them. Luca Eriksen appeared to be an experienced sailor and Mia was fearless – she loved everything that could move fast. She was grinning from ear to ear, her long black hair flapping in the wind, and she nodded encouragingly to Luca, which only caused him to accelerate even more. The spray stood around the bow of the white monster now. Thank God Luca had said that it wasn't far. Only ten or fifteen minutes and then Munch's feet would be back on solid ground.

'She's old,' he heard Luca shout over the wind. 'But she does a fair speed. She got new diesel engines a few years ago. Two 5.5-litre, six-cylinder Volvo Penta D6, 435 hp in each.'

'It shows.' Mia grinned. 'How fast can she go?'

Luca smiled and shouted something in response that Munch didn't catch.

'Push her harder,' Mia urged him.

'I can't do that in sheltered waters,' Luca responded.

Thank God for that.

'I'll take you out on the open sea one day!'

'Yes, please,' Mia said, her hair flying to all sides. 'Is she always moored in Viken?'

'Yes. But I can pick you up at yours,' Luca said. 'Do you have a deep-water jetty?'

'I think it might be too short – how long is your boat?'

'Thirty foot,' Eriksen said.

'I could always swim out to meet you,' Mia said and, for a moment, she looked as if she had forgotten why they were here.

The boat reduced her speed and ended up drifting calmly across the surface of the water. Luca docked and Mia jumped ashore, tied up fore and aft and stood with her hands planted on her hips.

'Wow. Cool.' She smiled broadly, then reached out her hand to help Munch up on the concrete jetty.

'It's not far,' Luca said, climbing up to join them. 'Just a few hundred metres.'

Munch considered having a cigarette, but he genuinely didn't fancy one right now. They left the life vests on the boat and walked up the road.

Victor Palatin's property was one of the few houses Munch had seen out here that was not located very close to the sea. A farm of an older design, it was situated in a dip on the west side of the road. There were two quaint residential houses, one on each side of the drive. A small barn and an outbuilding. An old Toyota was parked outside the door to the barn.

Mia caught up now, and looked at him gravely as they walked down the small road.

'What?' Munch said.

'Nothing,' Mia said, looking ahead as the door opened and a man stepped outside.

'Victor Palatin,' he introduced himself. He bowed nervously, then shook hands with them.

'Holger Munch,' Munch said, showing him his warrant card. 'This is Mia Krüger and Luca Eriksen – perhaps you have already met?'

'No,' Victor Palatin said, looking fearfully across the drive at the other house. 'But we have spoken on the phone.'

A door opened in the other house and an old woman in a wheel-chair rolled out on to the flagstones.

'Victor! What is it? Do we have visitors?' Her thin voice was strangely powerful, echoing across the drive.

'It's all right, Mother. Just stay where you are.'

Victor Palatin opened the door to his house for them.

'We had better go inside. She's not having one of her good days.'

'So you live out here alone?' Munch said when they had sat down in the living room.

'My mother lives over there. But, yes, in here it's just me and the little one.'

He nodded towards a cat that was asleep in an armchair.

A religious home: there could be little doubt about that. A crucifix on the wall. Pictures of Jesus. Moses with the tablets. A framed embroidery.

The word of God lights my path.

'Would you like something to drink?' Victor Palatin said, raking his hand through his dark hair.

He looked close to forty. Slim. Slightly drooping shoulders. A short-sleeved shirt buttoned all the way up and stuffed into light-coloured trousers that should have been a little longer.

'Nothing for me,' Munch said.

'I'm fine.' Mia nodded.

'I expect you're here to talk about the girl, Jessica.' Victor Palatin cleared his throat and sat down on a spindle-backed chair.

'I have spoken to the Lord and we have agreed that I should tell you everything. Because Jesus said: *I am the way, the truth and the life. No one comes to the Father except through Me.*'

Munch raised his eyebrows.

'No matter how shameful it is,' Victor Palatin said.

'So you knew her?' Mia said.

'Jessica Bakken, yes.'

'How well?' Munch said.

'Not very,' Victor Palatin said, folding his hands in his lap. 'We met a few times. At her place.'

Munch glanced at Mia.

'In the boat?' she said.

'Yes.'

'And you did what there?'

Victor Palatin covered his mouth with his hand and coughed.

'I'm not very comfortable sharing the details, but—'

'So you were sleeping with her?' Mia said.

'There was no . . . penetration, but other things, yes.'

He stared at the floor for a moment and then up at the religious images behind them.

'I know it wasn't right,' Victor Palatin said. 'And I have found a better way now. I live alone. No women's hands will touch my body again.'

Mia rolled her eyes and was about to say something, but Munch stopped her.

'So, Victor,' he said, leaning forwards on the sofa, 'just so I'm clear. You and Jessica Bakken were in a relationship?'

'Yes.'

'And this relationship involved you coming to the boat, the two of you doing what you had agreed and then you paying her for it?'

'Yes.'

'How much?'

'Five hundred kroner.'

'And how many times were you there.'

'Three.'

Munch looked to Mia, who nodded in response. The amount and the number of visits matched the entries in the black notebook.

'And you weren't at home on Saturday?' Mia said.

'No,' Victor Palatin said. 'I went to Tautra Abbey. My mother likes the soaps and creams the nuns make and I go there every now and again to buy them for her.'

'And this can be backed up by . . . well, the nuns?' Munch said.

Victor Palatin looked directly at them now for the first time since he had started telling his story.

'Yes, of course . . . surely you don't think that . . .'

There was silence for a moment while his gaze flitted between them.

'That I killed her? Oh, no, no, no . . .' He held out his hands. 'Ask the Lord. He knows the truth.'

'I'm not sure we'll get a reply there,' Munch said. 'But since you seem so keen on being honest, Victor, let me ask you directly: were you involved in or do you have any information about the murder of Jessica Bakken?'

'No.'

'OK, thank you. Then I think that we are . . .'

Munch looked at Mia, who nodded. She was already getting up from the sofa.

'One last thing,' Munch said when they were back outside. 'Would you be willing to give us a DNA sample? We're asking everyone who went to the boat. Would you?'

'Absolutely.'

'Good,' Munch said, and nodded to Luca.

Luca put on his gloves and swabbed Victor Palatin's mouth.

'Again, thank you,' Munch said. 'And good luck.'

Mia didn't say anything until they were halfway down the road.

'Good luck with what?'

'What else could I say?' Munch mumbled. 'Have you ever seen anything like that?'

'A few times, yes, sadly,' Mia said. 'The Lord moves in mysterious ways, isn't that what they say?'

'Don't ask me,' Munch said, and popped a cigarette in between his lips.

Fortunately the voyage back was calmer. Mia had switched from adrenaline junkie to being quiet and introspective in the seat next to him. Munch had often seen her like this and knew not to disturb her when she had that particular look on her face. She had probably thought the same as him on their way back from Victor Palatin's house.

Too easy, wasn't it?

All this talk of Jesus and the Lord?

If I confess to this, they'll go away?

Munch stayed silent and let her think. He didn't say a word until they were back ashore.

'So what's your verdict? Did we let him off too easily?'

She didn't have time to respond. A man was walking towards them.

'Munch?' he said, taking off his sunglasses.

'Yes, that's me.'

'Klaus Halvorsen, Kripos.'

He shook hands with Munch.

'And those men over there are Theo de Boer from the Dutch Police and John MacLaren from Interpol.'

He nodded in the direction of two men who were standing further along the quay.

'Is there somewhere we can talk?'

Chapter 48

In preparation for the parish council meeting Dorothea Krogh had laid the long table on the terrace with the white tablecloth and the china she only used for special occasions. She felt they needed something extra today after the recent terrible events. She had been tempted to ring everyone and cancel. The timing was all wrong, wasn't it? A shadow had been cast across the whole island after the murder on the boat. And now this? Rumour had it that Pelle Lundgren had been found dead last night out by the wildlife tower. That sweet, gentle soul, always riding his bicycle around the island. Dorothea shook her head in despair and set out the last few cups. She could sense it everywhere. In the shops. In the church. The tranquillity out here had been shattered. People were really scared. However, Beth Corneliussen, the chair of the parish council, had convinced her. *'Surely this is precisely the time we need to get together, don't you think?'* And she was right, of course: they had to join forces, try to find some light in these dark times.

The parish council had eight members. Four from the church: Thomas Ofelius, the new vicar; Nora Strand, who had arrived early for the meeting; Beth Corneliussen and Dorothea herself. Then three members of the congregation here in Sandstad and one person who, strictly speaking, belonged to Fillan Church.

'Did you get the notice of the meeting?'

'Indeed I did, Nora. I'm sure everyone got it.'

'Do you think it was OK? Should we have included the new roof as an item for discussion on the agenda?'

'No, no. We discussed it extensively the last time we met,' Dorothea said, and went inside to fetch the coffee.

In the meantime Thomas Ofelius had arrived in her living room, and he was looking just as lost, and snivelling, as usual.

'Are we sitting outside?'

'Yes, Nora is already here. Why don't you join her?'

They had gone through and approved the minutes of the last meeting and read aloud the agenda when Beth Corneliussen remarked that, strictly speaking, they should not have started yet as not everyone was here. Where was Lars Lolander?

Beth was a nice woman, but terribly pedantic. She had been one of the strongest advocates for accepting the new altarpiece, and that had not surprisingly led to people gossiping behind her back. She had to be a friend of the Prytz family, surely? And hadn't she just bought herself a new car? A very smart one at that. How on earth could she afford it? Sometimes people really had too much time on their hands, Dorothea thought. She, for her part, had argued in favour of the new altarpiece because it would save them money. It was as simple as that.

Fortunately, Lars Lolander arrived at this point and they were able to start properly. He apologized for his lateness and sat down next to the vicar. He had a bandage on one hand. And nosy Beth Corneliussen just had to ask him what had happened, and so more time was taken up by that. He had got a large splinter in his palm, he told them, and they all shuddered. Lars Lolander was a relatively new member of the congregation. He had been born on Hitra and had moved back only a few years ago. He had been something in finance, but he had retired from that and now sold firewood as a hobby, which explained his injury, an accident with a cut-off saw.

Right, that was that out of the way. At long last they could start.

Afterwards, when the meeting was finally over and Dorothea had herded most of her guests out of the door, she returned to the terrace hoping that she might soon get rid of the two last ones, but no, they had made themselves very much at home. Nora Strand and Beth Corneliussen. Didn't they have better things to do? They were whispering when Dorothea came back.

'So what are we talking about?' Dorothea said, and started to gather up the plates.

The two women looked at each other, somewhat embarrassed, as if Dorothea had caught them in the middle of an inappropriate conversation.

'Oh, I'm sure it's nothing,' Beth Corneliussen said, and cleared her throat.

'Isn't it? Well, never mind then.'

Dorothea arched her back and was about to say something about the sun, how lovely the sunlight was down by the gooseberry bushes, but she didn't get the chance.

'Have you heard what they're saying in town?' Beth Corneliussen said in a low voice, and leaned across the table.

'No, what are they saying?' Dorothea said as she flopped into a chair.

'The police, you know,' Beth Corneliussen continued. 'They're carrying out door-to-door enquiries, asking people about all sorts of things.'

'Yes, I know.' Dorothea nodded. 'They were here the other day. Two of them. A man called Munch like the painter and that woman who lives out by Kvenvær, the one who's been in the papers—'

'Krüger,' Nora Strand interrupted.

'That's right,' Dorothea said. 'Very nice and decent people, I thought. Seemed highly professional. I'm sure they'll get to the bottom of this.'

'Yes, but there are more,' Beth Corneliussen said. 'Investigators, I mean. Kari-Anne told me that one of them had been to her shop. Asking questions.'

'Rumour has it they're looking for someone,' Nora Strand interjected quickly. 'Some men.'

'Aha?' Dorothea heaved a sigh.

'They want to know about names,' Beth Corneliussen said in a hushed voice.

'Nicknames.'

'Yes,' Beth Corneliussen nodded. 'Kari-Anne said she was asked if she knew a man who might be known as Big B? And someone called Vic?'

'Well,' Dorothea said, getting up and putting teaspoons on top of the stack of plates, 'I'm sure they'll work it out.'

'There was another one,' Beth Corneliussen said, almost whispering now. 'A Mr LOL.'

The three women looked at each other.

'And when I saw his bandage, it suddenly occurred to me,' Beth Corneliussen said eagerly. 'Did I ask too many questions? Was it suspicious?'

'Whose bandage?' Dorothea said with a frown.

'Lars Lolander's,' Beth Corneliussen whispered.

'What about it?'

'Just think about it for a moment. Lolander? LOL? After all, we don't know him very well, do we? He used to work in a bank somewhere. He came here to retire.'

She mimed quotation marks with her fingers. Dorothea snorted.

'Oh, stop it, both of you. Right, I think it's time to wind this up. I need to water my flowers before they shrivel up in the garden. Good heavens, how hot it is today.'

At long last they left, but Dorothea could see them lingering on the steps to the church, still gossiping.

She went to the kitchen and put everything in the dishwasher.

Then she paused by the kitchen counter and gazed through the window.

Lolander? She shuddered.

No, it was impossible, surely? Should she give Luca Eriksen a call?

No. It couldn't be true.

Dorothea Krogh fetched a bottle of port from the cupboard, found a glass, picked up her crossword puzzle and her pencil on her way out and sat down, rather heavily, in a chair shaded by a parasol.

Chapter 49

Munch and Mia entered the meeting room on the fourth floor of Hjorten Hotel. Halvorsen from Kripos had been less than forthcoming; he seemed to be someone who expected people to follow his orders without asking questions. Munch, of course, had no truck with that. *'Listen, I don't give a damn about your operation. We're in the middle of a murder inquiry here. We can give you half an hour, max.'* Halvorsen had calmed down after that, mumbled something about shared interests and how it would be good for all parties if they could do this somewhere other than the police station. *'Highly sensitive. Absolutely no information can come out.'*

Munch found the light switch, ushered in the three new arrivals, and the men sat down at the round, white table.

'So,' Halvorsen began, 'I appreciate that this will come as a bolt out of the blue and that you're in the middle of your own investigation, but so are we, and we saw no option but to intervene and to let you know what is about to happen.'

He nodded towards the Dutchman and MacLaren from Interpol and continued in English. Halvorsen might come across as brusque, but he was clearly good at his job. He was direct and succinct and went straight to the point.

'For the last five years we in Kripos have been assisting the Dutch police and Interpol with an operation called *North.*'

The Dutchman produced a file from his briefcase and slid it towards Halvorsen, who spread several photographs across the table. Mia got up from her seat by the wall, pulled out a chair and studied the photographs with interest.

'This is a very complex case – we're talking cartel activities across the world. Plantations in Bolivia, factories in Vietnam. We've uncovered activities such as shipping and production. This is a big and so far very well-hidden organization with its headquarters in Rotterdam. In Kripos we have been focusing on the link to Scandinavia, to Norway specifically, of course, and primarily we're interested in this man . . .'

Halvorsen slid another picture across the table.

'Jacob Wallstedt?' Mia frowned.

Halvorsen nodded and continued.

'Which isn't his real name. His real name is John Gran and he has been a person of interest to us for some time. We first noticed him in Sweden some years ago and we have followed him out here to Hitra, where he now lives in a house on the southern side of the island, from where the Norwegian part of the operation is run.'

'Our witness in Svingen?' Munch said in Norwegian. Mia nodded.

'By now we have a pretty good idea of what's going on, but then we discovered that a police officer unconnected to our investigation had logged on to the system the confiscation of some of the products that this gang distributes,' Halvorsen said.

'Ecstasy, amphetamines, ketamine,' MacLaren interjected. 'They have fancy names such as Skywalker, Infinity . . .'

Munch looked to Mia, who nodded again.

'John Gran, or Jacob Wallstedt as you know him, is working with this man,' Halvorsen said, pointing to another picture. 'Steve Moore, originally from the UK, but he has lived in Norway for a while now. Moore is responsible for importation and distribution, and we also believe that he's involved with – how can I put it? – marketing the products. We noticed early on that some of the names they give their products have Norwegian origins.'

Munch recognized him immediately. Steve Moore was the man he had met at the former mink farm opposite the church.

'They probably decided that Hitra was the perfect hiding place,' Halvorsen continued. 'Isolated. Quiet. Close to the sea. Plenty of international shipping traffic. Easy to get the product in. The way they do it is they label their cargo as fish. Both ashore and at sea, it's the perfect cover out here, with so many fishing-related businesses. They have big ships which they meet in the open sea in speedboats that ferry the product to the shore.'

'And this is relevant to us because?' Munch wanted to know.

'We were aware of your investigation, but you really set off alarm bells when you looked up police records on Jacob Wallstedt. It's an alias, as I just mentioned, and we had created those entries in the database precisely to see if anyone with access to our systems might be interested in him.'

'You're wondering if they have someone on the inside?' Mia said.

'That's right,' Halvorsen said. 'I don't want to go into detail, but we have uncovered extensive corruption and bent officers in the Netherlands . . .'

He nodded towards de Boer.

'. . . and in Germany. And there was obviously a real risk that the same was true in Norway. We followed the trail in our records to someone called . . .'

He looked across to MacLaren.

'Gabriel Mørk,' the man from Interpol said.

'And from him to you,' Halvorsen said. 'I gather that he was working for you until quite recently?'

He looked at Munch, who nodded.

'We were aware that Wallstedt's name had previously come up in connection with a missing person case up here. He's in Kripos's database, nothing major, just as a witness, I gather?'

'Yes,' Munch said.

'And then you found drugs out here – not a lot, but definitely related to our operation. Because that's why you're here, isn't it? The girl you found last Saturday, and now another victim?'

'That's correct,' Munch said.

'I thought so,' Halvorsen said. 'We haven't reached the end of our investigation yet, we still have a few things to figure out, but given the circumstances, we thought we had better strike soon. We have set the starting time for our operation at zero five hundred tomorrow.'

'Tomorrow?' Munch said.

'Yes,' Halvorsen said. 'For my part, I would like to arrest them today, but we need a little more time to prepare. We are obviously keeping them under constant surveillance and we have yet to see any changes to their routines. So fingers crossed we'll get them.'

Halvorsen looked at both of them.

'Any questions?'

'So what do we do if we need to talk to either of them?' Munch said.

'Wallstedt and Moore?'

'Yes.'

'We'll accommodate you as far as we can, but I suspect they'll clam up pretty quickly. We're expecting their lawyers to arrive very soon once we have remanded them in custody. Is there any specific information you want from them? Again, it's my understanding that you don't believe the murder of the young woman is related to her involvement in drug distribution? That there are other factors at play here?'

He folded his hands in front of him on the table and looked at Munch and Mia again.

Munch shook his head. He loathed all those reports that were written and entered into databases every night. He preferred to keep his cards close to his chest for this very reason, otherwise anyone with access could snoop on his cases as much as they liked to.

It had annoyed Oslo Police Headquarters no end.

We need to see your reports, Munch.

But he had insisted on an absolute information blackout in his unit.

Not a word to anyone until everything has been solved.

'Am I wrong?' Halvorsen said when Munch didn't respond immediately.

'We're considering several angles,' Munch said. 'But we certainly can't exclude that drugs are the motive, especially now that we understand the bigger picture.'

'We're also still looking for the missing boy,' Mia said. 'Jonathan. His disappearance could be connected to all of this.'

'To drug trafficking?' Halvorsen frowned.

'It's just a theory,' Mia said. 'But it's definitely something we'll want to look into.'

'OK,' Halvorsen said. 'We will help you as much as we can, but our own operation comes first. As I said, we strike at zero five hundred hours tomorrow, and up until then it is extremely important, imperative in fact, that none of this is leaked. Understand?'

He looked at them again as if they were a part of his team now.

'It's just us here,' Munch said. 'You have nothing to worry about.'

'Good,' Halvorsen said, and got up. 'Then I think we're done here. Thank you for your time. And good luck.'

Halvorsen nodded and walked in front of the Dutchman and MacLaren out to the lift.

Munch took a cigarette out of the packet and stepped out on the balcony. Mia joined him.

'Right.' She whistled softly.

'Did we just kick a hornets' nest or what?' Munch said, lighting up.

'It looks like it.'

'Is that what you think? That the boy witnessed something?'

'I don't know,' Mia said quietly and, for a moment, she seemed lost in thought.

'OK,' Munch said. 'Let's give them some space while we think about whether we might want to set up an interview in due course.'

Mia just nodded.

'What?' Munch wanted to know, taking another drag on his cigarette.

She shook her head.

'No, I just . . .'

'Palatin?'

She nodded again. 'There's something about him, isn't there?'

'Do you want to pay him another visit?'

'Not necessarily.' She shook her head. 'It's about him being religious. The artefacts on his walls got me thinking. I wonder if we have made a big mistake.'

'OK? About what?'

'BABY WHORE.' She looked at him.

'Go on?'

'Rita, one of the crime-scene technicians, mentioned something I didn't pick up on at first, but which I now think could be important.'

'And what was it?'

'She said something about a dot,' Mia said, looking into the distance.

'A dot?' Munch said.

'On the cup. She said there was a kind of mark after the word *baby*. That it might be a full stop.'

'Could you be slightly less cryptic, please?' Munch heaved a sigh, then took another drag on his cigarette.

'Yes, sorry, I just—'

'Besides, what does any of this have to do with Victor Palatin?'

'No, I'm just thinking about all the religious imagery out there. *Whore*, that's an unusual word, wouldn't you agree?'

'Yes, but . . .'

She looked at him now, her expression was grave.

'When have you ever heard that word used? Mostly in a religious context, am I right? *Whore*. The Whore of Babylon?'

'You're right,' Munch said.

'Exactly. I don't think it says *baby*. I think it's an abbreviation for *Babylon*. The killer was sending us a message.'

'Damn it, Mia. Are you sure?' Munch said.

'It's got to be that. Because she wasn't pregnant, was she? So why mention a baby? No, it has to be Babylon.'

'Well done, Mia.' Munch smiled. 'I'll buy that. So where do we go from here?'

She shook her head.

'I'm not sure. Maybe we should take another look at Palatin after all. Ask the nuns if he really was at the abbey last weekend.'

'I'll get Luca to check right away.' Munch nodded, stubbed out his cigarette in an ashtray and went inside to get his mobile.

He had a new text message. From Lillian.

Call me, please?

Chapter 50

Hannah Holmen had not planned on staying very long, but Sylvia's mother had insisted. *'Of course you're eating with us, Hannah. I have a lasagne in the oven, and you love lasagne, don't you?'*

She was snapped out of her gloomy thoughts by Sylvia's mother, who had said something to her.

'What? Sorry, I—'

'You need to help yourself first, you're our guest.' Sylvia's mother smiled at her, then nodded to the lasagne on the table.

'Oh, yes, thank you.'

Hannah put a little on her plate, then passed the dish to Sylvia.

'Is that all you're having?' Sylvia's mother looked at her anxiously. 'I used the same recipe as the one you really liked the last time.'

'I'll have seconds,' Hannah said, but she probably wouldn't.

She wasn't hungry. She hadn't felt like eating for several days. Sylvia's mother gave Sylvia's father a worried look, but she made no further comment.

'By the way, where's Jonas?' Sylvia's father said, sticking his fork into the food. 'Surely he knows it's dinner time?'

Five o'clock on the dot.

It was how things were done in this household: you were on time and you had regular mealtimes. No one made a big deal out of it. The family did things together. It was how it used to be in Hannah's home. Hannah realized how much she missed it.

She picked at her food, making sure to pop small bites into her mouth every now and then, conscious that Sylvia's mother was watching her, observing everything she did. She was wondering,

Hannah reckoned, if everything was all right with her, which it quite clearly wasn't, but Hannah would prefer not to talk about it. *Just disappear.*

Fortunately the door to the terrace was opened at that moment and took the focus off her. Sylvia's younger brother came stomping inside. His shoes were muddy and he was carrying something heavy.

'Look what I found!'

'Jonas, really, what have we said about you coming inside with your shoes on? Look at the mess you're making.'

The eight-year-old boy looked at the linoleum.

'Oops, sorry, but take a look at this.'

Proudly he held up his treasure.

'It's a doll's house. Somebody has set fire to it.'

'Yuck,' Sylvia's mother said, getting up. 'Where did you find that? It's falling apart.'

'In the forest.' The boy grinned. 'Can I keep it? Please?'

'At least take it back outside,' Sylvia's mother said, herding him out through the terrace door.

'So.' Sylvia's father cleared his throat. 'I heard Sylvia say that you're thinking of going to Trondheim? To continue your education there?'

Don't mention Jessica. It was clear that they had made a decision not to. Just small talk. Life must go on. Something along those lines.

And that suited her fine.

'She's thinking about the Cathedral College.' Sylvia nodded. 'Very good science options there. Hannah is ace at maths.'

Sylvia smiled at her.

'Oh, right?' Sylvia's father said. 'I didn't know that. I wasn't too bad at it myself, I'll have you know. Which do you prefer? Algebra or—'

'Oh, a bit of everything,' Hannah said as Sylvia's mother returned.

'Right, you go to the bathroom and clean yourself up, Jonas.' She sat down and shook her head in resignation. 'Would you believe that boy? He has been playing *Zombie Apocalypse*. When did he start doing that? We have to cut his screen time even more, I think. Don't you agree?'

271

She looked at Sylvia's father, who nodded.

'I'll have a word with him.'

'Thank you.'

She ate another mouthful of lasagne, then she turned to Hannah and Sylvia.

'*Zombie Apocalypse?* I don't think we played that when I was eight years old. How about you?'

She laughed briefly. Hannah could practically hear the clock ticking on the wall behind her. She felt a huge sense of relief when she was finally outside the house again.

'Are you sure you don't want to stay over?' Sylvia said with a pleading look in her eyes.

'No, sorry. I need to get home.'

'Please call me tonight. Or tomorrow morning, OK?'

'OK,' Hannah said, getting into the car.

She put on her seatbelt and looked at Sylvia's mother.

'You really don't have to give me a lift home.'

Sylvia's mother looked at her anxiously.

'What? No, of course I'm going to take you home. I don't want you walking back on your own. Not the way things are now.'

It was quiet in their house. As usual. Hannah took off her shoes in the hallway and wandered into the living room.

'Hello? Mum?'

There was no reply. Hannah went into the kitchen, picked up a bottle of fizzy lemonade from the fridge and headed upstairs to her room. She slipped out of her shorts and got into bed. Reached for her laptop. Finally. She took a sip, set down the bottle on the windowsill and logged on.

BookFans. Several people in the chat room today. She quickly skimmed the list and smiled when she saw his name. Her fingers danced across the keyboard.

Hi, Ludvig. How are you?

272

SIX

THURSDAY

Chapter 51

Thursday morning, and Mia had set her alarm clock for three thirty. Just fifteen minutes later she was astride her motorcycle, heading for the town centre, then onwards out to Sandstad. She smiled faintly to herself behind the helmet as she passed through Fillan. The first time a local resident had mentioned the centre of Fillan to her, she had imagined a busy Oslo street. She had asked a passer-by if there was an off-licence here. *'Yes, sure, in the town centre.'* The images those words evoked. High-rise buildings, trams, traffic lights, street performers, flashing advertising, exhaust fumes, junkies begging. This was nothing like that. The centre of Fillan was possibly the nicest place she had ever bought wine. And it wasn't that small, really. They had quite a few shops here, perhaps as many as twelve, and the general mood of tranquillity everywhere was very attractive. A cinema, a library, even a public swimming pool. Campervans made up most of the traffic in the summer; the island was popular with tourists. And she could see why. She had read about people who spent their summer at Ikea. The parking was free and the food in the café was cheap. It was a far cry from waking up to the smell of the ocean, grazing deer and a heron taking off from the water's edge.

Five days. Since Jessica had been murdered. Munch had tried to boost the team's morale last night, emphasized how they mustn't get stressed, how an investigation was a marathon, not a sprint. That was a lie, of course. She had seen it in his eyes, she knew him too well.

The first forty-eight hours. The most important in any homicide investigation. The walls in her house were covered with photographs now. Jessica smiling in a Disneyland T-shirt with a can of cola in one hand. She had tried to prioritize the names around her.

Victor Palatin.

Thomas Ofelius.

Benjamin Prytz.

She had placed Pelle Lundgren nearby.

Jupiter? What was the connection between the two victims? Were they friends? She moved Pelle Lundgren's picture further away.

Ultimately he was collateral damage.

Several people had observed them together down by the boat. It was that simple, wasn't it?

Pelle Lundgren had seen something that night.

And that was why he had been murdered.

The others, however?

Benjamin Prytz. Was he just an idiot playboy or was there more to him?

And then the vicar.

Thomas Ofelius.

She would need to ring Gabriel later today to find out if he had discovered anything.

Mia parked her motorcycle by the recycling centre, then continued on foot through the fields and the forest down to Sandstad. She crouched down as she reached a hill about a hundred metres from the mink farm and crawled the remaining distance to a point from which she would have a good view. She made herself comfortable in the heather and took her binoculars out of her bag. It was very quiet.

She had originally joined the National Police Academy for one reason only: Delta, the armed response unit. No woman had ever met their entrance requirements and she had been determined to be the first. She had trained hard all summer. But then they were introduced to this test at the Academy. Photographs of dead bodies along the side of a road.

What do you see?

Her scores had been through the roof. She was headhunted by Munch and left the National Police Academy before the end of her training. She moved her binoculars from west to east. And there they were. Barely visible. Crouching figures that began to move silently across the field. She counted four. Helmets, machine guns, gloves and bulletproof vests. Discreet signals and gestures. *Come. Stop. Down.*

She retrieved her mobile from her pocket and checked the time.

04.57.

There was a second unit by the roadside at the foot of the hill moving stealthily upwards.

04.59.

And then it erupted. Cars appearing out of nowhere, driving at speed up the gravel track.

'Police!'

Doors being kicked open. It was over in a matter of minutes. Bleary-eyed, half-naked men kneeling on the ground. Their hands behind their heads. Mia smiled and returned her binoculars to her bag. She crawled quietly back across the heather, then walked along the forest and the fields the way she had arrived. At her motorcycle she stopped to take out her mobile and texted Simon.

It's sorted.

Your diving problem has gone away.

M.

Right.

Time to get a bit more sleep.

Mia put on her helmet, started the motorcycle and pulled out on the tarmac, which was slowly heating up in the morning sun.

Chapter 52

Munch put his sun hat on the table, passed his iPad to Luca Eriksen and stood up in front of his team.

'Good morning, all. Before I begin, does anyone have anything urgent we need to look at? Anything new?'

Munch looked across the room.

'No? All right. First up. We have received a tip-off which I think we should follow up. A very nice lady called Beth Corneliussen came to my hotel yesterday. I believe she is the chair of the local parish council. It would seem the abbreviations in Jessica's black book are already common knowledge across the island. Good job, everyone. Again we need to be careful and weed out the chaff – I'm talking about village gossip here. But this one seemed legit so, like I said, I think it's worth investigating. She gave me a name, Lars Lolander. Does that ring a bell with anyone?'

Everyone shook their heads.

'Not even you, Luca?'

'No . . . I don't think so. Lolander?' Luca echoed.

'Yes, Lars Lolander,' Munch said. 'An older man, I believe, and a recent arrival. He's also a member of the parish council. Our contact – I mean Beth Corneliussen – came across as credible. She stressed that she was definitely not trying to stir but felt strongly that this was a man we ought to take a closer look at. Obviously, his name, Lolander, but there was another reason. At a meeting yesterday, he turned up with a bandage around his right hand.'

There was murmuring around the room now.

'So,' Munch said, grabbing a dry-wipe pen. He wrote the name on the whiteboard. 'Lars Lolander lives in Hestvika, which I gather isn't very far from Sandstad. At the end of the road going north-east from the church. Am I right?'

Luca nodded.

'Mia and I will visit him.' Munch put down the pen and looked across at his team again. 'Another thing. We have checked Victor Palatin's alibi, which is his visit to Tautra Abbey. Luca?'

'Yes.' Luca took over. 'I spoke to a nun who could confirm that he was there last Saturday. I believe she knows him; he visits them regularly. They even had a cup of coffee together, so he definitely wasn't on Hitra at the time of the murder, no.'

'So,' Munch went on, 'Victor Palatin isn't our killer, but as we discussed yesterday, he admitted having met Jessica on the boat on three occasions, so he is our Vic. At least we have now identified one of the men in Jessica's notebook.'

Kevin Borg opened his mouth, but Munch stopped him.

'Sorry. I also want to add that this morning I had a very interesting phone call from a lawyer, whose name I can't remember, but he rang to tell me that he represents Benjamin Prytz and that they would like to meet with us today. So that they can explain, as he put it, *my client's part in this unfortunate business.*'

Ralph Nygaard whistled softly. He was wearing a Springsteen T-shirt again today.

'His part?' he said, looking around the room. 'That's an admission, isn't it?'

'Not necessarily,' Munch said. 'Mia and I had a quick word with Benjamin Prytz the other day and he has already told us that he knew Jessica. *A bit*, as he put it, but nothing more than that.'

'But his car was seen in the marina?' Nina Riccardo said. 'Last Saturday?'

'Correct,' Munch said. 'The owner of the boat saw Benjamin Prytz's car parked near the marina. It's a bright yellow Lamborghini.'

'I don't think that's his only car,' Kevin Borg remarked.

'Maybe not,' Munch said. 'But it was the one sighted by our man, the pirate captain Roger . . .'

Scattered laughter across the room.

'. . . But,' Munch went on, holding up a finger. 'Not at the time we're focusing on. This was earlier in the day.'

'But we still think that he's Big B?' Riccardo said.

'He's at the top of the list.' Munch nodded and looked back at Ralph Nygaard.

'How did you get on with your B? The bodybuilder? Any success?'

'Yes,' Ralph Nygaard said. 'Or rather, belated success, but no real success, no. He returned home yesterday after having taken part in the Sandefjord Open – it's a meet for bodybuilders. I wanted to check his alibi before I told you and, yes, it holds up. He won bronze in the category Men's Physique. I have a picture here, from the Internet, if you want to . . .'

He held up his mobile and looked around.

'So he wasn't at home,' Nina Riccardo said. 'But did he know her? He could still be our Big B, even if he wasn't on Hitra and so couldn't have killed her?'

She turned to Munch, who nodded.

'Yes, sorry, of course he could,' Ralph Nygaard said. 'He claimed that he didn't know Jessica, didn't know anything about the boat and had never heard of her until someone told him that a young woman had been murdered on the island.'

'OK,' Munch said. 'So we can't eliminate him yet, but I have a feeling that we might learn the identity of Big B once we meet with Benjamin Prytz and his lawyer today.'

'When are we meeting him?' Mia said.

'We've agreed ten o'clock,' Munch said, and continued. 'Pelle Lundgren's post-mortem report is ready and shows what we could see at the scene. Pelle Lundgren died from stab wounds to his neck.'

'Do we still think the two deaths are connected?' Claus Nielsen said.

'Yes,' Mia said.

'As you know, throughout yesterday we received several reports of previous sightings of Pelle Lundgren near Setervågen marina,' Munch carried on. 'Also in the company of Jessica.'

'And we think he was there the evening she was killed, is that right?' Nina Riccardo said.

'He must have been,' Mia said.

'He doesn't have to have been—' Munch began, but Mia cut him off.

'Yes, I believe so. I think he was there that evening and that he saw the killer. We know that only one road leads to the marina. I think that Pelle saw the killer, perhaps even spoke to him. Pelle couldn't know that Jessica's body was lying in the boat, but he would join the dots once the news of her death became public knowledge. So the killer decided to murder him, too, and time was of the essence.'

'OK,' Munch said. 'Like I said, we can't be sure, but let's explore that theory all the same. When did news of Jessica's murder become known across the island?'

He looked to Luca.

'Sometime Sunday morning.' Luca nodded.

'So we're looking for someone who met Pelle that Sunday or Monday?' Nygaard said.

'Yes,' Munch said. 'If our theory is correct. If Pelle Lundgren was murdered because he witnessed something, then he must have met the killer during that period.'

'Unless Pelle spoke to the killer on Saturday evening?' Nina Riccardo suggested.

'Good point, Nina,' Munch said. He could feel himself warming to this diligent investigator more and more. 'Either that conversation took place by the boat on the night of the murder or sometime during the next two days. What do you think, Mia?'

Mia had been lost in her own thoughts, but now she woke up again.

'Yes, let's say that. If it happened Saturday evening, we have no witnesses, so let's hope for our sake that it happened on the Sunday or the Monday.'

'Just so that I can keep up here,' Ralph Nygaard said cautiously, running a hand over his head, 'we're now discussing when the killer learned that Lundgren was going on his Jupiter trip, aren't we?'

'That's right,' Munch said. 'If Pelle didn't tell the killer on the Saturday, and Pelle thought he was leaving for Jupiter early

Tuesday morning, then it must have happened between Sunday and Monday. So who was it? That's our absolute top priority today. To whom did Pelle Lundgren speak in the period from Sunday morning to . . . how long did it take us to drive out to the nature reserve?'

'Twenty minutes. It would have taken him longer on his bicycle,' Nina Riccardo said.

'Good point. So let's say that he left his home an hour before,' Munch said. 'Then we're talking about all of Sunday until 2 a.m. Tuesday morning. Who was he seen with? I want us to go over this with a fine-tooth comb. Everyone will pitch in on this one, all right?'

Munch took his cigarettes out from his pocket.

'He didn't have a phone, did he?' Claus Nielsen said.

'No,' Munch said. 'For some reason Pelle Lundgren didn't have a phone, so he must have physically met the person in question. All hands on deck on this one.'

'Including me?' Luca said.

'Yes, especially you. You know the people out here better than any of us. It could be that some of the locals still resent us snooping around their island.'

He stuck a cigarette in his mouth.

'Are we all clear?' Nodding across the room. 'Good. I'll see you all here later.'

Chapter 53

Munch picked up a key from Ruth in the hotel reception, and he and Mia entered the lift. She pressed the button for the fourth floor, leaned against the mirrored wall, shook her head, then pointed to his hat.

'So what's that all about?'

'My hat?' He looked past her and studied himself in the mirror.

'Yes,' Mia said. 'It's not boiling hot today, is it? And yet you're still wearing it.'

'Don't you like it?'

'I don't know. Is that your signature look from now on? Sherlock Holmes has his deerstalker. Poirot has his moustache. And you have . . . well? A sun hat?'

She didn't even try to hide her smile as the lift doors opened and they let themselves into the big meeting room. Mia got a text message and stopped to check her phone while Munch hung his hat on a hat stand and stepped out on to the balcony. He looked across the landscape as he took a cigarette from the packet. Perhaps he should just move up here? Commandeer this room as his office? It was a tempting thought. He had called Lillian back, but she hadn't picked up. Instead she had sent him another text message.

It's about your stuff. I've packed your things.

You can pick them up at your convenience.

A convoy of trucks climbed the road below, making their way towards the centre of Fillan.

'What do you think that's all about?' Munch called out to Mia as he pointed.

Mia joined him and looked over the railings.

'A travelling fair, I think. SummerFillan.'

'SummerFillan?'

She took a bite of an apple she had taken from a fruit bowl on the table.

'An annual event on Hitra. A kind of summer festival. Stalls and tombolas and candyfloss and yes, a travelling funfair.'

She nodded down towards the trucks that had turned right at the roundabout and were moving slowly towards the town centre.

'And when will the festivities begin?'

'Saturday,' Mia said, munching her apple.

'So that means thousands of people here?' Munch heaved a sigh. 'There's the wedding, the media and drunken revellers all happening at the same time?'

The door to the meeting room opened. The lawyer was exactly as Munch had imagined him. Suit, tie, a mousy appearance with a pointy nose sticking out below a pair of round spectacles in a steel frame. Benjamin Prytz looked as he had the last time they had seen him. Grinning with his pearly-white teeth, his hair slicked back. White shirt, open with a cravat, a pink one today. He reminded Munch of the rich daddy's boys from Bærum, with access to so much money they thought they owned the world at the age of twenty.

He asked them to sit down at the table and took a seat opposite them.

'So.' The lawyer cleared his throat. 'As we all know, there was an incident here last Saturday—'

'Let's skip all that and get to the point,' Munch said. 'Did you meet with Jessica last Saturday?'

Benjamin Prytz glanced at his lawyer, who nodded.

'I did. Yes,' Benjamin Prytz confirmed.

'And when was this?' Munch said.

'Well, when was it? About noon? About that time.'

'And what was the purpose of your visit?'

The lawyer intervened.

'I would like to stress at this point that my client is not admitting

to an offence of any kind. Any references to such are purely theor-
etical and should be viewed only as an indication that my client is
keen to cooperate, that he would like to clear his name and help the
police in their efforts.'

'Now I don't understand half of what you just said, but we're not
talking about a criminal offence as such, are we?' Munch said.
'However, morally things might be a little different. Having sex
with a sixteen-year-old girl, I mean.'

'What?' Benjamin Prytz exclaimed. 'Having sex with her? Do I
look like somebody who needs to chat up chavs to get laid?' He
laughed. 'Are you out of your mind?'

'Benjamin,' his lawyer warned him.

'No, I mean it. Seriously, is that what you're thinking?'

'We think nothing at all,' Munch said. 'You were the one who
called this meeting. We're just here to listen to what you have
to say.'

'Good God,' Benjamin Prytz said, and shook his head. 'Is that
what people out here are saying now? That I was having it off with
Jessica Bakken in that trashy boat of hers? Bloody peasants. I can't
wait until this blasted wedding is over. Come Sunday I'm out of
here.'

He made a propeller gesture with one hand.

'So what were you doing in the marina?'

'Scoring drugs,' Benjamin Prytz said. 'What else?'

The lawyer intervened once again.

'Now it's important, as I said earlier, that we all understand that
at this point my client is not admitting to—'

'Sure, sure,' Munch said, dismissing him with a wave of his hand.
'For personal use?'

'Not my personal use, no,' Benjamin Prytz said. 'But I may have
sampled the goods from time to time.'

'Why go to her specifically?' Mia said.

'You mean, why did I buy drugs from her rather than anyone
else?'

'Yes.'

'Really good gear.' He raised his eyebrows. 'She was trash, but her drugs were class, if I can put it like that.' He grinned. And then he winked.

'Benjamin,' his lawyer warned him again.

'Yes, sorry,' Benjamin Prytz said, running his hand over his hair. 'I know that she's dead and RIP et cetera and all that – fine, I will control myself. Jessica Bakken sold great drugs. Everyone knew that. And that's why I was there that Saturday, all right?'

'Did you go there often?' Munch said.

'No, not often.' Benjamin Prytz hesitated. 'I wouldn't say so. I guess I've been there a dozen times, possibly.'

'But you don't live in Norway?' Mia said.

'No, I live in London.'

'And how many times have you been back home this year?'

Benjamin Prytz smiled wryly. 'OK, I see what you're doing. Fine. I tended to stop by whenever I was on the island, all right? There's nothing else to do out here. And, like I said, it was good gear. First class. That's not exactly illegal, is it?'

His lawyer heaved a sigh.

'It kind of is,' Munch said. 'But we have bigger fish to fry. Do you remember which dates you were home this year?'

Benjamin Prytz ran his hand over his hair again. 'The exact dates? No, I would need to check that.'

'Could it be these?'

Munch took out a piece of paper from his pocket, a photocopy of one of the pages in Jessica's black book.

Benjamin Prytz studied the dates.

'Yes, that sounds about right.' He grinned. 'Big B, is that me?'

'We think so.'

'Nice nickname. And who are the other guys? Vic? Mr LOL?'

'We were hoping you might be able to tell us.'

'The names of her other customers? I've no idea. I thought it was the whole island.'

He pushed the piece of paper back across the table.

'Try again,' Munch said, pushing it back. 'Mr LOL?'

Benjamin Prytz looked at the paper again. Then he shook his head.

'Did you go to the party?' Mia said.

Benjamin Prytz glanced at her sideways. 'Are you referring to that bunker party out in the nature reserve?'

'Yes? The costume party. Were you there?'

Benjamin Prytz looked at his lawyer. 'What do they take me for? Why would I hang out with a bunch of village idiots?'

'So you weren't there?' Munch said.

'Hmmm, let me think . . .' He rested his finger on his chin and laughed briefly. 'No, I didn't go to that party. Are we done? I need to get home and pretend to care about whales.'

'Whales?'

'Forget it. Are we done?' He looked at the lawyer again, who in turn looked at Munch.

Munch nodded. 'I think we have what we need,' he said. 'Unless you have something, Mia?'

'No,' Mia said.

'Then we would like to thank you for a constructive conversation,' the lawyer said, getting up. 'I hope I can count on all parties to appreciate that, given my client's position here on the island, then it is important for him and his family that everyone exercises discretion about our—'

'Sure, sure,' Munch said.

'Great.' The lawyer nodded. 'Here's my card, in case you need anything else from us.'

The lawyer then accompanied Benjamin Prytz to the lift.

'He was sleeping with her,' Mia said when the doors had closed.

'You think so?'

'Yes.'

She took another bite of her apple.

'How can you be so sure?'

'The black book,' Mia said, nodding towards the photocopy. 'He said it himself, didn't he? She sold drugs to a lot of people. But she only recorded three names. Vic has already admitted why he was there. Three clients. Benjamin, Victor Palatin and Mr LOL.'

'Loathsome little shit,' Munch mumbled.

'Spoiled brat,' Mia said. 'He's probably never done a day's work in his life.'

'So Lolander is next?' Munch said, taking his sun hat from the stand.

Mia nodded and followed him out through the door.

Chapter 54

'Goodness me!' Lissie's mother exclaimed, shielding her eyes under the brim of her red hat. 'Is that what we're going in?'

She pointed to the enormous white yacht anchored in the bay.

'Yes,' Lissie Norheim said, and slipped her arm around her mother. 'That will be fun, won't it?'

'I can barely believe my own eyes.' Her mother giggled and covered her mouth with her hand. 'It's like being in a movie. Don't you think so?'

Lissie smiled and nodded, except that wasn't entirely true. To begin with oh, yes. She had had to pinch herself over and over. Alexander had shown her a life she could never have imagined, even in her wildest dreams. But now? It was the strangest thing. She had grown used to it all so quickly. Though parts of her were still resisting, refusing to let go completely of her old self, she was slowly turning into someone else.

'Over here, Eva,' her father called out from further down the quay. 'The water is crystal clear. There are lots of crabs here. Come and have a look.'

'He's as excited as a little kid.' Her mother smiled and skipped across the concrete.

Alexander came walking towards her. He dropped his mobile into his pocket and shook his head.

'Turns out they won't be joining us after all.'

'Oh, no?'

He let out a light sigh.

'I must say I'm starting to have had enough of him.'

'Yes, what a shame,' Lissie said, but she didn't mean it, not really.

Soon Benjamin would be her family, too, but she just could not make herself like him. For starters, he had a tendency to brag and would frequently get very drunk, then there was the way he looked at her. It was unpleasant. Once the two of them had been alone during a garden party and he had leaned towards her, his gaze swimming.

'Do you really want to marry into this family? You've no idea what you're getting yourself into. Our lot? Good luck.'

Fortunately, Alexander had turned up and told Benjamin to go to bed.

Alexander waved across the bay to the captain on the yacht, who lowered a small boat into the water, climbed down the ladder and sailed ashore to pick them up. He glanced quickly at her parents, who were still pointing at the creatures in the sea.

'Listen, Lissie,' he said, pulling her aside. 'There's something I need to tell you.'

'Oh?'

'You know the other night when I said I had to go outside to take a call?'

'Yes?'

And there it was. She had lain awake almost the whole night worrying about it.

'That wasn't entirely true, I'm sorry,' Alexander said, looking very remorseful.

'You didn't get a phone call?'

'No, I got a text from Benjamin asking me to meet him in the garden. He said that something had happened.'

'Gosh,' Lissie said. 'What was it?'

'I don't know the details,' Alexander said, glancing at her parents again. 'But he had got himself mixed up in something. Something to do with Jessica Bakken.'

'The girl who was found murdered?'

'Yes. I'm really sorry that I lied to you, but he asked me, well . . . to keep it in the family, if you understand what I mean.'

She put her arms around him and gave him a big hug.

'Thank you.'

'For what?'

'For telling me.'

'Why wouldn't I? I don't want us to have secrets from each other.' He caressed her cheek and looked into her eyes.

'Of course not.'

'Just two more days,' he said with a smile. 'Then you, too, will be family. And then he can't use that excuse any more.'

'So . . . how did it go?'

Lissie took his hand and walked with him down towards the wooden jetty.

'How did what go?'

'You said just now that he had got himself mixed up in something. With that girl? Surely he had nothing to do with—'

Alexander stopped in his tracks and shook his head.

'What? No, no. Of course not. Benjamin is a problem in many ways, but he's definitely not violent. Drugs, however. He gets high a lot. He and that – pardon my language – tart he hangs out with. Jessica Bakken was dealing, I believe. I don't know what, but he used to go down there every time he was back home. Someone saw him there last Saturday. The same day she was killed.'

'Good heavens,' Lissie said. 'So what happens now?'

'Nothing, I don't think.' Alexander shrugged. 'Benjamin and our lawyer had a meeting with the police earlier today. Benjamin has just texted me "OK" so I'm guessing that everything has been taken care of.'

'Let's hope so,' Lissie said, squeezing his hand.

Her parents smiled and joined them on the jetty as the captain moored the small boat and climbed up to meet them.

'So?' the captain dressed in white said, and greeted them with a nod. 'Where would you like to go today? Iceland?'

'Iceland?' Her mother giggled. 'Did you hear that, Henrik?'

Her father chuckled and raised his camera from its strap around his neck. First he took a picture of the yacht in the distance, then one of the captain.

'I'm joking, of course,' the captain said. 'You wanted to go whale watching, am I right?'

'Will we see blue whales?' her father asked.

'That's unlikely,' the captain said. 'But we're very likely to see orcas and dolphins.'

'How about we sail to Smøla?' Alexander suggested.

'Yes, let's start there.' The captain smiled and offered Lissie's mother his arm. 'Shall we?'

Chapter 55

Hannah Holmen checked out the two books she had found using the scanner by the library door. She skimmed the list and nodded happily to herself when she realized that none of the books she still had at home were overdue. She put the books in her bag and went up to the counter.

'Hello, Hannah,' said Liv, the librarian.

'Hello, Liv,' Hannah said.

'Did you find something that took your fancy today?'

Hannah liked Liv. She reminded her of how her mother used to be. Funny, with warmth in her eyes. Hannah had a flashback to her old life.

'Look, Hannah, there are eggs in the bird's nest.'

'Wow.'

'Be careful not to touch them. Do you think we should tidy up or have fun today?'

'Have fun!'

'Yes, two. But I didn't find these,' Hannah said, taking out her mobile.

'Which ones?' the librarian said, and went over to her screen.

It was great that Hitra had a library, but it was quite a small one and they didn't have very many books. Hannah came here often; it was a place of refuge for her when everything outside threatened to overwhelm her. She had a corner where she tended to sit. It was behind the shelf with poetry, where no one ever went. There was a vending machine with hot chocolate and, sometimes, if Hannah didn't have any money, Liv would bring her a cup for free and would raise a finger to her lips and wink.

293

'Let's see,' Hannah said, scrolling on her phone. 'Do you have *The Magus* by John Fowles?'

'Oh,' Liv said. 'You want to borrow that? It's very good.'

'Someone recommended it to me.' Hannah smiled.

Several hours. Almost the whole evening.

She had left the chat window open, though they didn't have much to say to each other towards the end.

Each with their book. In separate beds. A short message from time to time, that was all.

How far have you got?

Page 67.

Is it still good?

Yes, very, and yours?

'Was it just the one? Or do you have others?'

'Quite a few, if you don't mind. Do you have *The Birds* by Tarjei Vesaas?'

'Good heavens!' Liv exclaimed. 'You're ordering some very grown-up books. How exciting.'

He had suggested several titles. Funny, really. How quickly you could get to know someone in such a short space of time.

'There,' Liv said when she had finished entering the order. 'Do you want me to call you when they arrive?'

'Yes, please.' Hannah smiled and went out to get her bicycle.

Trailers were lined up behind Hjorten Hotel and workers were already busy setting up. It was the same funfair that visited Hitra every year.

Hannah pushed her bicycle down to the common and took a seat on a bench. She felt sad again now. SummerFillan Festival. Family fun during the day, concerts for young people in the evening. She hadn't been for a long time. Not since Jonathan went missing. She had thought about going this year, but no.

Not after Jessica.

She was really struggling to cope with it all. She just wanted to be at home. In bed with her laptop. Hannah was about to get up when a door opened nearby and Cynthia Prytz appeared. She walked away quickly and looked about her as she did so. She was heading to her car, which was parked not far from the bench where Hannah was sitting, and as she did so, she took her mobile out of her bag.

Hannah looked up towards the door Cynthia Prytz had come through. It was Fabian Stengel's office. Her own psychologist. Something Jessica had said once popped back into Hannah's head. Jessica had practically whispered it.

'I know things about them. Secrets.'

At the time Hannah hadn't paid much attention to it, as Jessica had had a habit of saying outrageous things. But now? After everything that had happened?

Hannah quickly made up her mind, got up and pushed her bicycle closer. She lingered near a tree by the car park, then bent down, pretending to tie her shoelaces. Cynthia Prytz seemed upset. She paced up and down in front of her car, waving her free arm and talking irritably into a mobile.

'No, that's completely out of the question. I said *white* flowers, and that's what I want. No. Absolutely not. Everything in the church must be white. What do you think I'm paying you for?'

The wedding. She was just talking about flower arrangements. Hannah straightened up and shook her head at herself.

Phew. False alarm.

What was wrong with her? She was seeing ghosts everywhere. Hannah got on her bicycle and put on her helmet. Time to go home.

Chapter 56

Hestvika and its harbour showed Munch a rather different side to the island and gave him his first real insight into the local economy. Long, rectangular, anonymous buildings and a small industrial estate comprised what would appear to be warehouses. A large, rusty cargo ship was docked by the quay, men busy unloading something. Not fish, Munch thought, as he could see no cold-storage facilities nearby; besides, they were unlikely to unload fish on Hitra. It was more likely that fish was loaded on to ships and taken to export ports in the Netherlands and Germany before being sent on to the rest of the world. Munch had read somewhere that Norway exported more than 3 million tonnes of fish per year, worth 120 billion kroner. And the government's total income was around what? Around 1.2 trillion kroner? And that was before oil revenue, of course; that was in a league of its own. Recently he had looked at the website of the Norwegian oil fund, where the total value of the fund updated in real time on the screen. A dizzying number, constantly rising.

On the ferry to Hitra he had seen along the coast the numerous fish farms that had become such a contentious issue in recent years. Were they actually a good idea? There had been protests and demonstrations. Representatives from environmental organizations had appeared in heated debates on TV. But still it was hard to argue with 120 billion kroner. It was ten per cent of the government's income. No wonder that lobbyists could come and go as they pleased at the Storting. Except not every krone went into the government's coffers, of course, Munch had just seen evidence of that. The Prytz family and others like them. Vast fortunes in private hands.

Four big, grey-blue metal silos loomed behind the trees. Industry intruded on the otherwise beautiful landscape, but only for a moment. Munch and Mia rounded a corner and the idyll was back again. Small farms and houses, green fields and swaying trees against the calm, open sea.

Lolander's house was one of the biggest Munch had seen on Hitra. It was white, like most houses out here, with a large garden that reached all the way down to the water's edge. He parked in front of the house and, even at this distance, they could both hear it: the sound of a saw. There was evidence of felling in the yard as well – a tractor with a large log attached by a chain to its rear.

'A banker, was that it?' Mia said, looking about her. The whine of a saw blade echoed across the hillside.

'Retired, I believe.' Munch nodded and walked in front of her around the big house.

They could see him now, a man wearing an orange helmet with a visor and high-visibility utility clothes. Munch waved in his direction and the man waved back. The man removed his helmet, stuffed a glove into his back pocket and started walking down towards them.

'Was it you who called earlier?' he said, wiping sweat from his brow. The sun was behind a few clouds today, but it was still hot.

'Holger Munch,' Munch introduced himself. 'And this is Mia Krüger.'

'Nice to meet you.' The man nodded and held out his left hand.

'Are you Lars Lolander?'

'I am,' the man said, wiping his forehead again. 'Puh, perhaps I shouldn't be working in this heat, but I'm no good at just twiddling my thumbs. It's been a year, and I'm still not used to this life.'

'So you're retired?' Munch said when Lolander had shown them to a sofa on the terrace.

A jug of cordial and a bowl of biscuits sat on the table.

'Yes. Finance. I sell firewood now, as you can probably tell. I need something to keep me busy. Would you like some coffee?'

Munch shook his head and Mia did likewise.

'I've had to give it up.' Lolander smiled. 'Can't handle all that caffeine these days. The body is not the same once you start getting close to seventy.'

'We won't keep you long,' Munch said.

'Is it about that girl?' Lolander asked with interest.

'Yes, perhaps you've heard that we're looking for someone?'

'No,' Lolander said. 'Or should I say, I really hope that you're looking for someone, that you're not here on holiday?'

Another smile flitted across his tanned face. Munch looked for sarcasm in his voice, but the man appeared to be sincere.

'Did you know her?' Mia said.

'The girl, no,' Lolander said, helping himself to a biscuit. 'I don't spend a lot of time in there.'

He nodded towards the forest.

'In town, I mean. I'm a member of the parish council, but that's about it. I have had enough of people to last me a lifetime. Endless meetings, day in, day out. In the end you get fed up with it, and now I'm enjoying some peace and quiet.'

'And you're a man of faith?' Mia said.

'Yes, I would say so,' Lolander said. 'It's hard to believe that all this beauty happened by accident, isn't it?'

He nodded towards the water. The cargo ship that had been docked in the harbour had finished its business and was sailing slowly out towards the open sea.

'I notice you're wearing a bandage,' Munch said. 'An accident?'

'Ugh, yes, that was a close call.'

Lolander held up his hand and shook his head at himself.

'My wife is always on at me; she keeps telling me to be careful. And I've learned my lesson now, trust me – I could easily have lost a finger or two.'

He pointed up towards the cut-off saw.

'Fortunately it was just a splinter.'

'May we have a look?' Munch said.

'A look?' Lolander said.

Munch nodded towards the bandage.

'Yes. At what's underneath it?'

'You want me to take off my bandage? Why?'

There was an expression in his eyes now which Munch couldn't quite fathom.

'Just doing our job,' Munch said. 'We would like to eliminate people as quickly as possible.'

'Eliminate?' Lolander echoed, and frowned. 'Does that mean you think I'm—'

'No, no,' Munch said.

'Who told you I might have something to do with it?' Lolander said in a rather sharp tone of voice, and rested his bandaged hand in his lap.

'We're just following procedure,' Munch said. 'Please may we . . .'

Lolander heaved a sigh and placed his hand on the table.

'Is this really necessary? I've just put on a fresh one.'

'Just a quick peek,' Munch said.

'Very well.' Lolander grunted and removed the small clip that held the bandage in place.

He unravelled the gauze and showed them the palm of his hand. There was a circular wound in the middle of it.

'It went in here,' Lolander said, pointing. 'It went deep into my palm. A large splinter that came off a log. Satisfied?'

He shook his head and started putting the bandage back on.

'Where were you on Saturday?' Mia wanted to know.

'On Saturday? Here at home? Why?'

'Like I said, we're asking everyone we—' Munch began, but Lolander cut him off.

'And I think that's enough for now,' he said, getting up. 'I've got work to do. Is there anything else?'

'No, that was all. Thank you for your help.'

Once they were back by the car, Munch took a cigarette out of the packet.

'Waste of time.'

'Yes,' Mia said, looking across the field. 'Who tipped you off?'

'Beth Corneliussen. She's the chair of the parish council.'

'Perhaps we should take a closer look at her?'

'Her?' Munch laughed out loud.

'Yes?'

'I don't think she could even hurt a fly.'

Mia was about to say something, but they were interrupted by Munch's mobile ringing.

'Yes, Munch speaking.'

'It's Borg,' an eager Kevin Borg said on the other end. 'I think I've got something.'

'OK?'

'I've just been speaking to one of Pelle Lundgren's neighbours,' Borg continued breathlessly. It sounded as if he were running.

'This neighbour had seen Lundgren talking to someone. Sunday morning. She came out of his house.'

'Who?'

'Her name is Xandra,' Kevin Borg said. He appeared to have reached his car: Munch could hear the sound of a car door opening.

'Kassandra?'

'No, with an X. Xandra. She lives out on Fjellværsøya. I'm on my way there now.'

'I'm coming with you,' Munch said, getting into his own car. 'Meet me at the hotel.'

Chapter 57

Kevin Borg was waiting outside Hjorten Hotel, next to his car, its engine idling. He was so excited that he was practically bouncing from foot to foot. Munch parked his car and got out.

'Do you want to come with us?' He looked at Mia, who shook her head.

'I've got a few things to check out.'

'OK, call me later.'

She nodded and went to get her motorcycle.

'I'll drive,' Kevin Borg said, gesturing for Munch to take the passenger seat.

'So you know the roads out here well?' Munch said once he had put on his seatbelt and Kevin Borg had joined the main road.

The 714. Munch could visualize it now. The 714, which forked, going north-west to Frøya and north-east to Fjellværsøya. The 713 went only around Hitra.

He had pondered this repeatedly. He still couldn't work out how it was possible for no one to have seen anything. Not three years ago, and not last Saturday. True, they had got a few sightings from the Saturday, but nothing useful so far. A blue Ford with hollering passengers. A suspicious-looking cyclist, not near the crime scene but further away. It was day six and he could feel the clock ticking. He knew how people's memories changed even after a surprisingly short space of time. He had attended a fascinating seminar once about observations and memory. The more time passed, the more diffuse people's recollections became. Old memories would slowly be replaced by newer ones.

I thought I saw Olav down there?

An observation that could be real, only not at the right time.

Wasn't that Harald's car?

An entirely fictitious memory, created by the desire to be helpful, to contribute.

'Some friends of mine have a cabin out there,' Kevin Borg said, and took the fork to Fjellværsøya. 'I've visited them a few times. I think I might even have seen her as well, come to think of it. She might be the one who runs that Troll's Nest.'

'Troll's Nest?'

'Yes, that's its name. It's a house out there. Lots of . . .' He gestured in an effort to explain. 'Well, what do you call it? Colours and hippie stuff all over the place.'

'We're talking about Xandra?'

'Yes. And, oops, I almost forgot. You remember I paid a visit to the hairdresser's? After the break-in?'

'Yes?'

'That was her,' Kevin Borg said, snapping his fingers.

'The hairdresser?'

'No, no, the woman who collects the hair. Do you remember me telling you? That the hairdresser saves waste hair for an artist or something, who uses it for, well, I don't remember exactly what. That's her. She's the artist who wants the hair. You get me?'

He grinned at Munch, who opened his window. The sun was baking hot again, warming the landscape, which out here was even more magical. Windswept crags beyond green fields and the sea glittering below. Two deer skipped along a field before disappearing into a cluster of trees.

'I think we're on to something here.'

Kevin Borg nodded contentedly and turned on the radio.

'What do you think?'

'Do you mind?' Munch said with a glance at the radio.

'Silence?'

'Yes, please,' Munch said.

'Bloody good food down there,' Kevin Borg said, pointing to a sign. 'Prawns, crayfish and so on. They even do a box of seafood which you can have delivered to your cabin.'

'So you've been here often?'

'No, just a few times. They're friends of my ex-wife, so we're talking quite a few years ago. But then Luca mentioned Fjellværsøya and, like I said, I know exactly where that is.'

He changed gears, pulled out and overtook a campervan. Bridges now, two of them, as the landscape around them opened up even more.

'It's beautiful out here,' Kevin Borg said. 'If Hitra is the oyster, then this is the pearl.'

He turned down a gravel track and fell silent for a few minutes until they reached the water's edge, where a beautiful white sandy beach lined the bay.

'Welcome to Fjellværsøya,' Kevin Borg said as he got out of the car.

He arched his back and nodded.

'The hippie house is up there among the trees.'

'But you chose to park here?' Munch said.

'Always best to take people by surprise, don't you think?'

Kevin Borg winked at Munch and led the way across the road.

Chapter 58

Mia parked her motorcycle in the shade under a tree and paused in front of the church. A window high up on the side of the church was ajar and she could hear a choir of children. Beautiful, vibrating, delicate voices accompanied by a piano, which could perhaps have been played by more skilled hands. A large white van was parked in the car park. *Goldstar Events*. For the wedding, of course; the final details were being put in place. A woman was bossing about two younger women, who were busy fetching things from the van.

Mia walked over to the vicarage and rang the doorbell. She waited, but there was no reply. And why would there be? The sun was bouncing off the sparkling sea below the house. The old woman was probably in her garden or on the terrace; if she was even at home, that is.

Mia walked around the house and discovered that she was right. Dorothea Krogh was dozing in a chair underneath a parasol. Her spectacles had slipped down her nose and a crossword puzzle was lying on the terrace by her feet.

OK, better not disturb her.

She could do this later.

'Hello?'

Mia had just walked back around the house when she heard the voice.

'Hello?'

Mia returned and saw Dorothea Krogh push her glasses in place. She looked a little confused.

'Is anyone there?'

'I'm sorry, it's just me, Mia Krüger, from the police. I didn't mean to disturb you. I don't mind coming back later.'

'No, no,' the old lady said, gesturing for her to come closer. 'You're more than welcome.'

Dorothea Krogh looked about her with a frown before she realized that she was still wearing her reading glasses. She took them off and replaced them with another pair of spectacles in a case on the table.

'There, that's better.' She smiled. 'I must have nodded off for a moment. Come, take a seat. 'I'm afraid I'm out of coffee. Shall I make another pot?'

'No, there's no need,' Mia said, perching on the edge of a bench.

'I hope no more terrible things have happened? I think we've had enough of them.' She shook her head in despair.

'No, it's nothing like that,' Mia said. 'I just wanted to see you. You know absolutely everybody out here, don't you?'

'Oh, I used to. Not these days. Still, eighty years in the same place will give you some local knowledge. How can I help?'

'Anita Holmen? Do you know her?'

'Not well, but I know who she is, of course.'

The old woman nodded in the direction of the churchyard.

'She comes here often. She visits the empty grave. I've tried not to intrude, but I couldn't help myself the other day. I went over to see if there was anything I could do. But she wasn't terribly interested. Poor woman.'

'Who is the boy's father, do you know?'

'Jonathan's father, you mean?'

'Yes.'

'Well ...' She hesitated, looking at Mia over the rim of her spectacles.

'So you do know?'

'No, no,' the old woman said. 'I don't know for sure, but yes, there were rumours.'

'Go on.'

Dorothea Krogh leaned forward and whispered.

'Well, you didn't hear it from me, but rumour has it that it might be ... Roar.'

'What?' Mia exclaimed. 'Do you mean Roar Wold, who runs the garage?'

'I can't say for certain, but that's what people say.'

Dorothea Krogh winked and pointed to a dark bottle on the table.

'How about a glass of port? Can I tempt you?'

'I'm driving,' Mia said. 'And I don't want to keep you. Just a few more questions. Is that all right?'

'Of course. What do you want to know?'

'Beth Corneliussen? What can you tell me about her?'

Dorothea Krogh laughed out loud.

'Beth? Oh, I think you're barking up the wrong tree there. She's so law-abiding the good Lord must surely have a special seat reserved for her in heaven. Unless even He finds her a little too much. Oh, she makes the rest of us come across as regular villains.'

'OK,' Mia said. 'I have another name, and I'm sorry if this puts you in a tricky position.'

'Oh, don't worry about it. Nothing shocks me these days, my dear. Let me have it.'

'Thomas Ofelius,' Mia said. 'The new vicar.'

Dorothea Krogh fell silent at this point.

'Well,' the old woman said at last. 'What can I tell you?'

She interlaced her fingers and looked across her garden for a moment.

'I don't know about you,' Mia said, 'but I just feel that, well, there's something that doesn't quite add up about him, isn't there?'

'You can say that again,' Dorothea Krogh said with a cough.

'Do you know him well?'

'No, I wouldn't say that. He has barely been here a year.'

'Did he take over after your husband?'

'What? No, no. We had a woman vicar here after my husband. Impressive lady. I had to fight the parish council to appoint her, but I got my own way in the end. I usually do. But I don't think she ever really liked it here. It's a very small congregation. And many – how can I put it? – prejudices, you know. And then there was something about a sick mother down south, so it seemed a good excuse for her to go.'

'And how did Ofelius get the job?'

'Well, we advertised. *Vicar wanted.* And he was the only applicant.'

'You helped interview him?'

'Yes.'

'And what did you think at the time?'

'What can I say? He was very shy, quite nervous. He was straight out of the seminary and had never worked as a vicar before. Still, everyone deserves a chance, don't they? I thought that it would probably be all right in the end.'

'And how is it going?'

'All right, more or less.'

'Does he need a lot of support?'

'Well, what do you think? Now I mustn't sit here claiming to be better than everybody else. He does need a bit of help, but his sermons are good, I think. Give him a bit more time and he'll be just fine, you'll see.'

'There is paperwork involved in such appointments, am I right?'

'You mean an enhanced criminal-record check?'

'Yes? Did you ever see his?'

'Oh, yes, I did. There was nothing to see there, of course not, that's not what I was hinting at. He's just a bit . . . effeminate. Can I say that?'

'OK. That was all I wanted to know,' Mia said, getting up. 'Thanks for your help.'

'Is that it?' Dorothea Krogh said, she sounded almost disappointed.

'Yes, that was all.'

'That's a shame. I was almost starting to feel like a character in an Agatha Christie novel.'

Dorothea Krogh smiled, then she saw Mia out. Once Mia was back in the car park, Dorothea Krogh called out to her.

'Just let me know if you have any more questions.'

She smiled, then tapped her nose with her finger.

'Miss Marple, you know.'

'I will.' Mia waved to her.

And headed for her motorcycle.

Chapter 59

Kevin Borg hadn't exaggerated in his description of the location. While he might have been a bit pejorative, overall he had been pretty accurate. Munch didn't see any trolls, but he could definitely see a nest. There were several buildings, most of them crooked and very colourful. The place lay somewhat hidden, but it hadn't been hard to find. On their walk up here they had seen little hints of what they could expect. A garden gnome. A small, pink elk. A home-made sign with the wording *Nirvana 200m*. Munch could see no cars, but an electric bicycle with a trailer was parked in front of a building that actually looked like a nest. Woven twigs covered the walls. There was moss on the roof and, for some reason, a slalom boot.

'Oh, cripes, she's naked,' Kevin Borg yelped as they spotted a woman in a vegetable patch below the house.

'Hello!' the woman called out, and waved to them. 'Have you come to visit?'

'We're from the police,' Munch shouted back, and held up his warrant card.

'I'm on my way,' she responded, and started running towards them.

'Please would you get dressed first?' Munch called out to her.

'Pardon?' she said, and stopped.

'Some clothes?' he called back to her. 'Please would you put some clothes on first?'

The woman laughed and took a detour through the garden so that she ended up near the house without them seeing her.

She reappeared shortly in a dress that she had pulled over her head. It looked Indian, with intricate patterns and some fringing here and there.

'Right, so you're shy?' The woman laughed. 'I thought men were less uptight these days. And who do we have here?'

She stopped in front of them and planted her hands on her hips. Her hair was blonde and styled in long, thick dreadlocks which she had decorated with colourful feathers, a cork and a small bell; there was a rich display of ornaments in her fascinating mane. Kevin Borg stuck out his hand to her.

'Kevin Borg, investigator from Trondheim Police, and this is Holger Munch, a senior investigator from Oslo.'

'Er, all right?' Munch said with a nod.

The woman pressed her palms together and bowed slightly.

'Namaste, boys. So what are two nice police officers doing all the way out here? Did you get lost looking for Sasquatch?'

She had bright blue eyes and smiled at them with incredibly white teeth. Her face was beautiful, but could nevertheless do with a wash after her gardening.

'Sas— what?' Kevin Borg said.

'I think she means Bigfoot,' Munch said.

'Aha.' The woman winked. She pointed to Munch. 'I like you. But I don't really get you. A tie? On a day like this? Isn't that incredibly uncomfortable?'

Kevin Borg cleared his throat and nodded to the main building.

'Do you live here?'

'Yes.' The woman smiled and flung out her arms. 'Welcome to Nirvana. My own little paradise.'

'And your name is?' Kevin Borg said, taking out a pen and a small notepad.

'My name is Xandra,' she said, bowing again, more deeply this time.

'And your surname?' Kevin Borg said, putting his pen to the notepad.

'It's just Xandra.'

She showed them her white teeth again.

'But you must have a surname,' Kevin Borg insisted. 'One that is listed in the National Population Register, I mean. Do you have a passport or birth certificate we could see?'

He looked at her sternly.

'A birth certificate?' Xandra smiled. 'Well, I'm nearly forty years old. I honestly don't know where it might be.'

'How about a passport?' Kevin Borg grunted impatiently. 'Surely you have a passport?'

Munch had had enough. He pulled Kevin Borg to one side and pointed to the road.

'Go and wait in the car.'

'What?' Kevin Borg said.

'You heard me. I'll join you later.' He gestured towards the road again.

Kevin Borg scowled at him, but he did what he was told. He stuffed his notepad into his pocket and disappeared, still sulking, down the road.

'Oh, strict!' Xandra winked at Munch, taking his arm. 'We like that.'

She ushered him across the yard and inside a colourful verandah. A large dreamcatcher hung from the rafters along with some carved birds.

'Would you like something to drink? Rowanberry wine? I don't know if I have any clean glasses, but we can always drink from the bottle, can't we?' She smiled and started to walk barefoot towards the door.

'No, thanks. I'm all right.'

'Are you sure? Water? Nothing?'

'I'm quite sure.' Munch nodded.

Xandra flopped into a yellow rocking chair and pulled her legs up underneath her.

'So, Mr Policeman, what can I do for you today?'

'I just have a few quick questions.'

'OK?'

'Pelle Lundgren? Did you know him?'

'What do you mean, did I know him?' Xandra said. 'So it was true after all? They really did pick him up?'

'Who—' Munch began.

'The Martians? No, it was Jupiter, wasn't it?' She laughed for a moment. 'I visited him at home not all that long ago, and that's when he told me he had been given a time and a place. So it has finally happened? Who would have thought it?'

'No,' Munch said delicately. 'I regret to tell you that Pelle Lundgren is dead. We found him in Havmyran nature reserve in the early hours of Wednesday morning.'

She looked at him with a frown.

'They left behind his body? They only took his soul?'

Munch coughed.

'Well, he's no longer among the living, as it were.'

'Good for him,' Xandra said, and then she smiled. 'He didn't like being here on Earth very much. To be quite honest with you' – she leaned towards him, whispering – 'I never really believed him. But there you are. It just goes to show how wrong you can be.'

'Eh, yes,' Munch said, stroking his beard. 'So you visited him at his home. When was it?'

'Last . . . Sunday, I believe.'

'May I ask why?'

'You can ask me whatever you like,' she said, and winked at him. 'I was there because he had promised me some of his hair.'

'Yes, I've heard about that,' Munch said. 'That you collect hair? May I ask you what you use it for?'

'This and that. I knit and I weave. I had promised him a jumper. Well, not for now, obviously, but for the winter. I don't work very quickly, you see.'

'So you knit just with hair or with other materials?'

'No, I mix it with yarn. For protection, you know?' She laughed briefly.

'OK, I . . . I get it. We've spoken to Caroline, the hairdresser, and she said that she gives you hair from her clients?'

'Yes, for my loom. I'm working on a very exciting project. It's in the barn. Would you like to have a look?'

'Perhaps some other time,' Munch said. 'But what's it about, just briefly, please?'

'I'm weaving a community wall hanging. I'm trying to include everyone who lives out here in one work of art. These days everyone is so alone, if you know what I mean? It's not good. We need to be together.'

'Is it for an . . . exhibition, then?'

'Oh, I don't know yet. I'm hoping they might display it at the town hall, say. Or in the church? That would be nice. I hear it's all about fish down there these days.'

'The new altarpiece?'

'Yes, have you seen it?'

'I have.'

'Is it as awful as everyone says it is? The Prytz family and God, hand in hand?'

'I did see some salmon, but it wasn't too bad,' Munch said.

'I'm glad to hear it.' She smiled. 'We mustn't forget that they, too, are human.'

Suddenly the expression on her face changed and she stared at him.

'Oh, no!'

She got up from the rocking chair, then cocked her head.

'Grief?' She walked right up close to him and placed her hand on his chest. 'Gosh. Are you really feeling that sad?'

Munch coughed and removed her hand carefully from his shirt.

'I'm fine. Shall we . . .'

He gestured to the rocking chair.

'Hang on, I have something that will help.'

She rushed inside and soon returned with a small, polished black stone.

'Apache tears.' She nodded and slipped it carefully into his shirt pocket. 'Always keep it near your heart. It will help you. I use them myself whenever I'm feeling sad.'

She smiled wistfully and sat down in the rocking chair again.

'Where were we?'

'Right,' Munch said. 'Listen, I think that's about all I have. Oh, yes, I meant to ask, did you know Jessica?'

'The poor girl who was murdered?'

312

'Yes.'

She shook her head.

'No. But I know her mother. She has been out here a few times, looking for weed. The kind you smoke, I mean.'

'But you didn't have any?'

'Oh, yes, I have lots. I grow it myself in the greenhouse, but I didn't take to her. She was rude. And, well, how do I put it? Pushy, is that the right word?'

Munch nodded. 'But not Jessica?'

'No.'

'OK,' Munch said, and struggled to get up from the low chair. 'That was it. Thank you very much. It was nice to meet you.'

'Likewise.' Xandra smiled and walked him out.

Munch stopped and turned.

'Listen, Xandra, can I ask you one more thing?'

'Yes.'

He took a few steps away from her.

'Why do you have a bell in your hair? Isn't it very irritating?'

'What?' Xandra said. 'I have a bell in my hair? Where?'

'There,' Munch said, and pointed.

'So that's what it was.' She laughed. 'I thought the sound was coming from inside my head. Could you remove it, please?'

Munch stepped forwards and carefully freed the bell from her hair.

'Here,' he said.

'Keep it. As a memento of me. Come back some other day, won't you? And we can share that bottle of rowanberry wine.'

'Will do,' Munch said, and started walking down the road.

She waved to him from the yard.

'Remember the stone. Always keep it near your heart.'

Chapter 60

Hannah kicked off her shoes in the hallway and ran up the stairs. Then she had second thoughts and went back to line up her shoes neatly before returning upstairs. She took the library books out of her bag, placed them on her desk, hung her rucksack on the hook by the door and climbed into bed.

She turned on her laptop and waited. It was incredibly slow today; it took ages before the screen finally lit up at her. She clicked on the Internet browser and could feel her heart pound while she waited for it to load.

Friendz. Hannah went straight to BookFans. She could not wait to see who was in the chat room, but soon felt a pang of disappointment. He hadn't logged on. Hannah clicked on his profile.

Ludvig.

The circle by his name was red.

Not online.

Bother. Never mind. Surely she could think of other things to do. She got up and went over to the books she had left on her desk. Picked one and returned to her bed. Hannah turned to the first page and tried to lose herself in the story but found herself unable to concentrate.

She glanced at the screen. Nothing. OK. She pulled herself together; surely she could do better than that. She had cycled all the way to Fillan library, taken out two great books and now she was going to enjoy herself. She was halfway through chapter one when she heard a ping from her laptop.

Ludvig.

Hannah smiled and quickly typed.

Hi, didn't think you were coming today.
He replied quite quickly.
No battery. Had to look for the charger. My room is so messy . . .
He added an emoji of a face with its tongue sticking out.
Hannah replied.
I get you! I'm the same!
She chose the same emoji and pressed *send*.
Strictly speaking, that wasn't true, but so what? Her room was just as neat as it always was. Her mother had been up here again. Everything was in its right place and she could smell the green soap and the detergent her mother used.
Dots on the screen.
So what have you been up to today?
I went to the library.
Same here! Did you find some good books?
A few, but they don't have much out here. So I ordered some books from your list.
She put a big smiley at the end of that last sentence.
This time it took a while before he replied.
Hannah crawled over to the window and opened it a little bit.
There was his reply, thank God.
Is that Hitra? I think you said that's where you live.
She typed her reply quickly.
Yes. Why?
Another long break before his reply came. The dots took for ever.
That's funny. My parents are going there. They have some friends with a cabin. Knarrlagsundet. That's near you, isn't it?
Hannah smiled and typed.
Yes, it is. It's not far at all. When are they coming?
More dots, faster now.
Saturday.
Gosh? His parents were coming to Hitra in just two days? She thought about it, not sure if she should do it, but then she decided to throw caution to the wind.
And what about you? Aren't you coming with them?

315

She chose an emoji with an angel this time. She regretted it immediately, but it was too late now. This time his reply took even longer.
The dots would never end. Yes, now they stopped. But then they
started again. Hannah could feel her heart pound harder; she started
chewing a nail. There it was.

Well. I wasn't going to, but ... what are you up to on
Saturday?

Her fingers flew across the keyboard now.

Nothing special. Are they driving here?

More dots, faster now.

No, taking the express ferry. Their friends are picking them up at
the terminal.

Hannah reconsidered before she replied.

The express ferry? It would be a bit awkward, wouldn't it? His
parents were being met by their friends, and she would have to
stand there, looking stupid and making small talk with everyone
before they got into their friends' car and left.

No, it wasn't going to work. She heaved a sigh and didn't reply.
Another message arrived.

Are you there?

Yes, I'm here.

You've gone quiet?

She chewed her lip and then opted for honesty.

Yes. I was just thinking. It would have been good to meet up, but
it will be quite tricky. With the ferry and the car and everything.

It took a while before he replied.

I could always make them an offer, ha-ha.

What?

Well, I could tell them that I'll come with them if I can have some
time on my own. If they come back and pick me up when I call
them. My mum would be overjoyed.

Hannah smiled.

Why?

She's always on at me about getting some fresh air. She thinks I
spend too much time indoors ...

Hannah laughed to herself.

My mum is the same. So what do you think? How about we meet at the ferry terminal?

Again it took him ages to reply.

OK. I will check the ferry timetable.

Another message arrived.

I need to log off, but I will message you the time, OK?

OK!

She regretted the exclamation mark, but it was no big deal really. Some quick dots.

See you later.

Hannah smiled and replied.

See you later.

She put a big smiley at the end of her last message and turned off her laptop when she could see he was no longer online.

Wow. Meeting up? So soon? No, that was . . .

She leaned back in her bed and tried to focus on the book, but it was no use; she was too excited. Hannah stretched out her arms, then she got out of bed and wandered downstairs to the living room with a smile on her face.

'Mum? Are you in?'

Chapter 61

It was coming up for eleven o'clock at night. The orange sun was setting, still glowing, on the horizon. Mia was back on her island after another briefing. As usual, Munch had tried to keep the team's morale up, but she could tell from the look in his eyes that they were running out of time. Five days. She was an experienced investigator and she knew how it worked. As long as everything was fresh, there was no problem. But five days? Five days quickly turned into a week. One week quickly turned into two. Then a month. They would have nothing to show for their efforts. Some of the investigators would be reassigned to other, more pressing cases. And Munch couldn't stay on Hitra for ever. He had been flown up here because he was supposed to be the best. Because he got results. Who knew how much time they would give him if he failed to deliver?

She checked her mobile: she had two missed calls. Mia walked across the rocks to the jetty and pressed on the first number.

'Yes, Roar?'

The mechanic from the garage, it sounded as if he was eating.

'You called me?'

'Ah, there you are. Listen, I've got the spare parts. For your Jaguar.'

'You mean you've ordered them? From the UK?'

'No, it turned out there was no need. I found a guy in Oslo who has everything. A Rolls-Royce and Jaguar specialist, no less.'

'And when are they coming?'

'They're already here,' Roar said. He sounded like he was picking food out from between his teeth.

'That's amazing,' Mia said.

'Indeed it is. Top-class service out here, you know.'

'So when do you think my car will be ready?'

'It won't take long. I guess I'll be done on Saturday. Or Sunday. Depends how hard I fancy working over the weekend. I'll call you once it's ready, all right?'

'Great, thank you,' Mia said, and rang off.

She pressed the second number. Gabriel Mørk.

'Hi, Gabriel, how are you?'

He yawned at the other end.

'Good, I'm good. Did you get the email I sent you about that car?'

'I haven't checked my emails today. But I will, thank you.'

'I can see that you've been busy up there,' Gabriel said. 'That list of names you sent me was long. How many suspects do you really have?'

'I may be on to something,' Mia said. 'But we have no actual suspects yet, sadly. Did you check out the vicar?'

'The vicar, the vicar,' Gabriel said. It sounded as if he was shifting in his seat. 'I'm checking the list now. Is there a vicar on it?'

'Ofelius,' Mia said. 'First name Thomas.'

'There he is,' Gabriel said. 'No, I'm sorry I haven't got to him yet. But I'm making progress. I've sent you everything I have found so far, plus something about that car you asked about.'

'So nothing?'

'Not that I can see, no.'

'Please would you make him a priority when you have a moment?'

'Ofelius?'

'Yes.'

'Will do.'

'Great, Gabriel, and thanks again.'

Mia stuffed her mobile into her jeans pocket and went back to her house. She sat down on the floor in front of the walls with the pictures and tried to empty her head in order to look at everything with fresh eyes.

Jessica.

She got up and rearranged a few of the pictures.

Benjamin Prytz.

Thomas Ofelius.

She remained standing, holding a third picture in her hand, one she had got from the archives.

Lucien Frank.

That encounter still troubled her. It had looked just like a crime scene, hadn't it? The smallholding, the disgusting surroundings. The rubbish, the pig nearly drowning in her own excrement.

She picked up her laptop from the sofa and went outside to the doorstep; the signal was strongest there. She connected the laptop to her mobile and logged on to Facebook. Oh, yes. There he was. A more flattering picture this time; his mouth was closed in a kind of smile, a fishing rod in one hand, a perch in the other.

Lucien Frank.

76 friends.

Operator, Hitra port and freezer terminal.

Mia scrolled down the pictures. Two men at Ansnes Brygger restaurant, beer and prawns on the table. A selfie, grinning at a stadium, muddy motocross bikes in the background. From the port, wearing utility clothes and a white helmet, several photographs.

Mia's eyebrows shot up when she suddenly noticed the ship in the background. She copied one of the images and tried to enlarge it. It was an old ship, quite rusty, the name barely visible on the bow.

MS *Salazar*.

Bingo.

She got up quickly, picked up her mobile and found the list of incoming calls. A few seconds later she heard a sleepy voice.

'Yes, Lie speaking.'

'Hello, Daniel, it's Mia Krüger here.'

'Oh, hi, Mia, how are things up there?'

She walked eagerly across the rocks.

'Oh, they're good, thank you. Listen, I've come across something that might be of interest to you.'

'OK?' the friendly Kripos investigator said, his ears pricking up now.

'That trafficking case you worked on? I just wanted to double-check the name of one of the ships. It was MS *Salazar*, wasn't it?'

DEAD ISLAND

'Yes, why?'

'Now this might not be anything, but I have a name you may want to check out.'

'OK, super, hang on.'

He disappeared for a moment as if looking for something to write on.

'So who are we talking about?'

'The man's name is Lucien Frank. He works as a port operator. I'm not sure what specifically his job entails, but I have a picture of him with that ship in the background.'

'That's great. Do you have anything else? And why him?'

'Like I said, it might be nothing at all, just a feeling I got when I visited him. He has a criminal record, just for small stuff, but you will still be able to find him in our database.'

'OK,' Lie said. 'I'll look into it. Thank you so much. I'll keep you posted, all right?'

'Please do,' Mia said, and returned her mobile to her pocket. She went back to stare at the photographs in her living room and stood in the middle of the floor, utterly frustrated.

Jessica. And Jonathan. There was no connection, was there? No relationship?

Hannah?

Was she the connection? Mia reached for the Thermos flask, poured herself a cup of coffee, took it with her to the wall, where she rearranged the photos once more, placing the teenage girl in the middle now.

Hannah? No.

Or?

She was at the heart of it all, wasn't she? Jonathan was her brother. Jessica was her friend. The name in blood. Her brother had witnessed something that night. A drug deal. Had Hannah over-heard something, perhaps? Did she have the same motive as her mother? She was closer to Jessica, for obvious reasons.

A drunken conversation. A confession. Listen, Hannah, I've got to tell you something . . .

Die, whore.

Mia took a few steps back and shook her head. No.

Sod it.

She couldn't make it add up. She drained her coffee cup and re-organized the pictures yet again. Benjamin Prytz in the centre now.

Benjamin.

He had admitted to being in the marina that Saturday. He had admitted to knowing Jessica and buying drugs from her regularly. He had lied to them. And not just once. The way he had looked at her. Sized up her body. But ... No, it was a waste of time. Why would he write *Jonathan* in Jessica's blood? Where had Benjamin Prytz even been that evening three years ago?

Mia hurried to one of the archive boxes, flicked through the old files again, but she still couldn't find any mention of his name. He hadn't been a suspect back then. He was never interviewed. Had he even been on the island?

OK, I'll look into that tomorrow.

She shook the Thermos flask, but it was empty so she went to the kitchen to make a fresh pot of coffee. Back in the living room, she stood in the middle of the floor, now even more frustrated. For God's sake, Mia. Get it together. It's staring you right in the face.

Why can't you see it?

The sun had set on the horizon and the living room began to cool down. She shook her head and made up her mind. OK.

Start over.

All of it. Go right back to square one. Mia pulled a jumper over her head, walked up to the wall and started taking down all the photographs.

SEVEN

FRIDAY

Chapter 62

Holger Munch was having breakfast at Hjorten Hotel for the first time since his arrival on the island. Not because he was especially hungry, but because the fairground workers had woken him up. They had worked late into the night. It had sounded as if his room was right inside one of the carousels they were assembling. And they had started again at the crack of dawn. Clanging and hammering. Metal against metal. Hollering and shouting. There was no point in staying in bed. He had wolfed down some fruit and was now on his third cup of coffee. His notebook was on the tablecloth in front of him. He had to come up with a better plan. The investigation had become haphazard. Would they be *lucky* enough to get a lead they could follow up? Had anyone *accidentally* seen or heard something they had missed? Would one of the many fingerprints they had found in the boat provide them with a breakthrough? Would they *happen* to get a hit on one of the DNA samples they had taken? He hadn't factored in the difference between a city like Oslo and a small, tight-knit community like this one. Added to that, he was on an island. The mood. The pace of life. The flow of information. It was not something he was used to at all.

So a new plan was needed.

He got up to fetch himself some more coffee.

'Are you sure that's a good idea?' Ruth was standing near him, holding a tray of clean glasses, and shook her head. 'Your hands are shaking – have you noticed?'

'Thank you, Ruth.'

'Well, someone has to keep an eye on you. Have a cup of tea instead. It's better for you.'

Munch smiled and did as he was told. He carried his tea back to the table and bent over his notepad again. Ludvigsen had called him last night, his voice kind but firm.

'*So how are you doing out there, Munch? Can we expect the case to be solved soon? Have you considered that it might not be one of the locals? A lot of people pass through Hitra, you know, especially in the tourist season.*'

Yes, thanks for that. Of course it had crossed his mind. And that precise thought was his worst nightmare. A random person passing through. No relationship to the victim. Someone who just happened to visit.

Someone who was long gone by now.

Munch heaved a sigh and put down his pen. Admittedly he wasn't on his home turf, but they hadn't made any mistakes so far, had they? None that he could see. So should they just wait? No. He had to come up with something.

Munch was leaning over his notepad again when he detected a figure out of the corner of his eye that made him look up. A woman was watching him through the window. She waved at him. He recognized her from somewhere, but he couldn't remember where until she came inside and walked up to him.

'Hello, you're Holger Munch, aren't you?'

Blonde shoulder-length hair. Heavy eyeshadow, red lipstick. A blouse of some flimsy material with lace around the neckline. A beige skirt that reached to her knees.

'Ester Hundstad. I'm a freelance reporter.'

She extended a slim hand across the remains of the fruit on his plate.

'May I?'

She nodded towards a vacant chair but didn't wait for him to reply. She sat down and placed her camera on the table.

'I'm here for the wedding. Cinderella getting her Prince Charming. How nice to bump into you. Why are you so far away from your usual hunting grounds? Is it that girl? The one they found in the boat? And the other body? I've heard some rumours. Are you hushing it up?'

326

She leaned across the table and whispered: 'I wonder if the Prytz family is involved? Rumour has it Junior is something of a problem child.'

'No comment.' Munch wiped his beard with the napkin.

'Oh, come on, Munch.' She leaned back with a smile. 'We're old friends, aren't we? You must be able to give me something?'

He didn't notice her until she suddenly appeared at the table. Ruth threw her cloth over her shoulder and eyed up the journalist.

'Excuse me, are you a guest here?'

Ester Hundstad looked up.

'Eh, no . . . I was just—'

'Breakfast is for our guests only. We can't have people from the outside pestering our guests.'

Ruth nodded in the direction of the exit.

'All right,' Ester Hundstad said with a sigh, and picked up her camera from the table.

She took Munch's pen and scribbled down her number on his notepad.

'Call me, OK? If you should come across anything juicy.'

Ruth walked the reporter to the exit, then she returned.

'Thank you,' Munch said quietly.

'Like I said, someone has to keep an eye on you.' She winked at him, then returned to the kitchen.

Munch waited until he was sure that the reporter had gone before he stepped outside. He took a cigarette from the packet, lit it and looked across to the funfair, which was starting to take shape. Carousels and stalls. A stage further back. It looked as if they had almost finished setting up, but once they had, the noise level would only get worse, wouldn't it? SummerFillan Festival. Soon the whole area would be a cacophony of screaming and shouting. Perhaps he should have done what most tourists did and rented a quiet fisherman's cottage instead.

He took his mobile out of his pocket and called Mia. It rang a few times before she picked up.

'Hello, Holger. We did say nine o'clock, didn't we?'

'Any news?' Munch said, running his hand over his face.

'Not here,' Mia said. 'But did you get Gabriel's email? About Thomas Ofelius?'

'No,' Munch said.

'Right. He sent it to me this morning.'

'And?'

'Not a lot. It looks like our vicar might be gay, but I don't know if it's worth investigating that angle.'

'I couldn't care less if the guy is into men or monkeys,' Munch began, but then checked himself. 'Sorry, Mia, I didn't get a lot of sleep. How did he find that out?'

'An Instagram account, I think. He was tagged in a picture at a party. But it's a few years old. Want to look into it? Pay him a visit?'

'Is that everything we've got?'

'It's certainly everything I've got. Do you have anything?'

Munch rubbed his eyes. It was hitting him hard now. How tired he was.

'No, nothing my end, unfortunately. OK. Let's go and see him. After the morning briefing. Unless the others have discovered something, that is.'

'Good. See you shortly.'

Chapter 63

Munch parked in the same spot as before, then took out his cigarettes from his jacket pocket. Mia arrived just after him. She looked like an action figure on the smart, gleaming motorcycle. There was much activity in and around the church today, and it was teeming with people. There was a van from an events agency and a woman came running down towards a man in utility clothes who had just got out of his lorry.

'What are you doing with that ladder?'

'The roof?' the man said. 'We're here to put on the new roof?'

'Today?' the woman cried out, pulling at her hair. 'Forget it, we have a wedding here tomorrow, weren't you told?'

'But can't I just . . . How about I put up my ladder? Just to take a quick look at it?'

'All right, but go round the back,' the woman snapped. 'Where you'll be out of sight.'

She turned and called out to someone near the church.

'No, Monica, not there, it needs to go inside! For heaven's sake, why don't people listen?'

Mia hung the helmet on the handlebars and joined him.

'So the festivities have started already?'

'It certainly looks like it,' Munch said, lighting his cigarette.

The woman now came marching towards them.

'Are you the caterers? I thought you would be arriving in a van?'

'We—' Munch began, but she simply talked over him.

'The ceremony will start at twelve noon exactly. Before that I want a table up there – not near the steps, further up to the side. No, wait, let's put it in the garden over there. That works better.

Then people can help themselves when they come out. Did you get the menu? Canapés? And there has to be salmon on some of them, or caviar, preferably both. You were told this, weren't you?'

'Police,' Munch said, showing her his warrant card.

'Oh?' The woman smiled, then wiped her brow with her hand. 'Sorry. The wedding is tomorrow, you understand. It's the Prytz family.'

'So I've heard.' Munch nodded, and put the card back in his pocket.

'It's a bit frantic – again, I'm sorry,' she said, spinning around. 'No, Monica, not there! Jesus Christ, do I have to do everything myself?'

She shook her head and stormed off.

Munch followed Mia across the car park and into the church. Everyone might be stressed, but they had done a great job inside. The church was barely recognizable. Garlands and lush white flower arrangements: the place looked like a newly decorated ballroom.

'Is this normal, I wonder?' Munch said, and looked about him. 'Or legal? Are there even any rules for this? Laws relating to the appropriate use of a church? Did God say anything about that? On a tablet, perhaps?'

'Did you get out of the wrong side of bed again?' Mia said, and continued in front of him up the aisle.

The vicar was standing near the altar, mumbling, with his back to them.

'Excuse me, Vicar?' Munch said.

The young man turned. He seemed startled.

'Oh, hello. I didn't hear you come in. I . . .'

He showed them a sheaf of paper he was holding in his hand.

'Are you rehearsing for the big day?' Mia said.

Thomas Ofelius's gaze flitted and he coughed lightly.

'Yes. I just hope I can trust my voice.'

'Tea with honey,' Munch said. 'Never fails. Is there somewhere we could have a quiet word?'

'So not here?' the vicar said.

'Somewhere more private, perhaps?' Mia said.

'OK? Eh, yes. How about we go this way?' He pointed to a door towards the rear of the church.

'That's great,' Munch said, and followed him.

Once they were outside, the vicar stopped. He looked a little lost. 'So what's this about?'

Mia whispered something to Munch. It took a moment before he took on board what she was saying.

Cyanide.

All right, all right. Munch composed himself before he began.

'Thomas Ofelius,' he said, and attempted a smile, 'I want to start by saying that we have no interest in your sexual orientation. It's of no relevance to us.'

'What?' the vicar exclaimed, looking about him. 'But I'm not—'

'We've seen the pictures,' Mia said. 'Pride flag and leather cap.'

'But that was just for fun—' Ofelius began.

'Like I said, Vicar,' Munch cut him off, 'it's completely irrelevant. You live your best life. And more power to you.'

The vicar glanced around nervously once more as if to make sure that no one could overhear them.

'And, no, we aren't planning on telling anyone,' Mia said, 'if that's what you're scared of. We understand that it can be a delicate matter in this community. But as far as we're concerned . . .'

'It doesn't matter at all,' Munch said. 'There, now we have got that out of the way.'

This was a white lie. Munch had, of course, informed the rest of the team. Munch didn't want anyone to be left in the dark; it might actually lead them to a new line of inquiry, and that was exactly what had happened.

'Ofelius, yes, I'd forgotten him. Sorry.'

Ralph Nygaard. Munch had reprimanded him after their phone conversation.

'The vicar runs a youth club, and some people said that Jessica would go there from time to time . . .'

'Did you know Jessica?' Munch said.

'What?' the vicar said.

'Jessica Bakken, the girl who was killed?'

331

'No, I don't remember—'

'She came to the club you run. For young people?'

Thomas Ofelius still looked rather shaken, but he composed himself now.

'Oh, yes. I'm sorry. Of course. I'd completely forgotten. She came a few times. Not to hear about God, I don't think. We provide a hot meal. She was very hungry. But she didn't come very often. Three or four times, perhaps?'

'Did you ever go to her boat?' Mia said.

'No, never.'

'Really? Her boat in Setervågen marina? You never went there?'

'Setervågen?' Ofelius said. 'I don't even know where that is.'

'You've lived here for almost a year now, and you don't know where Setervågen is?'

'I haven't been around the island much. I've mostly been here in the church and in the town hall, where we have lots of meetings. Surely you don't think that I . . .' He looked at them with anxious eyes. 'No, you can't be serious?'

'You hide who you really are. It makes us wonder what else you might be hiding,' Munch began, but Mia moved her lips again and he backed down.

'I'm sorry,' Munch said, running his hand under his sun hat. 'Of course, I understand how difficult it can be.'

'Thank you,' the vicar said softly, and nodded. 'I mean, in a big city, sure, where everyone is more open-minded. But out here?' He looked around.

'It's a small island. We understand.'

'Was that all?' the vicar said in a trembling voice, then gestured to his sheaf of paper. 'I have to . . .'

Mia nodded towards the car park.

'Yes. I think that's everything,' Munch said.

'Thank you,' the young vicar said. He sounded relieved as he pushed down the door handle. 'I'll get back to rehearsals then.'

'You do that.' Munch nodded and followed Mia down to the car park.

'At first he didn't remember her, but then he remembered that she was very hungry? That's a bit weird, isn't it?'

'He isn't our man,' Mia said.

'Are you sure?'

She nodded and took the helmet from the handlebars.

'Day seven?'

'Yes, sod it,' Munch said, and took his cigarettes out of his pocket again. 'We have to get a break soon.'

'We will,' Mia said.

'Do you think so?'

'We always do.'

'Did we get anything from the list of locals with previous convictions?' Munch said.

'Are we about to have a repeat of your briefing from a few days ago?' Mia said.

'No, I'm just trying to . . .' Munch tapped his temple. 'We did a thorough check of all the local residents, didn't we, and we remembered to include registered owners of holiday cabins?'

'Three driving under the influence.' Mia sighed. 'Two convictions for embezzlement, one for importation of illegal drugs . . . do you want me to carry on?'

'No, I was just—'

'We can go over it all again if you think it will help,' Mia said, starting her motorcycle. 'However, there is something I need to check first. See you shortly.'

'What are you checking?' Munch said, but she had already joined the main road.

He popped a cigarette into his mouth and fetched the lighter from his pocket. Another hot day. The party planners were melting up by the church.

Yet another wild-goose chase.

What was it he was missing?

Think, Holger, think.

Munch leaned heavily against the car in the shade and lit the cigarette as his mobile rang.

'Hello, Munch, it's Luca calling,' Luca Eriksen said eagerly.

'What's up?'

'A young lad has turned up. He has just shown me a video he filmed at the party.'

'And?'

Luca Eriksen sounded breathless now. He appeared to say something to the young man before he came back on the phone.

'I think we've got something, Munch.'

Chapter 64

Mia parked the motorcycle and walked down to the jetty. It was quiet here now. The sea was dead calm. The rocks reflected in the water's surface a picturesque echo of the beautiful landscape that surrounded it. Mia glanced over her shoulder, then walked right to the edge of the jetty.

Jonathan's bicycle. Found here.

She shielded her eyes from the sun and looked beyond the line of rocks to where the road curved softly back across the island, out of sight.

The bend known as *Svingen.* The timeline on her wall at home. One hour and eleven minutes. From Anita Holmen's first phone call. Until she had called again. That was a long time, wasn't it? Or maybe it wasn't? She had ridden the distance twice. Slowly. Checked the stopwatch on her mobile.

Eighteen minutes.

Then add ten minutes for Jonathan to reach the road via the birch avenue.

No, that wasn't the problem. Or maybe it was? One hour and eleven minutes. That was quite a long time. Wouldn't a parent have acted sooner?

Mia lingered at the edge of the jetty.

Forget it, Mia, you've been through this already. You won't find the answer here.

She walked back and was heading up to the road when her mobile rang. She checked the display. Munch. She dismissed the call and put the phone back in her pocket.

What do I do?

He called her again.

'I'm a bit busy, Holger—' But she could tell from his voice it was important.

'You've got to see this.'

'What?'

'We have a recording of Jessica in the bunker.'

'A clear one?'

'Oh, yes. This you will want to see. I guarantee you.'

'OK. I'm on my way.'

She shook her head and put on her helmet. She looked around again. No, something was wrong.

She would have to check the distances again.

Every single one of them.

Mia parked the motorcycle by the entrance to the police station, picked up a bottle of water on her way in and walked down the corridor to the briefing room, where she detected the change in mood immediately. They had a break at last.

Munch was perched on one of the tables, looking at the screen with a smile on his face. Luca Eriksen was leaning against a window with his arms folded across his chest.

'So we can see her?'

'Yes,' Munch said. 'But not only that.'

He nodded to Luca.

'Play it again.'

Luca went to click the button on the laptop he had connected to the screen, then waited for further instructions. The recording began to play.

It was taken indoors. In the bunker. The person filming appeared to be holding the mobile above their head. Hollering and shouting. Loud music. Ten to fifteen people on the dance floor. Others clustered along the walls. Dark, brief glimpses of costumes under flashing lights in every colour. A witch with a green nose. An Elvis in a white satin suit with gold sunglasses. A red devil. A vampire with a white face and slicked-back hair. Goofy.

And there she was.

Mickey Mouse.

'Jessica.' Munch nodded, but didn't ask for the recording to be stopped.

Waving her arms in frantic movements to the pounding music. Hannah Holmen came into view now. Donald Duck. She bumped into Jessica, who almost fell over. Squeals and laughter before the crazed dancing resumed. The phone moved in a circle now, slowly scanning the walls for approximately thirty seconds, then it was over.

'Did you see it?' Munch said.

'See what?' Mia said as she twisted the cap off the bottle.

'Play it again,' Munch said.

Luca clicked the button.

The same scene. Thumping bass and white strobe lighting. Noisy young people packed into the low, fairly narrow room.

'Stop,' Munch said.

Luca paused the recording.

'There.' Munch pointed as he walked towards the screen. 'Recognize him?'

Mia walked closer to the screen. A clown at the back of the room. Stripy trousers. Wild, yellow hair. The clown removed their mask for a moment, a hand reaching up to wipe the undoubtedly sweaty face.

'Oh, wow,' Mia said.

'Quite.' Munch smiled.

'Benjamin Prytz.' Luca nodded.

'It is him, isn't it?'

'No doubt about it,' Munch said.

'But he wasn't there,' Mia said.

'No, he wasn't, was he?' Munch grinned.

'He made that quite clear. Thank God his lawyer was present. So he can confirm that Benjamin lied straight to our faces.'

'What an idiot,' Munch said. 'What was he thinking? That we wouldn't find out?'

'So what do we do?'

'What do we do?' Munch said. 'We bring him in, of course.'

'Now?'

'My car, OK?'

Mia nodded and followed him down the corridor.

Chapter 65

Lissie Norheim was standing in front of the big mirror in the dressing room on the first floor and could barely believe her own eyes. The beautiful white wedding dress had diamonds along the neckline and a delicate lace train that reached almost to the end of the room. She shook her head and smiled cautiously at the girl in the mirror, who smiled back, luckily.

'Let's see,' the seamstress said, returning with pins in her mouth. 'I just need to fix this bit. Stand very still.'

Lissie had tried on her wedding dress before, but it had been a different experience. In the studio in London. It hadn't been finished then, merely an indication of something. The design team had arrived by helicopter. They had carried the box containing the dress between them as if it were a priceless work of art.

She clasped her hand over her mouth.

Could this really be her?

There was a knock on the door. And she was here at last. Julia.

'Hello!' Lissie smiled and flung out her arms, forgetting the instruction not to move.

'Don't move,' the seamstress mumbled.

'Ta-da, your ring-bearer is here,' Julia exclaimed as she entered the room. Then she stopped in her tracks right inside the door, her eyes widening.

'Oh, my God, Lissie. You look so . . .' Julia walked slowly across the floor and lifted the train.

'Hands off,' the seamstress admonished her sternly.

'Sorry, I couldn't help myself . : . is it really you?'

Julia walked up to her, looking very much like she wanted to hug her but was scared to.

'Would you mind moving a little bit . . .' the seamstress said, waving her away.

'Sorry,' Julia said.

She returned to the doorway.

'Gosh, Lissie, it's absolutely . . .'

'Do you like it?'

'Like it?' Julia laughed. 'It's totally out of this world. You look amazing. I just want to cry.'

Julia ran a finger under her eyes. At last the seamstress had finished and Lissie could walk over to her.

'Julia!' She gave her friend a big hug.

'I'm sorry for getting here so late.'

'Don't worry about it. You're here now, that's all that matters.'

Lissie smiled and gave her another hug. Good old Julia. One of the few friends she had known since primary school. They had grown up next door to each other. Lissie had nearly dropped her architect's degree in Trondheim when Julia chose to study in Oslo.

This past year her life had been a whirlwind. She was surrounded by new people everywhere, not just at the university but also Alexander's circle of friends. It was so hard to know who was genuine and who just wanted to be her friend because she was marrying him.

But Julia? Best friends for life. She hadn't hesitated for a second when Alexander had asked her who her ring-bearer would be.

'Puh, it's hot out here,' Julia said, fanning her face. 'And it's quite a trek, isn't it? It was more than two and a half hours in the car from the airport.'

'We could always have sent the helicopter.'

'Would you listen to yourself, Lissie?' Julia laughed. 'Send a helicopter? Do I look like someone you would send a helicopter for?'

She looked down at herself. Torn denim jeans. A Ramones T-shirt. A nose ring and several ear piercings. She was perfect.

'Yes – for you, anything.' Lissie smiled and gave her friend another long hug.

'It's not my style.' Julia smiled. 'And it wasn't really that far, was it? But it's so hot. Do you have something to drink?'

'Over there,' Lissie said, nodding towards a small cupboard in the corner.

'You have a fridge in your dressing room? Fancy.' Julia winked and helped herself to a bottle of water.

She twisted off the cap and went over to the window.

'It's quite a place you have here.'

'Do you like it?'

'Like it?' Julia said. 'What's not to like? Please tell me that the fantastic building down there with water running down the wall is a spa?'

'It is,' Lissie said.

'Oh, fab. Guess who's hitting the spa tonight? We do have time for that, don't we?'

'Of course,' Lissie said. 'What did I just tell you? Anything for you.'

'You did indeed say that.' Julia smiled again.

They stood next to each other, facing the mirror.

'Beauty and the beast?' Julia said, fluffing her short black fringe.

'Oh, no, please don't say that.'

'I'm joking. You're very pretty. And I don't look too bad either, do I?'

'You're a star,' Lissie said, and kissed her on the cheek.

'Are you excited?' Julia wanted to know, and took her hand.

'Very.'

'It's going to be fine. I'm always here for you, you know that.'

'I'm really glad to hear that,' Lissie said, just as something kicked off outside.

There was shouting. The seamstress was already by the window.

'What's going on?' Julia asked with a nod towards the rotunda at the end of the garden.

Two police officers. Walking behind Benjamin. Was he . . . handcuffed?

'Oh, shit,' Lissie said, and walked as quickly as the wedding dress would allow her over to pick up her mobile.

Chapter 66

A car screeched to a halt outside the police station and Kevin Borg jumped out of it.

'Is it true? Have we got him?'

Munch nodded and took another drag on his cigarette.

'We're waiting for his lawyer.'

Kevin Borg ran his hand over his hair and grinned from ear to ear.

'I knew it. These rich bastards think they can do whatever the hell they like.'

'Let's take it one step at a time,' Munch said calmly. 'We're not home and dry yet.'

'No, no,' Kevin Borg said, stepping into the shade. 'But he was at the party? We're sure?'

'We have him on film,' Munch said.

'Dressed up as a clown, was that it?'

Munch nodded again.

'That seems appropriate.' Kevin Borg laughed. 'A bloody clown, that's what he is. Swanning around in his fancy cars that Daddy paid for – oh, this makes me so happy, I have to tell you.'

Kevin Borg put his hand on the knot of his tie and looked at Munch.

'I must admit that I had my doubts to begin with. When Ludvigsen said that he had brought you in, as if we weren't able to handle this ourselves. But I have to say, Munch, I've really enjoyed working with you. And as for what happened out on Fjellværsøya? I mean with Xandra? I think I need to apologize. I was a bit overexcited. I got carried away. That's what I'm like, you know. When the tiger in me wants to get out, then . . .' He winked and elbowed Munch.

'I understand,' Munch said.

'So your unit in Oslo has been closed down?'

'Yes, I'm afraid so,' Munch said.

'Any chance you'll be up and running again soon?'

'We'll have to wait and see. They're working on it. Behind the scenes.'

Kevin Borg elbowed him again.

'Let me know if you're recruiting. I'd be happy to move to the capital.'

'I'll bear that in mind.' Munch nodded and stubbed out his cigarette as the lawyer's car pulled up in front of the police station.

'Is he here?' the mousy lawyer said as he got out of his car.

He wasn't quite so friendly now. His face was hard behind the metal spectacle frames.

'In there,' Munch said with a nod of his head. 'We were just waiting for you.'

'And what have you charged him with?'

'Nothing. Yet.'

'You know that—' the lawyer began, but Munch cut him off.

'We can hold him for forty-eight hours. Without giving you any explanation at all. Once that time has passed we may have to charge him, but by my reckoning that's . . .'

He checked the time on his mobile.

'. . . forty-seven hours away, approximately.'

The lawyer looked grim as he picked up his briefcase from the gravel.

'Where is my client?'

'He's in here. Follow me, please.'

Munch led the way up the steps and down the corridor. He nodded to Mia, who was in the briefing room.

'We can start now.'

'Hold on,' the lawyer said. 'First I would like to talk to my client – alone.'

'Of course,' Munch said with a polite bow, and opened the door to the interview room.

He caught a glimpse of Benjamin Prytz's eyes as he turned to face them. He wasn't so cocky now. There was a slim glass panel next to the door through which they could observe the two men. Benjamin Prytz was sitting down while his lawyer paced around the room, speaking as softly as he could, but they could still gauge the tone of the conversation.

'I bet Daddy isn't happy now,' Mia said, taking a segment of orange from a plate in her hand.

'I doubt it,' Munch said. 'I wonder how long it'll be before he turns up.'

'I don't believe he's on the island,' Mia said.

'That's a shame,' Munch said. 'I would like to see the look on his face when he hears that we've nicked one of his golden boys.'

The lawyer had sat down now, and the conversation was more subdued.

'You do know that we have nothing on him, don't you?' Mia said quietly. 'He was at the party, but so what?'

'He lied,' Munch said.

'So we arrest him for lying? And what's the punishment for that? A slap on the wrist and house arrest? You can't drive the yellow Lamborghini any more, only the green one?'

'Forty-eight hours,' Munch said grimly. 'We'll find something on him within that time. Unless he decides to confess to it all, here and now.'

'Let's see,' Mia said, and wiped her fingers on her black shorts as the door to the interview room was opened.

'My client is ready,' the mousy lawyer said, and gestured for them to enter.

They sat down at the table. The lawyer took a seat next to Benjamin Prytz, who was sitting with his head bowed and his fingers interlaced.

'We—' Munch said.

'No,' the lawyer said. 'We'll start. Benjamin?'

Benjamin Prytz cleared his throat. 'I admit that I lied to the police. I shouldn't have done that. I did it to protect my reputation. I didn't want anyone to think that I mixed with those . . . well, the people out here. I was dressed up as a clown. I had a few beers. I spent a couple of hours in the bunker. Then I went home.'

Benjamin Prytz looked up at them now. The lawyer nodded contentedly.

'Had you been planning to go for a long time?' Munch said. 'Or did you just happen to have a clown costume lying around?'

'I—' Benjamin Prytz began, but his lawyer stopped him.

'That's all my client has to say at this point in time. We understand and accept that you have the right to remand him in custody for forty-eight hours. Which means that I'll be back here to pick him up' – he checked the gold watch around his wrist – 'in forty-six hours and thirty minutes.'

The lawyer got up and nodded to indicate to Benjamin Prytz to do likewise.

'Oh, no,' Munch said. 'We're not done yet.'

'Yes, we are. Where do you intend to keep him? I would like to remind you of his rights. Food and drink, fresh air. I would also like to remind you that my client's brother is getting married tomorrow and we're willing to go right to the top to make sure that Benjamin is able to attend the wedding. We will pick him up tomorrow morning. Given the position of my client's father, I regard the latter as a highly likely outcome.'

'OK.' Munch heaved a sigh and shouted out of the door. 'Luca?'

Luca came running down the corridor.

'Yes?'

'Take Benjamin Prytz down to the basement and put him in the . . . the drunk tank, is that what you called it?'

'OK?' Luca glanced nervously at the lawyer. 'In handcuffs or . . .'

'No, that won't be necessary. If he behaves this time.'

Munch watched Luca and Benjamin Prytz get ready while the lawyer whispered a few last words in Benjamin Prytz's ears before he left the police station.

'Shit,' Munch said when they were back in the briefing room.

'I thought that would happen,' Mia said. 'What's the plan now?'

Munch ran a hand over his beard.

'I'm not sure. But I want to visit the crime scenes again. And let's make a trip to the bunker where the party was held.'

'Should we split up?' Mia asked.

'OK,' Munch said. 'I'll go to the nature reserve and you take the boat? Then we'll meet up at the bunker later.'

Chapter 67

Munch had got a pair of his own wellington boots now; he put them on and paused to take in his surroundings. Everything looked different in the daylight. It had been murky, quite dark in fact, when they had found Pelle Lundgren. Munch had flashbacks to that night. The helicopter above them. The ambulances rushing to the scene. The stretcher they had struggled to get through the wetlands. The dark, rugged terrain had been sodden and the paramedics had tripped several times. Half of Pelle Lundgren's body had slid to the ground; the black body bag had ended up covered in soil and mud. He had sent some officers back later that morning, but he didn't quite trust them. An inbuilt defence mechanism after thirty years in the job. Don't trust anyone. At least not outsiders. Mia – of course he trusted her; that went without saying. But the newbies up here? No way.

Nina Riccardo had a good eye, though; she might prove to be the exception. But it was always best to see for yourself.

Munch followed the path to the big, bowing tree where they had taken a wrong turn the last time. He ducked under the heavy branches and stepped out on to the wetlands. A big bird took off and disappeared across the treetops. He had read somewhere that the whole area was protected by the Ramsar Convention, an international agreement on the preservation of such habitats. The nesting place for countless species of birds, especially migrating birds that would stop here, safe on their way to the south. The area measured approximately twelve kilometres square and included several lakes. Due to its size, they had not attempted to search every inch of it, but the crew he had out here had done a decent job, he was quite sure of that. But even so. It was never the same as seeing it for yourself. In daylight with your own eyes. An experienced gaze they didn't have.

Munch had reached the centre of the wetlands and stopped to look towards the crime scene. The wildlife tower. It had struck him as being the best place for the killer to wait. Departure at 0300 hours. But the killer couldn't be sure at what time Pelle Lundgren would get here, could he? So it was best to be early. Hide out somewhere with a good view.

Munch had climbed the tower twice that night with a torch, but even so. It was different during the day. He approached it in a big semicircle. There was wet, dark quagmire in front of him and he was taking no chances. He had seen people get stuck before, then sink helplessly into the viscous ground. Better safe than sorry.

His thighs were burning when he finally reached the bottom of the winding grey steps. So much for four weeks of exercise. His old body was slowly returning. He paused for a short breather. Then he walked up the steps and stopped at the top, resting his hands on the railing. The tower wasn't all that high, but he could see across all of the wetlands. A stag emerged from the edge of the forest before wandering off.

Munch bent down to examine the inside of the tower. This was what he had wanted to see for himself. The tower was not just of interest to birdwatchers, it was also a place where others might hide out. They had found beer cans, cigarette butts, scraps of tinfoil, Rizla papers. Teenagers, probably. With their exciting secrets.

Munch peered closely at the wooden planks as he tried to find what he believed he had caught a glimpse of that night.

It was somewhere in the back of his mind, but it hadn't surfaced until Mia had started to talk about Babylon.

The Whore of Babylon.

A religious reference. People had carved things in the wood.

Elling was here.

P and V, September –12.

Mona, I love you.

And there it was.

Isaiah 41:10

Munch took out his mobile, photographed it, then popped the

mobile back into his pocket. He put on a pair of gloves and carefully trailed his fingers over the wording. Someone had tried to mask it, make it look older than it really was by rubbing dust and dirt from the platform across it. But when he had brushed that off, he could see areas of fresh wood.

Bingo.

Munch smiled and got up. The knees of his trousers were dirty. He leaned against the railing and took out his mobile again.

He typed in the Bible reference. Munch waited while 4G slowly loaded the page on his mobile. He could really appreciate how Mia struggled with coverage out here. The signal quality was very poor. But finally it connected. Munch turned to avoid the glare of the sun bouncing off the screen. Isaiah 41:10 read:

Fear thou not; for I am with thee: be not dismayed; for I am thy God: I will strengthen thee; yea, I will help thee; yea, I will uphold thee with the right hand of my righteousness.

All right, steady on.

So the killer had waited here.

Under the cover of darkness.

He had watched Pelle Lundgren walk across the wetlands.

He scrolled to find the number.

'Kripos Forensics, Rita speaking.'

'Hi, Rita, it's Munch here. I need some people.'

'Right, where?'

'Havmyran nature reserve, where we found Pelle Lundgren. I want the wildlife tower examined again. Fingerprints, skin cells, hair – the whole caboodle.'

'But we've already checked it.' Rita heaved a sigh. 'It's contaminated. Too many traces, way too dirty.'

'I'm talking about a specific area,' Munch said, bending down again.

'How big?'

'Two centimetres by six, roughly.'

Rita disappeared for a moment. Then she came back.

'OK,' she said. 'I'm sending somebody now. They'll be there in a couple of hours.'

'Great, thank you.'

Munch returned his mobile to his pocket and took out his cigarettes.

Fear thou not; for I am with thee.

A message? To himself? For the strength? To do what he was about to do?

Munch lit his cigarette and gazed vacantly across the fairy-tale landscape.

Chapter 68

Mia walked down to the marina, where she found two technicians in the shade, leaning against the side of the boat.

'How is it going?' Mia asked.

'All right,' the man replied, scratching his neck.

They were no longer wearing white coveralls. They had finished the forensic examination, which Mia knew had been a rotten job. An old boat, examining it below deck, in the nooks and crannies, dust and filth everywhere. She had gone to take a look for herself while they worked away. Crime-scene technicians lying on their backs, constricted and hot, their heads twisting, arms contorting. These people didn't get enough credit. Many of the cases she had worked on had ultimately been solved by crime-scene technicians.

'I'm afraid we haven't found anything,' the woman said.

'We've gone over everything ten times at least.' The man nodded.

They had been looking for Jessica's diary. If it even existed, that is. Mia hadn't met Jessica's mother but, based on Munch's description, it could just be something she had made up.

'I'm not a bad mum.'

'I know things, I do.'

They had searched Laura Bakken's flat and the room that was supposed to be Jessica's bedroom yet again, but without finding anything.

'Let's call it a day,' Mia said.

'Sure?' the man said, sounding relieved.

'Thank you,' the woman said, then started to pack up.

'Would you mind leaving the light on down there? And come

back for the generator another time?' Mia pointed to the small diesel motor powering the crime scene.

'Of course. We can pick it up later. Just turn it off when you're done.'

'Will do,' Mia said, and nodded to indicate that they were free to leave.

She walked around to the other side of the boat and climbed up under the tarpaulin. It was different now, but memories of the first time she had been here came flooding back. The smell. Jessica's lifeless body down below.

The name written in her blood.

She made her way carefully into the hull of the boat and crouched down in the glare from the bright lights. The boat had been stripped. It was just an empty husk now. She had gone to see the crime-scene technicians a few days ago. They had commandeered the sports hall at the school and lined up several tables below the climbing wall.

Jessica's life in the boat. Item by item. A sock. An old magazine. A pair of knickers with hearts on them. Hundreds of objects laid out: the remains of someone's life, carefully labelled and sealed in small transparent bags.

It showed respect. For the job they did. She had felt invigorated when she left the sports hall.

We will find him.

Or her.

Nina Riccardo and her always questioning mind.

Are we sure that we're looking for a man?

No, of course not, but there was something about the brutality. The violence. Mia took a look around. What was she really doing down here? Hoping to get a sense of something? Was she trying to visualize the murder? But the technicians had gone over the whole boat with a fine-tooth comb.

She wasn't going to find anything here.

Mia shook her head and climbed back up on to the deck. She went down the ladder and flicked the switch that turned off the generator. The silence was noticeable. There were no sounds coming from anywhere except for a campervan driving slowly past up on the road above her. The campervan stopped, then turned into the car park. A woman got out and said something to the man behind the wheel. In Norwegian. Two children popped up their heads; one of them opened the van door. Mia had a flashback to her own childhood.

Camping trips often lasting several days, her father humming to himself with his fishing rod down by the water while her mother paced around the heather; she could never sit still for very long. All Sigrid wanted to do was sit inside the tent with her nose in a book while Mia explored the forests – she couldn't get enough of the outdoors.

She walked up towards the campervan.

'Hi, sorry, you can't park here.' She pointed to the cordon. 'There has been an incident, and this is a crime scene. I'm afraid you'll have to find somewhere else to park.'

Disappointment in their faces, especially in the children's, they sighed and climbed reluctantly back inside the vehicle.

'I'm sorry,' the woman said. 'We didn't realize.'

'There's plenty of parking further down the road,' Mia said.

'Thank you,' the woman said, getting back in the passenger seat. 'Have a good day.'

'You too,' Mia said.

The campervan turned laboriously and lumbered back up the road.

What was that?

Mia chased after it and banged on its side. The campervan jolted and came to a halt.

'Sorry,' Mia said as the woman opened the window. 'That mask, where did you get it?'

'What mask?' the woman said.

'She means the devil,' said the man behind the steering wheel.

'Oh, that one,' the woman said, turning around. 'Joakim, give me that mask you found, would you?'

The boy leaned forward between the seats.

'Please may I have a look at it?' Mia said.

She took it with a sense of butterflies in her tummy.

'Where did you find it?'

'Where did you find the mask, Joakim?'

'Where we were yesterday,' the boy said.

353

'On the other side of the island,' the woman chimed in. 'What's it called?'

'I'm not sure,' the man said. 'It was before Kvenvær. By the entrance to the nature reserve.'

'I'm a police officer. I'm afraid I have to keep it,' Mia said, showing them her warrant card.

'That's quite all right,' the woman said. 'It's horrible anyway. I'll be glad to see the back of it.'

'Do you have a number I can reach you on?' Mia said. 'We may need to know exactly where you found it.'

'Of course,' the woman said, looking a little worried now. She opened the glove compartment and wrote down a number on a piece of paper.

'He hasn't done anything wrong, has he?'

'No, no. Definitely not,' Mia said.

She waited until the campervan was back on the road before she took out her mobile and called Munch.

'Yes?'

'Where are you?'

'At the nature reserve. The technicians have just arrived.'

'Have you found anything?'

'Yes,' Munch said. 'And you?'

'Definitely,' Mia said. 'Can we meet?'

'Just the two of us or everyone?'

'The whole team,' Mia said, holding up the mask in front of her. The red devil grinned at her in the sunlight.

'OK. We'll meet in an hour.'

Chapter 69

Munch was connecting the iPad to the projector as his team filed into the briefing room. Curious faces rather than tired ones, summoned to a team briefing earlier than planned. Everyone was here except for Claus Nielsen, the police lawyer, who was still pacing up and down outside with his phone pressed to his ear.

'Has Ludvigsen called you? They're putting pressure on us. They want us to release the boy . . .'

Munch had expected as much. He didn't need a lawyer to tell him how the world worked. If you had money, power, status and contacts among the important men and women up here, then of course you could have things your own way. To be honest, he was surprised that it had taken this long; he had expected the first phone call to come within the hour.

'OK,' Munch said, sitting down at the table. 'I appreciate you all getting here at such short notice. I know you're busy, but as you have probably heard there has been a development, and I thought it best that we meet to discuss it.'

'I've heard a rumour that we'll have to let him go? Is that true?' It was Kevin Borg speaking, and he looked annoyed.

'There's a distinct possibility that we may have to let Benjamin Prytz go, yes.' Munch nodded. 'Unless someone has found something within the last few hours that would give us grounds for keeping him?'

He looked across his team. Everyone shook their head.

'Right,' Munch said. 'But that might not matter so much now. We may be looking for another suspect.'

He reached for the iPad.

'I was out at the nature reserve earlier today, where I examined the viewing platform of the wildlife tower again, and I discovered this. It was done quite recently, but an attempt had been made to conceal it.'

He brought up a photograph of the carving made in the wood.

Isaiah 41:10.

'A Bible quote?' Kevin Borg said.

'Yes,' Munch said. 'If we look it up, we find this verse.'

He touched the iPad again.

'All right,' Ralph Nygaard said. '*Fear thou not; for I am with thee?* What's that supposed to mean?'

'I think,' Munch continued, 'that the killer was waiting in the tower. He knew what time Pelle Lundgren thought he was going to be picked up, but he couldn't know how early Pelle Lundgren would arrive. Oversight. Control. He may have been sitting there for a while. Used the wait to stiffen his sinews.'

'So we're looking for somebody who knows their Bible well?' Nina Riccardo said.

'I think so,' Munch said. 'Then again, we were already aware of that angle, the religious one, I mean.'

He nodded to Mia.

'And we now believe that the abbreviation on the cup was for *Whore of Babylon*. I don't know how well you all know your Bible. We could do a survey.'

He looked around the room.

'How many of you here are familiar with the expression *Whore of Babylon*?'

Everyone raised their hands cautiously.

'And how many of you have heard of Isaiah 41:10?'

Everyone looked at each other, but nobody said anything.

'You see my point,' Munch said. 'If it was just *Whore of Babylon*, I think we would still have to treat most of the local population as suspects instead of looking for someone deeply religious, but this?'

He nodded towards the screen.

'This changes everything, in my opinion. All of us here might use the first expression, but to quote a Bible verse? I'm pretty sure that we're now looking for someone with strong religious beliefs or at least a good knowledge of Holy Scripture and a desire to live accord-ing to it.'

'That doesn't sound like Benjamin Prytz,' Nina Riccardo said.

'I agree.' Munch nodded. 'And as we're about to find out, it's possible that we're looking for someone other than him.'

Claus Nielsen came down the corridor and popped his head around the door.

'Sorry, but I think we have to let him go. Unless we have . . .' He looked at Munch.

'It's fine,' Munch said. 'Luca, would you?'

Claus Nielsen seemed relieved when Luca got up and took the keys to the holding cell from his pocket.

'All right,' Munch said when the two men had left the room. 'Mia?'

Mia stood up from her seat.

'I was out there recently – out by the boat, I mean. I happened to meet a family in a campervan who last night had camped not far away from where the bunker party took place. In the forest nearby they found this.'

Munch touched the iPad.

A photograph of the red devil mask appeared on the screen.

'On its own, it means nothing, perhaps. But take a closer look now . . .'

Munch started playing the recording from the bunker. Loud music once more. Flashing lights over the many costumes.

A witch.

Elvis.

Goofy.

Donald Duck.

A vampire.

And there was the red mask.

'The devil went to the party?'

'Yes.' Mia nodded.

'So what?' Kevin Borg said. 'So someone lost their mask on their way home?'

'Don't look at Jessica or Benjamin Prytz,' Mia said. 'Just watch the devil.'

She nodded to Munch, who played the recording again.

'As we can see, this person doesn't join in the dancing to begin with,' Mia said. 'She's standing by the wall. Here. Then suddenly she mingles with the crowd, dances a bit, or she pretends to dance, and then here . . .'

Munch paused the clip.

'She bends towards Jessica, and it looks like she whispers something in her ear. She probably has to shout – the music was quite loud, don't forget. Then what happens next is this: Jessica looks at her. That's an affirmative, isn't it? A slight nod. And the devil dances onwards, out towards the door, where she disappears.'

'You keep saying *she*?' Nina Riccardo said.

'Yes,' Mia nodded. 'We think it's a woman. If you watch her arms, her movements in general . . .'

'That's what I kept saying,' Nina sighed. 'We can't be sure that we're looking for a man.'

'The recording is time-stamped,' Mia said. 'It lasts thirty-four seconds and it was filmed Saturday evening at four minutes to nine.'

'As we already know, Jessica wasn't seen at the party after approximately eight o'clock,' Munch resumed. 'No one can give us an exact time, due to the state they were in, but it sounds about right. We have no sightings of her after that.'

There was mumbling across the room now.

'So we're looking for a devil?' Kevin Borg said. 'A devil who carved a Bible verse into the viewing platform of the wildlife tower the next day?'

'Play the footage again,' Nina Riccardo said. 'At 0.25.'

Munch looked puzzled.

'Play it at a quarter speed,' Mia said.

She bent down to show him. Again it appeared on the screen. The sound was now distorted as the music was played more slowly. The flashing lights came in short, more distinct glimpses over the costumes.

'There . . .' Mia said as the devil slowly appeared on the dance floor. Some arm movements. Then close to Jessica's ear. An affirmative nod in response. After which the devil retreated quietly from the crowd.

'It looks almost like a brief negotiation, doesn't it?' Ralph Nygaard said. 'Buying drugs? Something like that?'

'Well spotted.' Mia nodded. 'We think that this unidentified devil might have made Jessica an offer that was too good to refuse. A deal. And so they went to the boat together.'

'Again,' Munch said, gesturing towards the team, 'we don't know if this is exactly what we've been looking for, but it is definitely a lead we should prioritize. The devil mask has been sent to Forensics. It has probably been lying in the forest since Saturday, but they must be able to find something. Skin cells, a hair, an eyelash.'

Mia sat down.

'So a devil costume?' Munch went on. 'Where was it bought? From a toy shop? Online? Can we trace the transaction?'

There was nodding across the room now.

'And,' Munch said, 'someone must have seen this devil. At the party? In someone's home?'

'She must have been there for a while,' Nina Riccardo said, looking about her. 'Unless she knew in advance that Jessica was going as Mickey Mouse?'

'Good point,' Munch said. 'Really good, Nina. Did the woman know what Jessica would be wearing? Or did she have to spend time finding out? If it's the former, I mean if she knew in advance, then surely we should be able to identify her quite quickly. Is it a friend? An adult who knows Jessica?'

'But it can't be the two girls, can it?' Ralph Nygaard said.

'No,' Munch said. 'We can see both Goofy and Donald Duck at the party, so it can't be Sylvia or Hannah. So someone else in her circle of acquaintances. A regular customer?'

He paused the iPad and turned to the team again.

'I know it's Friday evening now, people. And that you're all exhausted. But we're going to find that devil. There may be a perfectly rational explanation for this, but we need to bring her in. If for no other reason than to eliminate her. It's the best lead we've had so far.'

'And the Bible verse,' Ralph Nygaard said.

'That too,' Munch said. 'We know that Jessica visited a Christian youth club. Did she meet this person there? I want the name of all participants, OK?'

'I really hope we get paid overtime for this,' Kevin Borg muttered, and got up.

Mia stayed in her seat as the others left the room.

'What do you think?' she said with a nod to the screen.

'I think the net is tightening,' Munch said, and broke into a cautious smile.

'Will we find her?'

'Oh yes, we will.'

He took a cigarette out of the packet.

'Even if I have to stay up all night.'

EIGHT

SATURDAY

Chapter 70

On Saturday morning, Sofia opened her eyes. She stayed under her duvet for a moment, feeling tingly all over. Today was the day. The day she would get to dress up and sing in the church. She leapt out of bed, went over to the window and drew the curtains. The sun was already high in the sky. Not too many clouds, just a few. She hoped it wouldn't be too hot today. After all, they were going to be inside the church, a lot of people there at the same time. During choir rehearsals it always seemed to get very hot inside the church, especially in the summer; the last time, they had had to open the doors, both the big ones at the front and the small one at the back. She crept quietly out into the corridor past her father's bedroom. The door was ajar and she could see him in his bed. He was still asleep. Sofia went downstairs and realized why when she saw the clock on the wall in the hall. Oh, it was only five thirty? That was annoying. It meant she had ages to wait. The ceremony would start at twelve noon exactly. But the choir had been told to turn up early, an hour before, so they could get ready. Two hymns, the first one 'Love Divine, All Loves Excelling'. They would sing that once everyone had sat down. And then the bride would arrive. Her father would walk her down the aisle. Oh, imagine the dress she would be wearing. Would she have a train? Sofia hoped so. She loved trains. And a crown. No, it wasn't called that, was it? What was the name of that thing you put on your head? A tiara. Sofia pulled on her shorts and a T-shirt which lay crumpled up on the chest next to the piano and went out on the terrace.

Flowers. Sofia would be wearing a garland of flowers on her head. The vicar had said that it wasn't necessary, but that she could

363

wear one if she wanted to, and Sofia had scoffed when he said that. Of course she was going to wear a garland of flowers. After all, their garden was full of lovely flowers. She had looked at them for days. Wondered which ones she would choose. They had to be white, of course, but which kind? Oxeye daisies. No contest. A beautiful green-and-white garland around her blonde hair, which she had washed last night.

Was she being childish?

She had wondered about it, most recently last night as she lay under the duvet, unable to sleep. Was she being silly? Caring about a wedding so much? Wasn't that just for little kids? For bridesmaids? But then she remembered the wedding of Prince William and Kate. In England. She and her parents had been at Granny's, watching the whole thing on TV. They had flags and cakes and sweets, and her mum and her granny had both celebrated as if it were Constitution Day. They had smiled and sighed and pointed to the TV, and Granny had even shed a tear.

Kate had worn a beautiful dress. Lace sleeves and a train. William a kind of uniform, a red one with bits of gold here and there and a blue sash across his chest. He had looked just like a tin soldier, hadn't he? No, Kate had looked much prettier.

Sofia went to the kitchen and sat down at the table. It was only a quarter to six. Why did time pass so slowly? She couldn't pick the flowers yet; she would have to do it just before they left or they would wilt. She had practised making garlands for weeks so she knew exactly how to do it.

Sofia spotted the green breakfast tray on the kitchen counter and smiled. She opened the fridge to get some cold cuts and took out a loaf of bread from the bread bin. She ran outside to pick a flower and put it in a small vase.

She walked upstairs, holding the tray. Carefully she nudged open the door with her elbow and walked over to the bed.

'Wake up, Dad. It's Saturday!'

Chapter 71

Hannah Holmen stepped on the pedals as hard as she could, but cycling in a dress was not easy. Oh, why had she worn this? Shorts would have been so much better. She stopped cycling, got off and glanced over her shoulder. Should she go back and change? No, she had come too far; she was almost halfway to the ferry terminal. And she would probably just end up agonizing in front of the mirror in her room again. Shorts or a dress? The white dress or the red one? Her hair up or down? And what shoes? Yikes, she had almost forgotten about them. She had run down to the hallway and carried every pair of shoes she owned up to her bedroom. Her trainers were definitely better for cycling, but were they pretty enough? Should she wear sandals instead? But then you could see her toes, and what were the rules regarding toes? Did you show your toes to people you were meeting for the first time? She wished the old version of her mum had been here now to guide her.

There you go, Hannah, don't you look lovely!

Finally she had settled on an outfit, then run out of the house, practically sweating already, only to change her mind, turn and race back up to her bedroom.

No, she had to stick with what she had chosen.

Her red dress and the white trainers. Though someone had once told her that it meant something special if a girl wore red. That red was an invitation. Which was not at all what she had in mind. They were just friends. Ludvig and her. After all, she had only just met him online. Like, a few days ago. And there had been no chatting about anything like that either. Not at all. Only about books. And about school. And yes, the world and the future, and so on.

They were incredibly alike. At times she felt that he already knew her. It was strange, but amazing and good at the same time. Ludvig was going to be an author; he had made up his mind. Even if every single publisher turned him down, he would never give up. Even if he had to live in a campervan and eat bird seeds for the rest of his life. It had made Hannah laugh. She had seen his photo and imagined him hunched over a laptop outside a campervan. In the middle of the forest, his mouth full of seeds.

And you?

She hadn't quite known what to say. It wasn't that she hadn't thought about it. Dear God, at times she thought of little else. First of all she would need to make some money. Get out of this house, move somewhere else. Far away. To Paris, perhaps? In a book she had read once someone had mentioned a university there, the Sorbonne. It had sounded amazing. She had imagined the Eiffel Tower and the Arc de Triomphe and the Louvre.

Hi, I'm Hannah, nice to meet you.

What do I do, did you say?

Oh, I study at the Sorbonne.

One day she would have to look into it. How you got a place to study there. But after that, no, she wasn't sure. An academic, perhaps? Something to do with mathematics? Or possibly astronomy? Black holes? Things like that.

She had seen a lecture by Stephen Hawking once where he talked about how people here on earth are slowly but surely being sucked into a black hole. That our whole galaxy will one day be swallowed up. In 20 billion years or so, but still. It was truly mindboggling.

Hannah sniffed her armpits. No, nothing to worry about. She had sprayed herself with deodorant for almost five minutes. She didn't want to risk sweaty armpits. Her hair was down, not up. Just friends.

The morning ferry was due in at 9.50 a.m. She had barely been able to sleep. She had woken up before six o'clock and paced the room. What would they actually do? Would they just stay down there? She should have organized a lift into Fillan. So they could wander round the town, maybe visit the funfair? Or the library? Have hot chocolate there?

She had considered asking her mum to give them a lift, but decided against it. Then there was Andres Wold, but she had quickly dismissed the idea. Imagine the gossip about her.

Hannah has a new boyfriend – from Trondheim.

So the boys out here aren't good enough for her, is that it?

And apart from her mum and Andres, she didn't know anyone else she could ask for a lift. It was better this way. Chat for a bit. Look at the sea. Just friends, nothing more.

Hannah looked about her, made sure that no cars were coming, then she got back on her bicycle and rode down the street with a smile on her face.

Chapter 72

Munch yawned and took another bite of the apple on the plate in front of him. He had had a reasonable night's sleep. When he finally woke up and staggered out of bed, groggy, he saw that they had finished putting up the funfair. They had still been at it when he had stumbled into bed just before 3 a.m. He had barely had the energy to undress. However, he had managed nearly six hours' sleep. That was enough. He took a sip of his coffee and looked around the restaurant, which doubled up as the breakfast room. It was busy today. Most of the guests were probably journalists. He could see cameras on several tables. The big wedding. Munch shook his head and realized how little he cared about it. The woman in the devil mask, however? Not a single lead. He had almost refused to believe it when one by one his investigators had returned to the police station, one more exhausted than the other.

'No. Sorry. Nothing.'

'OK, *we'll carry on tomorrow.*'

Frustrated, he had got into his car and driven the short distance to the hotel.

'Everything all right here?' Ruth appeared in front of him with a pot of coffee.

'Yes, thank you,' Munch said, holding out his cup.

'Are you sure?' The young blonde woman looked at him quizzically.

'Absolutely.'

'How many have you had?'

'Just this one,' Munch said, waving his cup.

'Oh, all right then,' Ruth said, filling it up. 'But no more.'

She disappeared with a smile to the other tables.

Where do we go from here?

Munch moved his notepad closer to his plate. Adults in Jessica's circle. Her mother, Laura?

No.

Anita Holmen?

Definitely a possibility.

Motive? *Yes.*

Opportunity? *Yes.*

Yet for some reason Mia had insisted: *No, it's not her.* He had challenged her: Why not? She had just shrugged her shoulders. Not given him a proper explanation.

So, yes. He would definitely pay Anita Holmen a visit today. Because what other connection was there between Jessica and Jonathan? The name in blood? By now they had interviewed countless people. And yet not a single person had even as much as hinted that Jonathan and Jessica had ever been seen together.

Hannah Holmen, yes. But only in passing, when Jessica had come to visit her, of course. But outside the Holmen family home? No one.

Munch emptied his cup, picked up his cigarettes and went outside. It was warm today, but not sweltering. Pleasant. He was about to light his cigarette when his mobile rang.

'Yes, Munch speaking.'

'Hi, it's Rita from Forensics.'

'Good morning, Rita.'

'Good morning, Munch. I have some good news for you. We have just had a match on the hair. The hair that was burned in the cup on the boat.'

'Go on?'

'It belongs to Victor Palatin.'

'What? Are you sure?'

'One hundred per cent. It's a full match.'

'OK, thank you.'

Palatin?

He shook his head, baffled, and rang Mia.

Chapter 73

Hannah Holmen arrived much too early at the ferry terminal. The ferry wasn't due for another forty minutes. She had miscalculated, but never mind. Being early was better than being late. That would have been so embarrassing. And awkward. Poor Ludvig, sitting there all alone in an unfamiliar place, on an island in the middle of the sea. No, it was just as well that she had set out early, even if it had stressed her out. Hannah parked her bicycle in the stand at the back of the terminal, walked around the building and took a seat on a bench. The terminal didn't look like it had anything to do with boats, really. It looked more like four mustard-yellow houses that someone had stuck together. It was probably to do with the museum, the Trøndelag Coastal Museum, which was housed on the first floor. Even so, Hannah had often thought that the terminal ought to be a bit fancier. Perhaps with a proper quay and a glass building, something that signalled *Welcome to Hitra!*

Maybe that was an idea? The Coastal Museum? No, she dismissed it. An exhibition about fishing in the old days? She was pretty sure that wasn't quite what Ludvig had in mind once he got here.

And here we have the old pioneers, the first to try to . . .

No, forget it, he would probably think that was really lame. Or maybe he wouldn't? Because Ludvig wasn't like that. Certain things were lame, others weren't. He seemed quite mature. Not like the boys on the island who were the same age as him.

Completely different.

No, stop it, Hannah.

Just good friends.

Oh, she had butterflies in her tummy now. When was it due? She checked her watch: still thirty-three minutes to go. Luckily she had brought a book. She moved to a shaded section of the bench and tried to read.

No. Too restless. She had to put the book away. Other people were turning up now; she knew most of them. People who rented out holiday cabins, who had arrived by car to pick up tourists. A man was parked with his engine idling while he sat inside his car, listening to music and smoking. Hannah could feel herself getting irritated.

Didn't he know how bad that was for the environment? Letting out all those exhaust fumes? She had just made up her mind to go over and tell him off when, fortunately, he turned off the engine. He stepped out of the car and went into the café.

She looked through the door as it opened. That would work. They could go there. The café didn't have a lot of stuff, but they had enough. Perhaps a cake and a fizzy drink. She had brought money in case he didn't have any.

My treat.

So they had something to do. If it became awkward. Because it could quickly turn awkward, couldn't it? When you met up in real life. She had heard horror stories, people who had dated online and, when they met in real life, it was like a totally different person who looked nothing like their pictures.

Hannah felt a lump in her stomach now. What if? What if he was nothing like he was on Friendz at all? Don't be silly. What was she thinking? Of course he would be himself. He was so very much like her. It didn't matter if he was shy or anything. Or if he didn't look quite like he did in that handsome picture. Because they had met the *inside* of each other, hadn't they? Nothing else mattered.

Ten minutes to go. The people waiting began to stir, and then she spotted the white-and-turquoise ferry in the distance.

Oh, no, no.

I'm scared, I'm scared.

She felt an urgent need to pee and rushed into the café. She sat on the loo, drumming her fingers on the sink while she finished. She quickly checked her appearance in the mirror as she washed her hands.

Hi, Ludvig, how nice to see you.

Hello, online friend!

No, definitely not the latter. Hannah stuck her head under the tap and drank some water. One final check in the mirror. Big smile.

Hi, hi, welcome to Hitra.

She had just stepped outside as the ferry began to dock. Hannah positioned herself by the bench and smiled again. There were few passengers on board. An old Japanese couple walked carefully down the gangway. They looked about them. Then they were picked up by their driver.

Another small group – she couldn't guess where they came from. Laughter and smiles. Another driver, then they were gone. Hannah looked on board, trying to see if any more passengers were still on the ferry. No. Disembarkation would appear to be over. The new passengers picked up their luggage and started to embark.

The ferry hooted. The engine started. The ferry sailed away again, slowly disappearing across the sea. Wasn't he coming?

Hannah felt cold inside. She slumped down on the bench, looking around again. Had she missed him? Had she nodded off for a moment? But, no. It was very quiet on the quay now. Everyone had gone.

Hannah continued to sit on the bench, staring into the distance, her eyes moist. For a moment she imagined the ferry turning around and coming back.

Oh, we forgot to drop off some passengers.

They didn't know where to get off.

She looked at her mobile, but she couldn't call him. They had not swapped mobile numbers. Hannah sat in silence on the bench for another ten minutes before she got up and walked back to her bicycle. She unlocked it and was about to mount it.

Oh, what was it now? Her rear tyre was completely flat. Had she had a puncture? Seriously! She could feel the tears well up in her eyes. No, she refused to give in to it.

She wasn't going to cry.

Hannah straightened her back, gripped the handlebars firmly and started pushing the stupid bicycle up towards the road. She had only got as far as the car park when she heard the sound of a car

372

horn behind her. Hannah turned. The driver waved to her. Who could that be? The driver got out, and she recognized him. Fabian Stengel. What was he doing down here?

'Hi, Hannah, are you all right?' The psychologist came over to her, looked at her tyre with a frown and then up at the road.

'Oh, dear, it looks like you have a flat tyre?'

It was getting harder. Holding back the tears.

'Is something wrong? Are you upset?'

Hannah nodded quickly, then stared at the ground.

'Poor you,' Fabian Stengel said, and carefully put his arm around her.

'Stupid bike.' Hannah sniffled and rubbed her eyes with her hand.

'Poor you,' Fabian Stengel said again. 'And what a long way you are from home! Listen, this is what we'll do. Follow me.'

'Eh?'

He walked around his car and opened the boot. 'Put your bike in the back and I'll give you a lift home. No, I've got a better idea. I have a repair kit at home. We'll drive to my house and I'll fix your bike. There must be an end to how much bad luck you can have. No, you need help now. Come on.' Fabian Stengel smiled and nodded towards the boot of the car.

'Really?' Hannah said tentatively. 'I'm sure you've got better things to do?'

'No, no,' Fabian Stengel said. 'I have no patients today. I have plenty of time. Come on, my friend.'

'OK.' Hannah smiled and pushed her bicycle towards the car.

'Thank you so much,' she said when they were both inside.

There was a nice smell in here.

'You really don't have to mend it. You can just drop me off at home.'

'It's no bother. I don't live far from here. It will take us no time at all. Are you thirsty? I have a cold cola here, if you want it?' Fabian Stengel smiled.

'No thanks, I'm fine,' Hannah said as Fabian Stengel turned the key and started the car.

Chapter 74

Mia had just mounted the motorcycle when her mobile rang.

'Hello, Holger. Did you get some sleep?'

'We have a match for the hair.'

'What hair? The hair in the cup?'

He flicked his lighter.

'Yes. Guess who?'

'No idea,' Mia said. 'Who?'

'Victor Palatin.'

'You're kidding me? They're quite sure?'

'One hundred per cent. I've just spoken to Rita.'

'I didn't see that coming.'

'Me neither,' Munch said. 'I'm off to talk to him now. Do you want to come with me?'

Mia mulled it over.

'Do you mind going on your own? I've got something I need to check.'

'Again? What is it you keep checking all the time?' Munch said.

I need to check the timings again.

And the distances.

All of them.

'Actually, that can wait until later today,' Mia said. 'I can come with you if you want me to?'

'Don't worry about it,' Munch said. 'I'll manage.'

'So what are you thinking now?' Mia said. 'After all, we know that Victor Palatin was at Tautra Abbey? So how did his hair end up in the cup?'

'I've no idea. Did we ask him about it?'

'About what?'

'About where he gets his hair cut?'

'No, I don't think so.'

'Bugger, OK. I'll ask him.'

'Call me afterwards, will you?'

'Will do,' Munch said, and rang off.

OK.

First distance: from the By family home and down to the jetty.

Mia put on the helmet, started the motorcycle and rode up the gravel road.

Chapter 75

Hannah Holmen got out of the car and her jaw dropped when she saw Fabian Stengel's house. Wow, it was big. And grand. She had never been here before. She had just seen the names on the letterbox down by the road when she had cycled past. *Karin and Fabian Stengel.*

'There.' Fabian Stengel smiled, lifting her bicycle out of the boot. 'We'll get you back on the road in no time.'

'Thank you so much,' Hannah said. 'That's so nice of you. You really didn't need to do any of this.'

'Oh, don't mention it,' Fabian Stengel said, parking her bicycle near his garage. 'Like I said, it's my day off. Karin is in town. Come in, come in.'

He gestured for her to join him by the front door.

'Inside?' Hannah said. 'I thought we were—'

'Sure, sure, but I keep the repair kit inside the house. Come on in.'

Hannah took a few hesitant steps across the flagstones and entered the porch.

'Would you like me to ...' she asked, gesturing towards her trainers.

'Just take them off and leave them on that shoe rack over there. Come this way, I have a present for you.'

'A present?'

'Yes.' Fabian Stengel smiled from the doorstep. 'I was going to give it to you at our next session, but this is the perfect opportunity. Come on in.'

He walked in front of her into the living room, then disappeared upstairs to a room on the floor above.

Wow. Hannah looked around. It was incredibly nice here. Almost like those interior-design magazines her mum used to subscribe to. Large windows overlooking the forest. A bookcase covering almost one entire wall. An open-plan kitchen which looked brand new. A beautiful white oval dining table. A blue designer sofa that looked as if it must have cost, well, Hannah didn't know how much money such things cost, but it was probably a lot more than the sofa they had at home, she imagined.

She walked up to the bookcase. She smiled as she read the titles. Good heavens, what a lot of books. She made up her mind on the spot to have a bookcase like that.

First the Sorbonne.

Then become an academic.

And then have a bookcase like this.

She smiled again as her eyes scanned the spines. She stopped suddenly, then put her finger on one of them.

Vurt by Jeff Noon?

How funny. That was the book Ludvig had recommended. There were several from the series.

Pollen.

Nymphomation.

Pixel Juice.

Gosh, he had all of them. She smiled. They hadn't even had them at the library in Fillan. The library needed to order them in and they had only had one of the titles. Perhaps Fabian might lend them to her?

Hannah continued to stand there, not really sure what to do with herself, but finally she opted for the sofa. She dusted the back of her red dress and sat down carefully. Fabian Stengel appeared at the top of the stairs and smiled as he walked down to her.

'Found it.'

He placed the present on the coffee table in front of her. She could see that it was a book. Beautifully wrapped with a gold ribbon and everything.

'Gosh, thank you so much,' Hannah said, a little embarrassed.

'It's the least I can do,' Fabian Stengel said, perching on the edge of the sofa. 'If anyone knows what a hard time you have had, then it's surely me. And you like books, don't you?'

'Yes, I do,' Hannah said cautiously.

'I didn't need to ask,' Fabian Stengel smiled. 'Because I already know everything about you, Hannah. We've been exploring your innermost thoughts together. Aren't you going to open it?'

Fabian Stengel smiled eagerly and moved closer to her. Hannah took off the ribbon and undid the tape. She removed the crackling paper and looked at the cover.

Lolita by Vladimir Nabokov.

'Gosh,' Hannah said. 'Thank you.'

'Have you read it already?' Fabian Stengel said, touching her shoulder carefully.

'No, I haven't,' Hannah said. 'But I've heard about it.'

'It's a classic. One of the great novels about true love. It's amazing. I've read it three times.'

'Thank you so much,' Hannah said, putting down the book.

'Perhaps we could read it aloud? To each other?'

'Eh, what?' Fabian Stengel moved even closer now, his thigh brushing hers. She jumped when she felt his hand on her back.

'You know, Hannah, as Nabokov so beautifully puts it, love has no age. Two people just find each other. They meet. Their souls meet. And, in time, then also . . . their bodies.' He trailed a finger down her red dress.

Hannah cleared her throat and stood up quickly. She walked over to the bookcase and looked hard at the titles. She was very cold now. She could barely breathe.

'I thought we were . . . fixing my flat tyre?' she said with her back to him.

'Oh, yes,' Fabian Stengel said, getting up.

Hannah continued to stare stiffly at the books. She read out the titles in her mind.

Moby-Dick by Herman Melville.

The Magus by John Fowles.

The Birds by Tarjei Vesaas.

What?

But they were the same books that . . .

She spun around. Fabian Stengel was standing in front of her. He had undone the top button of his shirt.

'It's not right to say no to love when it happens to you, you know. You just have to surrender to it.'

He smiled and then undid another button.

'Take Jessica, for example. She and I, we were so different really, but you can't say no when true love calls, can you? Just like the two of us, Hannah?'

Jessica?

'Did you know . . . Jessica?' Hannah said in a low voice.

She was feeling sick now. She wanted to run, but her feet seemed glued to the floor. Oh, shit . . .

Lolita.

Hannah looked at the book on the coffee table.

Mr LOL.

'A bit,' Fabian Stengel said, pulling his shirt out of the lining of his trousers. 'Not like you and me, of course. We're soulmates, aren't we, my love? So what do you say? How about we go upstairs?'

Fabian Stengel moved even closer to her. He traced a finger down her cheek and leaned forwards to kiss her lips.

Hannah felt an explosion inside her. She didn't think, she just reacted. Hannah pulled out a book from the bookcase and whacked him across his face with it.

'Ouch, what?'

And she was no longer glued to the floor. She ran to the kitchen as quick as lightning. She opened the kitchen door. And she fled in stockinged feet as fast as she could down towards the road.

Chapter 76

Mia pressed start on the stopwatch on her mobile and pulled down the visor on her helmet. She started the motorcycle and pulled out on to the main road. The 714. It was a Saturday and there was quite a lot of traffic today, but she would just have to try her best. She had to maintain a good speed. For a while she was stuck behind a tractor, but she was eventually able to overtake it. A campervan was coming towards her, but the motorcycle was fast and nimble and she managed to get out of its way in time. The campervan sounded its horn at her, a man giving her the finger through the window. 'It's an emergency,' Mia mumbled. She continued to the next exit. Took it. Joined the 713. She accelerated and flattened herself down even more behind the handlebars. The wind tore at her clothing.

Anita Holmen's house.

Done.

Onwards.

To Setervågen marina.

Done.

Full speed ahead.

The jetty.

Done.

She slowed down, pulled over on the verge, stopped and took out her mobile. Twelve minutes. OK. Plus the eighteen?

Not a chance.

Mia shook her head and put the mobile back in her pocket, turned the motorcycle around and drove back, more slowly this time. She had almost reached the exit to Fillan town centre when she spotted a girl running into the road in front of her.

Wearing a red dress. And socks? Wasn't that . . . Hannah? Mia rode towards her, stopped and dismounted.

'Hannah? Are you OK?'

The girl was shaking all over. She could barely speak.

'He . . . he . . .' She turned and gestured.

'Who?' Mia said, taking off her helmet.

'Fabian,' Hannah said, still panting. 'Stengel . . .'

'The psychologist?' Mia said, looking up in the direction Hannah was pointing.

'He killed Jessica – he's Mr LOL.'

'What did you just say?'

'Mr LOL. It's from a book. He gave it to me. *Lolita*.'

The tears were pouring down her cheeks now. Mia gave her a hug.

'You're safe now. What happened?'

'He tricked me,' Hannah sobbed. 'He pretended he was someone else. Online.'

'Did he hurt you?'

Hannah shook her head.

'No, thank God, I ran. He didn't hurt me, but he hurt Jessica. He killed her. Oh . . .'

She stared vacantly into the air for a moment, as if she had remembered something.

'That's why he asked . . .'

'Asked about what?'

'During my session. My last session with him before the party. He asked what costumes we would be wearing. I said they would be Disney. That Jessica would be Mickey Mouse.'

She looked over her shoulder, terrified, sobbing and trembling as she pointed.

'It's him. Fabian Stengel did it.'

Chapter 77

Munch turned off the main road and was about to light a cigarette when her number appeared on the display of his phone in its holder.

Mia. He pressed the button on the steering wheel.

'Yes?'

'Where are you?'

'I've just crossed a bridge. What's going on?'

'I think we've got him.'

'*Him?* I thought we had agreed that it was a woman?'

'We may have been wrong,' Mia said. 'I've just driven Hannah Holmen home.'

'From where?'

'I found her on the road without her shoes. She had fled from Fabian Stengel's house.'

'The psychologist?' Munch pulled over.

'He tried to have sex with her. He had already slept with Jessica. Munch, he's Mr LOL.'

'What? Are you sure?'

'Totally. He gave her a gift. A book. *Lolita* by Nabokov. He probably gave the same book to Jessica. And he owns weapons.'

'How do you know that?'

'Hannah is his patient. He has talked about guns. That he likes to go hunting. Do I have your permission to enter his house?'

Munch thought about it for a moment.

'Are you sure you don't want to wait until I get there?'

'And give him a chance to escape?'

'OK. But watch yourself. And make sure you're armed, OK?'

'I have the Glock,' Mia said, and rang off.

Munch quickly rang Luca.

'Yes, Luca speaking.'

'This is Munch. We have him. It's the psychologist, Fabian Stengel.'

'What? No, no . . . it . . .'

'Don't talk, just listen. Send every available unit to his house.'

'OK, but—'

'No buts. Everyone. Now.'

Munch lit his cigarette, turned the car around and accelerated back across the slim bridge.

Chapter 78

Mia parked the motorcycle by the side of the road, took out the Glock from the tail bag and moved stealthily up towards Fabian Stengel's house. Silence. The only sound was the wind in the trees around her. She crouched down, making herself as small as possible while holding the pistol in front of her. It was a big house. There was a garage. A grey Lexus was parked outside. So he was still at home. Unless he had other cars. Or had escaped on foot. Hannah's bicycle was there. Leaning up against the garage. The rear tyre was flat. *A side entrance leading to the kitchen.* Mia crept up to the wall. Listened out. Still nothing. She opted for the lawn, sneaked around the house and could now see the door Hannah had described. There was movement near it. She stuck out her head and caught a glimpse of him. He disappeared; a curtain fluttered. She crouched down again and made her way across the garden. A flower bed. Some berry bushes. A rake. A hat and a pair of gardening gloves on the grass. Was his wife at home? No, she was out. Fabian Stengel and Hannah had been alone, Hannah had said. Mia reached a small terrace; she was not far from the back door now. The kitchen behind it. She moved closer, and now she could see him again. He had his back to her. In front of a cupboard. A bottle of wine. Another cupboard. He reached for something, still with his back to her, a glass.

Oh, hell.

He's going to . . .

Fabian Stengel turned suddenly and his eyes widened when he spotted her through the glass door. He let out a small scream and dropped the bottle and the glass, which smashed on to the floor.

Mia made a quick decision. She ran across the terrace, opened the door with one hand while holding her pistol with the other.

'Police! Come towards me with your hands over your head!'

He was gone.

Damn.

Shards of glass. Wine everywhere. She walked around the mess and entered the living room. Was he upstairs? Or downstairs? She heard a noise from the first floor.

All right, upstairs.

Mia crept silently up the stairs with a firm grip on her pistol. First door. Bathroom.

No.

No one.

A second door, not fully closed. A wardrobe. She could see movement inside it.

'Police!' Mia called out, and entered the room. 'I can see you're in there, Fabian. Are you armed?'

There was a few seconds of silence before a squealing voice said: 'No.'

'Show me your hands.'

Two hands slowly appeared in the small gap between the wardrobe doors.

'OK. Nice and easy now. Step out on to the floor. Keep your hands where I can see them.'

He came out now, crawling on to the soft carpet.

'It wasn't me. It was her. She led me on. And she's sixteen. So I haven't—'

'Shut up,' Mia said, and grabbed her handcuffs from the back pocket of her black shorts.

Chapter 79

The sun in the bright blue sky made the diamonds on her wedding dress sparkle when Lissie Norheim emerged from the white limousine and stopped to wait for her bridesmaids. The church bells were ringing. It was twelve noon already, but everything was running late. Henry Prytz had arrived at the last minute by helicopter. *'So sorry, I'm here now. Where's my suit?'* As if the morning hadn't been stressful enough already. Manicure, pedicure, make-up; her hair alone had taken two hours. If it hadn't been for Julia, Lissie would have had a meltdown. *'Relax, gorgeous, you'll be fine.'* She was so kind and patient, and Lissie could not imagine how she would have managed without her. She felt better now. Much better. Lissie smiled and straightened her back. She looked over her shoulder and nodded to the bridesmaids, who were making sure that her train never touched the ground. They had practised yesterday in the Prytz house. Her shoes were uncomfortably tight, half a size too small. She had forced her feet into them. Walked as elegantly as she could across the floor with her bridesmaids and this delicate train behind her.

'Lissie, look here!'

'Lissie, this way!'

Reporters and cameras. But they were some distance away, thank God.

Her father was standing at the entrance of the church, waving to her. So handsome. A new suit and a flower in his buttonhole. They had gone over this many times. The groom must not see her dress, of course. Not until she reached the altar. So he was waiting inside the church. Along with all the guests. Only her father and her were outside.

Then the doors would be opened. The bridal march would play as her father walked her down the aisle. Flower girls first, of course. Scattering white rose petals where she would be walking. Alexander waiting by the altar. Then they would kneel in front of the vicar while a choir of children sang.

'Oh, Lissie, you look so beautiful,' her father said, kissing her on both cheeks. 'Do you have everything?'

'I think so.' She nodded nervously.

'Something old?'

'Well, I've got you,' Lissie said, squeezing his hand.

'Am I that old?' Her father laughed.

'No, of course not, but I thought you would do.'

'Thank you, sweetheart, how kind.' Her father smiled.

'Something new?'

'The dress.'

'And very fine it is too. Something borrowed?'

'Er, yes, sure.' Lissie nodded, but couldn't bring herself to tell her father what it was.

Julia had produced a pair of lacy knickers from her suitcase last night.

'There you go, something borrowed.'

'Oh, but I can't . . .'

'Of course you can – why not?'

'Something blue?'

'There's a blue sapphire in my engagement ring,' Lissie said.

'Great, then we're good to go,' her father said, taking her arm as the doors to the church opened for them.

Chapter 80

Munch closed the curtains in the interview room, returned to the chair and pressed the record button.

'Start of interview with Fabian Stengel. The date is 23 July and the time is 12.48. Present in the room are Holger Munch, Mia Krüger and the suspect, Fabian Stengel.'

'And I don't need a lawyer because I haven't done anything wrong,' Fabian Stengel said, speaking into the microphone.

'Nevertheless,' Munch said, 'at any point during this process you have the right to change your mind. Just let me know and we'll stop the interview.'

Munch leaned back in his chair.

'No, I want to explain myself,' Fabian Stengel said again. 'I haven't done anything wrong.'

He rubbed the palms of his hands together and stared at the tabletop for a moment. He was wearing a light blue shirt with a collar. Beige shorts. Brown sandals. He lifted his head and looked at both of them through his heavy, black-framed spectacles.

'OK, listen. Perhaps I went a bit too far with the girl, but I misread her signals, didn't I? You don't know how she has been looking at me during our sessions. She practically undresses me with her eyes every single time.'

'Are you referring to Hannah Holmen now?' Mia said.

'Yes, Hannah.' Fabian Stengel nodded.

'She was supposed to meet someone down by the ferry terminal,' Mia said. 'Someone she had met online. Was that you?'

'Me?' He pretended to be outraged. 'Me,' he said again, and shook his head. 'Online? What? I mean, how could that have happened? She's not on my list of friends on Facebook. Or any-where else.'

'So you didn't join a chat room and pretend to be a sixteen-year-old boy?'

'That's nonsense,' Fabian Stengel said. 'Why on earth would I want to do that? I'm a respectable man—'

'. . . who has sex with children,' Munch said.

'What? Of course I don't. I might have come on a little too strong, but I misread the situation, all right? And she's not a child. The age of consent in Norway was still sixteen the last time I checked. So even if I had done it, which I haven't, then it's not illegal, is it?'

Munch had to restrain Mia at this point. She looked as if she were about to leap over the table.

'So you don't think that you being her psychologist,' Munch said, 'would constitute an abuse of power?'

'Sure, sure, with hindsight one might argue that. That I ought to have known better. But I allowed myself to be carried away. In the heat of the moment.'

'In the heat of the moment?' Mia said, somewhat calmer now. 'So this wasn't planned? The online identity, the location, the timing, her bicycle?'

'I've no idea what you're talking about,' Fabian Stengel said, taking off his glasses. He held them out.

'Would you happen to have something I can . . .'

Neither Munch nor Mia lifted a finger. Fabian Stengel cleaned his glasses with his shirt and cleared his throat.

'Like I said. No. I haven't done any of the things you've just men-tioned. I'm utterly confused.'

'So why were you at the terminal just as the ferry arrived?'

'The exhibition,' Fabian Stengel replied without skipping a beat. 'At the coastal museum. *Old maritime pioneers*. It's very excit-ing. It's been on my mind for a long time, but I just haven't had time. Until today.'

Mia looked at Munch, who nodded in response.

He was good. She had to give him that. He had planned it care-fully. He even had an alibi of sorts if anything should go wrong.

'Let's leave Hannah for now. And talk about something else,' Munch said.

'OK,' Fabian Stengel said. He looked relieved.

'Jessica,' Mia said.

'Who?' Fabian Stengel said, but then thought better of it. 'Yes, of course, Jessica. What happened to her was awful. What a tragedy. I really feel for her family.'

'How many times did you have sex with her?' Mia said.

'What? But I haven't ever—'

'We have, remind me, how many witnesses do we have?' Munch wondered out loud.

'Five,' Mia said.

'Telling us that they have seen you enter her boat down in Setervågen marina,' Munch said.

That wasn't, strictly speaking, true, but Fabian Stengel was not to know that.

'Let me double-check,' Munch said, reaching for his notebook.

'OK, OK,' Fabian Stengel said, clutching his head for a moment. 'Fine. I admit it. Jessica Bakken and I had a sexual relationship. She liked older men and—'

'Money?' Mia said.

'What?' Fabian Stengel exclaimed. 'Are you insinuating that—'

Munch flicked through Jessica's black book.

'April 14, Mr LOL, 1,500 kroner. April 22, Mr LOL, 1,500 kroner. April 28, Mr LOL 1,500 kroner.'

Munch showed him the notebook.

'And Mr LOL, is that supposed to be me?' Fabian Stengel sneered.

'Vladimir Nabokov?' Mia snapped back. '*Lolita?* Did you give that book to all the little girls you were sleeping with, or just to Hannah and Jessica?'

Fabian Stengel was silent for a moment before he cleared his throat and spoke again:

'The book is a classic. Critically acclaimed all over the world. In Norway it's regarded as one of the one hundred best and most important books throughout the ages.'

'We're not arguing over the literary merits of the novel,' Munch said with a sigh. 'Rather your use of it. Was that your MO? Look, here's a novel about an older man who sexually exploits a young girl. And that's OK because it's a classic?'

'Listen,' Fabian Stengel said, taking off his glasses and rubbing his eyes. 'We really must stop using all these derogatory terms. *Little girls. Children.* They weren't minors. OK? I've done nothing wrong. Nothing at all. This is a free country. I can explore my sexuality in any way I like. Within the law, of course.'

Mia had to take deep breaths in order to stay on her chair at this point.

'Grooming, creating a fake identity, payment for sexual favours, I would say . . . what do you think, Munch?'

'Probably not very long? Two or three years in jail?'

'No, no,' Fabian Stengel said. 'This is all circumstantial. You can't prove any of it.' He pointed to the black notebook. 'Some girl's notes? A Mr LOL with a date and a number next to it?' He laughed. 'That could be anyone, absolutely anyone. No judge will accept that as evidence. And when it comes to Hannah.' Fabian Stengel leaned towards them now. 'What did she really tell you? Did she tell you that she fluttered her eyelashes at me? That she pulled down her red dress to reveal her shoulder? That she sat very close to me on the sofa? Does she have any physical injuries suggesting anything that could resemble an attack? No, you have nothing.'

Munch had to physically hold Mia back now. He placed a hand on her shoulder.

'We have a search warrant for your office and your home. I can't wait to see what your computers will reveal.'

'No, no, you can't,' Fabian Stengel said, shaking his head. 'Snoop around my files? No, out of the question. I have a duty of care. Everything is covered by patient confidentiality. Do you know something? I think I would like a lawyer after all. This must be stopped at all costs. For the sake of my patients.'

'The accused has requested legal advice. The interview is terminated at 13.06,' Munch said, and switched off the recording.

'There,' Munch said. 'So who do we call?'

'My mobile, please,' Fabian Stengel said, nodding to his mobile, which they had confiscated and which was lying at the end of the table. Mia slid it towards him with a piece of paper and a pen. Stengel wrote down a number and gave her the piece of paper.

'Won't be long,' Mia said, and left the room.

Munch leaned back in the chair again and took a cigarette out of the packet in his pocket.

'So, just between us boys, now that the lady has left the room.' Munch winked and offered Fabian Stengel the packet.

He declined politely with a faint smile.

'Saturday night?' Munch said. 'Were you down there? A quick trip to the boat?'

'Last Saturday?'

'Yes.'

'No. I saw my last patient at midday, then I flew to Oslo. My brother's fortieth birthday. Big party. Around fifty guests, I think. Great fun.'

'So you weren't on the island last Saturday?'

'No, not in the evening. I have plenty of photos on my phone if you don't believe me.'

But for pity's sake . . .

'Give me two minutes,' Munch said, and stomped out into the corridor, fuming.

Chapter 81

Sofia was standing in the front row of the choir and had the best view in the world. She could hardly believe it was real. So many people. And so many beautiful clothes. There were dresses in every colour. Except black – that was for funerals, of course. Or white, because only the bride could wear white. But every other colour, and she could not stop staring at them. Pink and pale blue and lilac. And the men were wearing suits, all of them, perhaps looking even finer than the English prince. Several girls in the choir were wearing garlands on their heads, but no one had thought of using oxeye daisies. Several people had commented on hers on the way in – '*Gosh, what a beautiful garland*' – including people she didn't know. And a man in a grey suit with a very strange moustache had even spoken to her in English. She hadn't understood very much of it, only the word *wonderful*, and she had curtsied and said '*Thank you very much.*' She could hardly recognize the church. There were flowers everywhere, literally everywhere. Even on the altarpiece where Jesus hung on the cross, surrounded by fish. It had been decorated with lots of flowers and above it were the capital letters 'A' and 'E', which were the couple's initials. Alexander and Elisabeth. Everything looked magical. Sofia could barely believe her own eyes. She had just stood in the middle of the church with her mouth hanging open.

They seemed to be starting now because Alexander had walked up to the altar. As did two other people, a man in a grey suit and a young woman with cropped hair and a pretty, short prom dress. They were the ring-bearers. Someone from the choir had said that her mother had read in a magazine that the rings were super-expensive.

She was tingling all over now as a hushed silence descended upon the church. The organ began to play. The doors were opened. And there she was. Sofia craned her neck. Walking slowly up the aisle with the bridal bouquet in her hands.

What a dress.

Lace and silk. Diamonds sparkled around her neck. And behind her was possibly the longest train in the world.

Oh, she was so pretty.

Sofia smiled with her entire being, and she was tempted to clap her hands. Nora stepped out in front of the choir.

'OK, everyone,' she whispered. 'Now remember what we've practised.'

She raised her hands.

'One, two, three.'

Sofia opened her mouth and sang at the top of her voice.

'*Love Divine, all loves excelling, joy of heaven, to earth come down!*'

Chapter 82

Mia asked Luca to call Fabian Stengel's lawyer and then returned to the corridor, where she was met by a fuming Munch, who signalled for her to step into the briefing room with a nod of his head.

'What is it?' Mia said when he had closed the door behind him.

He was practically frothing around the mouth.

'The bastard wasn't there.'

'What?' Mia exclaimed. 'Last Saturday night?'

'He was in Oslo. Celebrating his brother's fortieth birthday.'

'Crap,' Mia muttered. 'Are you sure?'

'He says he has photos. And an airline ticket. We'll confirm his alibi, of course, but we're stuffed. He knows that we could get him on that if it wasn't true.' Munch slammed his fist on to the table and flopped into a chair.

'OK,' Mia said. 'It's not the end of the world.'

'Not the end of the world?' Munch practically shouted. 'We have turned the island upside down to find this guy. Why didn't you check that . . .'

He realized he still had the cigarette in his mouth and he threw it on to the floor in his rage.

'Me?' Mia said. 'When would I have had time to check his alibi? I drove Hannah home, I spoke to her for ten minutes to get her story and then I called you. We were potentially dealing with an armed killer at large. I handcuffed him, put him in Luca's car and brought him straight here. Just when do you think I would—'

'OK, OK, sorry, OK,' Munch said, resting his head in his hands. 'I just . . .'

'So what do we do with him now?' She nodded towards the inter-view room.

'What?' Munch said, looking up at her again. 'Well, we keep him here, of course. For all the other stuff. I doubt his lawyer can get him out of that. The wheels have already been set in motion – we can get him on what he has on his computers. If the girl is telling the truth, that is.'

He stroked his beard.

'Do we believe her? Should we bring her in?'

'Why the hell shouldn't we believe Hannah?' Mia was outraged. 'And bring her here now? Are you out of your mind? Hasn't she been through enough today already?'

'Calm down,' Munch said, holding up his hands.

'Me?' Mia said. 'I'm not the one who needs to—'

'OK, that's enough,' Munch said, getting up. 'New plan. Just give me a moment to think. You wait here while he stews in there. I'm going for a smoke.'

Mia cursed softly under her breath and was about to help herself to some coffee when her mobile rang.

Gabriel.

'Hi, Gabriel, we're right in the middle of something here. Can I call you back?'

Nina Riccardo appeared outside now. She knocked on the door and waved a piece of paper.

'Of course,' Gabriel said. 'Only I've just discovered something I thought you would want to know.'

'What is it?'

'Do you want to hear it now . . . or later?'

'Give it to me quickly,' Mia said, shaking her head at Nina Riccardo.

'All right,' Gabriel said. 'Well, it's about that list of names you sent me. I've finally got through them all, and I didn't find much. Yes, there was the vicar, of course, but one person did stand out. At first glance everything looked fine – straightforward Facebook and Instagram accounts, very religious, but each to their own. The reason I had second thoughts about her was that her history was so short.'

'What do you mean by short?'

'Well, it only went back to December three years ago. There was nothing before. So I did a deep dive and bingo. Result. Three years ago she changed her name.'

'Who are we talking about?'

'Nora Strand.'

Shit.

The verger.

'She used to be known as Nora Vikmark Olsen. And I found quite a lot on her.'

'Go on?'

'Including an old page for a, well, what would you call it, a sect? I don't know. *God's Angels*. It doesn't exist any more, but when I looked into it, I found a range of activities. Different protests. Anti-abortion, torching a synagogue, conversations in various chat rooms about such issues . . .'

'Have you seen me or what?' Nina Riccardo said as she entered, still waving her piece of paper.

'I'll call you back, Gabriel,' Mia said.

'I've discovered something,' Nina Riccardo said. 'That list of members of the youth club was minors only, wasn't it? Here's one of the adults who was present.'

She placed the piece of paper on the table and pointed.

'Nora Strand?' Mia said.

'Yes? How . . . did you know?'

Damn.

'Follow me,' Mia said as she ran outside to find Munch.

397

Chapter 83

Nora Strand waited until the final note had reached the rafters and smiled sweetly at the choir. Lovely. Really beautiful. She sat down contentedly as the vicar appeared and positioned himself in front of the happy couple. What a prat. She had never seen the like. She was almost sorry that she wouldn't get the chance to see him make a fool of himself in front of everyone in the church. Not that she would call this place a church. It was nothing like it now. It was a shopping centre, that was what it was. Tarted up from top to bottom; she was surrounded by bad taste. Nora glanced up at the revolting altarpiece. Oh, well. Not long now. It had looked much better with the crows on it. Nora Strand covered her mouth with her hand and tried not to laugh when the clumsy vicar cleared his throat nervously and began:

'Grace be unto you, and peace, from God our Father, and from the Lord Jesus Christ. Dear Elisabeth and Alexander. You have come here to Sandstad Church to enter into holy matrimony. We're gathered here today to celebrate with you. We will hear your eternal promises to each other and ask for God's blessing for you and the home you are about to create.'

OK, that was enough of that. Nora got up and moved discreetly to the back door.

'Is that where the choir will be standing?'

'Yes, of course, the choir will positioned there.'

'Near the door, am I right?'

Nora smiled, stepped outside and closed the door softly behind her. She obviously hadn't said the last bit out loud.

She laughed to herself and lifted off the string around her neck. Two keys. One for this door and one for the double doors at the front. She locked the back door, then she walked over to the shed behind the garage and put on her overalls. And her gloves, of course. And a mask that covered her hair.

How she had reeked. It was just as well that she had carried out a dress rehearsal.

The little doll's house in the forest. OK, overalls, gloves, mask. She pulled aside the blanket that covered the two red jerry cans, picked them up and returned to the back of the church.

Normally it was completely unthinkable, of course it was, it would be sacrilege. But this place was no longer a church, was it?

The caps on the jerry cans were tighter than she remembered, but they came off eventually. She splashed a little of the petrol over the wooden walls and poured the rest on the ground alongside them. The insulation she had ordered for the new roof would help the fire take hold.

'Just leave it behind the church, would you?'

She laughed again and patted her pockets. Her matches? Where were they? She turned both pockets inside out. What the . . . Yes, there they were.

Nora struck a match and let it fall into the grass. She went back to the shed, took off the overalls, the mask and gloves, and walked to the front of the church. Ugh, all those stupid reporters. She had expected to be the only person outside the church at this point. But no, of course not. A dozen of them were hanging around the steps. She put on her stern voice.

'You can't stand here. No access to the church during the ceremony.'

She walked up the steps and locked the double doors.

'There,' she said as she passed the reporters.

One of them followed her down to her car.

'Who are you? Can I have your name?'

'Mary.' Nora smiled. 'I'm a bride of Christ and His protector.'

'Is that right?' the reporter made a note. 'And your surname?'

Idiot.

Nora Strand picked up the bag from the back seat and placed it next to her.

There.

She was ready. She turned the key in the ignition and smiled to herself in the rear-view mirror. And then she pulled calmly out into the road.

Chapter 84

They held a quick meeting outside by her motorcycle. Mia took out her pistol from the tail bag, stuck it into the back of her shorts and waited on the gravel, itching to get going.

'OK. Nora Strand. What do we do?' Munch said.

'The wedding,' Nina Riccardo said. 'She's conducting the choir, isn't she? The children's choir? They're singing at the ceremony.'

Oh, no. The choir. Mia had forgotten all about that.

Sofia would be there.

'Right—' Munch began, but Mia could wait around no longer. She put on her helmet.

'Call Gabriel,' she shouted through the visor. 'Get him to track her mobile. In real time. Then we can see if she makes a move.'

'Sure—' Munch said, and opened his mouth again, but she was no longer listening. Mia twisted the throttle open to accelerate and zoomed out into the road.

Sandstad Church. It wasn't far. Three minutes max. All she had to do was drive through the centre of Fillan. By now she knew the distances out here inside out.

A black SUV had stopped by the side of the road to drop off some children. Mia pulled on to the verge to get past it. The driver sounded the horn and clenched their fist. She quickly checked the mirror. Why would someone drop off children here?

Of course, the SummerFillan Festival. The town centre was packed. Laughter and squeals of excitement. She screeched to a halt as a crowd of people crossed the road. Leisurely, as if they had all the time in the world.

Oh, get a move on.

She could bear to wait no longer. She pulled on to the footpath and into the grass once more. The coast was clear. She leaned over the handlebars. The engine roared underneath her. The recycling centre. Not far to go now. There.

The church.

She pulled up in front of it just as someone came running towards her.

'It's on fire!'

Chapter 85

Sofia smiled as the bride and groom turned to face each other. Her eyes welled up and she rubbed them. Yes, it was emotional, but not that emotional, was it? She didn't usually cry. Not even that time she had fallen from the tree at Erik's house. She had broken a finger, but she still hadn't cried. Well, not very much, say. Just a little. She rubbed her eyes again. And then she coughed. Yuck, something foul was irritating her throat. And what was that strange smell?

The bride, Elisabeth, was now holding a piece of paper and was just about to say something when a man got up and shouted.

'Fire! Fire! We need to get out! Everyone out!'

Sofia looked around for Nora, but she was gone. And that was when she saw it. The smoke and the flames that were licking the wall behind the altarpiece.

'Everyone stay calm! One person at a time!'

Sofia coughed. She knew where the back door was. It was not far. She went over to it, crouched down, covered her mouth with her hand and turned the handle. How weird. The door refused to open. A spluttering man came up behind her. He nudged her aside and tried to open the door as well.

'The door is locked!'

High above her a window cracked, sending shards of glass everywhere. A girl from the choir touched her face, blood flowing between her fingers.

'Come!' Someone dragged her along with them.

There was another crack. Around her people were screaming. They crouched down on the floor, sobbing.

'Don't panic!'

The young woman was very close to her now. The ring-bearer. In her prom dress. The young woman put her arms around her, protecting her against the crowds.

'The bloody door won't open!'

The man was shaking the handle and banging on the door. There was another crack. People screamed out once more. A man stepped up on a pew and started smashing a stained-glass window while covering his mouth with his other hand. Sofia could barely breathe now; the smoke billowed around them on the floor.

'The loo,' Sofia said, tugging at the ring-bearer's dress.

'What?' The young woman bent down in order to hear her. 'What did you say?'

'The loo.' Sofia pointed and coughed again. 'There's a window in there.'

The ring-bearer in the prom dress took her hand and fought her way through the panicking crowd.

'Follow us! This girl knows a way out!'

'That way.' Sofia pointed.

There was yet another crack. Shards of glass rained down from the stained-glass windows.

'Here,' Sofia said, showing her the way to the lavatory. 'We can open this window.'

The young woman fumbled with the hasps before she finally managed to push open the window.

She stuck her head outside. Then she went back to the pews and shouted across the church.

'Here! Come in here!' She turned to Sofia. 'Come on, you go first.'

She helped Sofia up on to the lavatory and then up on the window-sill. Sofia looked down at the ground. And then she jumped.

Chapter 86

'Has someone called the fire service?' Mia shouted as she ran up to the church.

'Yes, they're on their way.'

Why the hell were people not trying to escape from the church?

She learned the answer when she reached the steps and heard banging from the inside of the white double doors.

'Help us! We're trapped!'

A shoulder crashed against the doors from the inside. Then several more. The doors creaked. There was a crack. Glass from a stained-glass window shattered over the gravel. Mia called out to the reporters.

'Move away! Get back!'

She spotted Dorothea Krogh. The old woman was in her garden. She looked horrified.

There was another bang. A shower of glass.

'Help us! The doors are locked!'

The flames were licking the walls now. Sirens in the distance. Mia ran down the steps and over to the vicarage garden.

'Come, Dorothea,' Mia put her arm around her. 'You need to move back.'

'Sofia is inside!'

'Do you have a crowbar?'

'What?'

'A crowbar. We need to force open the doors.'

Dorothea Krogh nodded towards a shed.

'You need to move further back,' Mia called out again as she ran to the shed.

There was another explosion. Glowing shards of glass cascaded all over the grass around her. She braced herself against the heat and entered the shed. A crowbar? There.

'Help us!'

She could hear people shouting from inside the church.

'One, two, three!'

The white doors were bulging now. Mia forced the crowbar under the lock.

'Again!'

They counted once more.

'One, two, three!'

She pushed as hard as she could.

'Again!'

'One, two, three!'

She could hear creaking now. A window was opened down the side of the church. Someone was climbing out. Sofia.

'Sofia!' Dorothea Krogh cried out. She ran up and grabbed her granddaughter and dragged her down towards the road.

'Again!'

They counted again.

'One, two, three!'

And finally it gave.

The wood splintered. The doors sprung open. People poured out. Everyone coughing and wheezing. The fire engines turned up with blue lights flashing. Followed by ambulances.

'Get out of the way! Let the emergency personnel through!'

Mia coughed and ran down to the road.

'Are you OK?' She bent down and stroked Sofia's hair.

'My hand,' Sofia said, showing her.

'It'll be fine. Granny will see to it. Won't you, Granny?'

Dorothea Krogh nodded.

A car horn hooted. Mia turned towards the sound. It was Munch. In a car not far away. She ran over to him.

'Is she here?' Mia said.

'No,' Munch said. 'She's on the move.'

He had Gabriel on speakerphone.

'The most recent triangulation of her mobile places it on Fjell-værsøya. Does that mean anything to you?'

Munch looked at Mia.

'That's where Victor Palatin lives,' Mia said, and jumped into Munch's car.

Chapter 87

Nora Strand drove down to the two neat little houses and parked in front of the garage. She checked the rear-view mirror once more and smoothed her fringe before she took the bag from the passenger seat and got out. What a place. What a man. Nora adjusted her dress and walked to the front door. She heard a voice behind her. Shrill across the drive.

'Who is it?' The crazy old woman in her wheelchair.

Nora heaved a sigh, turned and walked towards her.

'I thought it was you,' the old woman shrieked, jabbing her finger at her. 'You're not welcome here. Victor doesn't want you. I saw you the other day. The flowers on the doorstep. You went into his house, didn't you?'

Nora set down her bag, took out her revolver and shot the old woman in the face.

There. Peace at last.

Nora picked up her bag, opened the front door and stepped inside.

'Victor. Where are you?'

She entered the living room just as Victor Palatin came in from the garden through the back door. He stopped in his tracks and stared at her.

'Nora? Is that you? What are you doing here? Did you hear that bang?' He looked about him.

'The hunting season has started,' Nora said with a smile.

'No, it hasn't . . .' He looked over her shoulder.

'I'm here,' Nora said, and walked up to give him a big hug.

Victor Palatin stepped back, holding up his hands in front of him.

'I told you not to come here again, Nora. It's over between us. You know that.'

Nora tilted her head and smiled.

'I fixed it. You've heard, haven't you?'

'Fixed what?' Victor Palatin said, looking at her stiffly.

'The temptress,' Nora said. 'That little whore. Who ruined everything. You're free.'

She crossed the floor and stroked his cheek tenderly.

'God has forgiven you.'

'What?' Victor grabbed her hand, shaking his head. 'No, no, Nora. Please don't tell me it was you who . . .'

Nora smiled.

'But the angel said unto him: Fear not for thy prayer is heard.'

Victor pushed her aside. She nearly fell over and grabbed a chair for support. Nora stared at him.

'Why, Victor? That's no way to treat your beloved.'

He quickly crossed the room in order to reach his mobile, which was lying on the table. Nora set down her bag.

'Don't.'

She aimed her revolver at him.

Victor turned, and then he froze. Slowly he held up his hands.

'Nora, I—'

'Sit down on the sofa.'

Victor did as she said.

'Nora, dear. Think about this.'

'He that loveth not knoweth not God; for God is love.'

'Please, Nora, please.'

'You said that God had brought us together, didn't you?'

'Yes, yes, Nora, I did.'

'That heaven was for us and that we were heaven?'

He was sobbing now.

'Yes, Nora . . . we are heaven. You and I. For ever.'

'Let me look at you.'

He looked up warily. He trembled as he met her gaze.

'You're lying.'

'It's true. I swear it is.'

'No. You're lying to me.'

Nora Strand shook her head. And curled her finger around the trigger.

Chapter 88

Munch let the car roll quietly down the hill, then stopped halfway down the road. He took out his binoculars and aimed them at the two small houses in the dip. He nodded briefly, then passed the binoculars to Mia.

'A white Škoda,' Mia said. 'Do we think that's her?'

'We'll soon find out,' Munch said, and opened the car door.

He closed it softly behind him and took his pistol out of its holster. Mia took her Glock from her waistband and nodded. They made their way stealthily down the hill.

A crow took off from a tree, screeching as it flew up over the forest. A small potato field. A scarecrow swayed gently in the wind. They crouched down, holding their pistols in front of them as they moved carefully down towards the drive.

'Look,' Mia whispered.

'Oh no,' Munch whispered back.

The old woman in the wheelchair. Her head had rolled backwards and her mouth was hanging open.

'This way,' Mia said, and crept towards the barn.

Munch followed her. They reached Victor Palatin's house.

'Stay here,' Mia said, and continued alone.

Then she stopped and pressed her back against the wall. She lowered her pistol and stood up very slowly.

She took a quick look through the window. Then she squatted down again and nodded.

'Is it her?' Munch whispered.

'Yes, and Palatin,' Mia said in a low voice. 'She's sitting on the floor. He's tied to a chair.'

411

'Could you see her weapon?'

Mia shook her head.

'Are we waiting for back-up?' Munch said. 'Or—'

Mia didn't reply. Instead she ran, still crouching, along the wall to the back of the house. Munch followed suit.

The terrace door was open. They could see her inside now, kneeling on the floor. Her revolver in front of her.

'Police!' Mia called out, and stepped on to the terrace.

Nora Strand gave them a startled look.

'Police!' Mia said again as she moved forwards. 'Don't touch your weapon. I will shoot!'

Nora picked up her revolver from the floor.

'No, put it down!'

Munch glanced quickly at Victor Palatin.

His hands were tied to the chair. His mouth was covered with tape.

'Put it down!' Mia said, moving closer still. 'This is your final warning!'

Nora Strand smiled and looked up at the crucifix on the wall in front of her.

She pressed the revolver under her chin.

'Jesus loves me.'

And pulled the trigger.

Chapter 89

It was late Saturday afternoon and the mood in the briefing room was happy but restrained. Munch had originally summoned everyone for a debrief but then dropped the idea. His team was exhausted. *'Come in if you want to.'* Nina Riccardo was leaning against the wall. Ralph Nygaard was smiling faintly in a chair. The door opened and Kevin Borg entered carrying a six-pack.

'Anyone fancy a beer?'

'Yes, please.' Nina Riccardo grinned.

'I'm in,' Ralph Nygaard said, raising a finger.

'How about you, boss?' Kevin Borg asked, taking a can of beer.

'No, thank you,' Munch said, holding up his bottle of water.

'Oh, one won't hurt you, will it?'

Borg opened the can and flopped on to a chair.

'Absolutely not,' Munch agreed. 'You've earned it.'

'No Mia?' Kevin Borg said, looking around.

'She's on her way,' Munch said.

'Cheers,' Kevin Borg said, raising his can.

'Cheers,' Ralph Nygaard said. 'What a day.'

'We got her.' Nina Riccardo smiled and took a swig from her can.

'I just want to be sure that I have understood everything,' Ralph Nygaard said. 'Nora Strand? She went to Palatin's house and got his hair from a hairbrush or something?'

'Shower drain, I believe,' Nina Riccardo said.

'And then she went to the boat, where she killed Jessica and performed this little ritual? She burned his hair in the cup?'

'Or the other way round,' Kevin Borg said. 'She could have burned it first and then killed her afterwards.'

Ralph Nygaard looked at Munch.

'So she was the devil? At the fancy-dress party?'

'Yes,' Munch said.

'We found her costume in her home.' Nina Riccardo nodded.

'She didn't get rid of it?'

'Clearly not,' Nina Riccardo said, and stretched out. 'She thought God would protect her, I guess.'

'And what about Fabian Stengel, the psychologist?' Ralph Nygaard went on. 'What will happen to him?'

'He's in Trondheim now,' Munch said. 'Claus Nielsen and two officers took him there.'

'Will we be able to charge him with anything, do you think?' Kevin Borg said.

'Let's hope so,' Munch said.

'What a creep. Sleeping with young girls? Some men, really,' Nina Riccardo said, and shook her head.

'Are you looking at me?' Kevin Borg said.

'No, no.'

'Because I haven't done anything, have I?'

'You can be an idiot from time to time, that's all.'

'Yes, I know,' Kevin Borg said, and drank some beer. 'It's just when—'

'The tiger in you needs to get out?' Nina Riccardo said. 'Stop saying that. It makes you sound like a moron.'

'Now listen—' Kevin Borg began.

'We're celebrating now,' Munch said, reaching for his bottle of water.

The others raised their cans of beer.

'A toast,' Kevin Borg said. 'To us.'

'But what about the boy?' Ralph Nygaard went on. 'Jonathan? What happened to him? Did she say anything about that?'

Munch shook his head quietly.

'So will Mia be here soon or what?' Kevin Borg said. 'I want to celebrate with her.'

Munch walked up to the window and drew the curtain aside.

'She's on her way.'

Chapter 90

Mia pulled up on the drive outside the brown house and dismounted. The sun was low in the sky. The birch trees cast long shadows over the gravel. Luca Eriksen was sitting outside his front door.

'Hi, Luca,' Mia said, and hung her helmet on the handlebars.

'Hi, Mia.'

She crossed the drive and sat down on the doorstep next to him.

'So, Luca, how do you want to do this?' Mia said.

'I don't know,' Luca said, and buried his face in his hands.

'Did you write his name in the blood before you called me?'

He nodded quietly.

'Were you scared? That I would find out? About all of it?'

He nodded again.

'You wanted to throw us off the scent, didn't you?'

'I'm sorry,' Luca said. 'But I didn't know what else to do. When you moved out here, I mean. Everyone said how clever you were. And then you asked me for the files. You were going to re-examine the case. And I just—'

'You saw an opportunity to send me on a wild-goose chase?'

'Something like that,' Luca mumbled. 'How—'

He looked at her nervously.

'How did I work it out?'

'Yes.'

'The police boat,' Mia said.

'The boat?' Luca said.

'It was the timeline,' Mia said. 'Anita Holmen called you at 21.47. It was evening and you were at home. She called you at home. I have driven every distance relevant to that night dozens of times.

It's impossible. You didn't have time to drive from your house down to Viken, get in the police boat and reach Svingen by five minutes past ten. Not even a little after that, just in case your log wasn't entirely accurate. So you must have been in the area already.'

Luca sighed and buried his face in his hands again.

'I'm right, aren't I?' Mia said. 'You were there, both of you? You and Amanda?'

'Yes. She called me.'

'She was drunk?'

He nodded.

'It had happened before, hadn't it? Her driving under the influence?'

'Not many times, but . . .'

'And her fatal crash in the tunnel, am I right? Blood tests showed alcohol in her blood. A lot.'

Luca nodded softly. A tear rolled down his cheek.

'So on that evening, 16 July three years ago, Amanda called you at home, and then . . .'

'She was frantic. She said that she had hit him. With her car. That he was lying on the side of the road, dead.'

'So you drove to Viken, got in the boat and sailed out to Svingen to help her?'

'I had no choice, did I? A drunk teacher killing her own pupil? Out here? No, that—'

'You threw his bicycle into the sea?'

He shook his head.

'No, Amanda had already done that. She wasn't thinking straight. She was completely—'

'And his body?'

'I had a body bag in the boat. We carried him on board together. I picked up some rocks from the shore.'

'So where is he?'

'Out there somewhere. In the sea.'

'Luca . . .' Mia said.

'I know,' Luca said, covering his face again. 'But what could I do? What about Amanda? We're talking about Amanda.'

'So how did you get her car back home?'

'She drove it herself.'

'Drunk?'

He nodded.

'Rather that than—'

'Someone finding it in the area?'

'Yes.'

'So where were you really when Anita Holmen called you?'

'In the boat.'

'And you sailed back to the jetty near Svingen?'

'No, not immediately. I sailed around a bit at first so it wouldn't look as if—'

'As if you were already there?'

'Yes.'

'Luca . . .' Mia said again.

He stared vacantly into space. Then he buried his face in his hands once more.

'She was the love of my life.'

'I understand,' Mia said, stroking his back. 'Why don't you go and take off your uniform and pack a few things? Then I'll give you a lift into town?'

Luca nodded and got up.

'I should probably go with you,' Mia said. 'Is that all right?'

'OK,' Luca said quietly.

And walked slowly in front of her into his house.

NINE

SUNDAY

Chapter 91

Munch sat down for breakfast at Hjorten Hotel. He was allowing himself a prawn sandwich today. With extra mayonnaise. There was no Lillian any more, so why not? He was going to let it all hang out. He no longer cared. It was Sunday morning and the funfair was already in full swing. SummerFillan Festival. Happy people everywhere. People hollering and cheering on the merry-go-round. He had had an excellent night's sleep; it had been like sleeping on a cloud. Then he had treated himself to a lie-in. Ludvigsen had called him earlier and congratulated him. *'You can stay for a bit longer if you want to. The room has been paid for.'*

Munch smiled and wiped his beard with the napkin. It was another fine day. Trøndelag county had put on its best show while he had been here. He was no swimmer, but right now he was tempted to walk down to the rocks and dip his toes in the water. Munch pushed his plate aside and turned on his iPad. Checked out the online newspapers. Endless coverage of yesterday's events. Not the murder, no, there was little about that. Just the odd mention here and there. But the fire? That was on every single front page. *Billionaire heir in blaze drama. Chaos wedding. New wedding planned, Bahamas next?* Pictures of the church burned to the ground. And of the whole incident from start to finish. After all, reporters and photographers had already been at the scene – the scoop was handed to them on a plate. No fatalities, thank God. Many injured, yes, but no fatalities, it would appear. A miracle. Thank God, the little girl had taken action as quickly as she had. There wasn't much about her in the national newspapers. But there was locally. The local paper, the *HitraFrøya* had: *Sofia from Kvenvær saves the day*. Pictures of the eleven-year-old girl with her father. Munch smiled to himself again as Ruth appeared from the kitchen with the coffee pot. He put his hand over his cup.

'Is that it?' The blonde young woman smiled. 'Have you had enough already?'

'It's enough for today,' Munch said.

'I hear that you've cracked the case,' Ruth said, pulling out a chair. 'May I?'

'Yes, yes, sure.'

'People out here are singing your praises. You and the other—'

'Mia,' Munch said. 'But it's a team effort, it always is. There's no need to single anyone out.'

'Humble.' Ruth smiled. 'How charming. Where is your hat?'

'Well, I'm having second thoughts about it.' Munch smiled. 'I think I might retire it.'

'What a shame,' Ruth said, getting up again. 'I liked it. So what happens now? Are you going home to Oslo?'

'I'm not sure,' Munch said. 'I might stay here for a few more days. Do a bit of sightseeing.'

'Oh, yes? Then don't forget Frøya.'

'Even prettier than here,' Munch said.

'Let me know if you need a guide.' Ruth smiled and returned to the kitchen.

Munch got up and went outside. Spend a few days here? That might not be a bad idea. He stretched towards the sun, took the packet from his pocket and lit a cigarette.

Chapter 92

Mia drove the motorcycle down to the Deep South-style garage and parked by the entrance. The radio was on inside. Loud country music flowed through an open window. She patted the seat of the motorcycle as a thank you and carried the helmet into the office. Well, calling it an office was an exaggeration. It looked more like somebody had exploded a bomb inside a second-hand store, but there was a kind of counter and an old till which didn't look as if it had been in use for a while.

'Ah, there you are,' Roar said, turning down the volume on the radio.

'Is it ready?'

'The Jaguar is ready, indeed it is.' He nodded and wiped his hands on a rag.

'How much do I owe you?' She took out her credit card from her back pocket.

'Plastic?' Roar snorted with derision. 'No, I don't do that. Can I send you an invoice instead? I'm guessing you have an email address?'

'Absolutely,' Mia said, writing it down.

'So,' Roar said, tossing aside the rag. 'How about we take a look?'

'Yes, please,' Mia said, and followed him outside.

The Jaguar was parked around the back of the garage where she had met Roar for the very first time. It was a different Roar now, proud almost, when he showed her the car.

'Took less time than I had expected. Very nice motor, I must say.'

'Thank you,' Mia said, 'Good heavens. Have you given it a wash?'

The jade-green car gleamed in the sunshine.

'Washed and polished,' Roar said. 'I didn't do it, it was . . .'

He nodded to the small shack where his son lived.

'Andres? Please thank him from me.'

'Well,' Roar said, and picked at his teeth. 'He got the message, as it were.'

He moved closer to her now and lowered his voice.

'You know that break-in?'

'At the hairdresser's?'

He nodded.

'You didn't hear it from me, but this was his punishment.'

Roar winked at her, then he stuffed his hand into his pocket and pulled out the keys.

'There you go.'

'Thank you,' Mia said, and got in behind the wheel.

'Drive carefully,' Roar said, and saluted her by way of goodbye.

Mia pulled out on to the gravel, then she joined the road. She drove a few kilometres before she stopped. She got out and leaned against the car.

The sun was high above the white house down below. She could see Sofia in the garden. A ready-made family. Another life. There was a beep from her pocket. A message from Chen.

Are you coming?

She got back behind the wheel and texted her reply.

I'm leaving Hitra today.

Mia took one last look at the picturesque house, then she put her mobile on the passenger seat.

And started the Jaguar.

Samuel Bjørk is the pen name of Norwegian novelist, playwright and sing/songwriter Frode Sander Øien. The Munch and Krüger series features five books: the Richard & Judy Bookclub bestseller *I'm Travelling Alone*, *The Owl Always Hunts at Night*, *The Boy in the Headlights*, *The Wolf*, and *Dead Island*.